Lincolnshire
COUNTY COUNCIL

COMMUNITIES, CULTURAL SERVICES
and ADULT EDUCATION

**This book should be returned on or before
the last date shown below.**

0 8 MAR 2020

To renew or order library books please telephone 01522 782010
or visit www.lincolnshire.gov.uk
You will require a Personal Identification Number.
Ask any member of staff for this.

EC. 199 (LIBS): RS/L5/19

Christian Cameron is a writer and military historian. He is a veteran of the United States Navy where he served as both an aviator and an intelligence officer in the first Gulf War, Somalia, and elsewhere. He lives in Toronto with his wife and daughter, writing his next novel, while studying classics. To find out more, visit www.hippeis.com

By Christian Cameron

The Tyrant Series
Tyrant
Tyrant: Storm of Arrows
Tyrant: Funeral Games
Tyrant: King of the Bosporus
Tyrant: Destroyer of Cities
Tyrant: Force of Kings

The Killer of Men Series
Killer of Men
Marathon
Poseidon's Spear
The Great King

The Chivalry Series
The Ill-Made Knight
The Long Sword

Other Novels
Washington and Caesar
God of War

Ebook Exclusives
Tom Swan and the Head of St George Parts One–Six

TYRANT

CHRISTIAN CAMERON

An Orion paperback

First published in Great Britain in 2008
by Orion Books
This paperback edition published in 2009
by Orion Books, an imprint of The Orion Publishing Group Ltd
Orion House, 5 Upper St Martin's Lane
London WC2H 9EA

An Hachette UK company

5 7 9 10 8 6

A CIP catalogue record for this book is
available from the British Library.

ISBN 978-0-7528-8392-2

Typeset by Deltatype Ltd, Birkenhead, Merseyside

Printed and bound in Great Britain by
CPI Group (UK) Ltd, Croydon, CR0 4YY

www.orionbooks.co.uk

For my mother

Lincolnshire County Council	
04988757	
Askews & Holts	09-Jan-2015
	£6.99
4531840	LI42838

GLOSSARY

Airyanām (Avestan) Noble, heroic.

Baqça (Siberian) Shaman, mage, dream-shaper.

Daimon (Classical Greek) Spirit.

Epilektoi (Classical Greek) The chosen men of the city or of the *phalanx*; elite soldiers.

Eudaimia (Classical Greek) Well-being. Literally, 'well-spirited'. See *daimon* above.

Gamelia (Classical Greek) A Greek holiday.

Gorytos (Classical Greek and possibly Scythian) The open-topped quiver carried by the Scythians, often highly decorated.

Hipparch (Classical Greek) The commander of the cavalry.

Hippeis (Classical Greek) Militarily, the cavalry of a Greek army. Generally, the cavalry class, synonymous with knights. Usually the richest men in a city.

Hoplite (Classical Greek) A Greek soldier, the heavy infantry who carry an *aspis* (the big round shield) and fight in the *phalanx*. They represent the middle class of free men in most cities, and while sometimes they seem like medieval knights in their outlook, they are also like town militia, and made up of craftsmen and small farmers. In the early Classical period, a man with as little as twelve acres under cultivation could be expected to own the aspis and serve as a hoplite.

Hyperetes (Classical Greek) The *Hipparch's* trumpeter, servant, or supporter. Perhaps a sort of NCO.

Kopis (Classical Greek) A bent-bladed knife or sword, rather like a modern Ghurka knife. They appear commonly in Greek art, and even some small eating knives were apparently made to this pattern.

Machaira (Classical Greek) The heavy Greek cavalry sword, longer and stronger than the short infantry sword. Meant to give a longer reach on horseback, and not useful in the *phalanx*. The word could also be used for a knife.

Parasang (Classical Greek from Persian) About 30 *stades*. See below.

Peltastoi (Classical Greek) Literally, those who carry a small, light shield (LSJ). An intermediate class of warriors between the *psiloi* and the *hoplite*. Sometimes lightly armoured or wearing helmets or carrying shields.

Phalanx (Classical Greek) The infantry formation used by Greek hoplites in warfare, eight to ten deep and as wide as circumstance allowed. Greek commanders experimented with deeper and shallower formations, but the *phalanx* was solid and very difficult to break, presenting the enemy with a veritable wall of spear points and shields, whether the Macedonian style with pikes or the Greek style with spears. Also, *phalanx* can refer to the body of fighting men. A Macedonian *phalanx* was deeper, with longer spears called *sarissas*, which we assume to be like the pikes used in more recnt times.

Pous (Classical Greek) About one foot.

Psiloi (Classical Greek) Bare, naked men (Lexicon of the Homeric Dialect, 1924). Light infantry skirmishers, usually men with no armour and minimal weapons, slings or perhaps javelins, or even rocks. In Greek city-state warfare, the *psiloi* were supplied by the poorest men, retainers, or even slaves.

Sastar (Avestan) Tyrannical. A tyrant.

Stade (Classical Greek) 178 metres, about 1/8 of a mile. The distance run in a stadium. Sometimes written as Stadia or Stades in the *Tyrant* novels. 30 *Stadia* make a *Parasang*.

Taxeis (Classical Greek) The sections of a Macedonian phalanx. Can refer to any group, but often used as a company or a battalion. The Macedonian *taxeis* in the *Tyrant* novels has between fifteen hundred and two thousand men, depending on losses and detachments. Roughly synonymous with *phalanx*, above.

Thorax (Classical Greek) A breastplate or corselet. (Lexicon of the Homeric Dialect, 1924).

Toxotai (Classical Greek) Archers. In Greek warfare, usually trained men from the lower classes with a bow. Athens had a corps of them. Also, in some sources, horse archers or Scythians, who were also sometimes called *hippotoxotai* or horse-archers.

Xiphos (Classical Greek) A straight-bladed infantry sword, usually carried by hoplites or psiloi. Classical Greek art, especially red-figure ware, shows many hoplites wearing them, but only a handful have been recovered and there is much debate about them.

The sky above the dust was blue. In the distance, far out over the plain, mountains rose in purple and lavender, the most distant capped red by the setting sun. Up there, in the ether, all was peace. An eagle, best of omens, turned a lazy circle to his right. Closer, less auspicious birds circled.

Kineas felt that as long as he kept his attention on the realms of the heavens, he would be safe from his fear. The gods had always spoken to him – awake, in omens, and asleep, in rich dreams. He needed the gods today.

Noise and motion to his right distracted him and his eyes flicked down from the safety of the empty spaces to the banks of the Pinarus River, the flat plain, the scrub, the beach, the sea. And directly in front of him, separated only by the width of the river, waited thirty thousand Persian horsemen, their files so thick that they had raised a sand cloud, so deep that their rear ranks were visible over the cloud on the lower slopes of a distant hill across the Pinarus. His stomach clenched and rolled. He farted and grimaced in embarrassment.

Niceas, his *hyperetes*, gave a grunt that might have been a laugh. 'Look out, Kineas,' he said, pointing to the right. 'It's the boss.'

Horsemen, a troop of twenty or so, their cloaks flashing with gold ornament, their chargers heavy and magnificent, cantered along the plain toward the edge of the beach where the Allied Cavalry waited for their doom.

Only one was bareheaded, his blond curls as bright as the gold gorgon's head that pinned his purple cloak, his horse covered in a leopard's skin. He led them across the hard-packed sand to the General of the Left, Parmenio, just half a stade away. Parmenio shook his head and gestured at the hordes of Persian cavalry, and the blond curls shook with laughter. The blond shouted something lost on the wind and the Thessalians in Parmenio's bodyguard roared and shouted his name – *Alexander! Alexander!*

And then he cantered back along the beach until he reached the Allied Cavalry, six hundred horsemen all alone to the front of the left wing.

Despite himself, Kineas smiled as the blond rode towards him. Behind him, the men of the Allied Cavalry began to cheer, 'Alexander! Alexander!' It made no sense – few of them came from cities with any reason to love Alexander.

Alexander rode to the front right of the Allied Cavalry and raised his fist. They bellowed for him. He smiled, exhilarated, beamed at their approval. 'There's the Great King, men of Greece! And at the end of this day, we will be masters of Asia and he will be nothing! Remember Darius and Xerxes! Remember the temples of Athens! Now, Hellenes! Now for revenge!'

And he rode easily, his back straight, his purple cloak rippling in the breeze, every inch a king, cantering across the front of the cavalry, stopping to say this to one, that to another.

'Kineas! Our Athenian!' he called.

Kineas saluted, raising his heavy *machaira* across his breast-plate.

Alexander paused, holding his horse with his knees, a horse that was a good two hands taller than Kineas's and worth a hundred gold darics. He seemed to notice the great host of Persian cavalry for the first time. 'So few Athenians with me today, Kineas. Be worthy of your city.' He squared his shoulders and his horse sprang forward. As he crossed the front, the cheers began again, first the allied horse and then the Thessalians, and then along the plain to the phalanxes – *Alexander*. He stopped to talk again, motioned with his arms, his head thrown back in the laughter that every man in the army knew – *Alexander* – and then he was riding faster, releasing his white horse into a gallop with his escort streaming behind him like the cloak around his neck, and every man in the army was screaming it – *Alexander*.

Parmenio grunted dismissively and rode over. He motioned for the allied *hipparch* and his officers to join him. He, too, gestured at the mass of Persians. 'Too deep, too packed together. Let them get to the edge of the stream, and charge. All we have to do is hold until the boy does the work.'

Kineas was younger than 'the boy', and he wasn't sure that he would hold his food down, much less stop thousands of Medes from pouring over the plain then forcing their way into the flanks of the phalanx. He was excruciatingly conscious that he was here as a commander of a hundred horsemen because his father was very rich and very unpopular for his support of Alexander, and through no merits of his own. The Attican horsemen behind him included a number of his boyhood friends. He feared he was going to lead them to their deaths – Diodorus and Agis, Laertes and Graccus and Kleisthenes and Demetrios – all the boys who had played at being *hippeis* while their fathers made the laws and sold their cargoes.

Parmenio's voice snapped him back into the present. 'You understand me, gentlemen?' His Macedonian Greek grated even after a year of hearing it. 'The instant they reach midstream, you hit them.'

Kineas rode back to the head of his squadron almost unable to control his horse. Anxiety and anticipation by turns wasted and intoxicated him. He wanted it to be *now*. He wanted it to be over.

Niceas spat as he rode up. 'We're being sacrificed,' he said, fingering the cheap charm he wore around his neck. 'The boy king doesn't want to lose any of his precious Thessalians. And we're just rotten Greeks, anyway.'

Kineas gestured at his troop slave to bring him water. He caught Diodorus's eye and the tall, red-haired boy winked. He was not afraid – he looked like a young god. And beside him, Agis was singing an ode to Athena – he knew all the great poems by heart. Laertes tossed his throwing spear in the air and caught it with a flourish, making his mount shy, and Graccus smacked him in the side of the helmet to get his horse back in line.

The troop slave brought him water, and his hands shook as he drank it. Far away to the right, there were shouts – a long cheer and the sound of Greek voices singing the Paean. That could be either side. Plenty of Greeks over there. Probably more Athenians with the Great King than with Alexander. Kineas looked to his front, tried to put his mind back in the ether, but the Macedonian phalanxes were moving to his right, shaking the ground, more a disturbance to be felt than anything he could

3

see through the haze of dust they raised with their first steps.

The battle haze. The Poet spoke of it, and now Kineas could see it. It was terrifying and grand at the same time. And it rose to heaven like a sacrifice or a funeral pyre.

But he couldn't get his mind above the dust and into the blue.

He was right there on the beach, and the Persians were coming. And despite the shaking of his hands, his mind followed the actions of the battle. He could see the Macedonion *taxeis* in the centre moving through their clouds of dust. He could hear the shouts as the king moved the companions forward, and he felt the battle through all his senses as it flowed up the distant ridge. And the crash came as the centre engaged, the Great King's Greeks standing like a wall against Macedon's pikes.

The Persians to Kineas's front took their time. Kineas was able to watch the phalanx roll into the riverbed and struggle to cross the gravel and climb the bank on the other side, time to watch the Greeks and the Persian infantry meet them at the top of the bank and stop them cold, dead men falling back down the steep banks to trip the men in the next rank as they climbed. Cheers on the wind from farther to the right.

'Eyes front,' said Niceas. He kissed his charm.

Just a stade ahead of him, a single Persian rider trotted into the stream and began to pick his way across. He waved and shouted and the mass of Perisan cavalry moved slowly down the shallow bank and into the Pinarus River.

Phillip Kontos, the Macedonian noble who commanded the Allied Cavalry, raised a hand in the air. Kineas's whole body gave a great shake and his horse shied a step, and then another, his tension communicated to the beast through his knees. He'd faced Persian cavalry just once before. He knew they could ride better than most Greeks and that their horses were larger and fiercer. He prayed to Athena.

Niceas started to sing the Paean. In five words, every man in the front rank had caught it up, the volume of sound swelling and spreading like flame in an autumn field, a fire of song that sent sparks shooting across to the Thessalians behind them. The Persian cavalry was at midstream, a solid front of horsemen.

Kontos dropped his hand. The Allied Cavalry began to walk forward, the horses excited, heads up, tails lashing. Kineas transferred his light javelin from his bridle hand, determined to perform a feat of arms he had practised for five years – to throw his first javelin and fight with his second, all at the gallop. He measured the ground to the front of the Persian cavalry. The mass of Greek cavalry began to move faster, through a trot and into a canter, the Paean shredding away as the hooves of the horses pounded out the sound. Kineas's mount left the sand and started down the shallow gravel bank of the Pinarus. He clenched his fist, signalling the charge, and Niceas's trumpet rang out.

He was done being an officer. Now he would be a warrior. The wall of Medes in front filled his eyes and the tension in his shoulders, and his gut fell away. His mare's head stretched out with her stride, reaching a gallop. He jammed his knees and thighs like a clamp on her back and rose, his back straight, and flung his javelin at the closest Persian. And his weapon hand travelled down, following through, grabbing his second javelin and bringing it up as his horse's hooves bit into the water of the stream and she collided, almost head-on, with the mount of the man he'd killed – his javelin through the man's body – his little mare like an equine javelin, knocking the larger Persian horse down into the water, its hooves flailing. A blow against his unshielded left side connected with his helmet and his arms, pain – Kineas lunged at a big man with a red beard, swinging the head of his fighting spear like a long club, parried, and his own spear broke at the impact, the bronze head cutting the Persian's cheek as they passed so close that their knees touched. And red beard was now behind him and he was unarmed. His horse was up to her knees in the water, her momentum spent and one of the Persian horses slammed into her, chest to chest and head to head, so that both beasts rose out of the water like duelling personifications of the river god, droplets a fountain of fire in the sun. The Persian stallion's rider lunged with his spear and Kineas twisted away and lost his seat. In an instant he was under the water, the riot of sound cut off. In a beat of his heart Kineas had his feet under him despite the weight of his armour, and his sword found its way into his hand as his head returned to the air and the din.

His mare was gone, pushed aside by the bigger Persian horse. Above him towered a huge grey. Kineas hacked at the rider's leg – a clear blow, blood blew from the wound and then the rider was in the water and Kineas was scrambling to mount, one hand locked in the grey's long blond mane, the other with a death grip on the hilt of his sword, the water dragging at his legs and his heavy breastplate pressing him down at every attempt to mount.

A weapon rang off his helmet, turning it so that he was blind. A blade scored across his upper arm, scraped across the bronze of his cuirass and then bit into his bridle arm. The grey, startled, bolted forward and dragged him out of the stream and up the bank he had so recently left, hanging from her mane, which panicked her so that she tossed her mighty head. Luck, and the strength of her neck, dragged him a hand's breadth higher than his best effort had reached before, so that he got a knee over her broad back. Another horse rammed into his side – the blessing of the Goddess, as the new opponent served to push him up on to his new mount's back, although the stallion's teeth wreaked a toll on the bare flesh of his thigh. He struck out blindly across his own body with his sword and it bit into flesh. With his bridle hand he ripped the helmet clear of his head and flung it at the enemy he could now see, with his sword hand he cut again, this time with intent, and his man was down.

Kineas couldn't reach the reins. His knees were locked on the big mare's back but he couldn't get her turned, and his back was to the enemy, his breastplate a sure sign that he was a Hellene and an enemy. He couldn't even see another Greek. He cut at a man coming behind him with a levelled spear and missed completely, almost losing his seat again, but the man with the spear rode by.

Reckless – or hopeless – Kineas leaned out across his new mount's neck and grabbed at the dangling reins again – missed, again – had them – too hard a pull and his mount was backing, rearing, then down on four feet. He turned into the stream and cut at a Persian. The man shied. Kineas thumped his heels into the flanks of his horse and she moved deeper into the stream, bit savagely at a stallion in her path while Kineas killed his rider, pushed further forward into the mass of Persians, and then he was on gravel, across the stream, pressed into a mass of enemies who could neither advance nor retreat because of their numbers.

He was an evil surprise to them, pressed so close that their javelins were useless and even his sword was too long and his arm burned with effort every time he raised it. He was deep in their formation. He didn't think or plan. He hacked and hacked and when the heavy sword was wrenched from his hand by the weight of a victim and the fatigue of his hand, he took his dagger from his belt, pressing his next enemy close so that he could smell the cardamom on the man's breath as he rammed his dagger into his armpit. He hugged his victim to him like a tired wrestler and the body was struck a mighty blow that rocked him back on his mount. He let go and the body fell between the horses. A javelin hit Kineas at the edge of his breastplate, the head punching into the sinew of his neck muscles before falling free. He tried to parry another blow but his left hand wouldn't obey and the man struck his cuirass with a sword so that it bruised his side, and then his horse pushed ahead and the man was gone.

He was at the top of the bank. He had crossed the river and he felt as unafraid as if his spirit was high in the aether or already on the road to Elysium – detached, aware in the last instants of his life that he was alone in the midst of his enemies, wounded ten times.

The instants stretched – *this is how the gods feel time* – and he was not dead. Or perhaps he was – he could only see as if down a long hall, so that it was difficult for him to feel threatened by the Persian he could see at the end of the tunnel in his head. He wanted to shout back across the minutes to the boy who had started the charge – *We will be heroes, you and I.* The thought made him smile, and then the tunnel spun and he felt a great blow on his back, sharp pain biting on his neck and heels.

He didn't know until later that his boyhood friends Diodorus and Laertes stood over his body like Ajax and Odysseus and kept the Persians off until the battle was won.

He didn't know until later that his action had broken the Persian cavalry.

He recovered quickly, but not quickly enough to wear the wreath of laurel that Alexander awarded him as the bravest of the allies, or to hear his name cheered by the army. The wreath was pressed between boards of cedar in his baggage. Two years later another pair of cedar boards was pushed in beside it, pressing another wreath, one that cost him a scar five hands long down his right leg.

He learned about war – about how much pain his body could endure, about cold and heat, discomfort, desease, friendship and ambition and betrayal. At Guagemala he learned that he had a gift for *seeing* the battlefield as an organic whole, the way a physician might see a body, diagnosing its ills and proposing remedies. He read the Persians well enough to save his part of the front when the Persians pressed close and all seemed lost – and again he took a wound that put him down. A prostitute saved him from an ugly death on the battlefield, and he kept her for a while and then a while longer, and then they pursued the Great King to Ecbatana, where barbarian traitors brought the Great King's head to Alexander in a sack and the army knew that Asia was theirs and theirs alone.

Ecbatana smelled of smoke and apples. The smoke came from the campfires, as the whole army of conquest concentrated there after the death of Darius. The apples were everywhere, brought for the pleasure of the Great King and taken as spoil by the first units that came up the passes. For the rest of his life, Kineas loved the smell of apples and fresh-pressed cider.

Kineas was one of the first, and because of it there were another hundred gold darics in his baggage, he had a fine sword with a gold handle and he lay on a couch, his leman's breast under his hand, drinking cider from a silver cup like a gentleman instead of standing by a campfire drinking it from clay or horn like ten thousand other Hellenes. His woman wore a perfume that had come out of the palace, a scent that caught in his throat like the woodsmoke.

He was happy. They all were. They had beaten the greatest

empire in the world, and nothing could ever stop them. Kineas never forgot the feeling of that night, the smell of smoke and apples and her perfume, like a tangible Nike lying in his arms. And then his boyhood friend Diodorus, who had ridden with him from Issus to Ecbatana, an Athenian gentleman with a mind like a fox and red hair to match it, came in from his stint on guard duty, drank his cider and said they were going home.

'The war of the Hellenes is at its end,' Alexander said. He sat on an ivory chair and wore a diadem.

Kineas loved to follow Alexander, but the chair and the diadem made him look like a stage tyrant. He stood impassively with the other allied officers. If Alexander meant to impress them, his words fell flat.

'You have served the League brilliantly. There is a reward here for every one of you. If any of your men choose to stay, they will be enrolled with the mercenaries.' Alexander raised his eyes from the sacks of coins on the ground by his chair. He had heavy circles under his eyes from drinking, but the spark was still there, dancing away, as if something inside his head was on fire.

Kineas wondered for an instant if there had been a mistake in phrasing – if he, too, would be welcome to remain and conquer the rest of the world. And then Alexander's eyes met his and he read his dismissal. The officers were to go home. Alexander spoke on, ringing phrases of praise rendered empty by the bags of gold at his feet. *I'm done with you. Go.* He lingered by the door of the king's tent when the other allied officers filed out, hoping for a kind word, an exception, but Alexander rose without another glance and left by another door.

So.

Kineas wondered if Alexander knew how much political poison smouldered among his precious Macedonians, but he clutched his thoughts close. He kept his own counsel when his leman left him for a Macedonian cavalry officer – one of many Phillips – rather than travel home with him, and he was laconic when a deputation of his men came to him and asked him to remain and command them. Some suggested that they remain together and take service with Alexander's regent in Macedon, Antipater.

Kineas had no interest in serving Antipater. In a day he had realized that he had loved Alexander, not Macedon. He packed up his darics and his wreaths, sold most of his booty, retained some fine cups for friends in Athens and a wall hanging for his mother. He kept the sword, and the heavy grey horse, and his stained cavalry cloak, and prepared to be a rich farmer. He had been away for six years. He would return a wealthy man, take a wife.

The Athenians went with him. Kleisthenes and Demetrios were rotting in the ground, or walking in the groves of Elysium, but Laertes and Agis and Graccus and Diodorus had survived battle and disease and misery and hardship. And Niceas. Nothing could kill Niceas. They rode towards home together, and no bandit dared ambush their convoy. When they reached Amphilopolis on the Greek mainland, none of the other young men were ready to press on. They lingered in the wineshops. Kineas hurried home.

He found that he needn't have hurried.

In Attica, he found that his father was dead, and that he himself had been exiled for serving Alexander. He fled north, to Platea, where there was a community of Athenian exiles.

He'd only been there a day when he was approached by an Athenian with a proposition. Of course, the man came from the same faction that had arranged his exile. But Kineas had grown up with Athenian politics, so he smiled, and negotiated, and that night he sent Diodorus a letter, and another to a friend of his father's, another exile, on the Euxine.

PART I

THE SHIELD OF ACHILLES

'Therein fashioned he also two cities of mortal men exceeding fair. In the one there were marriages and feastings, and by the light of the blazing torches they were leading the brides from their bowers through the city, and loud rose the bridal song. And young men were whirling in the dance, and in their midst flutes and lyres sounded continually … But around the other city lay in league two hosts of warriors gleaming in armour. And twofold plans found favour with them, either to lay waste the town or to divide in portions twain all the substance that the lovely city contained within.'

Iliad, Book 18

1

The same squall that broached the pentekonter, knocking her flat against the waves and filling her sail with water, swamped the smaller trading ship to the south. The smaller trader's cargo shifted and she sank, the screams of her crew carried clear on the wind. The pentekonter lay broached, the standing sail a testimony to the inexperience of her trierarch and the unshifting cargo a tribute to her sailing master's skill. The ship should have gone down anyway, lost on the Euxine with all hands, except that the sailing master hurled himself over the side at the mast, taking a bronze knife from a sheath around his neck and sawing at the lashings that held the sail to the yard.

Under the awning in the stern, the trierarch lay in horrified paralysis against the stem, unable to cope with the consequence of his disastrous decision to leave the mast stepped. The chaos on the rowing benches was as immediate a crisis as the sodden sail – the trierarch had ordered the rowers to set the sweeps just before the squall hit, vainly trying to use the oars to keep her head before the wind, and when the ship broached the wind-driven water had forced the long wooden shafts back in through the tholes, ripping them from the rowers' hands and crushing heads and rib-cages. Two men were dead, one of them the oar master.

The ship's only passenger, a gentleman from Athens, had also lost his feet when the ship tipped, but not his head. He threw himself up, grabbing at the other side of the ship as it curved away from the stem above him, getting his feet under him. A glance showed him that the cargo had not shifted, another that the oarsmen were panicking.

'Hard in, there,' he bellowed. 'Oarsmen! Larboard side!' His voice carried over the wind of the dying squall with ease; the habit of command and the expectation of obedience as strong as the sound itself. Every man in the waist who had any command of himself obeyed, men scrambling over each other in the rising water to grasp the side that was still out of the water.

The sailing master cut the sail free. The passenger could feel the weight change, felt the deck move through a tiny arc towards an even keel. He flung himself over the gunwale, hanging by his arms with his whole weight outboard, and a few of the oarsmen copied him, adding their weight to his. The water in the waist shifted, the starboard gunwale rose above the surface, and the sailing master kicked himself clear of the sail and swam to the bow.

'He swims!' shouted the sailors and the oarsmen, to whom the ship was a man. Every sign of success rallied more men amidships.

'Bail!' shouted the passenger.

Two of the veteran oarsmen already had the olive-tree pump rigged, and water began to spurt over the side like arterial blood. Other men used helmets, pots, anything that came to their hands. By the time the passenger hauled himself inboard, the benches were no longer awash. The sailing master's attention was on the sea beyond him.

'Another gust and we're dead. I have to get the bow up to the wind,' he said with a murderous glance at the trierarch. He shouted orders at the oarsmen and the sailors, who began to cut the mast itself away. One of the seams in the larboard side had opened when the ship broached; water was coming in with every wave and a cross-wave with the impetus of the wind behind it flooded the waist again over the benches. The lack of an oar master told – the oarsmen hesitated, their hope destroyed by the second wave.

The passenger flung himself into the waist, taking his own helmet from his baggage in the stern as he passed, and scooped water over the side. 'Bail!' he ordered. And then as men turned to the task, he started pushing men to their benches. He didn't know their names, or where they belonged, but the force of his will was sufficient to move them. A long minute was wasted dragging unbroken oars from the larboard side across to the starboard and feeding them into the tholes and still the ship swam. At the first hesitant pull to the passenger's ringing shout, the ship moved a fraction of its own length.

'Pull!' he bellowed again, taking his timing from a bandy-armed professional on the bench under his feet. Only six oars a side in the water, the ship full of water and her bottom filthy with weed, and again the ship barely moved. He sloshed to another bench, pushed two frightened men down on to it and put the oar in their hands. Opposite there was a corpse filling the bench. He lifted the corpse, heavy beyond anything he could remember, and another pair of hands helped him fling his burden clear of the side even as he called 'Pull!' again. The oar shaft, free of the corpse, moved like a live thing and struck him a glancing blow in the shoulder that knocked him on to the bench. The man who had helped him caught it, lifted it clear of the water, and sat on the bench in one continuous motion. The passenger caught it on the return stroke, added his strength, and called 'Pull!' as the oar reached the top of the stroke. Around the shaft went, and down, the blade biting the water firmly – the oar felt alive under his hands. He raised his head and saw the sailing master aft, standing by the steering oar. He caught his eye and the sailing master took up the call for the stroke, leaving the passenger to pull, his smooth wet hands already feeling the weight of the oar.

'Pull!' called the sailing master.

The fourth stroke, or the fifth, and the man at the steering oar called, 'He steers!' and the sailing master gave him an order.

Then came an hour of physical hell for the passenger, without the rush of overwhelming danger, just the pain in his shoulders and the sight of his hands turning to bloody pulp as he pulled on and on, water rising around his feet and then his thighs. Another squall hit them and then another. They made no distance; indeed, the sail was visible to starboard with every rise of the waves. All the oars could do was keep the head of the waterlogged vessel up to the wind so that no wave could poop her.

They did all that men could do, and they prayed to the gods and just when the oarsmen were flagging and the heaves to keep her bow up to the wind were increasingly desperate, just when the second larboard oar caught a crab that threatened to endanger the stroke, the wind dropped, and before the passenger could look again at the ruin of his hands the sun appeared between clouds, and then the clouds themselves were rarer, and then they were rising and falling in the swell of a sunny day on the Euxine, and they were alive.

It was only when the wind fell off that the passenger could hear the thin cries from starboard, over the rail, where some poor soul was struggling with the sea.

'Rowed of all!' shouted the sailing master, his voice as raw as the passenger's hands. He was not used to calling the stroke for so long. The oars were tossed and pulled in, a ragged motion but an efficient one, so that they crossed the benches and tucked their handgrips under the opposite thwart, their blades held clear of the water. The passenger's bench mate fell forward on the headrest thus provided, his arms over the oars, his cheek against their shafts. He breathed in and out.

The passenger heard another cry from starboard. He pulled himself from under the crossed oar shafts, the residual salt water burning his hands like fire.

His bench mate looked up at him and smiled. 'Well pulled, mate.'

'There's a man in the water,' the passenger replied, pulling himself up on an empty starboard bench. The hold beneath their feet was undecked, and there was water over most of the cargo. They were still barely afloat.

The sailing master was seeing to it. He had the sailors, the deck crew, throwing bodies and anything else he deemed of no use over the side. Every minute lightened the ship, placed the thwarts a fraction higher out of the water.

The passenger looked under his hand at the empty blue sea, the sun reflecting with blinding intensity from the wavelets, and listened for another cry. When he heard it, it was closer than he had expected; a man, swimming weakly but still afloat just a rope's length from the bow. He dove before he thought the action through, and swam as best he could through the now smaller waves, the salt water chilling him and burning his hands all over again.

He reached the survivor quickly, but the man tried to fight him, surprised at the touch and fearing, perhaps, that Poseidon had come for him at last. The passenger shouted at him, took his

16

long hair in a fist and began to pull him towards the ship. The man's struggles endangered them both, but he took in a lungful of water and his struggles ended. The passenger got him to the side. He was surprised at the hesitancy of the oarsmen to pull the man inboard, but they did.

The man lay across an empty bench, alternating breathing and vomiting, for a long time. The passenger came aboard helped by more willing hands, to see the leather bag that held his armour and most of his tack being lifted towards the side. Slow from the sea's grip, he was still fast enough to get himself between the ship's side and his baggage.

'Don't,' he gasped. 'Everything – own.'

The sailing master stripped the bag from his crewman's hands and tossed it on the deck with a bronze clang. 'We owe ye that much,' he rasped. He pointed his chin at the long-haired man puking over a bench in the waist. 'They don't like him. Sailors don't take the prey from Poseidon. Shipwrecked men …' He left his thought unfinished, probably too superstitious to speak the belief aloud.

The passenger was Athenian; he had different views on Poseidon, Lord of Horses, and his 'prey'. 'I'll look after him. We'll need every man on the benches to get this boat on to a beach.'

The sailing master muttered something under his breath, a prayer or a curse. The passenger went back to his bench. It was only when he had wiped the long-haired man's face clean of vomit and heard a gasp of Lakedaemian-accented thanks, that he realized that the trierarch was no longer aboard.

They bailed and rowed all day until they were once again in sight of the land to starboard. This shore of the Euxine was notorious for its lack of beaches, just endless rock alternating with ugly low marsh. The sailing master didn't try to force the men to get the ship ashore, despite the slow bleeding of seawater from the open seam. They ate dried fish, sodden with salt water, and felt better for it. They slept in watches, even the passenger, and pumped and bailed through the night, and the sun rose the next day to more of the same. Breakfast was skimpier than dinner. Small trading ships beached at night and carried little in the way of provisions. The amphorae of fresh water were point down in the sand of the hold and most of their waxed caps were open, showing their empty innards to the blue sky. The passenger had no idea of the distance to their next port, but he had the sense not to discuss it.

By midday, the rescued man was better, bailing with a will. He was careful when he moved and quiet, obviously aware of his unwelcome status with the sailors and the oarsmen, clearly intent on earning a place by hard work. The fact that he was repeatedly seasick whenever the swell increased didn't help him. He was a landsman, and he didn't belong on the sea; he too had smooth hands and had never pulled an oar. And he had *Spartan* written on his head in every curling hair.

The passenger arranged to take his turn at the pump with the stranger. He had to do most of the work; the Spartan was weak from seasickness and ordeal and nearing the point of allowing events to overwhelm him.

'I'm Kineas,' he said on the upstroke of the pump. 'Of Athens.' Honesty forced him to add, 'Until recently.'

The Spartan was silent on the downstroke, putting all of his strength into it. 'Philokles,' he gasped. 'Of Mytilene. Gods, of nowhere.' He gasped again as the pump handle went up.

Kineas pushed down. 'Save your strength,' he said. 'I can pump. Just move your arms.'

The younger man's blood rushed to his face. 'I can pump,' he retorted. 'Do I look like a slave, not to honour my obligation to you?'

'Suit yourself,' said Kineas.

They pumped while the sun burned down on them for more than an hour, and they didn't exchange another word.

By nightfall, the last of the food and water was served out, and there was no hiding that the sailing master was at his wits' end. The mood of the oarsmen was ugly; they knew the way of things, and they knew that the trierarch was gone, and they didn't approve, however much they might have paid for his error with the mast.

Kineas had a lot of experience with men, men in danger, and he knew their mood too well. And he knew what the sailing master, who had already murdered the owner, would do to keep command. He took his bag to the bow early in the evening and sat on the bench there, ostentatiously cleaning the seawater from his cavalry breastplate and rubbing oil into his boots before putting an edge on his heavy cavalry sword and wiping the heads of his javelins. It was a display of deliberate intimidation. He was the best armed man on the ship and he had his weapons to hand, and he lost new friends in the crew by letting them know it.

Oblivious to what was happening, the Spartan lay opposite him on the bow bench, his anger spent in pumping. 'Cavalryman!' he said, surprised, his first word in hours. He pointed at the heavy boots, so alien to Greeks who went barefoot or wore only sandals. 'Where's your horse?' He gave a fraction of a smile.

Kineas nodded, his eyes on the men in the waist and the sailing master talking to two veteran oarsmen in the stern. 'They intend to throw you overboard,' he said quietly.

The long-haired man rose to a sitting position. 'Zeus,' he said. 'Why?'

'They need a scapegoat. The sailing master needs one, too, or he'll be the sacrifice. He murdered the owner. Do you understand?' The younger man's face was still green, and his mouth looked pinched and thin. Kineas wondered if he was taking any of this in. He went on, more to think aloud than make conversation. 'If I kill the sailing master, I doubt we'll get this pig of a ship into a port. If I kill sailors, they'll drag me down in the end.' He stood up, balancing against the swell, and hung the baldric of his sword over his shoulder. He walked sternward, apparently unworried by having half the crew at his back, until he knew he had the sailing master's attention.

'How long until we make port, sailing master?' he said.

Silence fell all along the benches. The sailing master looked around, gauging the mood of the crew, clearly unready for the conflict, if there was to be one. 'Passengers should mind their selves, not the working of the ship,' he said.

Kineas nodded as if he agreed. 'I was silent when the trierarch raised the sail,' he said pointedly. 'Look where that got me.' He shrugged, raised his hands to show the bloody welts – trying to win over some of the crew. He got a few chuckles, a thin sound. 'I have to be in Tomis in a ten-day. Calchus of Athens expects me.' He looked around, catching the eyes of men in front of him, worried about the men behind him because he knew from experience that frightened men were usually beyond persuasion. He couldn't say it more clearly – *If I don't reach Tomis, important people will ask this crew hard questions.* He saw it hit home with the sailing master and prayed, *prayed* that the man had some sense. Calchus of Athens owned half the cargo on this vessel.

'We got no water,' said a deck crewman.

'We need oars, and that seam is opening like a whore in Piraeus,' said one of the veteran oarsmen.

They were all looking at the sailing master now. Kineas felt the momentum change. Before they could ask more dangerous questions, he stepped up on a bench. 'Is there anywhere on this shore to beach and come at the seam?' he asked the question in a light tone, but his position above them on the bench helped his authority.

'I know a place, a day's easy row from here,' said the master. 'Stow it, you lot. I don't discuss orders. Maybe the *passenger* has more to say?'

Kineas forced a good smile. 'I can row another day,' he said, and stepped down from the bench.

In the bow, the sick Spartan had a javelin across his arm, the throwing loop on his fingers. Kineas gave him a smile and then a shake of the head, and the long-haired man relaxed the javelin.

'We'll need every man,' Kineas said conversationally, to no one in particular. His bench mate from the first hours after the broaching nodded. Other men looked away, and Kineas sighed, because the die was cast, and they would live or die on the whims of the gods.

He walked into the bow, his back to the sailors, and the sailing master called, 'You there,' and he stiffened. But the next was like music to him. 'You two fools by the mast! Back to the pumps, you whoresons!'

The two men by the mast obeyed. Like the first motions of the ship when the oars began to pull, the feeling on the deck moved a fraction, then a fraction more, and then, despite the muttering, the men were either back on their benches, or bailing. Kineas hoped that the master really knew where he was, and where they could beach, because the next time he didn't think his voice or his sword would be enough to cut the tangle of animosities on the deck.

2

The two old men who kept the harbour light at Tomis saw the pentekonter well out in the offing.

'He's lost his mast,' said one. 'Ought to have 'er stepped in this wind.'

'Rowers is done in, too. He'll have a job of it making the mole 'fore dark,' said the other.

They sat and shared their contempt for a sailor so foolish as to have lost his mast.

'Gods on Olympus, look at her side!' said the first as the sun crossed the horizon. The pentekonter was well in with the land, her bow only a dozen lengths from the mole. Her side was fothered with a length of linen and roughly painted in tar, a pitiful sight. 'Them's lucky to be alive.'

His companion had a pull at the nearly empty wineskin they shared, gave his cousin a black look, and wiped his mouth. 'Pity the poor sailors, mate.'

'Truer words never spoke,' said his cousin.

The pentekonter pushed her bow in past the mole before full dark, her deck silent as a warship's except for the call of the oar beat. The strokes were short and weak, and discerning eyes all over the port could see he'd pulled long past the ability of his oarsmen to look sharp or keep up speed. The pentekonter passed the long wharf where the traders usually berthed and ran her bow well up the pebble beach that fringed the river's mouth. Only then did the crew give a cheer, a sound that told the town all they needed to know about the last four days.

Tomis was a large town by the standards of the Euxine, but the number of her citizens was small and news travelled fast. By the time Kineas had his baggage over the side, the only man he knew in the town was standing with a torchbearer on the pebbles under the bow and calling his name.

'Calchus, by the gods,' he shouted, and dropped on to the shingle to give the man an embrace.

Calchus gripped him back, first hugging him, then grasping for a wrestling hold so that both men were grappling, down on the gravel in the beat of a seagull's wing, Calchus reaching around Kineas's knees to bring him down, Kineas grappling the bigger man's neck like a farmer wrestles a calf. And then they were both standing, laughing, Calchus adjusting his tunic over his muscled chest and Kineas rubbing the sand off his hands.

'Ten years,' said Calchus.

'Exile seems to suit you,' responded Kineas.

'It does, too. I wouldn't go back.' Calchus's tone implied that he would go back if he could, but that he was too proud to say it.

'You got my letter.' Kineas hated demanding hospitality, the lot of every exile.

'Don't be an idiot. Of course I had your letter. I have your letter, a string of your horses, and your hyperetes and his little gang of louts. I've fed them for a month. Something tells me you don't have a pot to piss in.'

Kineas bridled. 'I will repay you ...' he began.

'Of course you will. Kineas – I've been where you are.' He indicated Kineas's baggage with a negligent hand to his torch-bearer, who lifted the bag with a heavy grunt and a long sigh. 'Don't get proud, Kineas. Your father kept mine alive. We were sorry to hear that he died – and you were exiled, of course. Athens is a city ruled by ingrates. But we haven't forgotten you. Besides, the helmsman says you helped save the ship – that's my cargo. I probably owe *you*.' He looked past Kineas in the dim torchlight as another man leaped over the side to the beach.

The Spartan bent, his locks swinging to hide his face and loudly kissed the rocks of the beach. Then he came up behind Kineas and stood hesitantly at his shoulder.

Kineas gestured to him. 'Philokles, a gentleman of – Mytilene.' His pause was deliberate; he could see the confusion – even the anger – on Calchus's face.

'He's a Spartan.'

Kineas shrugged.

'I'm an exile,' said Philokles. 'I find that exile has this virtue; that no exile can be held responsible for the actions of his city.'

23

'He's with you?' Calchus asked. His sense of hospitality and etiquette had eroded in the Euxine, Kineas could see. Calchus was used to being in charge.

'The Athenian gentleman saved my life, pulling me from the sea when my last strength was nigh spent.' The Spartan was plump. Kineas had never seen a plump Spartan before, hadn't remarked it when they were at sea, but here in the torchlight it was obvious.

Calchus turned on his heel – a rude gesture at the best of times, a calculated insult now – and waved up the beach. 'Fine. He can stay with me, too. It's late to be out, Kineas. I'll save all my "whatever happened to so-and-so" questions for the new day.'

If the Spartan was offended, he didn't show it. 'Very kind, sir.'

Despite days of physical labour and several restless nights, Kineas woke with the last of the night and walked outdoors to find the first sleepy slaves carrying water from a well into the kitchen. Philokles had spent the night on the porch, like a servant, but it didn't seem to have affected him much, since he was still asleep, snoring loudly. Kineas watched the dawn, and when there was light enough to see, he walked down the lane behind the house to the paddock. The pasture beyond had two dozen horses, most of which he was pleased to see were his own. He walked along the paddock until he saw what he had expected to find, a small fire burning in the distance and a man standing near it with a short spear in his hand. Kineas walked over the broken ground until the sentry recognized him, and then all the men were awake, nine men with heavy beards and equally bandy legs.

Kineas greeted each in turn. They were professional soldiers, cavalrymen with dozens of years of war and accumulated scars and none of them had the money or the friends to aspire to the status of the cavalry class in a city – Antigonus, the Gaul, was more likely to be enslaved than made a citizen in any city, and he, like his friend Andronicus, had started with some other mercenaries sent out by Syracuse. The rest of them had once been men of property in cities that either no longer wanted them or no longer existed. Lykeles was from Thebes, which Alexander had destroyed. Coenus was Corinthian, a lover of literature, an educated man with a secret past – a rich man apparently unable to return home. Agis was Megaran and Athenian, a well-born pauper who knew no other life but war. Graccus, Diodorus and Laertes were the last of the Athenian citizens – the last of the men who had followed Kineas to Asia. They were penniless exiles.

Niceas, his hyperetes for six years, came up last and they embraced. Niceas was the oldest of them, at forty-some years. He had grey in his thick black hair and a scar across his face from a Persian sword. He'd been born to a slave in an Athenian brothel.

'All the lads who are left. And all the horses.'

Kineas nodded, spotting his favourite pale grey charger out in the paddock. 'All the best of both. You all know where we're going?'

Most of them were still half asleep. Antigonus was already stretching his calf muscles like an athlete. They all shook their heads with little interest.

'The Archon of Olbia has offered me a fortune to raise and train his hippeis – his cavalry bodyguard. If he is satisfied with us, we'll be made citizens.' Kineas smiled.

If he expected them to be moved, he was disappointed. Coenus waved a hand and spoke with the contempt of the true aristocrat. 'Citizens of the most barbaric city in the Euxine? At the whim of some petty tyrant? I'll just have mine in silver owls.'

Kineas shrugged. 'We're not getting younger, friends,' he said. 'Don't spurn the citizenship until you see the city.'

'Who's the enemy, then?' asked Niceas, absently fingering the amulet around his neck. He'd never been a citizen anywhere – the whole idea was a fantasy to him.

'I don't know – yet. His own people, I think. Not much up here to fight.'

'Macedon, maybe.' Diodorus spoke quietly, but with great authority.

Diodorus knew more about politics than the others. Kineas turned to him. 'You know something?'

'Just rumour. The boy king is off conquering Asia and Antipater is thinking of conquering the Euxine. We heard it in the Bosporus.' He grinned. 'Remember Phillip Kontos? He's commanding Antipater's Companions, now. We saw him. He tried to hire us.'

The other man nodded. Kineas thought for a minute, his head down on one fist as he did when something puzzled him, and then spoke. 'I'll get you the wherewithal from the house. Write a couple of your famous letters and get me some information. In Ecbatana and in Athens, no one ever mentioned that Antipater would march.' Diodorus nodded curtly. Kineas looked them over. 'We lived,' he said suddenly. There had been times when it seemed pretty certain that none of them would.

Niceas shook his head. 'Just barely.' He had a cup of wine in his hand, and he hurried to slop a libation on the ground for his apparent ingratitude to the gods. 'Here's to the shades of them that didn't.'

They all nodded.

'Good to see you all again. We'll ride together from here. No more ships for me.' They all walked out to the horses, except Diodorus, who stayed as sentry. It was one of their invariable rules – they always had a sentry. Learned the hard way. Justified too many times.

The horses were in good shape, their hooves hard from the rock and sand in the soil, their coats shiny. They had fifteen heavy horses and six light, as well as several pack animals – a former charger past his best years but still willing, two mules they'd captured raiding Thracians with the boy king and never quite lost. To Kineas, every horse had a story; most were Persian chargers from the spoils of the fight at the Issus River, but there was a bay he'd bought in the army market after the fall of Tyre, and the metal-grey charger, the biggest mare he'd ever seen, had been left wandering riderless after a skirmish at a ford on the Euphrates. The big horse reminded him of the other grey – the stallion he'd taken at Issus, long dead of cold and poor food. War was unkind to horses. And men. Kineas found himself moved by how few of them were left. But his chest was tight with the joy of seeing them.

'Well done, all. I need a day or two – we're not due in Olbia until the *Kharisteria*, so we have time. Let me get my legs under me, and then we'll ride.'

Niceas waved his arms at them. 'Leaving in a day? Lots to do, gentlemen. Tack, armour, weapons.' He began to issue suggestions very like orders, and the other men, most of them born to wealth and power, obeyed him, although he had been born in a brothel.

Kineas put his hand on his hyperetes' shoulder. 'I'll bring my kit down and join you this afternoon.' Another habit – every man cleaned his own kit, like hoplites. 'Send Diodorus to me. I'm going to the gymnasium.'

Niceas nodded and led the rest of them to work.

In what passed for the city, they had three things built of stone: the wharfs, the warehouses and the gymnasium. Kineas went to the gymnasium with Diodorus. Philokles joined them as they left, and Calchus insisted on acting as their guide and sponsor.

If the size of his establishment hadn't immediately given away his wealth, his reception in the agora and the gymnasium was ample evidence. In the agora, he was greeted with respectful nods and several men solicited his favour as he walked through. At the gymnasium, the other three men were immediately admitted free of charge at Calchus's insistence.

'I built this,' Calchus said with pride. He proceeded to catalogue the building's merits. Kineas, perhaps closer in his mind to Athens, thought it was satisfactory yet provincial. Calchus's boasting grated on him. Nonetheless, the gymnasium offered him the best opportunity to exercise that he'd had in months. He stripped, dropping his borrowed garment on top of his sandals.

Calchus guffawed. 'Too long in the saddle!' he laughed.

Kineas stiffened with resentment. His legs were a trifle over-muscled at the top, and his lower legs had never been much to look at. To his fellow Hellenes, who worshipped the male form, his legs were less than perfect, although he had to go to a gymnasium to be reminded of it.

He began to warm up. Calchus, by contrast, had a hard body,

27

carefully maintained, although he had the beginning of a roll of fat at his waist. And he had long legs. He began to wrestle with a much younger man on the sand of the courtyard. Spectators made ribald comments. The young man was apparently a regular.

Kineas gestured to Diodorus. 'Fancy a couple of falls?'

'At your pleasure.' Diodorus was tall, bony and ascetic looking. He was not any Hellene's idea of beauty either.

Kineas circled, waiting until the taller man stepped towards him to attack and pushed in to meet him and get inside the man's long reach. Diodorus took the momentum of the attack into his arms and threw it over his hip, and Kineas crashed his length in the sand.

He got up slowly. 'Was that necessary?'

Diodorus was embarrassed. 'No.'

Kineas gave a bitter smile. 'If you're trying to tell me that your wrestling is of a different order than mine, I already knew that.'

Diodorus raised his hand. 'How often do I get a chance to use that move? You walked into it. I couldn't help myself.' He was smiling, and Kineas rubbed the sore spot on his back and stepped forward for another hold. He felt a tiny twist of fear – the niggling fear that he carried into every contest, every fight.

He went for a low hold, got a piece of it, and he and Diodorus ended up in an ugly mess on the ground, neither man able to pin the other and both coated in sand and grit. By unspoken mutual consent, they both left off their holds and helped each other up.

Outside, Calchus had pinned the young man he was wrestling. He didn't seem in a hurry to let him up, and there was a great deal of laughter from the other citizens. Kineas faced Diodorus again and this time they circled and feinted and closed and recovered at a more normal tempo. It was almost dance, and Diodorus stayed to the movements of his gymnasium lessons, which kept Kineas comfortable. He even gained a fall.

Diodorus rubbed his hip and smiled. Kineas had fallen atop him, a perfectly legitimate approach to the game but one inevitably painful to the victim. 'Even?'

'Even.' Kineas gave him a hand up.

Calchus was standing with the young man and some other citizens. He called out, 'Come and wrestle with me, Kineas.'

Kineas frowned and turned his head, uncomfortable with all these strangers, the twinge of fear strong because Calchus was bigger, a better wrestler and as a boy in Athens had liked to use his advantages to inflict a little pain. Kineas disliked pain. Ten years of war had not accustomed him to dealing with sprains and bruises and deep cuts that took weeks to heal; if anything, ten years of watching men live or die at the whim of the gods had made him more afraid.

He shrugged. Calchus was his host, a fine wrestler and looking to demonstrate his superiority. Kineas gritted his teeth and obliged him, losing the first fall in some carefully fought grappling, taking the second fall by a matter of split-second timing that was more luck than skill, and which surprised both men. Calchus surprised him again by rising from the fall graciously, nothing but praise on his lips, and going on without rancour. Ten years ago, the adolescent Calchus would have come on for blood. The third fall was like the first; careful, at times more like dance than combat, and when Kineas was eventually pinned, the action caused the spectators to whistle in appreciation.

Calchus was breathing hard, and his arm circled Kineas's waist as he helped him to his feet. 'You give a good match. Did you all see him?' he called to the others. 'He used to be an easy mark for a fall.'

Men hurried forward to compliment Calchus on his victory – and to tell Kineas how well he had done. It was all a trifle sickening – a remarkable amount of praise lavished for so small a thing, but Kineas bore it in the knowledge that he had given a better guest gift than money, a memorable fight that left his host looking well.

The young man that Calchus had wrestled earlier was quite beautiful as he came up to pay respectful comments to the wrestlers. Kineas was unmoved by male beauty, but he appreciated it as much as any Hellene and he smiled at the earnest young man.

'I'm Ajax,' the young man said in reply to Kineas's smile. 'My

29

father is Isokles. May I say how well you fought? Indeed, I ...'
He hesitated, swallowed his words, and was silent.

Kineas read him easily – he was an observant youth. He was going to say that Kineas had looked the better wrestler. A smart boy. Kineas put a hand on the smooth skin of the boy's shoulder. 'I always imagined Ajax would be bigger.'

'He's heard that stupid joke his whole life,' said the father.

'I try to grow to fit it,' Ajax returned. 'And there was a smaller Ajax, too.'

'Do you box? Care to exchange a few cuffs?' Kineas gestured at the straps for boxers, and the boy's face lit up. He looked at his father, who shook his head with mock indignation. 'Don't get too cut up, or no one will want to take you home from the symposium,' he said. He winked at Kineas. 'Or should I say, get cut up, so you won't get taken home? Have kids of your own?'

Kineas shook his head. 'Well, it's an experience. Anyway, feel free to put a few welts on him.'

Diodorus helped them both wrap their hands, and then they began, starting as if by mutual consent with simple routines, blows and blocks, and then moving to longer exchanges and thence to sparring.

The boy was good – better than a farm boy in a Euxine backwater had any right to be. His arms were longer than they looked and he could feint, rolling his shoulders to telegraph a roundhouse that never came and then punching short with the off arm. He stretched Kineas, now fully warmed up and eager; a short blow to his cheek gave him some personal interest in the contest, and suddenly they were at it.

Kineas was unaware that they drew every citizen in the gymnasium. His world limited itself to his wrapped hands and those of his opponent, his eyes and torso. In one flurry, each of them jabbed ten or twelve times, parrying each blow with an upper arm, or taking one high on the chest to deliver one to the head.

The flurry ended in a round of applause that moved them apart. They eyed each other warily, still charged with the *daimon* of combat, but the surge of spirit soon dwindled and they became mere mortals in a provincial gymnasium again. They shook hands warmly.

'Again?' said the boy, and Kineas shook his head.

'Won't be that good again. Keep it as it is.' Then, after a pause, 'You're very good.'

The boy hung his head with real modesty. 'I was going as fast as I could. I don't usually. You are better than anyone here.'

Kineas shrugged and called over the boy's head to his father, proclaiming how talented his son was. It was an effective way of making friends in the gymnasium. Everyone wanted to congratulate him on his skill, on the beauty of the moment. It made him happy. But he needed a massage and a rest, and he said so, declining innumerable offers of further contests until someone said they were all going to throw javelins and he couldn't resist. He followed them outside and felt a pang – Philokles, forgotten or ignored, was running laps outside around a big field full of sheep.

Kineas didn't know what to do with the Spartan, who seemed to have become a dependant. Gentlemen weren't supposed to be so bereft, but Kineas suspected that he himself wouldn't have been much different if he had washed up on an alien shore with no belongings and no home. He waved. Philokles waved back.

A slave herded the sheep well down the field and the men started to throw. It wasn't a formal game; older men who were disgusted by their first throw took a second or even a third until they were satisfied, whereas younger men had to suffice themselves with one throw. It would never have done at the Olympic games, but it was comfortable, as the shadows shortened, to lie on the grass (mindful of the sheep turds) and watch the whole community of men compete. Kineas was conscious of his legs and the imperfections of his body, but he'd proven himself an athlete and was one of them now, making easy conversation with Isokles about the olive harvest in Attica and the problems of shipping olive oil.

Calchus threw with a great cry, and his javelin came close enough to make one of the sheep move with unaccustomed speed. He laughed. 'That's the best so far. I have a mind to throw again – they're my sheep, we could all eat mutton tonight.'

Kineas was to throw next to last and Philokles last, places of honour because they were guests. Diodorus had thrown early

– a good throw, with no grunt or cry, beaten only by Calchus. Most of the other townsmen had been competent, but the youth Ajax had surprised Kineas by his poor throw. Isokles had beaten it, throwing well, if short of the final mark, and he'd teased his son.

Kineas was used to throwing from horseback, and he threw too flat, but it was still a long throw – again the sheep started as his javelin landed close to them.

Calchus winced. 'You've become an athlete while I run to fat in exile,' he said.

Philokles picked up several javelins before choosing one. He walked over to Calchus, who was talking business with another man. 'This is scarcely sporting. I'm a Spartan.' He said it with a smile, an overweight Spartan showing a sense of humor.

Calchus didn't understand. He indicated with a flick of his head that he had been interrupted. 'If you can do better than we have, let's see it.'

Nettled, Philokles gestured at the sheep. 'How much for the straggling ewe?'

Calchus ignored him, returning to his conversation and then jerked his head around in time to see Philokles throw, arching his body and almost leaving the ground. The javelin leaped from his hand, flew high and descended fast. It knocked the ewe to the ground, all four feet splayed, the bolt from heaven pinning her to the ground through her skull.

There was a moment of shocked silence and then Kineas began to applaud. Then they all applauded the throw and teased Calchus about his ewe, suggesting various prices for her, some obscene, until Calchus laughed. Most of the town's social interaction seemed to revolve around keeping Calchus pleased. Kineas didn't like to watch it.

Isokles pointed down the field. 'Let's have a run,' he said. And they set the distances and were off, running for a while in a pack until the better runners grew bored and took off. They circled the field three times, a good distance, and finished in the yard of the gymnasium. Kineas was close to last and took some good-natured teasing about his legs, and then they headed for the baths.

32

Tired and clean, with a couple of bruises and a general sense of *eudaimia*, well-being that inevitably came to him from the gymnasium, Kineas walked beside Calchus. Diodorus had gone off with some younger men to see the market.

'You could do well here,' Calchus said suddenly. 'They like you. This fighting you do – it's no job for a man. In defence of your city, that's different. But – a mercenary? You squander what the gods have given you. And one day some barbarian's sword is in your gizzard, and there you are. Stay here, buy a farm. Take a wife. Isokles has a girl – she's pretty enough, smart, a housekeeper. I'd put you up for citizenship after the festival of Herakles. By Zeus, they'd accept you today after that boxing.'

Kineas didn't know what to say. It appealed. He'd liked the men. The citizens of Tomis were a good lot, provincial but not rustic, given to gross jokes and amateur philosophy. And all good sports. He shrugged. 'I owe it to my men. They came here to join me.' Kineas didn't add that something in him looked forward to another campaign.

'They can just as easily move on and take up service elsewhere. You are a gentleman, Kineas. You don't owe them anything.'

Kineas frowned. 'Most of them are gentlemen, Calchus.'

'Oh, of course.' Calchus waved dismissively. 'But not any more. Not really. Perhaps Diodorus? Could be a factor, or your steward. And those Gauls – they should be slaves. They'd be happier as slaves.' Calchus spoke with authority and finality.

Kineas frowned again and allowed himself to be distracted by a man lying in the street. He didn't need to quarrel with his host. 'A barbarian?' he asked, pointing.

The man in the street was plainly a barbarian. He wore trousers of leather and had filthy long hair hanging in plaits, and a leather jacket covered in a riot of colourful decoration, and he wore gold. His jacket had several gold ornaments, and showed spaces where other bangles had been removed. He had an earring in his ear. And a cap on his head like a Thracian.

And he stank of urine and vomit and bad sweat. They were almost on top of him. He wasn't asleep – his eyes were open and unfocused.

Calchus looked at him with deep contempt. 'A Scyth.

Disgusting people. Ugly, stinking barbarians, no one can speak their language, and they don't even make good slaves.'

'I thought they were dangerous.' Kineas looked at the drunk with interest. He imagined that at Olbia there would be a lot of Scyths, born to horseback, a dangerous enemy. This one didn't look like a warrior.

'Don't believe it. They can't hold wine, can't speak, can't really walk. Scarcely human. I've never seen one sober.'

Calchus walked on and Kineas followed him, albeit unwillingly. He wanted a better look, but Calchus was uninterested. Kineas looked back, and saw that the drunk was rising unsteadily to his feet. Then he toppled again, and Kineas followed Calchus around a corner and lost sight of the Scyth.

He heard a lot about Scyths at the symposium because he was the senior guest and he introduced the topic. The wine flowed; the inevitable flute girls and fish courses folllowed each other in the approved manner, and then the older men settled in to talk, moving their couches together so that the younger men could relish the more amorous of the flute girls with a degree of privacy. Eyeing a black-eyed girl, Kineas had a brief pang that he was now considered old enough to make conversation, but he pulled his couch to the side, and when he was asked, he suggested that they all tell him about the Scyths on the plains to the north.

Isokles took the pitcher of wine from a slave and looked at Kineas. 'You're not proposing we drink in the Scythian fashion? Unwatered wine?'

The young men yelled for it, but the older men held the day, and the wine was mixed at a sedate two waters to each measure of wine. While Calchus mixed the wine, Isokles looked thoughtful.

'They're barbarians, of course. Very hardy – they live on their horses. Herodotus has a lot to say about them. I have a copy at my house if you'd care to read it.'

'Honoured,' said Kineas. 'We read Herodotus when we were boys, but I had no idea I'd end up here.'

'The thing about them is that they fear nothing. They say they are the only free people on the earth, and that all the rest of us are slaves.'

Calchus snorted derisively. 'As if anyone could mistake us for slaves.'

Isokles, one of the few men who seemed willing to risk Calchus's displeasure, shrugged. 'Deny it if you will. Anarchises – does that name mean something to you?'

Kineas felt as though he was back in school, sitting in the shade of a tree and getting interrogated on his reading. 'Friend of Solon – a philosopher,' he said.

'A Scythian philosopher.' Philokles spoke up from the end of the room. 'A very *plain*-spoken man.'

A whisper of laughter honoured his pun.

'Just the one.' Isokles nodded at Philokles. 'He told Solon that the Athenians were slaves to their city – slaves to the walls of the Acropolis.'

'Nonsense,' said Calchus. He started passing cups of wine around the circle of couches.

'Oh, no, not nonsense, if I may.' Philokles was leaning on his elbows, his long hair framing his face. 'He meant that Greeks are slaves to their notions of safety – that our incessant need to protect ourselves robs us of the very freedom we so often prate about.'

Isokles nodded. 'Well put.'

Calchus shook his head vehemently. 'Crap. Pure crap. Slaves can't even carry arms – they have nothing to defend, nor can they defend anything.'

Philokles waved to the butler who had brought the wine service. 'You there,' he said. 'How much do you have in savings?'

The slave was middle-aged. He froze at being singled out.

'Answer him,' said Isokles. He was smiling.

In fact, Kineas realized that not only did Isokles not mind twisting Calchus's tail, he positively relished it.

The slave looked down. 'I don't exactly know. A hundred owls? Sirs?'

Philokles dismissed him with a wave. 'Just my point. I have just lost all of my possessions to Poseidon. I do not have a single owl, and this bowl of wine, the gift of my esteemed host, will, once in my gullet, be the sum total of my treasure.' He drank it. 'I am now as rich as I'll be for some time. I do not have a hundred owls of silver. This slave does. May I take it from him?'

Calchus ground his teeth. As the slave's owner, he probably held the man's cash. 'No.'

Philokles raised his empty cup. 'No. In fact, you would prevent me from taking it. So, it appears that this slave holds property and can defend it. And so would Anarchises say of us. In fact, he would say that we are slaves to the very act of holding our property.'

Isokles applauded with a trace of mockery. 'You should be a lawyer.'

Philokles, apparently immune to the mockery, replied, 'I have been.'

Kineas sipped his wine. 'Why are the Scythians so free, then?'

Isokles wiped his mouth. 'Horses, and endless plains. They don't so much defend their territory as wander it. When the Great King tried to make war against them, they melted before him. They never offered him battle. They refused to defend anything, because they had nothing to defend. In the end, he was utterly defeated.'

Kineas raised his cup. 'That I remember from Herodotus.' He swirled the wine in his cup thoughtfully. 'But the man in the street today ...' He paused.

'Ataelus,' Isokles put in. 'The drunk Scyth? His name is Ataelus.'

'Had a fortune in gold on his clothes. So they have something worth defending.'

The conversation grew much duller as the merchants present squabbled over the source of the Scythian gold. After another cup of wine, that gave way to a mock-scholarly debate on the reality or fiction of the tale of the Argonauts. Most of the men present insisted that the golden fleece was real, and debated which river feeding the Euxine had the gold. Philokles insisted that the entire tale was an allegory about grain. No one listened to him.

No one told Kineas anything useful about the Scythians, either. He drank four cups of watered wine, felt his internal balance change, and passed on the next cup.

'You didn't use to be such a woman about wine,' Calchus laughed.

Kineas didn't think he had done anything to react, but Calchus flinched from the look on his face and the room fell silent.

In a soldier's camp, that would have been an insult demanding blood. Calchus didn't mean it as such, Kineas could see, although he could also see that the habit of power had robbed Calchus of his social conscience.

Kineas bowed and forced a smile. 'Perhaps I should go sleep in the women's quarters, then,' he said.

Guffaws. Outright laughter from Isokles. Calchus's face grew red in the light of the lamps. It was his turn to resent an insult – the suggestion that his women might enjoy a visit from Kineas, however oblique. Kineas saw no reason to apologize. He upturned his cup and slipped away.

3

The next morning he was up with the dawn again. He didn't have a hard head and he didn't like to drink too much wine, however good the company.

Once again, Philokles was snoring on the portico. Kineas walked past him, thinking that the man was certainly a nested set of surprises, contrasts within contrasts, and he barely knew the Spartan. Fat athlete, Spartan philosopher.

He walked out to the paddock. One of the Gauls was standing sentry. This morning Kineas raised a hand in greeting and then went out to the paddock and got the grey stallion to come to him with a handful of dates. Then he was up on his bare back, his thighs clenched on the animal's ample sides, and the chill air of the morning was rushing past him as he cantered the length of the paddock. He jumped over the paddock rail without much effort on the stallion's part and headed north, off Calchus's farm and on to the rolling hills of the plains. He walked until the sun stood clear and red above the horizon, and then he made a garland of red flowers and sang the hymn to Poseidon, which the grey stallion liked. The stallion ate the rest of the dates and spurned the grass as too coarse, and then Kineas mounted and rode back towards the town, gradually pushing the stallion to his extended gallop, until he was a god, floating on a carpet of speed. The stallion was scarcely winded when he pulled up at the edge of the market. He dismounted and led the grey along the street until he found an early stallholder with a jug of watered wine for sale by the cup. He drank deeply of the sour stuff until he came fully awake. The grey watched him, waiting for a treat.

'Good fucking horse,' the Scythian said. He was standing by the stallion's rump. Kineas turned and saw that he was stroking him and cooing. The grey didn't resent it.

'Thanks, I think.'

'Buy me for wine?' the Scythian asked. The phrase rolled off his tongue as though he had said it a thousand times.

He didn't smell so bad this morning and he fascinated Kineas. Kineas paid for more wine, handed a cup to the Scyth, who drained it.

'Thanks. You ride for her? I see you ride – yes. Not bad. Yes. More wine, please.'

Kineas bought more wine. 'I ride all the time.' He was tempted to boast, but couldn't see why. He wanted the Scyth – a drunk, a beggar, but one with the value of a farm in gold about his person – to like him.

'Thanks. Rotten wine. You ride for all times? Me, too. Need for horse, me.' He looked comical, with his pointed hat and his terrible Greek. 'You got more horse? More?' He patted the grey.

Kineas nodded gravely. 'Yes.'

The Scyth patted his chest and touched his forehead – a very alien gesture, almost Persian. 'I call Ataelus. You call?'

'Kineas.'

'Show horse. More horse.'

'Come along, then.' Kineas mounted with a handspring, a showy, cavalry school mount. Before he could think about it, the Scyth was mounted behind him. Kineas had no idea how he had mounted so quickly. Now he felt ridiculous – he hadn't intended to let the man ride with him and they doubtless looked like fools. He took a back street and kept the stallion moving, ignoring the glances of a handful of early rising citizens. Something for Calchus to twit him with when he was up.

They cantered up to the paddock. All of his men were awake and Niceas had the paddock open for the grey before Kineas could call out.

Niceas held the grey's head as they dismounted. 'He's been here before. Seems harmless. Might make a good *prokusatore*.'

Kineas shrugged. 'I have a hard time understanding him, but I think he wants to buy a horse and get out of here.'

Diodorus was stretching his legs against the paddock wall. His hair was a tangle of Medusa-like red snakes in the morning, and he kept pushing the more aggressive locks off his forehead. 'Who can blame him? But if he's a Scyth, he'd be a good guide.'

Kineas made a quick decision and went over to the Gaul. 'Cut the white-faced bay out and bring him here.'

Antigonus nodded and started pushing through the horses. The Scyth walked over to the paddock wall and sat with his back against it, his leather trousers in the dirt. He didn't seem to mind. He seemed content just to watch the horses.

When Antigonus brought him the bay, Kineas walked it over to the Scyth. 'Tomorrow, we go to Olbia,' he said slowly.

'Sure,' said the Scyth. Impossible to tell if he understood.

'If you will guide us to Olbia, I'll give you this bay.'

The Scyth looked at the horse. He got to his feet, ran a hand over her and leaped on to her back. In one stride, he was moving at a gallop and off, over the wall of the paddock and up the road to the plain.

For a group of professional soldiers, it was an embarrassment how totally he had taken them by surprise. He was gone, just a thin tail of hoof dust hanging in the morning sun, before any of them thought of mounting or getting a weapon.

'Uh,' said Kineas. 'My fault. He seemed harmless.'

Niceas was still watching the dust, his hand on his amulet. 'He didn't exactly do us harm.'

'He certainly knew how to ride.' Coenus was watching the last of the dust under his hand. He grinned. 'The Poet called them centaurs, and now we know why.'

There wasn't anything useful to be done about it. They didn't know the plains and they didn't have the time to chase a lone Scyth for days. Niceas put them all, even Kineas, to cleaning their tack and packing it tight for the next movement. They agreed that they'd leave the next morning. It wasn't that they were a democracy – it was just that they took orders better if they had participated in shaping them.

Of course, Kineas took a good deal of teasing from the citizens – he'd lost them their pet Scyth, didn't he know better than to let a Scyth up on a horse? Would he let a child play with fire? And more such. Calchus just laughed.

'I wish someone had woken me up to see you riding with that drunk. The things I miss!' If he held any rancour about the night's revel, it was clearly dispelled by his guest's embarrassment of the morning.

'I'll be off in the morning.' Kineas was indeed embarrassed, and caught his fingers smoothing the hem of his tunic, an old habit.

Calchus watched the men around the paddock oiling leather. 'I can't make you see sense and stay?'

Kineas turned up his hands. 'I have a contract, my friend. When it is done, and I have a talent or two in silver – why, then I'd be pleased to have this conversation again.'

Calchus smiled. It was the first really happy smile that Kineas had seen in two days from the man. 'You'll think about it? That's good enough for me. I have Isokles coming tonight, and his daughter will visit to sing for us. Family evening – nothing to shock a girl. Take a look at her.'

Kineas realized that Calchus, for all his overbearing ways, was working quite hard to make Kineas welcome. 'You, a match-maker?'

Calchus put an arm around his shoulder. 'I said it when you first came. Your father saved our whole family. I don't forget. You're fresh from the city – you think I'm a big frog in a little pond. I see it. And I am. Isokles and I – we argue about every-thing, but we are the men of substance here. And there's room for more. The pond's not that small.'

For Calchus, that was a long, emotional speech. Kineas hugged him and got a crushing squeeze in return.

Calchus went off to watch slaves being loaded for Attica. Kineas went back to working on his tack. He was sitting with his back against the outside of the paddock, using the wall for shade, with his bridle laid out in pieces and a new headstall to sew on, when young Ajax loomed above him.

'Good day to you, sir,' he said.

'Your servant, Ajax. Please accept the accommodation offered by this tuft of grass.' Kineas waved to it and passed a skin full of sour wine, which Ajax drank as if it were ambrosia.

'My father sent this for you to look at.' He had a bag of scrolls over his shoulder like a student in the agora. He hoisted it to the ground.

Kineas opened one, glanced at the writing – a very neat copy-ist – and saw that it was *Herodotus*.

'It is only Book Four – the part about the Scythians. Because – well, my father says you are leaving – leaving tomorrow. For Olbia. So you won't have time to read much.'

Kineas nodded and picked up the headstall. 'I probably won't have time to read the first scroll,' he said.

Ajax nodded. He then sat in silence. Kineas resumed his work, using a fine bronze awl and the backing of a soft billet of wood to punch a neat row of holes down each side of the new headstall. He looked at Ajax from time to time from under his eyebrows – the boy was anxious, fidgeting with scraps of leather and bits of thread. But silent. Kineas liked him for his silence.

He kept working. When the holes were punched, he waxed a length of linen cord and fitted it to a needle – the needle was too large for the job, but it was the only good needle in the camp. Then he began to sew.

'The thing is ...' Ajax began. But he lost heart and the words just hung there.

Kineas let them dangle for a bit while he finished his length of cord and threaded a new one. 'The thing is?' he said gently.

'I want to see the world,' Ajax announced.

Kineas nodded. 'Laudable.'

'Nothing ever happens here.'

'Sounds good to me.' Kineas wondered if he could live in a place where the festivals and the gymnasium were the sum of excitement. But on this day, facing the loss of a horse, an uncertain journey and the tyrant of Olbia, he felt that a life of certain boredom looked preferable.

'I want to – to join your company. To ride with you. I can ride. I'm not much with a javelin but I could learn, and I can box and wrestle and fight with the spear. And I spent a year with the shepherds – I can sleep rough, start a fire. I killed a wolf.'

Kineas looked up. 'What does your father say?'

Ajax beamed. 'He says that I can go with you if you are fool enough to take me.'

Kineas laughed. 'By the gods. That's just what I expect he said. He's coming to dine here tonight.'

Ajax nodded vigorously. 'So am I. And Penelope – my sister – is going to sing. She sings beautifully, and she weaves wool better than merchant's wool. And she is beautiful – I shouldn't say it, but she is.'

Kineas hadn't encountered this level of instant hero worship before. He couldn't help but bask in the admiration for a little while. But not long. 'I shall be pleased to meet your sister. I will talk to your father tonight. But Ajax – we're mercenaries. It's a hard life. Fighting for the boy king – that was soldiering for the city, in a way, even if we got a rough reception when we came home. Sleeping rough, aye. And worse. Days without sleep. Nights on guard, on horseback, in enemy country.' His voice trailed off, and then he said, 'War isn't what what it was, Ajax. There is no battle of champions. The virtues of our ancestors are seldom shown in modern war.'

He stopped himself, because his words were having the opposite effect from what he had planned. The boy's eyes were shining with delight. 'How old are you?'

'Seventeen. At the festival of Herakles.'

Kineas shrugged. Old enough to be a man. 'I'll talk to your father,' he said. And when Ajax started to stammer thanks, he was merciless. 'By the crooked-minded son of Cronus, boy! You could die. Pointlessly, in someone else's fight – a street brawl, defending a tyrant who despises you. Or from a barbarian arrow in the dark. It's not Homer, Ajax. It's dirty, sleepless, full of scum and bugs. And on the day of battle, you are one faceless man under your helmet – no Achilles, no Hector, just an oars-man rowing the phalanx toward the enemy.'

Wasted words. He hoped they were not prophetic, because he still had some Homer in him after ten years of the real thing. He dreaded the pointless death in an alley, or a wine-shop squabble. He'd seen them happen to other men.

Late afternoon and his tack was clean and neat, the horses were inspected, the other men as ready as they needed to be, the armour and cornell-wood javelins packed in straw panniers for the baggage animals. He'd moved from the paddock to the base of the farm's lone oak tree with a blanket to repair, but Kineas found it difficult to keep his eyes open. The coming dinner reminded him of the girl, Ajax's sister, and what she would have meant – home, security, work. And her mere mention reminded him that it had been months since he had lain with a woman. Probably not since he left the army. And the contrast seemed vivid. Without even meeting Ajax's sister, he could see her, at least in the guise of his own sisters. Demure. Quiet. Beautiful, remote, devout, cautious. Intelligent, perhaps, but certainly ignorant, without conversation.

His longest liaison in the army had been with Artemis. Not, obviously, her real name. She was a camp follower, a prostitute, although she insisted on being called *Hetaera* and claimed that she would be one in time. Loud, opinionated, violent in her loves and hates, given to drinking undiluted wine, she had seen more war than most of the soldiers, for all that she wasn't yet twenty.

She'd stabbed a Macedonian file-closer who tried to rape her. She'd fucked most of the men in his troop, adopted them and been adopted. She had her own horse, could recite whole passages of Homer and dance every dance the men could – all the Spartan military dances, all the dances of the gods. The night before a battle, she would sing. Like Niceas, she was born in a brothel near the agora in Athens. She made the whole company, even the Corinthians and the Ionians, learn the anthem of Athens, to which she was fiercely patriotic.

> Come, Athena, now if ever!
> Let us now thy Glory see!
> Now, O Maid and Queen, we pray thee,
> Give thy servants victory!

She turned their drab followers into part of the company, got them messes, dealt with their squabbles and ruled them. And gave them value. And she had said to Kineas one night, 'Two things a girl needs to make it in this army: a hard heart and a wet cunny. That's not in Homer, but I'd wager that it was the same for the girls at Troy.'

Artemis was well known to pick a unit she liked and go to the strongest man in it, until he died or she grew restless or he didn't provide for her. She wouldn't abide a non-provider. Kineas had kept her a year, in camp and city. She'd left him

44

for Phillip Kontos, a Macedonian hipparch, a good professional move, and he didn't hate her for it, although it occurred to him behind closed eyelids under a tree on the Euxine that he had expected her to stay with him.

Like the women, the life. He didn't see much hope of becoming a farmer.

He fell asleep and Poseidon sent him a dream of horses.

He was riding a tall horse – or he was the horse, and they flowed together on an endless plain of grass – floating, galloping, on and on. There were other horses, too, and they followed, until he left the plain of grass for a plain of ash. And then they neighed and fell behind, and he rode on alone. And then they were at a river – a ford, full of rocks. On the far bank was a pile of driftwood as tall as a man, and a single dead tree, and on the ground beneath his hooves were the bodies of the dead ...

He awoke with a start, rubbed his eyes and wondered what god had sent him such a dream. Then he rose and went to the house's bath, handed his best chiton to a slave to press and gave the woman a few obols to do a good job. She brought him ewers of warm water to bathe. She was attractive – an older woman with a good figure, high cheekbones and a tattoo of an eagle on her shoulder. Sex crossed his mind, but she was having none of it, and he didn't press the issue. Perhaps because he didn't, he got his chiton beautifully pressed, with every fold opened and carefully erased, the wool shining white, so that he looked like the statue of Leto's son on Mytilene. She accepted his thanks with a stiff nod and stayed out of his reach, which made him wonder about the habits of the house.

He walked naked back to where the men were camped. He had some good things in his baggage, to go with his good chiton. He had good sandals, light and strong with red leather bindings that helped disguise the scar on his leg, but the only cloak he had was his military cloak, which had once been blue and was now a faded colour between sky-blue and dust. He did, however, have an excellent cloak pin; a pair of Medusa's heads in bright silver from the very best Athenian sculptor and castor. He pinned it to the old cloak with a muttered prayer and slung the cloak over his shoulder anyway, out by the fire with Diodorus and Niceas.

The other men had gone to the market to drink. They hadn't been invited to the symposium, and since most of them were as well born as Calchus, they chose to resent it. Agis and Laertes and Graccus had known Calchus as a boy. They were angry at being treated as inferiors.

Diodorus had a flagon of good wine, and he Coenus and Niceas passed it around while Kineas finished dressing.

Niceas held out a good brooch to put on his cloak, loot from Tyre, meant as a guest gift for Calchus. 'Save the Medusas for a more worthy host,' he said.

Kineas wondered what Calchus would think if he knew that the slave-born Athenian on his back farm considered him a poor host. Probably snort in contempt. His ruminations on Calchus were interrupted.

'Look at that,' Niceas exclaimed.

Kineas turned and looked over his shoulder. A lone horseman was trotting to the paddock. Coenus laughed.

'Ataelus!' bellowed Kineas.

The Scyth raised a dusty hand in greeting and swung his legs over the side of the horse so that he slipped in one lithe movement to the ground. He touched the flank of the horse with a little riding whip and she turned and walked through the gate into the paddock.

'Horse good,' he said. He reached out a hand for the flagon.

Coenus handed it to him without a moment's hesitation. The Scyth took a deep drink, rubbed his mouth with his hand. Then Coenus caught the Scyth in a bear hug. 'I think I like you, barbarian!' he said.

Kineas shook his head. 'I thought you stole the horse.'

The Scyth either didn't understand or ignored the subject. 'Where for you go? Leave tomorrow, yes? Yes, yes?'

Kineas was conscious of the sounds of conversation from the drive. Isokles and his family were arriving. It was late. 'Olbia,' he said.

The Scyth looked at him. He handed the flask to Diodorus as if he had always been part of their circle. 'Long,' he said. 'Far.' His Greek wasn't barbaric. He pronounced his few words well, but had no notion of the complex rules of cases that governed nouns.

'Ten days?' asked Diodorus. That's what the merchants had said.

The Scyth shrugged. His eyes were back on the horse.

'You'll guide us?' asked Kineas.

'Me *go* for you. You *go*. Horse good. Yes?'

'I think that's a deal, boss.' Niceas nodded. 'I'll just keep an eye on the bugger, shall I?'

Coenus shook his head. 'Ataelus and I share a hobby. Let's go get drunk, my friend.'

Ataelus grinned. 'Think for like you, too, Hellene!' he said to Coenus. They walked off together toward the wine shops of town.

Niceas looked at Diodorus. 'I guess we get to watch the camp.'

'While I go to a dinner party? Excellent.' Kineas grinned. 'He'll make a superb scout if we can keep him.'

Niceas waited until Coenus and the Scyth were out of earshot before going on. 'He's plenty smart.'

Kineas had seen some intelligence in the face, but he was surprised to hear Niceas confirm it. 'Smart just how?'

Niceas pointed at the horse. 'If he had just stayed here with us, would we trust him on the plains? But he's already shown he *could* ride off, right? Stands to reason we'll trust him more.'

Kineas saw it, put that way. 'You're as much a philosopher as that Spartan kid, Niceas.'

Niceas nodded. 'Always thought so. And if he's a philosopher, I'm a hipparch in the Guards.'

'Enlighten me.' Kineas was actually standing on the balls of his feet, that eager to be in Calchus's house on time, but Niceas was not much given to bursts of conversation and when he spoke it was worth listening to.

'I heard from Dio about his javelin throw. He swam for an hour, maybe more, before you rescued him, or so I heard it. Spartan bastard. Out of shape – don't know why. But he's officer class – Spartiate. The tough ones. Fucking killing machines.'

'I'll bear that in mind,' Kineas said.

'Don't marry the girl until we've done our contract,' said Niceas.

Dismissed by his own hyperetes, Kineas headed for the house. He was still thinking about Niceas's comments when he found himself lying full length on a wide couch with the Spartan himself.

'I hope you don't mind sharing with me,' Philokles said. 'I asked Calchus to put me here. I think he was going to give you Ajax.'

'Thanks.' The Spartan's breath was heavy with wine already. Kineas moved a fraction away.

'You are leaving tomorrow?'

'Yes.'

'For Olbia?'

'Yes. That's where we have our contract.' Kineas was finding it hard to talk to Philokles, a man who seemed immune to social convention, while the other guests, Isokles, Ajax, and a robed and veiled figure that had to be a woman all stood, obviously waiting to be introduced to the principal guest before taking their ease.

'Will you take me?' Philokles clearly resented having to ask. A good deal of suppressed arrogance was very close to the surface.

'Can you ride?'

'Not well. But I can.'

'Can you cook?' Kineas was in a hurry to end this – Isokles had just shifted his weight, they were being very rude to the other guests, why couldn't Philokles have kept this until the end of the meal? But he didn't want to say yes.

'Not if you want to eat it. Otherwise, yes.'

Kineas raised his eyes to Isokles and tried to pass a message. *I know I'm being rude, I'm being importuned by someone whose life I saved.* Isokles winked. The gods only knew what he thought was happening.

'I'll take you. It may be dangerous,' he added weakly, too late to make any difference.

'All the better,' said the Spartan. 'Goodness, we're being rude. We should greet the other guests.'

Isokles and Ajax greeted them and took their places on

couches. The girl had vanished, probably taken to the women's rooms on the other side of the house.

Dinner consisted of fish, all very good; lobster, a little under-cooked, and then more fish – the sort of *opson*-filled meal that moralists in Athens complained of. Watered wine made the rounds, a series of slaves bearing in the ewers of wine and Calchus mixing in the water himself. He was the only one alone on a couch, and he started conversations to include all of his guests; the wars of the boy king of Macedon, the hubris of the boy king claiming to be a god, the lack of piety in the younger generation, with the exception of Ajax. Despite his best intentions, he tended to launch monologues on his views on each of these matters. Ajax was silent and respectful, Isokles didn't rise to the arguments as Kineas had expected he would, and Philokles applied himself to the fish courses as if he didn't expect to eat this well ever again.

After the last food course basins of water were brought and all the men washed their hands and faces.

Calchus raised a wine bowl. 'This is really a family gathering,' he said. 'To Isokles, my rival and brother; and to Kineas, to whom I owe everything I have achieved here.' He poured a libation to the gods on to the floor and then drank the bowl to the dregs and upended it to show it was empty. 'Since we are just family, it will outrage no god or goddess for your daughter to sing for us, Isokles.'

'I couldn't agree more,' said the older man. He took a full bowl of wine and raised it. 'To Calchus, for hosting us to this excellent dinner, and to his friend Kineas, who we all hope will grace us with his presence for long years to come.' He, too, poured off a libation.

Kineas realized that it was his turn. He felt out of place, shy, unaccustomedly foreign. He took a full bowl and rose to a sitting position. 'To the hospitality of Calchus, and to the making of new friends – for new friends are gifts from the immortal ones on high Olympus.' He drank the cup down.

Philokles took his bowl and stood with it. Kineas could see on the faces of Isokles and Calchus that Philokles had it wrong

– he was not supposed to raise a toast any more than young Ajax – but he did.

'Poseidon, Lord of Horses, and Kineas saved me from the sea, and Calchus's hospitality made me a man again.' His libation to the gods was half the cup, and then he drank the rest. 'Surely there is no bond dearer than guest to host.' He subsided back on to his couch.

Ajax recognized the quote and applauded. Isokles raised his bowl in salute. Even Calchus, who at best tolerated the Spartan, gave him a nod and smile of thanks.

Two women entered the back of the room, unveiled, their hair piled high atop their heads and wearing fine linen. The older had to be Calchus's wife, although this was the first time Kineas, who had lived in the house for three days, had laid eyes on her. She was tall, well built, long of limb and elegant in her movements, and she carried her head high. Her face would not have launched a thousand ships, but her expression of pleasure and her obvious intelligence took the place of beauty. She smiled at all of them.

'This is Penelope,' she said quietly, without raising her eyes. 'Daughter of Isokles. I will just sit by and listen, if I may.' She never raised her eyes, never mentioned her own name – the very picture of a modest matron – except that surely Calchus had no children or Kineas would have seen them.

Penelope had large, round eyes that darted around the room like excited animals. She would lower them when she remembered modesty, but just as suddenly they would start, rise up and seek new quarry.

Kineas decided that she had probably never been out in public before, perhaps never seen men having a private dinner. He himself had often taken a meal with his sisters and told them the news of the day or the gossip from the gymnasium, but not all girls got as much.

Her hair was very black and her skin fairer than most. She had a long neck, long arms, well-shaped hands. She was quite attractive, obviously the female twin to Ajax, but Kineas found her furtive curiosity disturbing – too much like a caged animal. And after Artemis, modesty no longer appealed to him as much.

He felt a vague disappointment. What had he expected?

She began to sing without any warm-up, and she had a clear, light voice. She sang a harvest song from the festival and she sang a love song he had heard in Athens, and then she sang three songs that were quite new to him and whose cadences sounded foreign. Her singing was good, confident, if a little quiet and breathy. She sang an ode and finished with a hymn to Demeter.

They all applauded. Philokles punched his arm and smiled broadly.

Isokles stood. 'Not every father indulges his children like this – I mean, that she sings songs meant for men. But it seems to me that she has a gift, sent by Leto's son, and that she should be allowed to polish it and even show it off, if she does so with modesty. Which, I may be excused for thinking, she has done.' He looked at Kineas.

Kineas once again fretted to be the centre of attention. He saw that Calchus's wife was looking straight at him – she had lovely eyes, perhaps her best feature – they were all looking at him expectantly. *I've only been here three days and you've cast me in the role of the suitor.*

'Nothing more suitable or modest in the eyes of the gods than for Penelope to show the talents they have given her to friends and family,' he said. He could see from their reactions that he had not hit the right note – years of commanding men had taught him to read expressions that quickly, and these reactions were not of the best. But what was he to say? To praise her singing or her appearance would be to break the artificial constraints of this being a 'family gathering'. Was he supposed to take that plunge, moved by a sudden passion, and declare himself her suitor?

Sod that, he thought, suddenly angry.

Philokles shifted on the couch next to him and rose unsteadily to his feet. 'In Sparta, our women live in public with our men, so I'll ask you to excuse me if I am uncouth. But surely Penelope is the very image of modest accomplishment; the muses must love a girl who plays so well.'

Kineas looked up at Philokles, who swayed a little as if drunk although he had taken very little wine. *His* compliment was well received; Calchus's wife, for instance, smiled and nodded. Isokles looked pleased.

Well shot, Philokles. Kineas punched his arm lightly as he sank back on to the couch, and Philokles grinned at him with a look that said, *You're a slow one, I'll explain all this later, you dolt.*

Isokles rose again. 'And while I'm indulging my children, I will ask a favour of Kineas here, since he is my fellow guest and the man of the evening. Favour me and take my son with you to Olbia?'

Right in public, where I can't refuse. By contrast, Philokles' request was the soul of courtesy. Kineas stole a glance at Calchus's wife. She looked interested. Kineas said, 'I am a soldier. The life I lead is dangerous, and the campaigns are long. I fear to take the responsibility for your son and leave his bones in some field. I fear the anger of the gods if I take him from you, and I fear your wrath if some untoward thing might happen. Don't men say: "In peace, sons bury their fathers, but in war, fathers bury their sons"?'

Isokles was sitting on his couch with his hand on Ajax's shoulders. 'He needs to see something of the world. His head is full of Achilles and Odysseus and nothing but the mud and flies of a real campaign will cure him.' Isokles's eyes met his own. 'There is always risk, when you are a father. I let Penelope sing here – I have risked her reputation, and mine. The risk is small, the company near and dear – I accept it. You might say I have known you only three days, but I say, you are the boyhood friend of Calchus and Calchus, for all we are rivals in everything – I speak bluntly to please the gods – for all that we are rivals, Calchus is the closest man to my heart. And your reputation precedes you, too, Kineas. Were you not sent to the boy king with fifty men to be hostages for Athens? And did you not succeed in winning his praise as a man, as a soldier, to the credit of your city? Calchus says that you have made five campaigns in six years, and that only the jealousy of the assembly at your father's wealth sent you to exile. I have met you. You are a man I could trust with my child.'

'Or both of them,' whispered Philokles.

Kineas didn't want all the praise, nor did he think they knew what little glory he'd garnered with Alexander. Trusted cavalrymen were on mighty charges that shattered Persian armies. Greek cavalry were lucky to be assigned to scout a ford on the flank of the army.

'You praise me above my merits. I will take Ajax to Olbia and show him a little war, and cure him, as you ask.' Kineas sighed. Philokles hit him in the ribs quite hard with an elbow.

Calchus sprang up. 'Enough family business. Wife, be off with you – it is time for men to speak of men's things and drink some wine.'

His wife took Penelope by the hand and she rose gracefully, nodded her head to the guests, and withdrew. She had never spoken a word. She was what – fifteen? Sixteen? Kineas watched her go and noted the scowl on the face of Calchus's wife.

'Does Ajax have a good horse?' Kineas asked.

'Not as good as any of yours. Ours are lighter, really just for a race behind the agora.'

Kineas looked to Isokles. 'If he's coming with me, he'll need money to buy equipment in Olbia – you don't have the items here, I looked in the market. Two heavy chargers and a light horse – probably his racehorse is too fine for the work. Several heavy tunics. A big straw hat like slaves wear in the fields – the bigger, the better. Two javelins – good ones, with cornell wood shafts and bronze heads. Boots to protect his legs when we manoeuvre. And a sword. I'd like him to carry a cavalry sword. I'll teach him to use it.' He looked at the boy. 'You ride well?'

Ajax looked down modestly. 'Well enough.'

'Chair seat? On the rump of the horse?'

'No. Like the Dacae. I learned to ride from one when I was a boy.' Ajax looked up to see if this was the right answer.

It was. 'Good. And armour. The panoply will be as much as a hoplite's – heavy breastplate and back, and a helmet with cheek pieces.'

Isokles was fingering his beard. 'How much? I want him to have good equipment and good horses. They can keep a man alive.'

Kineas nodded sharply, all business on familiar ground.

'Exactly. I have no notion what things cost in Olbia, but with all the Scyths there I hope that good horses are plentiful and cheap. Still – a hundred owls?'

Isokles laughed. 'Ouch. Look, Ajax, why didn't you just ask to have a ship built for you?' He held out his hand. 'No, I jest. A hundred owls in a purse, and another fifty for you, Kineas, against expenses.'

Kineas knew it was customary for hipparchs to hold extra money on campaign for the sons of the rich, but he had never benefited from it. 'Thank you.'

'I don't want him to seem poor besides the sons of the rich in Olbia. Send for more if things are expensive.'

Calchus rose from his couch. 'I, too, have something for you, Kineas.' He beckoned to the doorway, and a young male slave came in. 'This is Crax. A Thracian. He claims to be good with horses, and he can handle a spear. You need a slave – a man of your position looks naked without one.'

'You are too generous,' said Kineas, who had not owned a slave of his own in years. He didn't know what to say. Crax looked more like a potential recruit than a slave – good carriage, good muscles, young, and his stance suggested that slavery had not beaten his aggressiveness out of him.

'Well, I insist. We all want you to succeed – go, please the tyrant, win a few talents, and come back here. And I'll be honest – Crax is a bit much for my foreman to handle. Nothing for you, I'm sure.'

Crax stood like a soldier at attention. Cavalrymen had a saying – no worse gift than an unbroken horse. 'Thank you, Calchus. Thank you for the hospitality and the care you gave my men and horses, and now this. I'll repay you when I can.' He gestured to Crax. 'Fetch my cloak and sandals, will you?'

Crax marched out of the room.

'So soon? You and Philokles have so much to add to spice our conversation,' said Isokles.

'I apologize for leaving you so early, but I'll be riding with the dawn.'

'And taking my son. Well, I'll enjoy his company another hour.'

Kineas nodded to Ajax. 'Join us when the sun is rising by the paddock. I'll provide you a horse until we can buy you a string of them.'

Ajax looked as though it was all too good to be true. 'I can't wait until morning.'

Kineas looked at Isokles and shook his head. 'I can.' He nudged Philokles.

Philokles showed no sign of feeling the nudge. 'I'll just stay here and enjoy my last night of civilization,' he said. He raised his wine bowl to have it filled.

4

The sun shot over the distant hills between one girth strap and the next, and suddenly the light was different and every blade of grass in the yard had its own shadow. Kineas counted heads – all present, all looking eager, even the old soldiers. Ajax had a slave with his own horse, which he had insisted on bringing, a pretty Persian mare. Crax went up on one of the spare chargers as if born to the saddle, which he probably was, and carried Kineas's two javelins easily in the same hand as his reins. Ataelus had a bow on a belt at his hip and a riding whip, and he moved his bay around the grass like most men walk, the man and the horse a single animal. Niceas mounted and passed the reins of the baggage animals to the slaves. Kineas rode with him up and down the column. A dozen men, twenty horses and baggage – too big a target for bandits, all the men obviously armed. Kineas liked the look of them, felt happy to have them all. He left Niceas in the middle of the column with the remounts and the baggage and rode to the head where the Scyth waited.

Calchus was not up. Only a handful of slaves were moving around the house, most of them carrying water. Isokles was there to see his son leave, leaning on the paddock wall and chewing grass.

'Embrace your father,' Kineas said to Ajax.

Ajax dismounted and they embraced for a long time. Then he came back and vaulted into the saddle.

Kineas raised his hand. 'Let's ride,' he said.

The road from Calchus's farm became a track the width of two cart wheels within a few stades, and continued as such all day as it turned inland from the sea and headed north and west. At first, Greek farms lined the road, each house set well back amid olive groves and fields of wheat. After a few hours, the Greek farms vanished, to be replaced by rustic villages where the women worked in the fields and men wore barbarian dress, although there were plenty of Greek goods to be seen at every house – amphorae, bronze goods, blankets and wool fabric.

'Who are they?' asked Kineas.

Ataelus didn't understand the question until it was repeated with a gesture. 'Bastarnae,' he said. He said a good deal more, with occasional Greek words interposed in his own barbarian tongue – *bar bar babble* smash *bar bar bar* destroy! And *bar babble* warriors. From which Kineas understood that they were fierce warriors when roused. He had heard as much.

They didn't seem particularly fierce.

When the sun was sinking, they found a bigger house in the third village and asked for lodging. They were well received by an obvious chieftain and his wife, and one silver owl of Athens paid for fodder and food for the whole party. Kineas declined to sleep in the house, but accepted dinner, and despite the barrier of language, enjoyed himself. Philokles declined dinner.

'My fucking thighs are bleeding,' he said.

Kineas winced. 'You're a Spartan.'

Philokles swore. 'I gave up on that closed-mouth, endure-the-pain shit when I was exiled.'

Niceas laughed. 'You'll be fine,' he said. 'In about a week.'

But they provided him with salve, and Niceas saw to it that the salve made its way to Ajax as well.

In the morning, they were away again at first light. They continued to ride past villages and fields. Twice they passed Greek men with carts headed into the town they had left with goods for market.

Late afternoon brought them to the ferry at the Danube. The river, just one of its many mouths, was as wide as a lake. The ferryman had a small farm and had to be summoned to his duty. It took them an hour to unpack the horses and pack the ferry and then they were away, rowed by the ferryman and his slaves while the horses swam alongside. It was a difficult, complex operation, but Kineas and his veterans had crossed too many rivers to be unprepared, and they made it without the loss of baggage or horse.

The mast of the ferryboat cast a long shadow by the time they were across. Niceas put the men to unpacking, and Kineas, done with the worries of the crossing, sat under a solitary oak tree and watched. The ferryman took no part in the unloading, although he did encourage his slaves to help.

Ataelus didn't touch the baggage. Neither did he show any signs of drinking wine. He recovered his wet horse, curried her, and mounted. Then he sat, an immobile centaur.

The ferryman spoke good Greek, so Kineas waved him over. 'Can you tell me about the next two days' travel?'

The ferryman laughed grimly. 'You just left civilization, if you call Aegyssus civilization. On the north bank it's just you and the Dacae and the Getae and the Bastarnae. That boy of yours – Crax? He's Getae. He'll run tonight, mark my words – and cut your throat if he can. The Getae will want your horses. If you keep following the edge of the hills over there and keep clear of the marches, you'll come to Antiphilous in four or five days. There's not a farm or a house between.'

Kineas turned his head to watch Crax. The boy was working hard under the orders of Antigonus the Gaul. They were laughing together. Kineas nodded. 'Fair enough.'

'Your party is too small. The Getae will be stuffing your heads with straw by tomorrow.'

'I doubt it. But thanks for your concern.'

The ferryman shrugged. 'I'll take you back over. Course, I'll have to charge you again, but you can wait at my place until another party comes.'

Kineas yawned. It wasn't feigned, he found the ferryman's scare tactics dull. In fact, he had heard it all before. 'No, thanks.'

'Suit yourself.'

Before the sun had dipped another degree, the ferryman and his boat were gone. They were alone on the north bank. Kineas called Niceas to him. 'Camp here. Watches, picket and hobble the horses, and watch Crax. He'll try to run tonight, says the ferryman.'

Niceas glanced at the boy and shrugged. 'What else did he say?'

'We'll all be killed by the Getae.'

'Like as not.' Niceas said philosophically, but his hand went to his amulet. 'What's a Getae?'

'Crax's folk. Thracians with horses.' Kineas looked at the horizon under his hand. He beckoned to Ataelus, who rode over. 'We camp here. Take Antigonus and Laertes and ride out, check the area, come back. Yes?'

Ataelus said, 'It's good.' He patted the flank of his horse. 'She want to run. Me too.' He waited for Antigonus to mount up. Laertes, the best scout in the company, was already up, and the three of them rode out on to the plain, heading north-west to the horizon.

The other men built two fires and put their cauldron on one. They made up beds from the grass all around. They argued over setting up the two tents and Niceas made them do it, his gravelly voice and imaginative curses a counterpoint to their work. Kineas took no part – barring a crisis, he acted the part of the officer and watched them. Niceas gave most of the orders, settled the disputes and allocated the watches. The three mounted men came back just before the fall of full night and reported horse tracks in all directions to the north, but no immediate threat.

So easy to forget. When he wasn't on campaign, Kineas mostly remembered the good times and the danger. He never remembered the nagging weight of casual decisions and their mortal consequences. For instance – double the watch and double their chances of detecting an attack, with the consequent fatigue for all of them tomorrow. Or keep normal watches and know that any one man could fall asleep and the first they'd know of an attack was the rush of hooves and the spike of iron in the belly.

He compromised – always an added danger – and ordered that the last watch at dawn be doubled, and put himself on it. Then he summoned Crax and ordered him to put his blankets down next to Kineas's own, placed Antigonus on the other side, and dismissed the subject. They ate quickly, set their watches and lingered – too early in the campaign to go to sleep automatically. Instead, they sat up with their last amphorae of wine from Tomis, telling each other stories of their own exploits, reliving and laughing. Ajax sat and watched, silent and polite, his eyes wide as if he were sitting with Jason and the Argonauts.

Agis recited lines from the Poet:

'"But come now, change thy theme, and sing of the building of the horse of wood, which Epeius made with Athena's help, the horse which once Odysseus led up into the citadel as a thing of guile, when he had filled it with the men who sacked Ilios. If thou dost indeed tell me this tale aright, I will declare to all mankind that the god has of a ready heart granted thee the gift of divine song." So he spoke, and the minstrel, moved by the god, began, and let his song be heard, taking up the tale where the Argives had embarked on their benched ships and were sailing away, after casting fire on their huts, while those others led by glorious Odysseus were now sitting in the place of assembly of the Trojans, hidden in the horse; for the Trojans had themselves dragged it to the citadel. So there it stood, while the people talked long as they sat about it, and could form no resolve. Nay, in three ways did counsel find favour in their minds: either to cleave the hollow timber with the pitiless bronze, or to drag it to the height and cast it down the rocks, or to let it stand as a great offering to propitiate the gods, even as in the end it was to be brought to pass; for it was their fate to perish when their city should enclose the great horse of wood, wherein were sitting all the best of the Argives, bearing to the Trojans death and fate. And he sang how the sons of the Achaeans poured forth from the horse and, leaving their hollow ambush, sacked the city. Of the others he sang how in divers ways they wasted the lofty city, but of Odysseus, how he went like Ares to the house of Deiphobus together with godlike Menelaus. There it was, he said, that Odysseus braved the most terrible fight and in the end conquered by the aid of great-hearted Athena.'

They cheered his performance, as the veterans always had, and made jokes comparing red-haired Diodorus to wily Odysseus. The first watch was done before any of them were in their blankets except Philokles, who all but fell from the saddle straight into bed.

Kineas caught Ajax as he rolled in his cloak. 'You'll want this,' he said, and nudged Ajax with a sword.

Ajax took it, hefted it in his hand and tried to look at it.

Kineas said, 'Sleep with it under your head or in your hand.' He smiled invisibly in the dark. 'You get used to it after a few nights.'

Kineas was asleep as soon as he was under his cloak. It was like being home. He had a dream of Artemis – neither long nor precise, and certainly not one of those dreams that Aphrodite sends to men, but a happy dream none the less, and he awoke when the watch changed and men shifted in the tent, alert as soon as his eyes opened and then relaxing, remembering the dream and wondering if some hint of her was in his cloak. He smiled and went to sleep again and awoke with a start when something heavy fell across his legs. He remembered a loud noise – he had his heavy sword in his hand and he was on his feet before he was awake, the sword clear of the scabbard.

Antigonus spoke softly at his ear. 'It's nothing – Kineas – nothing. Your slave boy tried to run and I knocked him cold. He'll be sore in the morning.'

The weight that had landed at his feet was Crax; the boy was deeply unconscious. And other sleepers were now awake, pushing him from where he had fallen. They wrestled him into his own blankets.

'Where was he headed?'

'I didn't wait to see. When I saw him get up, I knocked him flat with my butt-spike.'

Kineas winced. 'I hope he isn't dead. Wake me for next watch.'

'Never fear. You can have rosy-fingered dawn all to yourself.'

Kineas fell asleep thinking that Antigonus, who couldn't read or write, probably hadn't ever read the *Iliad*. He was awakened the third time to throw water on his face and hands. His hands swelled at night, and his joints ached when he woke, and waking up seemed harder every year. Campaign aged a man too quickly.

He took the heavy javelin from Antigonus's hand. Ajax was up, too – Kineas had decreed a double watch for dawn and Niceas had put Kineas on with the least experienced man, and the most expendable – decisions, decisions.

'Before you turn in, find him a javelin,' Kineas said to Antigonus, who burrowed in the equipment and came out with one. He handed it to Ajax, who looked quite self-conscious with it in the first grey light of morning, as if he were wearing the wrong costume for a party. He also looked absurdly young, pretty, and well-slept, and Kineas thought, I'll bet his joints don't swell.

'Anything to report?' Kineas asked.

Antigonus peered off to the north. 'I heard something – distant, could have been a wolf taking a buck, but it was heavy movement. It was an hour back.' He gestured at a dim shape by the tree. 'Don't trip over our barbarian. He's asleep with his horse.'

Kineas nodded and pushed the other man towards his sleeping spot. It was light enough to crawl into the tent without waking everyone else and Antigonus was snoring before Kineas had walked the perimeter of the little camp. Ajax followed him, clearly at a loss as to what to do.

Kineas took him around the camp again, showed him the two slight rises which would give a sentry a few stades more view, stopped with him to smile at the sight of Ataelus asleep with the reins of his horse in his hand, ready for instant action. Then Kineas told Ajax to build up the fires. 'When that's done, curry the horses.'

Ajax gave Kineas the first look of displeasure Kineas had ever seen him wear. 'Curry the horses? I'll wake my slave.'

Kineas shook his head. 'Build up the fires and then curry the horses. Yourself. Do a good job. Then you and I will take a little ride before we wake the others. And Ajax – don't imagine you can discuss orders.'

Ajax hung his head, but he said, 'Other men do.'

Kineas laughed and swatted him. 'When you've killed a dozen men and stood sentry a thousand nights, you can debate with me.'

He liked being on watch and he stood under the tree, immobile, and watched the grey horizon to the north-west. He listened to the rising birds, watched a rabbit move across the light grass where the ferry had landed and then watched a falcon stooping out over the estuary of the Danube. He felt they were safe – in wild places, it was usually easy to feel the approach of an enemy.

For an hour, he watched Ajax bring up the horses one at a time, curry them and then hobble them again. The lad was thorough, although he had a rebellious set to his back that Kineas hadn't seen before. But he checked hooves, rubbed each horse with straw, looked in their eyes and their mouths. He knew what he was about. Kineas went back to watching the horizon, and he was surprised when Ajax started walking towards him with a pair of horses – the time had flown by. But his hands were back to normal, his neck felt less strained and he was ready for a ride. Once mounted, he walked his horse to the near tent and tapped the poll with the butt of his javelin. Niceas put his head out.

'We're riding a dawn patrol. Have the slaves start the food. We'll ride in an hour.'

Niceas buried a yawn with one of his big hands. 'I'm on it.'

Kineas turned his horse and rode out with Ajax at his side. He rode straight north along the river, staying in low ground when he could and showing Ajax what he was doing at every step – keeping the rising sun from silhouetting him and his mount, using the brush along the river for cover and background, coming to a dead stop when he had to cross a rise. They made their way along the bank and then Kineas led them inland, almost due north, until they reached some high ground that he had seen while he was standing watch. They were almost a stade from the camp, and he slid to the ground, tossed his reins to Ajax and crawled to the crest on his hands and knees. He was showing off for the boy, but the cause was good – the boy needed to see how to do a dawn patrol correctly.

From the crest he could see an enormous arc of ground, all of it empty. Of course, every fold of it could contain a Scythian horde, but Kineas knew from experience how hard it was to keep men and animals in ambush without motion and dust for any length of time. He slid back down to Ajax. 'Hobble your mount and keep watch up there until I come for you. I'll have your slave bring you something to eat. If you see movement, run like the furies were on you.'

Ajax nodded, very serious. 'Am I – in trouble?'

'Certainly not. This is what we do on the dawn patrol. I have work to do – you already did yours. So you can loaf up here, watch the whole horizon, and wait for the men to have breakfast. It'd be the same if I had Diodorus here.'

Ajax let a smile break through. 'Oh. Good. I'll watch, then.'

Kineas rode back to camp by a different route, still keeping his silhouette away from prying eyes. He ate a bowl of reheated soup from the night's dinner, re-curried his own charger and then put her into the remounts, choosing a smaller, lighter horse for his day's work. He told Diodorus, Lykeles and Graccus to be prepared to hunt. They were eager for it.

Crax was working on the baggage animals under the careful eye of Niceas. He didn't seem the worse for his misadventure, but when Kineas checked the baggage, he found that every girth the boy had done was loose or sabotaged. Kineas summoned the boy with a wave and knocked him flat on his back with a single blow of his fist.

'I don't like to hit a slave,' Kineas said evenly. He paused to lick some blood where he had split the skin over a knuckle. 'You tried to run last night. Fair enough. If I were a slave, I'd run for home, too. Then you rigged the baggage to slip – lost work and a late start for us. Bad job both times. If you try something like this again, I'll just kill you – you didn't cost me a copper obol and I don't need a slave. Understand?'

The boy looked dazed – probably was, after two heavy blows.

'But I do need more cavalrymen. Show me you can do the job and take the crap, and I'll put you up as a groom in Olbia and free you in the *gamelia*. Or die. I hate to waste manpower, but I don't like sloppy knots.' Kineas turned away and rolled heavily on to the back of his light horse. He didn't feel like vaulting, and his split knuckle hurt like fire.

He sent Ataelus to bring Ajax in, and then they were off across the plains of the Getae.

They made good time after they started, although Crax remained dazed and he had to be tied over a horse. By noon they were clear of the marsh to the east and riding on a broad, flat grass plain dominated by a line of low rocky hills to the west. Lines of wind moved the tips of the grasses in waves. The sea of green rolled on and on over hummocks and low hills, all the way out to the horizon. It was terrain built for horses by the gods, and Kineas stopped at the top of the first low ridge and looked out under his hand while the sun crept up a finger's breadth.

The magnitude of the view kept them silent, and then Ataelus dismounted, knelt, and kissed the ground, before giving a screech that vanished in the vastness of the sky.

'Someone's home,' said Coenus with a grin.

When they found some tracks Ataelus rode all the way to the base of the hills and came back with a heavy black arrow that he handed to Kineas without comment.

'Getae?' Kineas asked.

Ataelus shrugged expressively and rode out ahead.

In early afternoon they flushed a small herd of roebuck in a deep gully cut by a small stream, and the three hunters rode ahead of them, cut out a big buck and brought him down with javelins. It was a pleasure to watch, and the aristocrat in Kineas appreciated how professional cavalrymen had mastered the mounted hunt in a way that few aristocrats would ever see, much less learn. He rode on, thinking of Xenophon, whose works on horses and hunting he had read in his youth. Coenus – an educated man, and often out of place in a company of mercenaries – doted on Xenophon, and could quote great swathes of his works. Seeing the returning hunters, he rode up next to Kineas, pointed, and said, '"Therefore I charge the young not to despise hunting or any other schooling. For these are the means by which men become good in war and in all things out of which must come excellence in thought and word and deed."'

Somehow, that reminded him that he still had Isokles's scrolls of the fourth book of Herodotus, and that pained him, because he couldn't imagine having the time to read and he dreaded the scrolls getting soaked to illegibility.

Philokles came abreast of him. 'Is this spot sacred, or may I ride here?'

Kineas snapped to full awareness. 'Sacred?' he said.

'Only Niceas ever rides with you – or Ataelus, I suppose, and Coenus, when he needs a vent for his scholarship. And I'm bored, and my thighs are burning, and a little gentle conversation might get another few stades out of me.'

Kineas was looking over the Spartan's head. 'I think you've come to the wrong place for gentle conversation. *Niceas!*' He raised a hand. 'Halt! Chargers and armour, *now!*'

The orderly column fell apart. The old soldiers were the fastest – Niceas was in his armour and up on his best warhorse while Ajax was still fumbling at a basket pannier for the sword he'd been lent. Philokles had no armour, so he sat on his horse and watched Kineas don his own.

'What did you see?' he asked.

'Ataelus. He's coming in towards us at a flat gallop, and shooting behind him – a nice trick if you can learn it. No – farther away. Look up the valley.' Kineas had his breast and back plate fastened, his helmet locked and the hinged cheek pieces down, and was trying to get control of his charger, who was not having any of it.

Another minute passed as men forced their helmets on or fought with straps and buckles. Niceas served out javelins. Kineas finally got up on his warhorse, embarrassed by looking like a new recruit in front of his men. The grass here grew in heavy tufts that formed small mounds and made walking nearly impossible and mounting even more difficult. Horses on the other hand seemed to walk easily among the tussocks. From a distance, the hilly plain stretched away to the hills beyond like a rippled green cloth, with no sign of the treacherous ground under the lush green grass.

Ataelus was one grassy rise away, and Kineas could see riders pursuing him a few stades back. They were small men on small horses. A few had bows, most had javelins, and none had armour. There were quite a few of them. Even as they watched, Ataelus changed direction, riding wide of Kineas's troop and heading north beyond bowshot.

'Diodorus! Take – take Ajax and support the Scyth. Get on their flank and harry them if they ignore you. The rest of you, knee to knee. Now! Two lines, and move!'

He had ten fighting men – a tiny number, but they had some advantages and the Scyth had brought the Getae in close. He thought that he'd have one chance to charge them and scatter them, force them into close action where his big, grain-fed military horses would overpower their ponies.

'On me. Trot.'

The Getae were still coming on. At this distance they might just be seeing the armour, and the horse size would be hard to judge ...

'At them!' Kineas had his horse in hand, was ready for the change to the long surge of the beast's powerful hindquarters. He trusted the stallion to know how to gallop over the tussocks – if he misjudged, they'd be dead in a heartbeat. 'Artemis!' he cried, and the veterans took it up – *Artemis, Artemis!* It was a pale, thin remnant of the sound that three hundred of them had made, but loud enough.

The initial charge was going to be successful. He could feel it already in his balls, see the next act of the play as easily as if he had written it himself. He rose a little in his seat, pressed his horse's sides with his knees and threw his light javelin into the side of a Getae. The next one pivoted his pony on its haunches, pulling her mouth viciously, but he was too slow, and Kineas's warhorse rode the smaller horse over without changing gait. A boy – brave, or perhaps simply frozen – waited for him, sitting on his horse with his bow drawn. Kineas put his head down to take the point of the arrow on his helmet and leaned forward with his heavy javelin. The bow twanged, a singular sound even in the mêlèe.

The arrow missed – it went the gods knew where – and Kineas reversed his javelin in both hands and swung it like a staff, knocking the boy clear of the saddle. At the end of the stroke he reversed the staff again and turned his head. He drew rein, used his rein hand to push the helmet back on his head so that he could see and snapped his head right and left looking for friends and foes.

Niceas was right by him, mumbling a litany of prayers to Athena, his heavy javelin reversed and held short in his fist, dripping red on to the ground. Antigonus was on his other flank with his heavy sword out. His horse was giving him trouble, skipping and hopping. Smell of blood. New horse. Kineas didn't have to think about these details, he just knew them, just as he could see the shape of a fight in his mind.

Coenus and Agis were side by side, a few horse lengths away. Coenus was just finishing a man in the grass. He had a long red mark down his right thigh. None of the others appeared to be hurt.

Kineas used his knees to push his horse around in a tight circle. One man was down – his count was one short. There were dead and dying Getae all around him in the grass and a double handful already a hillside away. Even as he watched, one of them took an arrow full in the back from Ataelus's bow and the man fell slowly, losing his seat and finally collapsing to the ground. His horse stopped and began to crop grass. The other Getae continued to run. Agis tried a long javelin throw from horseback, missed, swore, and then the surviving Getae were swallowed by a hillside and the fight was over.

No time at all had passed since Kineas had first spotted the Scyth coming back. The blink of an eye. Kineas had done something to his back and had the pain of a pulled muscle in his shoulder. He felt as if he had pushed a plough in a field for a whole day. He turned to Niceas. 'Who's down?'

Niceas shook his helmeted head. 'I'll find out, sir,' and he rode away.

After a few moments. Niceas rode back, his shoulder hunched like an old man. 'Graccus,' he said. He turned away, hand on his amulet, then looked at Kineas. 'He got an arrow in the bole of his throat as soon as we went to the gallop. Dead.'

Kineas knew that Niceas and Graccus had been friends – sometimes more than friends. 'What a waste. Stupid barbarians – we must have killed ten of them.'

'More than ten. And three prisoners. The boy you levelled. You want him?'

Kineas nodded. 'That's why I didn't kill him, yes. He and Crax can plot behind our backs.'

Niceas nodded heavily. 'The other two – they're wounded.'

Kineas could hear someone making a horrible, pitiful mewling alternating with a full-throated roar of anguish. He rode back to the first man he had downed, it was a good throw – the javelin was through his chest and had probably cut his heart. He gave the shaft a half-hearted tug without leaving the saddle. It didn't budge. He kept going, riding carefully over the tussocks until he came to the wounded men. The loud one was hit in the guts by a throwing javelin. He might live a long time, but it would be horrible. The other man had lost a hand to somebody's heavy sword. He was bleeding out, his face empty. He was trying to stop the flow of blood with his other hand, but he wasn't really strong enough. He had also soiled himself from the pain.

It was like the end of every action. War in all its glory. Kineas rode over to the screaming man and thrust his heavy javelin through the man's upturned face. Thrust, twist. The man fell forward across his own lap, instantly silent. The other man turned and looked up at him. He raised his eyebrows a little, as if surprised. 'Do the thing,' he said in weak, guttural Greek.

Kineas saluted his courage and prayed to Athena that when it was his turn he'd be as brave. Thrust. Twist. The second man died as fast as the first. 'Graccus can have them to work the ferryman's oars. Poor bastards. Niceas, get the slaves moving. We need all the javelins back – I left mine about a stade deep in that poor bastard over there. Anyone else hit?' He looked around. 'Put Graccus over his horse.'

Ajax was looking at him with loathing. He was clutching his arm.

Kineas pointed at him. 'Ajax. Show me your arm.'

Ajax shook his head. But the corners of his mouth were white.

'Antigonus, get Ajax off his horse and see to his arm. Ajax, that's what war is. That's all it is, boy. Men killing men – usually the strong killing the weak. Right. The rest of you, dismount, except Lykeles and Ataelus. You and the Scyth collect the horses.' Lykeles was one of the best riders, and horses loved him. He rode out. The Scyth was already out on the plain, using his short sword to take the hair off men he had killed. It was a grisly piece of barbarism and Kineas didn't spare him more than a glance.

Kineas stayed mounted, in his armour. He rode from man to man, exchanging a few words, a jest or a curse. Making sure they weren't wounded. The god-given spirit that flooded a good man in a fight could rob him of the ability to feel a wound. Kineas had seen men, good men, drop dead after a fight, pools of blood around them, without ever knowing they had taken a wound. Horses could go the same way, as if they, too, were touched by the *daimon* of war.

Coenus's wound was minor, but Kineas set Niceas to look after it while he tended Ajax. When he had seen to the others, Kineas cantered his horse to the top of the next rise and looked past the slope towards the hills in the distance. Carrion birds were already coming in to the feast of Ares. The smell of blood and excrement lay over the smell of sun and grass, polluting it. His shoulders sagged and his hands shook for a while. But the Getae didn't come back and in time he had control of himself. The Getae horses were rounded up, the few wounds coated in honey, and the column moved off across the sea of grass.

They made camp early because the men were tired. They found a small stream with a handful of old trees growing on the bank with enough downed wood to make a fire. Crax was working, Kineas was happy to note. He moved heavily, but he moved. The other Getae boy was still out. Ajax's slave was cooking, a stew of deer meat and barley from their stores. The men ate it hungrily and then sat quietly.

Niceas didn't speak except to ask about the burial of his friend, but Kineas shook his head. 'Town tomorrow,' he said. 'We'll give him a pyre.'

Niceas nodded slowly and went to take a second helping of food. Ajax avoided Kineas, staying around the fire from him. Philokles, who had played no part in the fight, came and lay on the ground next to him where he sat with his bowl of stew. The Spartan indicated Ajax with a thrust of his jaw. 'He's in a state,' he said. 'You should talk to him.'

'No. He watched me kill the captives. He thinks …' Kineas paused, searching for words. *I'm in a state, too.*

'Bah, he needs to grow up. Talk to him about it or send him home.' Philokles took a mouthful of his own food, dropped a heavy piece of campaign bread into his bowl to soften it.

'Maybe tomorrow.'

'As you say. But I'd do it tonight. You remember your first fight?'

'Yes.' Kineas remembered them all.

'You kill anyone?'

'No,' Kineas said, and he laughed, because his first fight had been a disaster, and he and all the Athenian *hippeis* had ridden clear without blooding their weapons and hated themselves for it. Hoplites disdained the hippeis because they could ride out of a rout.

Philokles pushed his jaw at the boy while chewing. 'He cut that man's hand off. One blow. And then the poor bastard lived and you had to put him down. See? A lot for a boy to think about.' He took a bite of his bread and chewed, some of the stew clung to his beard.

'You're the fucking philosopher, Spartan. You talk to him.'

Philokles nodded a few times, silently. He took another bite of bread and wiped his beard clean with his fingers. And he looked at Kineas while he chewed. Kineas held his gaze, irritated at being badgered but not really angry.

Philokles kept chewing, swallowed. 'You're not as tough as you act, are you?'

Kineas shook his head. 'He's a nice kid. You want me to go tell him what everyone else around this fire knows. Yes? Except that once he knows, he'll never be a nice kid again, will he?'

Philokles rolled over so that he was lying on his stomach and staring at the fire, or maybe the contents of his bowl. 'If that's what you tell him. Me, I'd tell him in the terms he understands. Honour. Virtue. Why not?'

'Is that really honour and virtue in Sparta? Killing prisoners because they're too much trouble to save?'

'If killing those two is eating your liver, why did you do it? I wasn't close, but it looked to me like they should have wanted a quick end.' Philokles slurped some soup from his bowl. 'Ares and Aphrodite, Kineas. The boy isn't suffering because you put those two down. That's just what he'll tell himself. It's because he knows that he's responsible. He did it – he cut the hand off, he fought, in effect he killed. How many fights have you seen?'

'Twenty. Or fifty. More than enough.' Kineas shrugged. 'I see where you are leading the donkey, though. Fair enough, philosopher. I'm old enough to ignore the men I kill and I still feel it – so it follows that the boy will feel it worse and blame me. Why not? His blame lies lightly enough on me.'

'You think so? He worshipped you this morning.' The Spartan rolled back to look at Kineas. 'I think you'd both be happier if you talked. Happier and wiser. And he'll be a better man for it.'

Kineas nodded slowly. 'Why are you with us?'

Philokles smiled widely. 'I'm running out of places to go where they speak Greek.'

'Angry husbands?' Kineas smiled, getting to his feet. Best to get this over with.

'I think that I ask too many questions.' Philokles smiled back.

'Honour and virtue ...' Kineas began, and looked at Ajax across the fire.

'Admit it, Kineas. You still believe in both of them. You want what is good. You strive for what is virtuous. Go tell it to the boy.' Philokles waved him away. 'Get going. I intend to eat your stew while you are gone.'

Kineas snatched his bowl from the other man and refilled it at the common cauldron as he passed. By tradition, the captain ate last, but everyone had eaten, most men twice, even the slaves. Kineas scraped the side of the bronze with his wooden bowl. While he filled his bowl, Antigonus came up and refilled his own. 'Fair haul, for barbarians. Twelve horses, some gold and silver, a few good weapons.'

'I'll divide it after dinner.'

Antigonus nodded. 'It will make the men feel better,' he said.

Diodorus, listening in, nodded. 'Graccus lived through all

those years with the boy king just to die on the plains in a gang fight with stupid barbarians. Sticks in our throats.'

Kineas nodded. 'I'll keep it in mind,' he said, and went and sat by Ajax. He did it so suddenly that the boy didn't have time to bolt. He was just rising when Kineas put out a hand. 'Stay where you are. How's your arm?'

'Fine.'

'Long gash. Does it sting?'

'No.'

'Yes, it does. But if you keep honey on it and don't go mad from the flies, it'll heal in a week. It won't hurt in two weeks. And by then, you'll have forgotten his face.'

Ajax took a quick breath.

'I'm sorry I killed him without asking you. Perhaps you would have kept him. But he was a man of my age, and he had never been a slave. Missing a hand, like a criminal? No way for him to live as a crippled slave.'

'Does that make it right?' Ajax asked. His voice was steady, even light, as if the question had no consequence.

'Right? They attacked us, Ajax. We were crossing this land on the plain, below their hills. They came for our heads and our horses. Next time, we may be the ones in their territory – going right up to their huts in the hills and putting fire to their thatch. That's what soldiers do. That's a different kind of right – the right of strength, of one polis against another, where you trust that the men who voted for war had their reasons and you do your duty. This was a simpler right – the right to resist aggression. Like killing a thief.'

'You killed both of them. And then you said ... you said that that's all there was, the strong killing the weak.' Less steady.

'Let me tell you the truth. It's a rotten truth, but if you can handle it, maybe you'll make a soldier. Ready?'

'Try me.'

'I'm the captain. Yes?'

'Yes.'

'Rank means you do what is hard. Killing unarmed men is rotten work. Sometimes we all do it. But usually, I do it, so that other men don't have to.'

73

Ajax watched the fire for a while. 'You make it sound like a virtue.'

'I'm not done yet.'

'Go on, then.' Ajax turned and looked at him.

'Mostly, when the polis makes war, or all of Greece, or the whole Hellenic world goes to war – think about it. Do all the men go to war?'

'No.'

'Do all of the warriors go? All the men trained to war?'

Ajax laughed without happiness. 'No.'

'No. A few men go. Sometimes more than a few. And the only thing that makes their profession noble is that they do it so that the others don't have to.'

'You're a mercenary!' spat Ajax.

'You knew that before you came.'

'I know. Why do you think I find myself so craven now? I knew just what happened here and I came anyway, and now I have no stomach for it.' Ajax had tears running down his cheeks.

'I fight for other men. And for my own profit. It is a hard life, full of hard men. I don't recommend you become one of them, Ajax. If you wish to leave, I'll send someone back to the ferry with you. On the other hand, if you wish to stay, you have to answer for yourself if you can do this and be a good man.' Kineas rose to his feet, felt the age in his knees and thighs. 'You won't like the next part. The ugliest part, after the killing. But you should watch.' He rubbed at his unshaven chin. 'Besides, the division of spoils is part of war. And it's in the *Iliad*, so it can't be wrong.'

Kineas put a hand on his shoulder and Ajax didn't shrug it off. Then he walked off, dropping his bowl by a slave, washing his hands in a leather bucket, and then stood by Diodorus and the string of captured horses. Crax had the sum of all the valuables from the bodies on a bloody tunic at his feet. His face betrayed no emotion, but Kineas could see tension in his stance and in his shoulders – recognition, perhaps, of the origin of the brooches and pins on the blanket at his feet.

Kineas didn't have to speak to gather the attention of the men.

He raised a hand for attention. 'Gentlemen. As is our custom, we will divide the spoils of our enemies by share, in turns. For the good of the company, I take these.' Kineas reached among the brooches and took both of the large gold ones. They were worth twenty owls apiece and would feed the horses for several days in a city. No one demurred, although they were easily the most valuable objects in the pile.

Then he pointed to the Scyth. 'Ataelus discovered their war party and gave us warning. He also slew four of them. I say he gets the first share.'

It was uncommon for a new man, or a barbarian, to be given the first share. There was a buzz of talk, but not an ugly one. On the one hand, there wasn't much spoil to divide, and first choice wasn't a matter of heaps of gold. On the other hand, the buzz seemed to say, the Scyth had probably saved all of them, or at least saved them from a harder fight.

Antigonus, himself a barbarian born, raised a fist at the Scyth. 'First share!' he rumbled. Other men took up the cry.

Ataelus looked around as if making sure he was being chosen. He grinned from ear to ear. Then he went to the string of captured horses and leaped astride the tallest, a pale bay mare with a small head and some Persian blood in her. He gave a loud *yip yip!* and then dismounted to release her from the string.

It didn't surprise Kineas that the Scyth took a horse, but it pleased the men, who wanted the ready cash in the form of silver and coins. The tradition of a first share to the man judged most worthy was often a two-edged sword, causing resentment as easily as it rewarded military virtue. But Ataelus's choice made him popular, or perhaps more popular.

The rest of the division was by strict seniority. Niceas chose second, and whatever grief he might feel for Graccus, he chose carefully from the pile, a heavy silver torc with a chain attached that was worth a month's pay. Ill armoured as the Getae had been, they wore good jewellery and carried coins.

The other men each took a share in turn, and there were plenty of items left after the first share had passed. Ajax did not join in the sharing, but Philokles did and no one complained – the Spartan was already accepted.

Kineas allowed them to circle around again, so that most men had at least a dozen owls' worth of silver and some had more. What was left on the tunic after the second sharing was mostly bronze, with a few small silver rings.

'Slaves,' Kineas said. He pointed at the tunic. Ajax's slave came forward willingly – he had become the head slave by age and experience and he didn't hesitate, but took the largest silver ring and put it on his hand. Then he winked at Crax.

Crax's face in the firelight showed the tracks of tears like rivulets on a hillside after a storm. Nonetheless, he reached down and took another silver ring. Then they divided the bronze coins between them. No one noticed this last division, because they were examining the horses, bickering over their small size and complaining that the Scyth had taken the only good one. The sun slipped under the hills to the west while they divided the horses.

Ataelus came up to Kineas. 'Me look?' he asked, pointing at the two heavy brooches in Kineas's hand.'

Kineas handed them over. The Scyth looked at them in the last light, the red sun colouring the gold so that it looked like new minted copper. He nodded. 'Make for my people,' he said. He pointed to the horse and stag motif that ran through both. They were very fine for barbarian work, the haunches of the horse well worked, the head of the stag noble and fine.

While Ataelus looked at the brooches, Kineas glanced at Ajax twice, but the young man showed nothing but weary resignation at the evils of an older generation. Ataelus handed the brooches back and returned to gloating over his horse. Kineas shrugged, took his cloak and rolled in it on the ground. He didn't think of Artemis, and then it was morning.

5

Dawn patrol brought no surprises. The girths were well attached, the baggage loaded, and Ajax's slave whistled while he scraped the cauldron. Ataelus had curried both of his horses until their coats shone. His example got others to currying, which pleased Kineas who liked men to look their best every day.

Kineas rode off apart to have a moment to himself. He watched them working, watched the last items roped down to the packhorses – plenty of them, now, and lighter loads for each, which meant they'd move faster.

Ajax's slave waited patiently by his knee. When Kineas noticed him, the slave bowed his head. 'Par'n me, sir.'

Kineas felt that the man's whistling had helped to set the tone of the morning, that sharing the booty with the slaves had somehow pleased the gods. 'I don't know your name.'

The slave bowed his head again. 'Arni.'

Kineas chewed the barbarian name a little. 'What is it, Arni?'

'Par'n me fur askin. I wunnert if we – if'n there'd be more fight'n.' He looked eager. 'I cin fight. If'n you were to want it. Could take a swort or a knife. Plenty left a' yesterday.'

Arming slaves was always a dangerous business. Crossing the plains, however, was the immediate problem. 'Only until we reach a town. And Crax?'

The slave smiled. 'Give 'im a few days. Aye. E'll come round.'

Kineas nodded. 'Watch he doesn't take your weapon and kill us all before he does so.'

Arni smiled, shook his head and withdrew.

Horses shining, richer and with a score of remounts, the column rode across the plains.

Three days of uneventful travel brought them to the scatter of Greek homesteads surrounding Antiphilous. Antiphilous was a settlement so small it could barely be thought of as a colony – indeed, it was the colony of a colony, guarding the southern flank of the more prosperous towns of Tyras and Nikanou, both centres of the grain trade with the interior because they controlled access to a bay so deep it was like a small sea. Kineas had never seen any of them, but he'd heard enough to have a sense of the area. He gave an inward sigh of relief when his horse's hooves were on the gravelled dirt of a Greek road.

Their arrival made an instant stir in Antiphilous. It was easy to see that not many caravans crossed the sea of grass, because householders stood on their porticoes to watch the column pass, slaves gaped, and the men of the town hurried for their spears and stood in the sun of the small agora, ready to repel invasion. When they discovered that Kineas had no ill intent, they hurried to wring every possible profit from him, asking a grim price for their grain – the cheapest grain in the world, right at the source, at Athenian famine prices.

A scuffle in an ugly wine shop caught Kineas's attention. He motioned to Niceas. 'Get a day's grain for the horses. Don't budge an obol on our campaign price. I'll be back.' He raised his legs over the horse's back and slid off, checked his sword and pushed through the curtain of wooden beads that masked the entrance of the wine shop. Inside, Lykeles and Philokles had swords in their hands. Coenus had a man down and was tickling his throat with his sword.

'He tried to cheat us on the measure,' Lykeles said defensively. He knew that Kineas hated any kind of incident with 'citizens'. Lykeles considered himself a gentleman, although he wasn't as well born as Coenus or Laertes.

'So you hit him and drew your swords? Get outside, all of you.' Kineas's hands didn't leave his belt, but his voice was cold.

Philokles stood up straight and drank off the measure of wine in his hand. He seemed disposed to argue the point.

'Now!' said Kineas.

Philokles met his eye. His eyes shone with ferocity, like an animal's, and he gave Kineas a slight nod, as if to say that he would obey *this time*. He looked like a different man entirely. But he went.

Outside, Kineas could see that the shopkeeper was, in fact, a slave. A grimmer-looking specimen he had seldom seen. He threw him some bronze coins. The slave swore and demanded more, lies frothing from him like spit bubbles. Kineas stood his ground until the slave was silent and then went back inside. Niceas was still dickering with a grain factor and a crowd of men had started to gather in the agora, many with their spears – again.

Diodorus pushed forward through the horses of the column. 'The ferry's closed. Some nonsense. They want to gouge us for the price. If you want my guess ...'

Kineas nodded.

'I'd say they didn't like us. Trade with the Getae? The gods only know. And they don't like Ataelus.'

Kineas nodded again, his eyes flicking up and down the column. 'Mount up,' he said. 'Let's get out of here.'

They were out of Antiphilous as quickly as they had entered. And they weren't going to be crossing the ferry to Nikanou, which meant that they were about to ride for days into the heartland of more barbarians in order to go around the bay. Kineas thought he might have just made a hurried and foolish decision, but there had been something rotten about Antiphilous, and some god had whispered to him that it was time to move, a whispering he never ignored.

Ten stades south of the town, when he was questioning his decision and trying to ignore the sullen silence of the company, they came across a lone Greek homestead whose farmer was busy trying to unbury a plough with two young slaves and a horse. Before the sun had slipped another finger towards the west, they had struck a bargain and were camped amidst the man's olive trees, and the whole string of horses were gorging on grain at a price that pleased everyone so much that most of the men stripped off their tunics and threw themselves at the recalcitrant plough, pushing and calling and laughing until the blade pulled free, and then running down to the sandy shore of the bay and flinging themselves in the water with the noise of a cavalry charge – *Artemis, Artemis!* Kineas accepted a proffered cup of wine from the farmer, Alexander, and sat with his legs crossed on a finely carved stool in the farm's courtyard, enjoying the shade of the one and only tree.

'No one much comes this way except the grain ships looking for a load,' the farmer said. 'Can't remember the last time I saw a party going around the bay the long way.' He nodded to the west. 'I see you have a Scyth with you – that's good thinking. They're everywhere west of here another twenty stades. You'll be intercepted every day by a band.'

Kineas sat listening with his chin on his hand. 'Are they trouble?'

Alexander shook his head. 'None to me, and don't let some fools tell you otherwise. I give 'em a cup of wine when they ride by and I'm civil and that's all it takes. For barbarians, they're a good lot – they are hellions when they drink hard, and they are mean when crossed. So don't cross 'em, says I. My wife's afraid of 'em – she's Sindi, so stands to reason, don't it?'

Kineas thought that the man was starved for conversation. 'Sindi?' he asked.

The farmer jerked a thumb over his shoulder in the direction of the coast. 'Scythians is no more native here than you an' me. The Sindi was here first, or so they say. They do the farming – the Scyths just tax the grain they grow. And then the Greeks tax it again at the towns, but for all that, it's cheap.'

'Not for us. We tried to buy grain in town. They wanted Athens prices.'

Alexander laughed. 'They figured you had no other choice. Riding across the plains! You're either damn smart or a born fool. I see you tangled with the Getae.'

Kineas nodded.

'Nice ponies. I'd be happy to buy a couple.'

Kineas sipped his wine. 'They are the property of my men. You'd have to bargain with them.'

'Easier if I bargain with you. I'll give you fifty measures of grain and two silver owls per pony.'

Kineas reckoned quickly. 'With bags?'

'Baskets. No bags. I'm short on cloth as it is, but they're good baskets.'

'Done. I can sell four.' Kineas was calculating what price to give the grain so that the men made a profit on their ponies. Easy money.

If you lived.

The next day dawned bleak and rainy, with heavy clouds in the west and waves rolling across the bay.

'Better by night, but you'll be soaked by then,' said Alexander. 'You should stay. Those nags of yours could use a day to eat. We could bake you all some fish. Come on, Kineas. Stay a day.'

Kineas had forgotten what it was like to feel welcome. So few men would welcome a troop of mercenaries – but that sort of trouble had never happened here. Alexander had taken a few precautions; his gates were locked at night and although he had daughters, Kineas had not laid eyes on them. They were probably locked in a basement or restricted to the upper rooms of the farm's *exedra*.

Sons were a different matter. Alexander had half a dozen sons, ranging from the quiet, hard-working eldest, a tall, modest man of twenty-five with a young beard, to Ictinus, whom they all called 'Echo'. Echo could be heard at all hours, trailing the soldiers, repeating anything they said, trying to help. He was fifteen and tried to sport a beard. All six sons appeared together to build a fire on the beach in the afternoon when the sky, as predicted, showed signs of clearing. The clearing had happened so fast that the sky was blue and clear and the tents were dry before the afternoon began to wane. All the men looked forward to eating fish. Barley and meat were good enough, but hard food to have to face every day.

When their gear was clean and repaired, all the men gathered wood for Graccus's pyre. Alexander, the farmer, was kind enough to allow them to take wood from his orchards, and there was driftwood on the beach. They built him a pyre as tall as two men, and laid his body atop it in the old way. He already stank of death, but they washed his body and arranged his limbs anyway. Graccus had been quite popular.

The sons prepared the fish with their mother in a remarkable way. First, they had one single, enormous fish acquired in late morning from a passing log boat. They layered the whole fish in clay, built a fire pit in the sand, burned a bonfire over the pit as soon as the rain ceased and then buried the clay-coated fish in hot coals with iron shovels. Kineas spent most of the day pushing his men to cleaning and oiling their tack, currying horses and mending. The farmer was remarkably forthcoming with the requirements of mending, from flax thread and oil to bits of leather.

His hospitality made Kineas suspicious. He disliked having to be suspicious of such favour, but he was. He posted a sentry on the horses. He arranged the sale of four of the Getae ponies and transferred them to their new owner, watching with satisfaction as basket-woven panniers full of grain were arranged for the other ponies. He would leave the farm with more grain than he had started the expedition.

Returning from reviewing the proceeds of the sale, he lay down on his cloak inside his tent to discover that his light throwing-javelin had been polished, the head gleaming like a mirror, the wood shaft carefully oiled so that the grain of the wood swam like fish in a stream. His heavy javelin lay beside it, equally well cared for.

He found the slave, Arni, sitting with the other slaves playing knucklebones. They all got to their feet sheepishly, Crax avoiding his eye and the new boy, the Getae whose life he had spared, wincing as he rose.

'I usually care for my own weapons, Arni. But I thank you for the care you lavished on them.' Kineas offered him a bronze obol.

Arni shook his head and smiled, showing a number of gaps in his teeth. 'Warn't me. Soldiers' weapons is their tools, I tell 'em. Not our work. Boy wouldn't listen though.' Arni looked at Crax fondly.

Crax looked Kineas in the eye. 'I cleaned them. The throwing javelin was damaged in the fight. I cut the shaft a few fingers and reset the head. One of the farm boys drove the rivets.'

So you've decided to grow up, Kineas thought. He tossed the younger slave the obol. 'You did a beautiful job, Crax. You remember what I told you? Good job, you'd be a free man.'

'Yes sir.' He was very serious.

'I meant it. Same for your new little brother there. I don't need slaves. I need men who can ride and fight. And I need to know which you both plan to be by the time we ride into Olbia. Ten days – two weeks at the outside. Understand?'

Crax said, 'Yes, sir.'

The new boy looked terrified. Crax nudged him and said something barbarian, and the new boy coughed and mumbled something that might have been 'yes, sir' in what might have passed for Greek.

Kineas left the slaves to their share of the day of rest and walked back to the beach, where couches of straw had been prepared for twenty. He could smell the fish baking through the embers in the ground. He wondered if the clay would turn to pottery around the fish. It did.

As the Charioteer prepared to drive the sun under the world, they sat down to feast on the fish, with proper sauces and some wine – heavy red wine, a little past its best days but heady stuff. Alexander toasted and drank and so did his sons, as did every man of Kineas's troop, until the last light was gone from the sky and the bones of the giant fish were picked clean.

Diodorus, on the next couch of straw, gave a yawn and stretched, his hair a halo of fire in the last of the sun. 'Better day than I expected when we was in that rotten little town. Thanks to you, Alexander, and the blessing of the gods on you and yours for your hospitality.'

Kineas poured a libation on the ground and raised his *kylix* high. 'Hear me, Athena, protector of soldiers! This man has been our friend and given us sacred hospitality. Bring him good fortune.'

One by one, other soldiers added their benisons. Some spoke with simple piety, others with aristocratic rhetoric. When the cup returned to Kineas, he again poured a libation. 'This is the best we'll come to a funeral feast for Graccus. So I drink to him and may his shade go down to Hades and dwell with heroes, or whatever fate he might best enjoy.' Unlike Kineas, Graccus had been a devotee of Demeter. Kineas was not an initiate and had no wish to know what fate such men imagined in the afterlife, but he wished the man's shade well.

Niceas begged the host's indulgence, and then told a few tales of Graccus's courage and a comic one of his boastfulness and all the men laughed, the eyes of the farmer's younger sons shining like silver owls in the firelight. And then they were all telling tales of Graccus and other men who had fallen in the last few years.

Coenus rose and stood with one hand on his hip, and told the story of the fight on the fords of the Euphrates, when twenty of them on a scout caught the tail of Darius's army in the moonlight. 'Graccus was the first to take a life,' he said in the phrasing of the Poet, 'and a Mede splashed into the river at his feet when he plunged his spear into the man's neck.'

Laertes told of how Graccus fought a duel with one of the Macedonian officers – on horseback, with javelins. It had made him famous and notorious in a day, and what Kineas best remembered was the time he'd spent averting King Alexander's wrath. But it made a good story.

Alexander the farmer listened politely and mixed the wine with lots of water like a man who was being well entertained, and his sons sat and drank it all in. The eldest listened like a man being visited by men from another world, but Echo listened like a hungry man watching food.

Finally Agis, the closest they had to a priest, rose and spilled wine on the sand. 'Some say it is a bitter thing when the bronze bites home, and the darkness falls over your eyes. Some say that death is the end of life, and some say it is the start of something new.' He raised his cup. 'But I say that Graccus was courteous and brave; that he feared the gods and died with a spear in his hand. Hard death is the lot of every man and woman born, and Graccus went to his with a song on his lips.' Agis took a brand from the fire – pitch-filled pine that flared in the wind – and every man there, even the farmer's sons, took more, and they walked along the beach to the funeral pyre. They sang the hymn to Demeter, and they sang the Paean, and then they flung their torches into the pile. It burst into flame as if a bolt from Zeus had struck it – a good omen.

They watched it burn until the heat drove them back, as well as the smell of roast meat. Then they drank again. Later, they rose from the straw and bowed, the better-born soldiers offering well-turned compliments to the host, and went off to sleep on the straw pallets in their tents. Kineas walked back with Niceas, who had tears running down his face. He had cried quietly for an hour, but the tears were drying now. 'I can't remember a symposium I liked so much.'

Kineas nodded. 'It was kindly done.'

Niceas said, 'I'll give him my booty horse in the morning. Let it be from Graccus, for his feast. And thank you, sir, for thinking of him. I was afraid you had forgotten.'

Kineas shook his head. He punched his hyperetes in the shoulder and then embraced him. Other men came and embraced Niceas. Even, hesitantly, Ajax.

In the morning the pyre still smouldered, and the sun rose in splendour, casting a pink and yellow glow across everything before he was halfway over the rim of the world. Kineas heard the phrase 'rosy-fingered dawn' a dozen times before he had his horse bridled.

Niceas arranged with young Echo to fetch the hot bones from the pyre when they cooled, and then bury them in the family graveyard.

The column formed quickly and neatly, every packhorse bulging like a pregnant donkey with baskets of grain. Everyone knew their place by now and things happened more quickly – the tent came down fast, cloaks were rolled and stowed, horses fetched in from hobbles. Neither Kineas nor Niceas had to oversee the process. So, rosy fingered dawn had not yet given way to full day before Kineas, mounted, was saluting Alexander in his yard. Niceas had already given him a horse.

It was a pleasure to leave a place with friends left behind.

Niceas looked back as they rode over the first hill. 'That boy will tend his grave as if he was one of the heroes,' he said. Tears were running down his cheeks.

'Better burial than any of us have a right to expect,' Kineas said, and Niceas made the peasant sign to avert an evil fate.

A stade later, Philokles rode up beside him. 'Think you'll ever be that man?'

Kineas grunted. 'A farmer? Wife? Sons?'

Philokles laughed. 'Daughters!'

Kineas shook his head. 'I don't think I could go back.'

Philokles raised his eyebrows. 'Why not? Calchus and Isokles would have you in a flash.'

Kineas shook his head. 'You ask the damnedest questions. Does some god whisper in your ear "go and torment Kineas?"'

Philokles shook his head. 'You interest me. The Captain. The soldier of renown.'

Kineas sat back on his horse, his ass high on the horse's rump, and crossed his legs. It gave his thighs a rest at the cost of his behind. 'Oh, come on. You're a Spartan. You must have had a great deal of opportunity to plumb the thoughts of soldiers of renown.'

Philokles nodded curtly. 'Yes.'

Kineas said, 'So I command what – twelve men? Why me? Soldier of renown. Flatterer. May your words go to Zeus.'

'But my Spartans would all claim they pined for a farm. So many would say it that it has become the norm to say it – perhaps even to think it. Perhaps I ask you because you are not a Spartan.'

'Here's my answer, then. Once, I wanted a farm and a wife. Now, I think I'd die of boredom.'

'You love war?'

'Pshaw. I love not-war. I love the preparation and the riding and the scouting and the planning – camaraderie, shared success, all that. The killing part is the price you pay for the not-quite-war part.'

'Farmers have to plan as well. At least, good farmers do.'

'Really?' Kineas raised both his eyebrows in a parody of a tragedian's look of surprise.

Philokles went on as if Kineas had spoken with genuine surprise. 'Really. Good farmers plan carefully. Good farmers prepare and scout, their whole farm is like a file of hoplites, all trained to work together. But that's not for you?'

Kineas shrugged. 'No.'

Philokles nodded as if to himself, his eyes on the distant hills. 'Perhaps it is something else.'

Kineas shook his head. 'Spartan, do you ever talk about the weather? Or about music, athletic events, poetry, women you've bedded – any of those things?'

Philokles considered a moment. 'Not often.'

Kineas laughed. 'Why exactly are you with us?' he asked again.

Philokles had begun to fall back along the column. He waved. 'To learn!' he shouted.

Kineas cursed and looked around for Ataelus. The Scyth had avoided the beachside symposium, but he was otherwise now comfortable with most of the men, especially Antigonus and Coenus – a former slave and a former nobleman. He had ridden off at the first blush of dawn to scout. Kineas wanted him back. It was time to begin to worry.

Kineas realized that he hadn't worried about anything in a day, and he thanked the gods for Alexander the farmer again, calling down blessings on the man. And he thought about being a farmer, and he thought of the man's instant friendliness, and wondered if he should have asked ...

Ataelus appeared on the crest of a hill, well to the front, sitting confidently on his Getae horse and waiting for the column to reach him. Already Kineas could recognize him at a distance, just from his posture on the horse, so un-Greek, so relaxed. He might have been asleep.

Closer up, it became plain that he was.

Kineas rode up to him, cantering up the last rise. Ataelus was awake before he reached him, a hand waved in greeting.

'Have a nice nap?' Kineas asked.

'Long ride. Many things. Yes?'

Kineas nodded. 'What did you see?'

'For me? I see many things, grass and hills. Also tracks of horses, many running horses. My people. No stinking fuck themselves Getae.'

Kineas felt a frisson of fear. 'Your people? How recent? When were they here?'

'Yesterday. Maybe yesterday. Two days if not for rain.' The Scyth had a poor command of Greek's complexities with nouns, and he tended to stick to the form he liked, the dative. 'For rain?' he said again, as a question.

'Did it rain? Not yesterday.' Kineas looked back at the column breasting the slope. 'Your people – will they harm us?'

Ataelus slapped his chest. 'Not for me.' He grinned. 'To go find them?'

Kineas pointed. 'You are going to find them? And come back? Back to us?'

Ataelus nodded. 'Find for them, come back for you.'

Kineas nodded. 'I want to keep moving.' He gestured at the column. 'Keep moving?'

'Come back for you,' said Ataelus, still grinning. He waved at the column, turned his horse and rode off, heading north.

Kineas pulled his horse's head back towards the column and ambled over to Niceas, who was watching the Scyth ride.

'He's found some of his own, and he's going to meet them. Then he'll come back. At least, that's what I think he's saying.'

Niceas swatted a fly with his hand. 'More like Ataelus? All in a band? That'll be exciting. Ares wept – mutter a prayer we don't annoy them. Look at the fucking tracks!'

Kineas's eyes followed Niceas's pointing hand. They were riding over the ground that Ataelus must have spotted, a low trough between two hills that had the prints of hundreds of horses, all moving together. He realized that he was holding his breath.

'Two hundred horses, easy.' Niceas swatted at the fly pestering his horse's neck, caught it and crushed it between his fingers, then flung the corpse of the thing from him in disgust. 'Better hope they're friendly, Captain.'

They rode the rest of the day without incident, it was a sunny, pleasant day on the plains. Water was sparser than Kineas had expected and with Ataelus gone, he had to use Lykeles as a scout for a camp. He came back late, near dusk.

'Nothing but the beach,' he said. 'There's a trickle of water coming in – enough to water us and the horses if we don't foul it. It's not much. I've been fifteen stades.'

Kineas nodded. 'See any tracks?'

Lykeles nodded. 'We're following them, like as not. Next ridge over – it's like the path to a horse fair.'

It was near dark by the time they dismounted. The tents

bloomed immediately; the horses were hobbled close in. Antigonus and Laertes took first watch immediately and stayed mounted.

The slaves collected driftwood on the beach for a fire while Kineas debated with himself. A fire was a clear signal for many miles, especially on the shore of the bay. On the other hand, Ataelus seemed confident that his people were no threat. And yet – Ataelus was a barbarian, for all his qualities.

Nonetheless, Kineas gave Arni the nod and watched him use a steel to raise sparks on charred linen for the fire. On balance, two hundred horses' worth of bow-wielding Scythians would obliterate them if it came to that, a force so strong compared with his own that it really wasn't worth worrying about.

As the flames rose, however, he watched them and worried anyway.

Niceas had put him on watch with Ajax at dawn. Ajax didn't avoid him any more, but he was distant, careful, different from the eager youth of the first mornings. On the other hand, he knew his business now, and he posted himself on a low ridge above the beach without the exchange of a word. Kineas curried the horses. There were twenty-eight of them, a good string for twelve men and three slaves. He curried his charger first and then his riding horse, then Niceas's horses, and then all the other chargers. Diodorus was up by then. He woke the slaves and roused the fire and then lent a hand to the horses. They were all up, the work done, their cloaks rolled and the baggage loaded before the sun's chariot was full over the rim of the world. The beach stretched away in a curve for a dozen stades, and Niceas elected to follow it. He wanted to cross a decent stream and get water for the horses. Water was his current worry. He waved to Ajax on the ridge above them, who waved back. Lykeles left the column and rode to join the young man and the pair of them flanked the column as they rode along the beach.

They crossed two tiny rivulets in the sand, too easily fouled by the first horses to reach them. By the third, he was more careful, sending dismounted men to lead their mounts one at a time to drink, digging a pit in the sand for flow and letting it fill. It still wasn't a good drink. He sent Laertes riding up the beach for water. It felt odd to be so worried when the hillsides were damp between tufts of grass and their flank was covered by the sea, but the smaller horses were already flagging.

Laertes returned at noon. 'Decent-sized river at the bottom of the bay. Plenty of water, fresh as fresh. Lots of hoof marks, too.'

'Good job.' Kineas rode back along the column. 'Right, no lunch, gentlemen. We'll push through.'

'There's another of these little streams in a few stades,' added Laertes.

'Hades! We lose time every time and the horses scarcely get a drink worth a mention. Straight through. How many stades to this river?'

'Twenty. I had a hard ride.'

'A morning gallop over the sand!'

'Fair enough, Captain.' Laertes grinned his characteristic grin and pushed his big straw hat back on his head. 'You'll be there by late afternoon at this rate.'

'Then we'll camp there.'

Ajax caught his attention, waving his hat from the ridge. Lykeles rode for them flat out, his seat far back on his horse's rump as she descended the ridge.

'Company coming,' Kineas said. His men were at the base of a steep ridge, with the sea at their backs, on jaded horses that needed water. 'Armour and chargers. Now!'

He swung down from his riding horse and got his helmet and breastplate from bags on a packhorse. Other men and horses nudged him, bumped him – the column was in chaos. He hoped that it would sort itself out.

Lykeles shouted from his left. Kineas had his breast and back plates fastened and was wrestling with the leather cords that padded the crown of his helmet. It was already growing warm from the sun, promising to bake his head in a few minutes.

'Scythians!' Lykeles called. 'Hundreds of them!'

Kineas used his heavy javelin to lever himself up on to his charger. 'Where's Ataelus?'

'No sign of him.'

Kineas got his seat, always difficult in armour, and managed to gain control of both of his reins. Crax appeared out of the dust and picked up his javelins and handed them up.

Kineas pointed to the baggage horse with more javelins. 'You want to be free?' he asked. Crax nodded. 'Take my riding horse, mount it, and take a pair of javelins and form on me. You are now a free man.'

Crax was gone into the dust before he was done speaking.

'Two ranks on me! Form up!' Kineas yelled. The beach sand was kicking up with all the activity and he couldn't see. The damned helmet didn't help. He folded the cheek pieces back and tipped it up on his head. Lykeles had fallen in and Niceas next to him, and now others were coming up at speed. Crax pulled in behind him, clumsy at keeping in formation like any new man, but a born rider.

Lykeles hadn't bothered with his helmet. He turned to Crax. 'Welcome to the Hippeis, boy!' and to Kineas, 'You freed him?'

Kineas felt a particular joy on him and the whisper of the god was clear; freeing the boy had been the right act. 'He made a lousy slave,' Kineas barked, and all the men laughed.

Ajax finished a headlong flight down the ridge and pulled up on the left of the line. At the top of the ridge there was a rustle of movement and the laughing stopped. Then, in the blink of an eye, the ridge was full of horses and riders, the flash of coloured harnesses and the unmistakable gleam of gold repeated again and again so that the whole host of them glittered in the sun, which also flashed off iron armour and bronze and spear points.

'Blessed Athena stand with us now in the hour of our need,' intoned Lykeles at his side.

Niceas cursed, profane and long.

Kineas felt their appearance like a blow. They were more splendid than any Persian cavalry he had ever seen, and better mounted. They made his fourteen riders look poor and cheap.

Too bad, he thought. Better to have died on the boy king's campaign.

Nonetheless. 'Silence. Sit at attention. Don't twitch. Be Greeks!' Persians had always been impressed by displays of discipline, especially when facing odds. Kineas slammed his helmet down on the crown of his head and the cheek pieces bounced against his cheeks.

Two riders separated themselves from the mass at the top of the hill and began to ride down. A deep-throated trumpet sounded three times and the rest of the mass began to descend the hill at a sedate pace, two horns growing from the flanks and cutting off the beach to north and south while the main body halted well within bowshot.

Kineas thought that it was an impressive manoeuver, especially for barbarians. But he was breathing again, because one of the approaching riders was clearly Ataelus, and the other was almost certainly a woman.

As they crossed the line of the beach, they slowed. Kineas could see that Ataelus's companion was slim, straight-shouldered and wore a pale leather coat with a blue lined design. She also wore a gold neck plate that covered her from her throat to the middle of her chest. Her hair was tied back in two heavy braids. Closer yet and he could see she had dark blue eyes like the sea and heavy black brows that had never been plucked and which gave her a serious look. And she was young.

Kineas turned. 'Sit here like statues. I think we're going to live to tell this tale. Niceas, on me.'

Kineas and Niceas rode out on to the soft sand and met the approaching Scythians.

Ataelus raised his hand in greeting and said something to the woman. She was silent. Then she said a few words, like a gentle reminder, it seemed to Kineas.

'Greetings, Ataelus. These are your people?' Kineas tried to sound commanding and confident. The woman was looking attentively past him at his little company.

'No, no. But like for my people. Yes? and *she* says, "Not for liking not for seeing face. Yes?"' Ataelus spread his hands wide as if unable to explain the ways of women, or commanders.

Kineas handed his spears to Niceas and took off his helmet. 'Greetings, mistress,' he called.

She smiled and nodded her head. She half turned her horse and motioned to the main line of horses. Another rider left the line and approached. While watching the approaching man

– woman, Kineas saw now – she spoke softly to Ataelus. It wasn't a short speech.

Ataelus nodded. Halfway through the flow of words something surprised him and he remonstrated, and in a second the two of them were spitting at each other in the barbarian tongue.

Hermes of travellers! thought Kineas. Whatever she wants, Ataelus!

She stopped spitting and went back to the gentle voice. Ataelus began to nod again. The second woman approached at a trot – the trumpeter. Very Persian. Except that Kineas had heard it whispered …

Ataelus turned back to him. 'She says "pay tax for riding over my land".' He paused. 'She say "two horses taken from Getae bastards" and she say "half a talent of gold". And I say "we have nothing for half-talent of gold". Yes? So she say "for me, gold?" and I say "Kineas for gold". So give her gold. And two horses. And we friends and make feast and ride in peace.'

So much for the company treasury. 'Arni? Get the black leather bag from my pack horse and bring it here.' He pointed at the baggage horses. 'Ask her if she would like to choose her horses,' he said.

Ataelus translated. She spoke.

'She say you choose,' Ataelus shrugged again.

Kineas rode back to the baggage, took the black bag from Arni and picked the two finest of the Getae horses – Lykeles' and Andronicus's. They would have to be refunded from whatever was left in the common store. He led them back on short reins and handed them to the woman, who took them. She put her hand over his for a moment. Her hand was very small compared with his, fine-fingered but with heavy joints – from work, he thought. Her hands were rough. She had a heavy gold ring on her thumb and a green stone ring on another finger. Up close, he could see that the blue linear decoration on her leather coat was worked in fine blue hair. The gold cones full of coloured hair that dangled from the seams of her coat made music when she moved. She was wearing a month's pay for a full company of cavalry. Her horse was excellent – as good as Kineas's own and that horse had been the charger of a Persian nobleman.

He smiled at her, as one professional to another, as if they shared a joke. She returned it in kind.

He opened the company treasury bag and handed it to her. 'Tell her that is what we have. Tell her to take what is fair – I am not hiding anything.'

She exclaimed. In fact, it didn't take any understanding of her barbarian tongue to understand that she was cursing like Niceas. She held up one of the gold brooches and her trumpeter barked something. Ataelus spoke briefly and pointed at Kineas. The Scythian commander looked at him. She took the two brooches and handed him the bag. She spoke directly to him, her eyes on his.

'She say, "These for us. These stolen. You kill for Getae – good. And more than you owe for tax these two. So come and eat and I give you gift for these." And she angry, Captain. Angry hard. But not for us. Yes?' Ataelus sat on his horse, nodding.

Kineas blessed the moment in which some god had sent him the Scyth. Hermes – almost certainly the god of travellers and thieves had sent him the Scyth as a guide, because without him this woman would have killed them all. He could feel it. He could feel the anger rolling off her, making her ugly and hard.

She had a golden whip on her saddle and she waved it at him and spoke again, just a few words, and then whirled and galloped back to her main body with her trumpeter on her heels.

Ataelus shook his head. 'Pity for Getae bastards,' he said. 'Did something fucking stupid. Killed someone – I not knowing for whom. But fucked up, going to die.'

Kineas took a deep breath. 'You *did* tell her that we killed the man who was wearing these and scattered his riders?'

'She not care. Angry and young. Hey! You owe me, Captain!' Ataelus looked happy.

'No shit,' said Niceas, his first words in ten minutes. 'We all owe you.'

Ataelus grinned, showing some bad teeth. He liked being the centre of approbation. 'Where you camp?'

'We're going to camp at the river.' Kineas pointed down the beach towards the site Lykeles had located.

Other Scyths from the main body were riding down on them. They didn't seem threatening. In fact, they seemed curious. Two of them rode right up until their ponies were nose to nose with the two Greeks. One of them pointed at Kineas with his whip and called to Ataelus.

'He say – good horse!' Ataelus said. Ataelus looked around, turned his horse and looked up the hill. He seemed upset.

Kineas had other things to occupy him. In a few moments the company was surrounded by Scythians riding around their formation, pointing at things. One whooped and suddenly they were all whooping. They galloped off down the beach a stade and came to a halt.

Ataelus rode back over. 'Gone,' he said. He shrugged. 'She say camp and eat but she gone.' He shook his head. 'Getae bastards for trouble are.'

'You think she's going against the Getae right now? Just like that?' Kineas had his eyes on the other Scythians, about twenty of them, who were waiting down the beach. He looked back at his men and the horses, and he caught a glimpse of his captive, the Getae boy, and an ugly thought came to him. 'Niceas, get the men moving. In armour. Now. Gentlemen, right along the beach. Ignore the barbarians. I have to bet they won't make trouble. Hermes, send they do not make trouble.' The company moved off in double file.

Kineas pulled his charger over to Crax, who was riding his mare. He had to hold the charger hard; his stallion liked the smell of the mare, wrinkled his lips and snorted. 'Crax, the moment we make camp – I mean it – you get the Getae boy into a tent and stay there. These barbarians ...' He realized that there wasn't much he could say. The barbarians were after the Getae. He'd just fought them himself. The distinction was likely to be lost on Crax.

But Crax understood. He nodded. 'The amazon wants blood.' Just like that.

'Amazon?' Kineas asked, astonished at the former slave's erudition.

'Amazon. Women who fight.' Crax looked back at the Getae boy. 'I'll protect him.'

'Don't make trouble, boy.' Kineas wished he had time to explain, wished he understood *anything* about the politics of the plains or where those thrice-damned brooches had originated from. The column was moving. The Scyths were keeping their distance. 'You are Getae?' he asked.

Crax glanced at him sideways and spat. 'No,' he said. 'Bastarnae.'

Kineas had heard of the Bastarnae. 'But you know these people?' he asked.

Crax shook his head. 'The Getae are thieves. The Scyths are monsters. They never take slaves, only kill and burn and go. They have magic.'

Kineas rolled his eyes. He wasn't the only one listening and he heard some comments behind him. 'Magic – Crax, magic is a story to scare slaves and children.'

Crax nodded. 'Sure.' He looked around. 'They have men ...' He paused, clearly uncertain about what to say. 'They are horrible. Everyone says so. The Getae are just thieves.' He looked at Kineas. 'Am I really free?'

Kineas said, 'Yes.'

Crax said, 'I will fight for you. For ever.'

They made camp by the river before the sun had slanted far down the sky. The tents went up quickly after Kineas and Niceas had made the reason plain to everyone, and Crax disappeared with the Getae boy while the Scythians were busy with their own camp. Ataelus didn't go with them. He picketed his horses with the Greeks and squatted down by the first fire to be lit. Kineas sat by him.

'Who is she?' he asked, pointing to the eastern horizon for emphasis.

'Young, for angry woman?' Ataelus shrugged. 'Noble.' He used a word that usually meant 'virtuous' in Greek. Kineas puzzled it out.

'She's well born? A queen?'

'No. Small force. Big tribe. *Assagatje*. Tens of tens of tens of riders they can put on the plains and still have many for camp, again. They for Ghan – Ghan like king for them. Yes? Ghan of Assagatje big, big man. Has nobles, yes? Three tens of tens, nobles. All Assagatje.'

Kineas took a deep breath. 'The king of these Assagatje has thousands of warriors and this is just a small band under a noble?'

Ataelus nodded.

'And she is young and angry and maybe eager to make a name for herself, and she took her troopers and went after the Getae, who are four days' ride away?'

'Getae feel fire tomorrow,' Ataelus said.

The flatness of his answer gave Kineas a chill. '*Tomorrow*? That ride took us three days.'

'Assagatje are *Sakje*. Sakje ride over grass like north wind for blow, fast and fast and never for rest.' Ataelus thumped his chest. 'Me Sakje.' He thumped his chest. 'Ride for day. Ride for night. Ride for day again. Sleep for horse. More horse for fight – like Captain, yes?'

Niceas cut in from across the fire. 'Ares' balls – so she's going to hit the Getae tomorrow and come back?'

Ataelus nodded vigorously. He pounded his right fist in his open left hand, making a noise like a sword hitting a body. 'Hit – yes.'

Kineas and Niceas exchanged a long glance. Kineas said, 'Right. Up in the last watch, move as soon as there is light in the sky. Everyone not on watch get in your cloak.'

Kineas curled up next to Diodorus, who was not asleep. 'What are we afraid of? You paid the tax – with our horses, I'll hasten to add.'

Kineas considered feigning sleep and not replying, sure that every man in the tent was attending to a question only Diodorus could ask him. Finally he said, 'I don't know. She was pleasant. Straighter than many an oligarch. But when she saw those damned brooches – I am afraid we've started something. And I want to get to Olbia ahead of whatever it is.'

Diodorus whistled softly. 'You're the captain,' he said.

Too right, thought Kineas, and went to sleep.

Artemis, naked, her broad back and narrow waist he so well

remembered. He came up behind her, his prick stiff as a board, like
something an actor would wear, and she turned and smiled at him
over her shoulder, but as she turned she was the Assagatje noble-
woman, the gold gorget hiding her breasts, and she spoke words in
anger, words that sounded like a snarl, and in each hand she held
one of the brooches, and she slammed the pins into her eyes ...

He awoke with Diodorus's hand over his mouth. 'You were
screaming,' Diodorus said.

Kineas lay and shook. He knew he had stronger dreams than
other men, and he knew the gods sent them, but they often
disturbed him nonetheless.

When the fit passed, he rose, took his own silver cup from a
bag and poured wine into it from his own flagon, walked well
down the beach and poured the whole cup into the sea as a
libation, and he prayed.

6

Olbia stood out from the low shoreline of the Euxine like a painted statue in a dusty marketplace. From where Kineas sat on a low bluff across the great Borasthenes River, he could see a long peninsula projecting from the far shore. A pall of smoke from thousands of fires coated the town like dust, or soot, but the temple of Apollo rose in pristine splendour atop a steep hill at the base of the peninsula and the town filled the tip, with solid walls as high as three men – the highest walls Kineas had seen since the siege of Tyre. The walls seemed out of place, out of proportion to the size of the place and the position of the town. And the town spilled over the walls, small houses and mud buildings filling the ground from the base of the walls to the temple hill, an ill-defended suburb that would have to be sacrificed in the event of a siege. Olbia had two harbours, one on either side of her peninsula, and dolphins, the symbol of the town, sported in the water below him and gleamed gold on distant marble pillars at the town gates.

The golden dolphins reassured him. Almost at his feet was a proper polis: gymnasia, agora, a theatre – and a hippodrome. Kineas was glad to see that he had not led his men into a howling wilderness for nothing. But the tall walls and the slovenly suburb were at odds – either the city needed to defend itself, or it did not.

Niceas coughed and a cloud of breath formed in front of his mouth. It was cold. The summer was long gone. 'We'll need—' He coughed again, this time too long. 'We'll need a ferry. Hermes, I'll be happy to be in a bed with some straw.'

Kineas spotted what had to be the ferry crossing, more than a mile from the mouth of the river, well clear of the traffic in the harbour. 'Let's get you indoors.' Niceas wasn't the only sick man.

Only Ataelus was immune to the cold. He had a fur-lined hood, taken at a dice game with the other Scyths, and a longer cloak. The hard, clear air didn't give him sniffles or a cough and he still slept outside with his reins in his hand. The other Sakje had ridden away two days before, returning to their woman leader wherever she was once they had taken Kineas to the mouth of the Borasthenes. They had been good guests, good hosts and everyone had dined on their hunting skills night after night. Most of the men had picked up a few words of their language and the deep grunt – *uuh-aah* – they made when they won at dice.

As they rode down to the ford, the horses picking their way through long grass silvered with late morning frost, Kineas trotted over to Ataelus. 'We all owe you a debt of thanks. You are a fine scout.'

Ataelus smiled, then shrugged. 'It is for good for with you.' He looked at his riding whip as if finding some flaw to cover his embarrassment. 'Good with you. Me, I stay, you give a more horse. Yes?'

Kineas had not expected this. It made his morning. 'You want to stay with us? And you want me to give you another horse?'

Ataelus held up his hand. 'More horse, and more horse. You chief, yes? Bigger chief in city, yes? I get more horse when you get more horse.' Ataelus shrugged as if this was the most obvious thing in the world. 'Diodorus more horse. Antigonus more horse. Even Crax more horse. Why else fight for city? Yes?'

Kineas reached out and they clasped hands. In this respect, the Scythians and Greeks were brothers – they clasped hands to show friendship and agreement. 'I'm very glad you wish to stay.'

Ataelus nodded, smiled again almost flirtatiously. 'Good. Let's go drink wine.'

But it wasn't that simple. Their arrival at the ferry caused a commotion – a dozen obviously armed men with no trade goods and a Scythian. It took all of Kineas's various skills as a leader and as a bully to get the ferryman to load his men, and when they arrived on the other side with thirty very cold, wet horses, soldiers met them.

'Please state your business,' said the officer. He was a big man with long dark hair, a dark complexion like a Levanter or an African, a huge beard and expensive armour under a voluminous black cloak. And his men were well armed and well disciplined. The officer wasn't rude, but he was direct. 'You have scared a number of people.'

Kineas was ready with his letter, and he held it out. 'I was hired to come here and command the Hippeis. Here is my letter from the archon.' The letter was a little the worse for having travelled from this spot to Athens by sea and back again in a saddlebag, but it was still legible.

The officer read it carefully, Kineas had time to wonder how many things might have gone wrong in six months – another man took the commission, the archon died, the city had changed government … The big man returned his letter. 'Welcome to Olbia, Kineas of Athens. The archon hoped it was you, but we expected you by boat, many weeks ago.' Now he was regarding Kineas carefully. Kineas knew the look – every officer in Alexander's army watched his rivals just that way. Kineas stuck out his hand. 'Kineas son of Eumenes, of Athens.'

The officer took his hand firmly. 'Memnon, son of Petrocles. You served with the Conqueror?'

'I did.' Kineas motioned to his men to start unloading.

'I was at Issus – but with the Great King.' He turned and bellowed an order and his men brought their spears to the rest, then down butt first on to the ground. 'Take your ease!' he called. His voice was not as low as his size had led Kineas to expect and he gave his orders in a curious sing-song Greek. His men stopped being automatons and became quite human, dropping their heavy shields and pulling their cloaks around them, looking with undisguised curiosity at Kineas's men.

Town slaves came from behind the hoplites and began to make bundles of their gear and place it on their heads. They were mostly Persians. Kineas watched them – he had seldom seen Persians used as slaves.

Memnon followed his interest. 'The Great King made a foray against a local brigand a few years back and the result was a market glutted with Persians.'

Kineas nodded. 'A Scythian brigand?'

Memnon smiled out of half his mouth. 'Is there another kind?'

Kineas saw that Niceas, in betwen coughing fits, had the men currying the cold, wet horses on the spot – good. He put a hand on Niceas's shoulder. 'This is Niceas, my hyperetes. And Diodorus, my second in command.' He looked through the group again. 'Where is Philokles?'

'He was just here,' said Diodorus.

Memnon watched them all carefully. 'One of your men is missing?'

Diodorus laughed. 'I imagine he headed for the nearest wine-seller. We'll find him.' He gave Kineas a minute shrug.

Kineas interpreted the gesture to mean that Philokles was on an errand or had business of his own. Diodorus apparently knew what was happening. Kineas did not – so he merely said, 'We'll find him soon enough.'

'Never mind, the archon is waiting.' Memnon smiled un-pleasantly. 'He hates to be kept waiting.'

It took an hour for all of Kineas's men to find their quarters. They had been put in the city's hippodrome, in a newly built barracks by the stables. The rooms were new but small and none of his men, least of all the gentlemen, was in a mood to be pleased.

He gathered them all in the stable. 'Stay here, clean the place, get it warm and bathe. I want Niceas and Diodorus with me to attend the archon. The rest of you – this is where we are. I suggest you find a way to like it.' He spoke sharply – perhaps more sharply than he meant. 'And find the Spartan.' Then, unbathed, he changed into a clean tunic, good sandals and combed his hair and beard.

In the entryway of the barracks he met with Diodorus, who looked clean and neat as a newly forged pin, and Niceas, who looked like a man with a serious head cold. A soldier and a town slave waited outside, the slave to carry anything that might be wanted, the soldier to take them to the archon.

The soldier led them to the town's citadel, a stone-built tower with heavy bastions and walls a dozen feet thick. Memnon's men guarded the entrance, forbidding in their cloaks. More of them guarded the closed doors at the end of a long, cold portico.

The walls and the guards prepared Kineas to some extent for what awaited him. No archon of a free city needed mercenary guards, a citadel, and an antechamber. The archon of a free city would be at his house, or in the agora, doing business. And so he wasn't surprised when the guards at the doors indicated that his men were not welcome. He gestured that they should wait for him and passed on. A guard took his sword – a barbarian in a torq.

Kineas watched the closed doors open and heard the clash of arms within – more guards – and followed his guide into a warm, dark room decorated in gold with a heavy hand: statues of the gods, their clothes picked out in gold; Persian hangings shot with gold thread; gold lamps suspended on chains from the ceiling that gave a faint gold light; an iron brazier with gold legs that glowed red and vented scented smoke; a gold screen; a table set with gold cups and a huge golden bowl. And behind the table, almost invisible in the scented murk, a man with a diadem was seated on a chair. Memnon stood behind him, his armour appearing to glow in the ruddy light. Flanking the man in the diadem stood a pair of heavily muscled men in lion skins, holding heavy clubs.

'Kineas of Athens?' The voice was soft, very quiet. The smoke from the brazier and the darkness made the voice appear to come from throughout the room, like the voice of a god. 'You are late by fifty days.' A soft laugh. 'It is not easy to travel to the end of the earth, is it? Please, help yourself to the wine at your elbow. Tell me about your adventures.'

'There is little to tell, Archon. I sought to bring my own horses and I have. I apologize for being late.' Kineas found himself off balance. The incense in the smoke was cloying – it bit at his throat unpleasantly. And the men in skins – more barbarians – seemed to be a direct threat.

'You have no need to apologize, young man. At least, for being late. These things can happen. Please tell me how you came here.'

'I came by sea to Tomis and then by land with my horses.'

'Come, young man. More detail.'

'What can I say? We had a brush with some bandits. We met

with a group of Sakje.' Kineas was wary. He had the sense that a trap was being laid for him.

'The bandits you fought were Getae, yes? Unfortunate that they are allies of this city. And the Sakje – truly, the worst bandits of the lot. You were lucky to escape with your skin.'

'The Getae were a few men under a local leader. They attacked us for our horses.' Kineas grabbed a handful of his beard as he often did when puzzled. 'I had no idea they were allies of this city.'

'Nor did they suspect that you were in my service. A most unfortunate circumstance. Still more unfortunate that you then turned the Sakje on them. They lost ten villages, burnt. We trade with the Getae and the Getae are allies of Macedon. You have hurt our trade.' The archon rested his chin on his hand and looked up at Kineas. 'And perhaps you did not know that my own family are of the Getae?'

Kineas winced. 'I had no idea.'

'A pity. and the Sakje – did they ask a toll of you?'

'Archon, you seem already to know these things.'

'Please answer the questions as they are put. You are in my service and the service of my city. We require your cooperation in all things.'

Kineas took a deep breath and coughed. Then he said, 'The Sakje asked a toll. I paid it – two horses from my herd and some gold.'

'And the lord of the Sakje – a red-bearded man?'

'A woman, Archon.'

The archon's surprise was evident. His voice became louder, more focused. 'A woman? That I had not heard. That is interesting news. What was her name?'

Not for the first time Kineas regretted that he had not learned it. 'I don't know.'

'A pity. It is my lot in life to follow the careers of these petty brigands. Often it becomes a matter of state security to know which of them is developing ambitions. Young man, we do not pay tolls to the brigands on the plains. Please be sure never to do so again. Ah – and I'm told you have one of them in your train. Please dismiss him.'

Kineas had kept his temper on a long leash, but he'd just reached the end of it. 'I'm afraid you have sent for the wrong man, Archon,' he snapped. 'I am a gentleman of Athens, not a dog.' He tossed the letter on the table. 'Perhaps a dog can be ordered to dismiss his men in Olbia, but not an Athenian.'

The archon smiled. His teeth gleamed like ivory in the light. 'Not so obedient. But loyal to your men. Will you be as loyal to me, I wonder?' His tone changed, the smile folded and put away, the teeth gone back into the darkness. 'You brought horses. Why? There are few things we need less, here. The brigands sell us what we need. They breed them like maggots. You came fifty days late and antagonized an ally so that you could get a few Greek horses into my city? That's not good judgement. I only want men with good judgement.'

Kineas tried the wine and found it excellent. It cut through the smoke in his throat. 'You do not have a single cavalry mount in the city stables.'

The archon paused. For the first time he glanced at Memnon. 'Nonsense. I have twenty horses there, all superb animals. They had better be superb, I paid well for them. If you advise me, I shall get more if required. No need for your Greek beasts.'

Kineas nodded. 'All twenty are excellent horses. Not one is trained for war. I brought twenty chargers and with them as a foundation I can train a hundred more this winter.' And start a stud, he thought, but kept it to himself.

The archon cocked his head to one side and put his chin in his hand. 'Humph. Perhaps there is truth in what you say. That's why I wanted a cavalry officer. So, here you are. I'll fob the Getae off, then. And the brigands, what did you think?'

'I think they are a little more than brigands. Very good cavalry. I would not want to tangle with them.'

'Brigands, I tell you. They pretend we owe them tribute and tolls. Humph – wait until you try and trade with them. But they have their uses and they don't cost us anything. Unlike your gentlemen, who are quite expensive.'

Memnon smiled. 'Security is never cheap, sir.'

'Humph. Kineas, you know the terms. You brought men with you – that was never in the contract. I wish you to train the gentlemen of my city.' A deep breath and then the voice went on in a whisper. 'Make them useful, stop them from being such a thorn in my side. They waste my time with their plotting and their lawsuits. But I didn't want to hire another troop of mercenaries.'

Kineas nodded. 'I took the risk that you would accept them. They are excellent soldiers, gentlemen of family from Greece and elsewhere. And I must have some experienced men as file-closers and as trainers. Those men must be well born or your Hippeis will not accept their direction. I brought a dozen men, sir – they will not empty the treasury,' Kineas pointed at the gold lamp, 'which seems well stocked.'

'Don't count my treasure before you've earned it,' snapped the archon. His voice, rich and mellow when calm, was sharp as a sword when aroused. Money clearly aroused him. 'Memnon? What do you think?'

'I think he's got a point. I wouldn't offer to train a city's hoplites to be better soldiers without a staff.' Memnon caught Kineas's eye.

'What do you expect them to be paid, these *gentlemen*?' asked the archon.

'Four drachma per day, payable every month,' Kineas was happy to be on firm ground, rattling off the figures he had pondered for a month. 'A month in advance for every man. Double wages for my hyperetes and one other senior man. A bonus for combat duty and for each year of good service.'

'Double the wages of my men,' said Memnon. But he gave Kineas the tiniest of nods.

'Your men don't provide their own mounts which they have to keep, nor all the tack. I think that you'll find that after deductions for living, the wage is about the same.' Kineas had, in fact, asked for more money than his men were expecting.

Memnon gave a short laugh, like a bark.

The archon shook his head. 'Humph. Very well. I expect good service and I expect that when I learn to trust them, your men will be at my disposal.' He rang a small bell, the noise sharp in the heavy air. A slave in a long robe responded immediately.

The archon gestured at Kineas. 'Do the maths and get this man a month's pay for his men.'

The slave was well dressed, thin as a pole and heavily bearded with deep-set eyes. He bowed. 'As you command, lord.' His Greek was accented with Persian. He looked at Kineas. 'I am Cyrus, the factor of the archon. I understood that you have twelve men, two of whom are to receive double pay, at the rate of four drachmas a day. Is this correct?'

Kineas nodded. The Persian was very formal. He had probably been a nobleman. Nothing in his demeanor indicated what he thought of his current status. Kineas bowed. 'Cyrus, I am Kineas of Athens. May we be well met.'

Cyrus held his eye throughout the greeting – not the sign of a born slave – and was visibly pleased to be greeted in such a way.

Kineas continued. 'My hyperetes is waiting beyond these doors. Please give him the money.'

'As you wish, sir.' Cyrus walked through a side door.

Kineas turned back to the archon. 'I also desire the city rank of Hipparch, as you stated in your letter.'

The archon hesitated. 'I am hiring you to train my nobles—'

'And you will expect me to lead them in the field,' Kineas interrupted.

'Don't be so stiff-necked. There is a man of the city, a powerful man, Cleitus, who holds the post of Hipparch. I do not wish to offend him.'

'Neither do I, Archon. Nonetheless, no squadron can have two commanders. Either I am, on the one hand, his superior, in which case it is my job to make him understand and obey me, or he is, on the other hand, my superior, in which case neither he nor any other gentleman of this city has any reason to listen to a word I say.'

The archon fiddled with his beard. Memnon said nothing. His eyes were fixed on one of the gold lamps hanging over Kineas's head. Silence reigned.

'You will both be Hipparchs,' said the archon. 'That is my word on it. My law. You will be equal in rank. If he is not willing to learn your ways, perhaps you will bring word of this to me. And another thing . . .' He raised a hand to forestall Kineas's protest. 'From time to time, you will no doubt hear rumours of plots against me from these men. You will bring these plots to me. You will win their respect so that they expect to confide in you. In this way you will strengthen my rule and the city itself. Do you understand?' He lowered his voice again. 'And if these men miss musters, or refuse to serve under you – that is a crime, on the rolls of this city long before my time of rule. You will report each misdeed to me at once.'

It was Kineas's turn to stand silent. In effect, he was being asked to inform on his own troopers, a situation so repugnant that he was tempted to give a hot answer. On the other hand, it was just the sort of petty crap any soldier expected when serving a tyrant. Kineas balanced the one against the other – the good of his men, that of his own and his view of himself as a man of honour.

'I will tell you if I believe a man to be plotting against the city,' he said carefully. His choice of verbs was exact, the product of his childhood training in rhetoric. 'Or committing any serious crime.'

If the archon caught the hedging in his reply, he made no comment. 'Good, then. I like that you have not made some horrible demand for your own pay. What do you expect?'

'What you offered to get me to come here,' said Kineas.

'Please note that I do not subtract the bonus because you are fifty days late.' The archon's voice was warm, amiable. 'I will start the pay of your men from the time they entered our lands.'

'Thank you, Archon. You are generous.' Kineas now longed to be free from the room, the stink of the brazier and the atmosphere of restriction and fear. 'When do I begin my duties?'

'You began them when you reported to me. I expect I will have errands for your men soon. I will summon the Hippeis for the day after the feast of Apollo. It is their custom to be on the parade of the hippodrome at the ninth hour. Please inform me by name of every man who fails the muster. Cyrus will provide you with a complete list.' He waved his hand in dismissal. 'I look forward to great things from you, Kineas – now that you have come.'

Kineas held his ground. 'How shall I address you?'

'As Archon – at all times.' The archon lowered his head and waved his hand again in dismissal.

Even Alexander had used his name with his companions. And he said he was a god. Kineas allowed himself to smile. 'Very well, Archon.' He turned on his heel and left.

Niceas was waiting with two hefty leather sacks and a scroll. Diodorus looked through the closing door at all the gold and whistled. 'Well?'

'We're hired.' Free of the room, Kineas began to think of the many things he should have said, and several he had not said. He picked up a sack of coins and thrust the scroll through his sword belt, then recovered his sword from the guard. The guard summoned a guide who led them back through the citadel and out to their quarters.

Diodorus waited until their guide had left and asked, 'Tyrant?'

'Oh, yes.' Kineas wanted to wash.

'You smell like a Persian girl. We staying?' Diodorus indicated the coins. Niceas started to say something and was lost in coughing.

Kineas opened a bag and began counting out coins. 'Yes. First, because the pay is excellent. Second, because we have nowhere else to go.'

Diodorus laughed. 'Got that right.'

Kineas put a hand on Niceas's shoulder. 'How sick are you?'

'I'll be fine.'

'Good, then go round up the men. Let's get some things straight.'

When they reached the hippodrome, almost clear across the town from the citadel, Diodorus poured them both wine. Kineas called for Arni and put him to mulling wine with spices for Niceas. By the time the room, the largest in the barracks, was full of the aroma, all of the men were gathered. Diodorus remained by Kineas and Niceas joined him, wiping his nose on a rag. The others brought stools. Lykeles sat in front with Laertes and Coenus. Andronicus and Antigonus stood by the door. Crax hovered at the edge of the hearth. Ataelus sat on the floor and Ajax stood with Philokles against the window.

Kineas raised an eyebrow at Philokles, who smiled in return. Kineas didn't have time just then to discover where the Spartan had been. He rose to his feet and addressed them all.

'Gentlemen. Our first payday since we left Alexander. And time for some rules.' Kineas held out a hand for silence as the word 'payday' was greeted with happy murmurs. 'First – we serve a tyrant. I will say nothing beyond this – every man here must swear before leaving this room to be loyal first to his messmates and his friends, before any other loyalty. I ask this of you because I already suspect that we will be spied on, that our words may be relayed, and that our position here could become very difficult. Instead of living in fear, I propose that we agree to speak freely among ourselves, whatever silence we choose to keep outside the walls of the hippodrome.' He sipped his wine. They were stone silent, now.

'We will be training the Hippeis of this city – provincial gentlemen with large sums of money, large estates, and no experience of taking orders from anyone. I will speak frankly. Those of you who were men of property in your cities – Lykeles, Diodorus, Laertes, Coenus, Agis, and Ajax,' at his name, Ajax's head came up as if he were surprised to be included in any way, 'will have the greatest duties as trainers. You will understand best the manners and the motivations of our noble soldiers, and while being firm on matters of discipline, you will exercise judgement as to how to apply them.'

Lykeles nodded. 'Don't antagonize the rich?'

'Lead through example. That's why I brought you. We will offer prizes for accomplishment from the first. We will not stint with genuine praise, but we will not flatter. We will strive to always be better men than our pupils without embarrassing them. If possible, we will meet them socially and bury them under the weight of our accumulated war stories.'

Most of them laughed, even Ajax.

Antigonus raised his hand. 'Are the rest of us to curry horses?'

'No.' Kineas looked around. 'We are a company of equals. I command, yes. Diodorus will be my second and Niceas my hyperetes, as always. After them, every man will take his turn at every duty. First, however, I intend to accustom our recruits to the idea that we *are* their social equals. After we have them broken to the saddle, then we will use the rest of you to train them on squadron work, skirmishing, all the things at which you excel.' Kineas had piled the Olbian drachmae on the table while he waited for Niceas to bring the men. 'Pay will be at the rate of four drachmas per day. Each month is paid in advance. This is your first month's pay. Diodorus and Niceas get double pay. Is that acceptable to everyone?'

It was better than acceptable to everyone except Ataelus, who began counting on his fingers, and Ajax and Coenus, who shrugged.

'Very well,' said Kineas. 'Agis the Megaran – one hundred and twenty drachmas. Make your mark. One hundred and twenty drachmae to Andronicus, plus fifty drachmae for the loss of your horse to the amazon. No deductions. One hundred and seventy drachmas. Make your mark, you are a rich man. One hundred and twenty drachmas to Antigonus, no additions, no deductions. Make your mark. Coenus ...' And so he went through them, leaving Crax beaming at the pile of silver in his hands and Ajax bemused at what to do with so much pocket change. He paid them all while Niceas made marks on a scroll and Diodorus watched.

'Tomorrow we have our first parade. I want every one of you up and sparkling for this and every other parade we have. Remind them by your bearing that you are a professional soldier and they are hopeless amateurs. Once your tack is clean and your armour shined, you may go spend your money any way you like. Fill the barracks with whores – gamble it all away. Be warned, though – we are under discipline now. Discipline with us means don't make an ass of yourself outside the barracks.' They were laughing, the poorer men unable to take their eyes off the small piles of heavy silver coins. 'But first,' Kineas's voice snapped like a banner in the wind, 'you will all swear.'

They stood in a circle – all twelve, and raised their hands, putting them over Kineas's in turn, so that he could feel the weight of their arms on his. 'By Zeus who hears all oaths, by

Athena and Apollo and all the gods, we swear that we will remain loyal to each other and the company until it is dissolved by us all in council.' Kineas spoke the words and they repeated them with gusto, no voice lacking. Ajax surprised Kineas with his eager voice rising above the others. At that moment he loved them. He tried not to show it.

'Clean your armour. Then let's get some wine.' He wriggled his toes by the warmth of the fire, glad to be off the cold plains and sitting in a decent chair.

But he wished he had learned the name of the Sakje woman.

In the morning, if there were any long heads from drinking, they were hidden well. First, Kineas read off to all of them his intended course of inspection and instruction. They laid out butts for throwing javelins, set aside space for the practice of mounting and dismounting, and built fences to simulate riding over rough country. After the field of the hippodrome was ready, Kineas inspected his dozen veterans. All of them had spent money the day before on tunics and buckles and they looked the better for it. They wore blue tunics under their armour, the colour of the city, and every man had a silver buckle on his sword belt. Their horses shone. Kineas gave them a smile to show that he appreciated their efforts. He himself wore a new cloak of deep blue, and had a blue horsehair crest on his plain bronze helmet. He had shaved his beard from the shaggy mass of hair it had become to a neat brush in the new style.

They exercised for an hour in the sharp air, their manoeuvers easily accommodated by the field of the hippodrome. Kineas turned to Niceas after the first run with javelins. 'We shall need more room for three hundred gentlemen. Have Ataelus scout the ground around the city and find us a decent field.'

'I'll go with him,' said Niceas, and coughed. He wiped his nose with a rag and coughed more.

'I want you to go to bed. You look terrible.'

Niceas shrugged. 'I'm fine,' he said, and began to cough again.

The exercises were quite competent. Kineas kept them at it until the horses had all been worked to a lather and the men had brushed the cobwebs off their skills. Ajax could throw one spear at the gallop but couldn't yet manage to get his second javelin transferred to his throwing hand before he passed the target. He tended to drop the second in his haste. Philokles could throw far and accurately, but he couldn't throw quickly and he could just manage his horse. His riding had improved, but not to the standard of the other men's.

Kineas chose not to single Philokles out – the Spartan was perfectly aware of the shortcomings of his riding. But when the exercises were done, he summoned them all.

'I want you to think that we are now in a land of horsemen. The Sakje are not the only men here who ride. Our Hippeis are likely to be better riders than most Greeks, as good as Thracians or Thessalians. That was good work today. Get those horses stabled and warm. When that's done, I'd like Philokles, Diodorus, Lykeles, Laertes and Coenus to accompany me to the gymnasium. The rest of you should wander the city. Accustom yourselves to the streets. Learn where the gates are and the posterns – not just the wine shops.'

The Getae slave, Sitalkes, took Kineas's horse and began to curry it, which earned him a glare from Niceas. Kineas ignored the glare and went to change for the gymnasium.

Their barracks was small, but it had amenities. The central hall off the porch was lined in pegs for cloaks and equipment and gave on to the kitchen where two city slaves cooked, as well as a meeting room and Kineas's own pair of large rooms and a hearth at the back of the building. Stairs on the outside of the building gave on to a passage with doors that led to six small rooms with sleeping racks for soldiers. The rooms were unheated, but better than any tent and the men had taken the two rooms directly over the kitchen. Kineas entered through the portico and stripped in his own chamber, wiped the cold sweat from his breastplate, cleaned his helmet and set them on a stand by his bed. He hung the baldric of his sword belt over the breastplate. Clothed in a decent but unmilitary tunic and sandals, he met Diodorus in the central hall.

'Now we show ourselves to be gentlemen,' Kineas said.

'I'll see what I can do,' said Diodorus.

Coenus gave a sneer. 'I'd rather the locals proved *themselves* to be gentlemen. So far, they look like hicks.'

While waiting for the others, Kineas sent a slave to the gymnasium to request permission to use it with his men. As mercenaries, they had some status, but they were not citizens. It was best to be sure.

Lykeles came in rubbing his head. 'I have a good mind to buy a slave to curry my horse,' he said. 'The stink!'

The town slave returned with a handful of clay discs. 'These are for your honours' use. They mark you as guests.'

Kineas gave the boy an obol. 'Shall we take some exercise?' he said to his gentleman troopers.

Olbia's gymnasium was a finer building than that in Tomis, if gaudier. Bronze dolphins adorned the stone steps and the façade was stone as well. The building had heated floors and warm baths, and a heavy gilt-bronze plaque in the portico declared that Archon Leucon son of Satyrus had built it as a gift to the city.

Kineas read the plaque, amused to see that here, at least, the archon used his name.

Town slaves took their cloaks and sandals. They walked through a short passageway to the changing room and stripped in the chill air, leaving their tunics in wooden cubbyholes. Two other men stopped their conversation and watched them strip, silently. They began a hushed exchange as soon as the five soldiers left the changing room for the exercise floor.

The silence was repeated there. At least a dozen citizens stood about the sanded floor, a few exercising with weights, one man using his strigil on another, but their conversation died when Kineas entered.

Diodorus looked about him. Then he shrugged. 'Care to wrestle a fall, Kineas?'

It was too chilly, even with the heated floor, to pause for long. Kineas squared off against Diodorus, while Coenus and Lykeles began to exercise, carefully working their cold muscles. Laertes set to lifting weights.

Diodorus feinted a grab at Kineas's legs, caught an arm and threw him, but Kineas got hold of his head on the way down and they fell in a tangle of limbs. In a second they were both on their feet again. In the second engagement, Diodorus was more careful, but he couldn't get Kineas to overcommit and it was Kineas who trapped one of Diodorus's hands and went for a throw. Diodorus struck Kineas a sharp blow to the ribs, but Kineas got a foot behind Diodorus's leg and tripped him. Diodorus rolled out of the fall and they were both on their feet again, now warm and breathing harder.

Kineas raised his hands, palms out, in a high guard. Diodorus kept his low, close to his body. They circled. Out of the corner of his eye, Kineas saw that they were being watched by most of the men in the room. He grabbed at Diodorus's head with both hands. Diodorus's hands shot out, parted Kineas's hands and hit him, open-handed, on the forehead, rocking him back. In a second, Diodorus was on him, his left leg between Kineas's legs and Kineas was down, this time with the weight of his friend solidly atop him. The sand on the floor was none too deep and the fall bruised his hip. Diodorus got to his feet and Kineas stood, dripping with sweat and rubbing his hip.

'Well struck,' he said ruefully.

'I certainly thought so. You make me work harder and harder, Kineas. You may make a passable wrestler yet.'

They wrestled three more falls, two of them by Diodorus, and then Lykeles and Coenus began boxing. Neither of them was as fast as Kineas or as athletic as Ajax, but they were competent and a little showy.

None of the other men in the room offered a contest or even a wager, and none of them approached Kineas's men. They stood silently by the gymnasium's fountain, watching in a group.

Kineas crossed the floor to them. He was reminded of the efforts he had made, fruitless efforts as time proved, to be social with the Macedonian officers in Alexander's army. Despite his doubts, he approached the oldest of the men, a lean, athletic old man with a beard nearly white.

'Good morning, sir,' Kineas said. 'I am only a guest here and I desire to run. Where do I go to run?'

The older man shrugged. 'I run on my estate outside the city. I imagine that's what any gentleman does.'

Kineas smiled. 'I'm from Athens. Our estates are generally too far from our houses to visit for exercise. Many times I have run around the theatre, for instance, or early in the agora.'

The old man cocked his head, examining Kineas as if he were a ram for sale at auction. 'Really? You have an estate? Frankly, young man, that surprises me. I imagined you were a freebooter.'

Kineas began stretching. He looked up at the old man – and his crowd. 'Before he died, my father was among the largest landholders in Athens. Eumenes – you must have heard of him. Our ships traded here.' And as he switched sides to stretch the other leg, he said very deliberately, 'My friend Calchus still sends ships here, I believe.'

Another man, thinner, but with a paunch that suggested a serious lack of exercise, leaned forward. 'I trade with Calchus. You know him?'

Kineas brushed sand off his thigh and said, 'We grew up together. So you don't run in the city?'

The best-looking man in the group, younger and harder, said, 'Sometimes I run around the gymnasium. It wasn't built on the best site – well, it wasn't! I'm not attacking the architect or the archon! The new gymnasium doesn't have room for a running event, is all.'

Other men edged away from him as if he had a disease.

Kineas extended a hand to the man. 'I'd like some company. Care to run with me?'

The man looked around at the rest of the group, but none of them met his gaze and he shrugged. 'Certainly. Let me stretch a moment. I'm Nicomedes.'

They ran longer than Kineas might have wished. Nicomedes was an accomplished distance runner and he was interested in going faster and farther than Kineas had planned, leaving little wind for talk. But it was companionable enough, if cold, and when they had run as far as Kineas could manage without collapsing in public, they returned to the gymnasium and the baths, and Nicomedes invited Kineas to dinner – his first invitation in the city.

Luxuriating in the first decent bath he'd had in a month, Kineas asked, 'Are you in the Hippeis, Nicomedes?'

'I certainly qualify by property, if that's what you mean. I have a horse, but I've never served. My people have always served on foot.' Close up, Kineas could see that Nicomedes was a bit of a fop – he had the remains of make-up on his eyes and the cheeks of a heavy drinker. He was older than he had first appeared, and very fit, and his preening indicated that he knew how good his body was – but he was a pleasant companion for all that.

Kineas chose his words carefully. 'A word to the wise, Nicomedes. The archon has given me a full list to muster the town's cavalry and he seems to expect compliance.'

Nicomedes' shoulders came out of the water so fast the drops flew. 'That's not fair – we've always served as hoplites.' And then: 'How fucking typical.' And after another pause: 'I shouldn't have said that.'

Kineas shrugged and scrubbed. 'You might pass the word.'

Nicomedes said, 'Have you met the hipparch, Cleitus?'

Kineas thought, I'm the hipparch. And then he thought back to the archon's hesitation on the subject. *Ahh, now I begin to see.* 'I have not. I'd like to – we will have to work together to accomplish anything.'

Other men were coming into the baths and busy slaves were filling the other wooden tubs. The rooms began to fill with steam. It lent a comforting anonymity. The chatter grew louder. Kineas could hear Lykeles flattering somebody's physique, Diodorus asking questions and Coenus quoting Xenophon's views on horsemanship.

Nicomedes said, 'He sometimes shares a cargo with me, and we are occasionally allies in the assembly – when the archon lets us have an assembly, that is. Hmm, shouldn't have said that. Anyway, I could ask him to dinner – give the two of you a chance to meet. We were only told that the archon was hiring a mercenary.'

Kineas motioned for a slave to rub his shoulders. 'I can imagine,' he said.

Clean, dressed and pleasantly tired, Kineas led his men back to the barracks. His damp beard seemed to freeze as soon as they went outside and his cloak would not get him warm. 'That went well,' said Kineas.

'They expected us to be monsters,' said Lykeles. 'Makes me wonder about Memnon and his lot.'

'It'll take more than a couple of dinners and some visits to the gymnasium to settle them,' said Kineas, rubbing his beard.

Diodorus said, 'There's more going on here than I expected. It's not just the old bloods against the archon, either. My sense it that there are three, or even four factions. Does Athens support the archon? It's not like Athens to support a tyrant, even in these decadent times.'

'Athens needs the grain,' said Coenus. 'I heard a debate on granting citizenship to the tyrant of Pantecapaeum, once, in the assembly. It was all about grain subsidies.' He rubbed his beard. 'I thought your Nicomedes was a fine man, if a bit of a fop. I bored one of the older men with my erudition – laid it on a bit thick. Petrocolus, his name was. Fine old fellow.'

'They're a cautious lot,' said Lykeles. 'Hermes, they're a close-mouthed crew – all except your Nicomedes. Handsome man. Did he run well?'

'Better than I ever will, or want to,' said Kineas.

'Bit of a hothead, by local standards. I wonder how soon the archon will hear you are dining with him?' asked Diodorus.

One of Memnon's men was standing in the entryway to the barracks.

'There's your answer,' said Kineas.

Kineas had to struggle to enjoy dinner with Nicomedes. His food was excellent and his wine passable, but the men around the circle of couches were either silent or spoke in what appeared to be a code.

Nicomedes' house was colourful, decorated in the latest style, except for an antique mosaic over the floor of the main room, which showed Achilles killing the queen of the Amazons at Troy in grisly detail. His furnishings and his food were on a par with the richest men in Athens.

Kineas revised his view of Olbia. The grain trade made these men very rich indeed.

He was introduced to Cleitus immediately – a short, dark-haired man with a long beard and deep-set eyes and a fair amount of grey hair – but he couldn't seem to start a conversation with any of them. All of them lay alone to dine and the couches were set far enough apart that conversation was difficult. A trio of Nubian dancers reminded him uncomfortably that a bath wasn't the only thing he hadn't had in a long time, but they also served to kill any talk that might have sprung up after the main course.

Unable to leave his couch due to the prominence of his approval of the dancers, Kineas watched the other men, trying to identify why the situation seemed so normal and yet so alien. On the one hand, everything was just as it should be in a well-run Greek home – the men being served, the side dishes, fish sauce, wine on the sideboards, busy slaves. On the other hand, the silence was oppressive. Kineas tried to remember a time in Athens, even under the most repressive governments, when his father's table had not rung with angry denunciations, violent protests, if only against the taxing of the rich, and political argument.

The last dishes were cleared away and more wine was brought. Without being asked, Kineas rose and pulled his own couch closer to that of Cleitus. Cleitus glanced at him while he moved his couch, but said nothing.

Kineas lay back down and held out his cup for filling. Nicomedes rose, said a prayer and poured a libation. The other guests added their own prayers and libations. Again, they behaved just like Greeks, but there was no ribaldry, no jokes, no suggestions. Odd.

'Nicomedes,' called Kineas. 'I checked the rolls. You are listed for service in the cavalry.'

Nicomedes sat up on his couch. 'By all the gods – well, I suppose it can't be blamed on you. I can ride well enough – when is this muster?'

'The day after the feast of Apollo, I believe. Cleitus – you are the hipparch?'

Cleitus shook his head. 'I act as the hipparch. Only the assembly of the city can appoint the hipparch. They have not met … they have not … that is to say.' Having gone so far, Cleitus halted and drank his wine.

Nicomedes smiled. 'Cleitus doesn't want to say it, but the council has not met since the archon dismissed them. Since then, the hipparch, Cleander, died. Cleitus does the duty.'

Kineas frowned at his wine cup. 'So you are not the hipparch and I am not the hipparch. Who can command in such a situation?'

Cleitus glared at him, stung. 'What is there to command? The last time I mustered, only sixteen men came with their horses and armour. Many others came on foot, to see and be seen.'

Kineas nodded. Athenian cavalry often showed the same contempt for authority. He had himself, once. 'When were you last in the field?'

Nicomedes snorted. Cleitus actually blew some wine out his nose. 'Field? In the field? What, against the Scyths? They'd eat our brains. The Getae? Another city? You must be joking.'

Kineas looked around the room. 'Are you all Hippeis, then?'

The youngest man shook his head and declared that he fell far below the property qualification, although he had a horse and liked to ride. The rest were all of the cavalry class.

Kineas said carefully, 'Wouldn't it be better to have a well-trained, well-led body of cavalry in this city than a rabble of rich men?'

'Better for your pay, perhaps,' said Cleitus.

Nicomedes nodded. 'Who would it serve? What faction would control this well-trained cavalry?'

'For the good of the city,' said Kineas.

They all laughed. But Nicomedes fingered his short blond beard thoughtfully.

All his life, Kineas had heard the phrase 'for the good of the city' used in a number of ways – with deliberate sarcasm, with political amorality; to flatter, to cajole, or to demand. He'd heard the phrase abused, but he'd never seen it ignored. Who are these men? he thought. What kind of city is this?

'Have a good night?' asked Diodorus when Kineas came into the barracks.

'The wine was good. The company was a little dull – what are you reading? In fact, what are you doing in my rooms?'

'It's warmer here and I wanted to talk to you as soon as you came back. I thought that the archon told you to avoid Nicomedes?'

Kineas laughed mirthlessly. 'Actually, the archon asked me to be careful in making friends. I always have been, so I chose to take his words as a compliment. You waited up to worry about my relations with the archon?'

'No, this.' Diodorus held up a scroll. 'I had several letters from friends waiting for me, and you need to know the contents. Antipater has made Zopryon his satrap in Thrace. He's putting gold and men into Thrace even now. They're building an army there.'

'Headed where?'

'I can't say for certain and neither can my sources. The word being given out is that it's an army of reinforcements going out to the Conqueror.'

'That could be true, certainly.'

'They could be aimed here, too. These are rich lands and Antipater needs cash. Alexander may be conquering the world, but he hasn't sent a lot of money home and Antipater has a lot of enemies. Look at Sparta.'

Kineas nodded. He pulled at his beard and started to pace the narrow confines of the chamber. 'Is Sparta planning war?'

'Sooner or later. What choice do they have? And Macedon is mighty, but they need money. What better place to get it but here?' Diodorus made a rude gesture. 'And there goes my bonus.'

'If they are poor and yet sending money and men into Thrace, then the move can't be far off. They won't have the money to pay mercenaries for long.' Kineas stopped and poured himself some wine. 'Want a cup?'

'Please. Until next summer, I expect.'

'How many men?'

'Two taxeis of phalanx, some mercenaries and some Thracians – perhaps fifteen thousand foot. Companions and Thessalian cavalry – perhaps four thousand horse.'

Kineas whistled. 'We'd best get out of the way, then.'

Diodorus nodded. 'That's why I thought I should tell you immediately. You don't seem surprised.'

Kineas shrugged. 'You suggested as much at Tomis, just not in the same detail. And,' after a minute's hesitation: 'I heard something about the possibility in Athens.'

Diodorus nodded. 'Yes you denied any knowledge of it at the time.'

Kineas met his eyes and they stared at each other for three heartbeats.

'I see. So that's not open to discussion.' Diodorus rubbed his forehead, clearly annoyed. 'So what did the dinner guests say? You met the hipparch?'

'He's not really the hipparch,' Kineas said. He explained why and revisited the conversation.

Diodorus looked thoughtful. 'I think I see where this is going.'

'You are not the only thinker here, Diodorus. I can see through a brick wall in time. The archon is trying to appoint me so that he can usurp yet another power of the assembly. I see that.' Kineas gestured with his wine cup. 'And then he uses me to keep the rich men in line.'

Diodorus nodded. 'Worse than that, really. I think he expects to use you to cull some of the rich – those who conveniently break the muster laws, for instance, will doubtless be arrested, tried, and exiled – or worse. But you may have ruined that by warning them. The worst of it is, though, that the archon no doubt plans to use the Hippeis as hostages.'

Kineas choked on his wine. 'Hostages?'

'Certainly. Once they are under your command, he can threaten to send them off – to fight, to patrol – he'll have control of them. Remember – there is no assembly, no council – this man can make war and peace on his own word. He can send these rich men out of their city on the pretence of public service, and keep them out as long as he likes.' Diodorus drank the rest of his wine and wiped his mouth. 'Really, I'm surprised no one has thought of it before.'

'Gods help us all if you ever achieve political power,' said Kineas.

'It's nice to have my skills admired. I'm going to bed. But I have another point to raise,' Diodorus looked at his wine cup as if the design surprised him.

'Go ahead.' Kineas rubbed his chin, which didn't seem to have enough hair on it.

'Philokles.'

'Is he a problem? I thought everyone liked him.'

'He's good company. But he comes and goes – Ares' balls, it's hard to put a finger on this. He's out most of the time, and he's not whoring. I think he's got some business of his own.' Diodorus shrugged. 'I don't mean to spy on him, but ...'

Kineas swirled the wine in his cup. 'I'll think about it. I don't watch any of you – I try not to know who's got a lover and who might drink too much. You're suggesting what – that Philokles is a spy?'

Diodorus looked at his wine for a long time. 'I don't know what I'm suggesting. He clearly didn't want to be seen coming into the city – remember?'

Kineas nodded. 'The atmosphere of this place is going to get to us all. Let's allow the Spartan to live his own life for a while.'

Diodorus nodded, but he was clearly unconvinced.

'Diodorus,' said Kineas. 'Thanks. I'm happy to be told – I don't always see things the way you do. And sometimes, no action is the best action.'

Diodorus frowned. 'I'm beginning to suspect that everyone here has a secret. I'd best go find one of my own.'

PART II

LOTUS AND PARSLEY

'His people along the sea-shore took their joy in casting the discus and the javelin, and in archery; and their horses each beside his own car, eating lotus and parsley of the marsh, stood idle ...'

Iliad, Book 2

7

The autumn feast of Apollo, the Paenopsion, was a noisy festival. A day of sacrifices and feasts was followed, at least in Olbia, by an evening torchlight parade of children holding aloft the produce of the city and garlands of a special wheat cake made in the form of Apollo's lyre. As they walked, they sang.

> The Eiresione bears rich cakes
> and figs and honey in a jar, and olive oil
> to sanctify yourself, and cups
> of mellow wine that you may drink and fall asleep.

When full dark fell, the parade gave way to dancing, drinking and horse races. Kineas thought the sacrifices were too showy; someone had spent a great deal of money on elaborate pageantry. The archon appeared only at the great sacrifice, closely guarded by Memnon and fifty soldiers.

Most of Kineas's men attended, wearing their best off-duty clothes and mingling with the city's elite. Ajax made his first public appearance in Olbia's society and was immediately at the centre of a circle of admirers – his beauty drew them regardless of his status as a mercenary and their political factions. Kineas didn't need to stand near the boy to watch the ripple of comment as the admirers discovered who the boy's father was – most Olbian traders did business with Isokles of Tomis.

In fact, his men circulated so freely that Kineas found himself virtually alone at the torch race, attended only by the Getae boy, Sitalkes. He didn't have an urge to break into a new group and he couldn't see Nicomedes or any of the local men he had met. Coenus was visible taking bets, but his new friends were not Kineas's sort.

Kineas began to wander through the crowd. He considered going home. He wanted to find Cleitus, but the man didn't seem to be in attendance. Kineas saw Philokles shout a greeting to someone in the torch-lit gloom and was envious. Philokles made friends easily.

Cleitus was, of course, entering a horse in the race. Kineas felt like a fool for failing to realize that every wealthy horse owner would put up a horse. He walked down to the edge of the track around the temple and pushed through a crowd of slaves and workers, all staring at the horses and trying to work out the best wagers.

When he found the not-quite Hipparch, he called, 'Good fortune to your horse, Cleitus.'

'The blessing of Apollo on your house,' Cleitus replied. 'She's so skittish I'm afraid she won't run. Doesn't like the crowd.'

Kineas watched two slaves hold the mare while she tossed her head and rolled her eyes. 'Is she trained to the torches?'

'Before this, I'd have said she was immune to fire.' Cleitus shrugged, clearly unwilling to solicit advice, but at his wits' end.

Kineas watched her again. 'Put blinders on her, as the Persians do.'

Cleitus shook his head. 'I've no idea what you're talking about.'

Kineas bent down so that his head was level with the Getae boy's. 'Run and find me a piece of rawhide – at least this big.'

Sitalkes screwed up his face in thought. 'Where getting this thing I am, sir?'

Kineas shrugged. 'I have no idea. It's a difficult task. Surprise me. Or, run to Ataelus at our stable and get some from him.' The boy was off before he finished speaking. 'I'll also need a knife and some thread,' Kineas shouted after him.

Cleitus watched his mare try to rear. 'I don't know. Better to scratch my name off than to injure her. And the race will start as soon as the sun's rim goes below a certain mark – too soon.'

'Try my way. If the boy doesn't make it back, you can always scratch then.' Kineas watched the horse – a beauty, with a deep chest and proud head – and added, 'Scratching would be ill fortune indeed at a temple festival.'

'Too right,' said Cleitus. 'In the meantime, I'll try something of my own.' Cleitus called for a slave and they began to rub the horse down together, murmuring endearments. Kineas was glad to see Cleitus working himself – too often rich men lost the knack of work and expected their slaves to do everything.

Sitalkes appeared at his elbow. He wasn't even breathing hard. 'See it, sir. See it – good?'

'Good. Well done. Where did you get it so quickly?' Kineas took a sharp knife from another slave and began to cut the rawhide in half.

'Stole it,' said the boy, not meeting his eye.

Kineas kept cutting. 'Anyone see you?'

The Getae boy stood tall. 'Look idioting? No!'

Kineas cut strap holes carefully with the point of the knife. 'Bring me her head stall,' he called.

It wasn't perfect – when it was on, one of the blinders stood correctly and the other flapped, disturbing her more. Kineas took the thread and stitched both of them in place. As he finished, the horses were called for the race. It was distinctly darker and he could just see his work.

'Thanks for trying so hard, but I'll have to scratch.' Cleitus was watching anxiously. 'They've called the horses.'

'Here. Wait just a moment – one more twist of thread. There. Put it on her head. See?' Kineas looked around for the rider – Cleitus's son Leucon, hurriedly introduced moments before. 'She won't be able to see to her sides. Remember that when you try and pass another rider.'

Already, the mare was calmer. Cleitus and Leucon walked her away into the crowd and Kineas followed the rest of Cleitus's slaves to the finish line, where all the owners and their retainers stood in the light of one of the temple bonfires. Torches were lit from the fire and tossed up to the riders.

Kineas was unable to follow the progress of the race beyond the sound, the chorus of shouts and cheers that moved like fire itself around the temple precinct. But as the horses finished, they presented a brilliant spectacle, crossing the line in a close-knit pack with their torches streaming fire behind them. Cleitus's mare finished third and Leucon was presented with a wreath of laurel leaves.

'I wanted to talk to you about the muster tomorrow,' Kineas said when the congratulations and thanks were tapering away.

'I don't plan to give you any trouble. You're the professional.' Cleitus was rubbing down the mare.

'I'll need your help to get any of these men to do any training.' Kineas thought that straight talk was the right course with Cleitus.

Cleitus turned and leaned one hand against the rump of his mare, crossed his feet and smiled. 'You always in such a hurry, Athenian? It's going to take time – and luck – to get these boys to practise anything. Look, tomorrow will be a shambles – we'll be lucky if everyone on that damned list comes. You come back to dinner with me tomorrow night – bring your officers, we'll all get to know each other. And some advice? Don't be in such a hurry.'

Kineas took a brush from one of the slaves and began to work on the other side of the mare's rump. 'Sound advice. I have my reasons for hurry.'

'I really should thank you for the blinders. Dangerous in a night race – but the chance was worth the result, eh? But I still had to wait for you to get the blinders done. You see? Let's get through tomorrow – Apollo send that all the men are wise enough to come; if some fool gets arrested we'll never have a day's peace.'

'Your words to the god. May every man come.' Kineas handed his brush to the waiting slave. 'I'll take my leave. Until tomorrow.'

'Goodnight, then. Leucon, say goodnight to the gentleman.'

Kineas had his men up at cock's crow and they flogged the stable floors dry, set up more exercise butts and curried their horses until they shone. Mounted, in armour, with new plumes and cloaks, they made a fine show. Kineas had them at the barracks end of the hippodrome half an hour before the appointed time.

The city's gentry arrived all together a few minutes before the appointed hour. They rode or walked into the hippodrome in a long column and immediately spread over the sand, forming groups of ten or twelve, with a few loners and one large group of two dozen, all well mounted, gathered around Cleitus.

Kineas left his men to Diodorus and rode up to Cleitus. As he rode, he watched the local men. They were excellent riders – far better than their equivalents in Athens or Corinth. They rode as well as Macedonians or Thessalians, just as he expected. They had an odd taste in accoutrements, as well. More than one of them wore Sakje trousers, or Thracian-style caps, and their horse harnesses were often more Sakje than Greek.

Cleitus glanced at him and turned his head away, then glanced back and shouted for his men to wheel and join Kineas's men at the far end. The tail of the column was still entering the hippodrome, little knots of men without horses.

Behind the laggards, Kineas saw the dark cloaks of Memnon's soldiers. 'There's trouble,' he said, pointing his whip at them.

Cleitus pulled his heavy Corinthian helmet back on his head so that he could see better. 'Those idiots had better all be here. How do you want to do the muster?'

Kineas gestured to the end, where Cleitus's horsemen had joined Kineas's men, making an imposing front. 'First we muster the properly turned-out men. Then we line the rest up and muster them – first those with horses, then those with armour and no horses, then those with neither armour nor horses. It makes the least prepared waste the most time.'

'You've done this before.' Cleitus smiled mirthlessly.

'Twice a year in Athens.' Kineas gestured with his whip to Niceas, who galloped across the sand to him, nearly oversetting two portly men. 'You have the roll?'

'Right here.' Niceas stifled a cough.

'Start with the men who just fell in. Then do our men. Once a man is mustered, he may dismount and relax. Cleitus and I will start culling the herd,' Kineas gestured at the hundreds of men milling about, 'for more to muster, and we'll send them to you at the end.'

Niceas nodded and saluted.

'Who is your hyperetes?' Kineas asked Cleitus.

'My son. Leucon. You met him last night.'

'May I send him to help Niceas so that it doesn't look like it's all my doing?'

'Good thought. Leucon!' Cleitus clamped his horse's back

with his knees, rose in the saddle and roared. His son was resplendent in a deep-blue cloak and gilt breastplate – one of the
best turned-out men in the city. Kineas sent him to Niceas.

As it turned out, the muster itself was uneventful. Three men
of the cavalry class were absent, but all for acceptable reasons
– one at Pantecapaeum on business, two known to be ill, and
both had sent substitutes. When the muster was complete, they
had all gathered at the far end of the hippodrome. It was a cold
day and the crowd huddled for warmth.

Kineas inspected them from a distance. Less than one quarter
had any armour, although many claimed that they had such
stuff at home. About one half had come mounted, mostly the
younger men.

'Want to say something?' asked Kineas.

'You're burning to do it,' said Cleitus. 'Be my guest. Just
remember that antagonizing them will serve no one.'

Kineas rode to the head of the crowd. His voice, when he
started, was a roar that squashed interruption.

'Men of Olbia! We are gathered today to serve this city! I
serve her for pay – and you from love of your homes. Is it possible that some of you love the city more than others? Or that
the gold you pay me is dearer to me than your love of your city?
Or is it possible that some of you are really too poor to bear
the burden of cavalry service and lack the horses and arms that
make a cavalryman?'

He lowered his voice, because he was the only man talking.
'Anything worth doing is worth doing well. Socrates said so,
and so did my father. There is no point pretending to have a
troop of city cavalry. There is no point in wasting your valuable
time mustering you for a service you can't perform – and make
no mistake, gentlemen – at the moment you cannot perform it.
Even if the gods gifted you this second with fine Persian chargers,
trained from birth for war, with armour crafted by Hephaeston
himself and weapons fresh from his forge, you wouldn't last a
minute against real cavalry.' He smiled. 'With nothing but a
little work, we could change that. With a little work, we could
make you gentlemen good enough to participate in city parades,
as the Athenian cavalry does. Perhaps good enough to rival the

precision of Memnon's men.' Kineas pointed down the field where Memnon stood with fifty soldiers – a palpable threat. And by pointing them out, Kineas hoped that he had been sufficiently subtle in suggesting that they could be bested.

'I wish to show you what cavalrymen look like. Perhaps, having seen them, you will say that professional soldiers have the time to practise such things – but I'll tell you that these skills can be taught to you, and you can master them and serve your city with pride.'

Kineas rode in silence to the head of his own men. He pitched his voice low, hoping the gods would carry his words to his own men only. 'Gentlemen, I'd appreciate it if you'd put on the finest display of horsemanship in history.'

Diodorus smiled coldly. 'At your command, Hipparch.'

'Start with the javelins,' he said. 'At my command, form file from the left and throw at the gallop. Then form your front and halt just short of Memnon's line. And gentlemen, when I say just short, I mean the length of a horse's head. Throw both javelins if you think they'll both hit the target – Ajax, Philokles, throw just one. Ready?'

A shifting, some glances.

Kineas looked around, found Arni waiting by the barracks door. 'Collect the javelins as soon as they score and bring them back here.'

Arni nodded.

'File from the left, *skirmish!*' Kineas shouted, and led the way.

All the way down the sand to the target, Kineas had time to consider whether he could have handled them any other way – and then he was ten strides from the butts, his first javelin away, his second just as he passed – not his best throw, but in the target and he swept by, curbing his charger and bringing her to a canter so that Diodorus caught him up easily, and then Crax fell in behind him. He refused to turn his head and count the hits. The Hippeis on the sand were watching closely – Lykeles fell in, and then Coenus behind him, and then Philokles and Ajax – *gods send they hit something* – and then the Gauls, and the line was formed. Kineas shouted, 'Charge!' and the line went back to a gallop. Just short of Memnon's waiting men, he shouted, 'Halt!' They were knee to knee, aimed at the center of Memnon's line. Memnon's men flinched – more at the back than in front. Kineas's men had their own troubles – Ajax nearly lost his seat and Philokles, despite the month of practice on the road and a week's drill in the hippodrome, had his horse rear under him and threw his arms around her neck to keep his.

The hoplites had lost their ordered ranks and Memnon was bellowing at them, his voice high with real rage. Kineas ordered his men to face about and led them sedately down the sand to the waiting Hippeis.

Diodorus leaned over to him. 'Memnon will make a bad enemy.'

Kineas nodded. 'I didn't see much choice. Perhaps I can sweeten him later – but they all hate him. And I need them to be united.'

Diodorus shook his head. 'Why? Why not just collect the money and let them rot?' But then he smiled and shook his head again. 'At your command.'

'Many of your mounts are untrained for war,' Kineas called to the men waiting on the sand. 'Many of you are not expert at mounting, or throwing the javelin, or staying in ranks. We can teach all of these things. We would like to teach you. And every man who loves his city should want to learn. At the next muster, I expect every man in armour and atop his horse. At the next muster, we will throw javelins until the sun sets. Cleitus?'

Cleitus rode to the head of the muster. 'I intend to learn what this man has to teach.' He turned and rode back to the ranks of the fully armed men. It wasn't a long speech, but it had its effect.

When Niceas declared the muster complete and announced the next one at the new moon in just three weeks, there was a buzz of talk, but no angry shouts. Kineas was greeted afterwards by at least twenty men, many of whom found it necessary to stress excuses as to why they were not mounted today, but would be next time.

As the last of them trickled out of the hippodrome, Diodorus unfastened his chinstrap. 'The town's armourers will be busy men for three weeks,' he said.

And then came the summons from the archon. Kineas heard it from one of the palace slaves and nodded curtly. To Diodorus, he said, 'We dine tonight with Cleitus. You, Ajax, and one of the gentlemen.' Nodding at the retreating figure of the slave, he shrugged. 'If I survive meeting the archon.'

Diodorus raised an eyebrow. 'The archon can hardly be offended by a minor scuffle between mercenaries. Is this dinner purely social?'

'Nothing in this city is purely anything, Diodorus. Bring Agis. He's a talker.' Kineas decided to wear his armour. He rode to meet the Archon.

This time, the Archon was not in the murk of his private citadel. He was sitting in the open in the agora, flanked on both sides by files of fully armoured soldiers, giving justice at the courts. The market was full of people: men walking arm in arm, talking; men doing business, from the sale of a farm by the fountain to the dozens of stalls set up by merchants along the sides. Kineas was surprised by the scale of some of the sales – one stall seemed only to be an office selling cargoes of late-season wheat to ship owners anxious to beat the first winter storm on the Euxine. And there were women. Women doing their market shopping, attended by a string of male slaves; slave women on the same errands, or buying for their households, or talking by the fountain. Finally, there were beggars. Dozens of children begged by the foot of the statue of Hermes and grown beggars sat by every stall.

Kineas had to wait while the archon heard a boundary dispute – lengthy arguments on both sides appealing to various customs and the views of various neighbours. Kineas gathered from the arguments that when land had been taken from the local tribe of Sindi, the demarcations of land grants had never been firmly settled.

Kineas had time to watch the archon. He was not a tall man and tended to slouch his shoulders and hunch his back as he listened to the debate before him, his chin resting on his right fist. He wore a simple white tunic with a red border and a heavy gold ring on one thumb, had a diadem on his head, but otherwise wore no sign of rank or ornamentation. Despite the cold air and an icy wind blowing from the north, he didn't don his cloak. He had a heavy, dark beard shot with grey and his hair had begun to thin on his forehead. With the exception of the diadem, he looked every inch a Greek magistrate.

He settled the grievance in favour of the smaller farmer who had brought the charge that his boundary stones had been moved, and ordered that a cup of wine be brought. Then he motioned for Kineas to attend him.

'Greetings, Kineas of Athens,' he said formally.

'Greetings, Archon,' Kineas replied.

'I'm told that the muster of the Hippeis went well. Here, stand close by me. You have the muster?' The archon was convivial. Kineas thought he was about to place his hand on Kineas's shoulder.

'I have the full account of the muster to present to you, Archon.' Kineas held up a scroll. 'I was satisfied.'

The archon frowned. 'I understand you took steps of your own to see that the muster would be full. Yes?'

Kineas hesitated and then said, 'Yes. I asked several gentlemen to see to it that the importance of the muster was understood throughout the city.'

The archon grunted. 'Harrumph. Kineas, perhaps I failed to make myself clear to you – or perhaps you have your own designs. In the first case, I am at fault; in the second case, you have done me a wrong. Had I wanted the men of this town informed of the importance of the muster, do you not think I could have passed that word myself? If I did not, perhaps you might have thought that I had my reasons?'

Kineas recognized that he was on dangerous ground. 'I sought only to improve the quality of your cavalry, Archon. The first step on the road to training them was to draw them to the muster.'

The archon sipped his wine. 'Perhaps,' he said after a few long seconds had passed. 'Kineas, you have come here to serve me and this city. You think, perhaps, that you understand us already. You see a tyrant on his ivory chair and some noble gentlemen who seek to keep the tyrant within the bounds of the law. Hmm? Very Athenian. I asked you here today – to the court – to see another thing. These cavalrymen of the city, these "gentlemen", are the rapacious landlords who will try to gouge my small farmers. I must protect the farmers; without them, we have no grain. If I let the great ones enslave them, I have no hoplites. And the small men – they have rights too. I protect them.'

Kineas thought, the law protects them. But he remained silent, only nodding.

'Many of your gentlemen do all in their power to impede the running of this city – even its security. Hmmm? When I hired you, I was not aware of your many *connections* – and I wonder if I have made an error. Have I?'

At the word 'connections', Kineas felt, for the first time, the touch of fear.

'Nicomedes is a dangerous man, Kineas of Athens. Dine with him at your peril. Very well, you have mustered my gentlemen and now you will train them. In the meantime, I have a use for you. You will please take the men on this list,' and he handed Kineas a tablet, 'and find the bandits who wish to send me an embassy. You will escort their ambassador to me. I understand that they are north of the city above the great bend in the river, about three days' ride. As you have set your next muster for three weeks hence, I recommend that you proceed immediately.'

Kineas glanced at the tablet. There were seven names and none of them was familiar to him. 'I would rather take my own men.'

'I'm sure you would. Feel free to take – two. Not more than two. Am I clear? I would dislike having my orders misunderstood again.' He smiled. 'And please apologize to Memnon, who feels that you insulted him in the hippodrome.'

Memnon emerged from the nearest file of soldiers. 'We can settle in private, Archon.'

'That's just what I don't wish,' the archon snapped. 'No private feuds, no quarrels. Kineas, apologize.'

Kineas considered for a moment. 'Very well. I apologize, Memnon. Know that I hold you no ill will. However, your ill-considered arrival at the hippodrome, armed and unannounced, could have had serious consequences for my command.'

'Don't be a fool,' snapped Memnon. 'I was there to save you, horse master. They could have turned on you in a second – don't think any of them loves you. I was there to provide *you* with some security, and you embarrassed me.' He leered. He was missing some teeth, and up close he was a scary man. 'Is that what passes for an apology in Athens? Because in my city – Heraclea – it'd get your balls cut off.'

Kineas shook his head. 'No. You were there to intimidate the Hippeis – and me. And don't hold *me* to blame if your men flinch from a cavalry charge – sounds like a professional problem.'

'Fuck your mother,' said Memnon, flushing red. His voice was quiet, almost eerie. 'Don't play games, Athenian.'

The archon stood up. 'Kineas, you are not impressing me. Neither one of you is. Perhaps I should try raising my voice. *Apologize at once.*'

The three of them stood in a triangle, now surrounded by Memnon's soldiers who were blocking the crowd. Memnon's whole posture showed that he was ready for violence. His thumbs were hitched into his sword belt and his right hand was twitching – he was that close to drawing his sword. Kineas expected he looked the same. He was on the balls of his feet, ready to fight.

The archon's eyes flicked back and forth between them. 'Kineas, apologize now.'

Kineas made his decision and felt smaller for it. 'Memnon, I apologize,' he said.

The archon grunted. 'I ordered Memnon to support you, you fool. You think you know us – you know nothing. Think about hubris while you escort the barbarians through the plains. Now go.'

Kineas, humiliated, turned and pushed through Memnon's men.

'Let's take our mounts and go!' said Niceas, his hand on the amulet of Athena's owl at his neck. He coughed long and hard.

Crax and Arni had settled him on a couch in front of the brazier. He was quite sick.

'You can't travel,' snapped Kineas. It sounded more like an accusation than he had meant. 'Winter is almost on us – you want to ride back down the coast in winter?'

'We could leave the horses and take a ship out of here,' said Diodorus.

'We could all cut our throats. Look, it's my fault – first, that we are here and second, that I cannot guard my tongue. For now, we stay. I'll take Lykeles and Ataelus with me. Diodorus, stand ready for anything and keep our men out of trouble with Memnon's.'

Philokles pushed through the curtain from the hallway. 'Private party?'

Kineas glared at him. Philokles' comings and goings were a constant irritation to him; the Spartan was with them when it was convenient and distant when it suited him. 'Yes.'

Philokles moved over to the table and poured a cup of wine. 'Voices carry. Trouble with the archon? And you have been sent on a mission? Very sensible of the archon – he's getting you out of town for a few days. That suits me as well – I'd be happy to accompany you.'

'I've already chosen my men,' Kineas said. 'The archon has only allowed me two.'

'The rest of us,' said Diodorus, 'will make good hostages.'

Philokles smiled. 'Well, I'm not really one of your men,' he said. 'I can't really imagine that the archon meant to deprive you of my company. So I'll just ride along. Or perhaps I'll meet you on the road.'

Kineas, angry and still smarting from the scene in the agora, was both touched and incensed. A hot answer came to his tongue, but he bit down on it and swallowed it with some wine. 'I can't stop you,' he said, but his voice had a little more warmth in it.

'My point exactly.' Philokles drank off his wine. 'When do we leave?'

'As soon as I can find the men on this list.' Kineas pointed to the tablet on the table.

Philokles read the list and nodded. 'I know most of these – they're all young. Several are friends with Ajax – two of them would like to be better friends, if you take my meaning. Send him to gather them up and take him along – the thing is as easy as that,' and he snapped his fingers.

Diodorus nodded. 'I'd be happier if I could keep Lykeles, anyway. He knows the locals as well as I do.' He looked at Philokles. 'Young rich men. The sons of the richest, perhaps?'

Philokles shrugged. 'The archon is no fool. Neither are you, Kineas – when you don't lose your temper. I've heard a rumour – perhaps you've heard it too? That the archon is going to allow the assembly to meet to confirm his taxes.'

Diodorus nodded. 'I have heard the same rumour.'

Philokles threw a leg over the table and reclined as if on a couch. The sturdy oak table groaned under his weight. 'If I had to guess, I would say that the archon is sending away the sons of the most powerful men as a method of controlling the assembly. Hmm?'

Diodorus ran a hand through his hair. 'Of course he is. I should have seen that.'

Kineas looked from one to the other. 'Nice of the two of you to keep me informed like this. Any other gorgon's heads to drop on me while I pack for the plains?'

'The town's croaking like a chorus of frogs about the cavalry muster. People were very impressed – with us, and with you, and with your little performance against Memnon's men. They are widely hated. So far, we are not. Now, shall we send for Ajax?'

Kineas said, 'I hate being mothered.' He smiled ruefully. 'What a fucking idiot I was.'

'Which time?' said Philokles sweetly, and dodged through the curtain.

The dinner with Cleitus was uneventful, decorous and professional. By chance or design, most of the other guests were men whose sons he was taking out into the plains at dawn. Kineas sensed no hostility from them, and he was at pains to make clear that they would train and ride hard, but that he would see to their safety.

Cleitus himself raised the possibility of an assembly. 'It's all over the agora – the archon will summon us to vote his new taxes.'

Kineas remained silent and tried to catch the eyes of Diodorus and Philokles to keep them silent. He failed.

'When is the last time the assembly met?' Philokles asked, sipping wine.

Cleitus glanced around and shrugged. An older man, Cleomenes, one of the city's richest merchants, rose a little on his couch. 'Almost four years, sir. An entire Olympiad has passed since we were last allowed to assemble.'

His son was a very young man – Eumenes, who had presented himself at the muster horsed and in armour, as Kineas remembered. He was not so young that he couldn't speak at a dinner. He sat up on his father's couch and said, 'It was not always so, sir. When the archon was first appointed, the assembly met regularly.'

Cleitus motioned to a slave to bring around more wine. 'We're loyal to the archon here, poppet – so watch your insinuation. I'd like to think that the possibility of an assembly is a good sign.'

Eumenes looked about a little wildly. 'I meant no disloyalty!'

Kineas felt that the whole conversation had subtext – even Cleitus's declaration of loyalty seemed to have a coda. Just watching the men's eyes and facial expressions told him something of the tensions between them.

'Perhaps things will be different after the assembly,' offered another gentleman. Kineas knew the man was the largest ship-owner in the city and that his son, Cliomenedes, was barely old enough to serve in the cavalry and was coming on the expedition in the morning.

It seemed an ominous statement, the more so as it was left to lie with the spilled wine. None of the other men took it up – not even Philokles. Instead, Cleitus turned the talk to the success of the muster.

Kineas gathered praise – too much praise, he felt. 'We haven't begun to train,' he said. 'None of you will think of me so highly when your butts are sore.'

That got a laugh, but Clio's father – Petrocolus – shook his head. 'We expected another mercenary, like Memnon. We were surprised that you are so clearly a gentleman. I think I can speak for many men when I say that we'll be happier for the training – at least, come spring. This notion of winter exercise has my old bones creaking already!'

The party continued on a lighter note from there. Cleitus, despite his public gruffness, was an excellent host. There were dancers – tasteful and skilled – and acrobats, and a dark-skinned freeman who mimed several of the city's important men – Memnon, Cleitus himself, and finally, Kineas.

Even Kineas had to laugh at the gross parody of his legs and autocratic hand motions. He knew himself immediately – it wasn't the first time he'd been imitated. The others present roared, and he collected several smiles.

At the end of the evening, Philokles performed on the Spartan harp and Agis recited a section of the *Iliad*. It was a nice re-minder that Kineas's men were gentlemen of accomplishment, and both performances were well received.

Huddled in their cloaks, trying to avoid puddles in the street as they walked back to the hippodrome escorted by a pair of Cleitus's slaves, Philokles laughed. 'That went well,' he said.

Agis laughed as well. 'I expected my old tutor to appear at the door and point a bony hand at me if I missed a word. Not like performing at the campfire!'

Diodorus was more sombre. 'They're hiding something.'

Kineas nodded agreement. 'Steer clear of it, whatever it is,' he said to Diodorus. 'Don't get involved. Is that clear?'

Diodorus nodded. He looked at the sky, paused, and then said, 'We're in for a weather change. Feel it? It's colder already.'

Kineas pulled his cloak tighter. He was already cold. He coughed.

8

They left as the dawn reddened the frosted grass north of the city, under a cold blue sky. The seven young men were well mounted and each of them had a slave; the two eldest each had two slaves and half a dozen horses. They were well turned out, with good armour and heavy cloaks. And they were all eager to go.

Their eagerness made the situation easier to bear. Hostages or not, they were city cavalry and his men, and Kineas found himself enjoying their company as they followed the narrow track out of the city and up the bluffs beyond to the plain. For stades, the track wound along the stone walls that edged grain fields, now a blasted desert of stubble and broken stalks where the harvesters had cut the crops. Heavy stone farmhouses dotted the landscape and as the morning went on they began to pass farmers making their way into town, most on foot with small carts, a few more prosperous on horseback. Their breath left plumes in the cold air, and the farmers didn't seem happy to see so many soldiers.

The young men chatted, pointed out farms that belonged to their families, discussed hunting in this or that copse of woods and rehearsed their views on philosophy with Philokles – until Kineas began to ask them questions.

'How would you ride up to that farmhouse,' Kineas indicated a distant stone building with his hand, 'leading twenty men, so as not to be seen in your approach?'

They took him seriously and they talked about it, waving their hands excitedly. Finally the leader, Eumenes – his leadership was obvious to Kineas, less to his friends – pointed. 'Around the woods and up that little gully, there.'

Kineas nodded. It was interesting to see the change in Eumenes from the timid boy of the night before. Among his own, he seemed quite mature. 'Good eye,' Kineas said.

Eumenes flushed at the praise. 'Thank you, sir. But – if you don't mind my asking – isn't cavalry warfare more of, well, fighting man to man? It's for the *psiloi* to sneak around – as I understand it. Don't we cover the flank of the hoplites and fight it out with the enemy cavalry?'

Kineas said, 'War is about having an advantage. If you can gain an advantage over the enemy cavalry by sneaking, you should do it, don't you think?'

Another youth, Cliomenedes, Petrocolus's son stuttered, 'Is that – is it – is it – I say, can it be, I mean, right? Right to take an advantage? Did Achilles do such things?'

Kineas was now riding easily in the midst of them. Ajax had stayed on his right hand, Philokles had dropped back with an amused look that suggested that mundane matters such as war were beneath his notice, and Ataelus had already galloped off ahead – lost in the morning glare.

'Are you Achilles?' Kineas asked.

'I should like to be,' said another boy, Sophokles. 'My tutor says he is the model for a gentleman.'

'Are you so good a man of arms that I can expect you to cut down any number of enemies?' Kineas asked.

The boy looked down. Another boy – Kyros – cuffed him.

'Real war is to the death. And dead, you lose everything – liberty, love, possessions, all lost. To preserve them, a few tricks are required. Especially when your enemies are numerous and better trained than you are.' He said all the words that old soldiers say to young ones, and was greeted with the same respectful disbelief that he had offered his father's friends who had fought at Chaeronea.

They dismounted for lunch and the slaves set out a magnificent meal fit for a party of princes on a hunting trip. Kineas didn't complain – the supplies would be gone soon enough and then they'd be eating the rations that Kineas had on two mules under Arni's supervision. Philokles ate enough for two and turned the conversation back to philosophy.

'Why do you think there are rules in war?' he asked.

Eumenes rubbed his bare chin.

Philokles motioned at Kineas. 'Kineas says that you must be prepared to use subterfuge. Should you use spies?'

Eumenes shrugged. 'Everyone uses spies,' he said with the cynicism of the young.

'Agamemnon sent Odysseus to spy on Troy,' Sophokles said. He made a face, as if to indicate that he might say such things, but put no faith in them.

'If you take a prisoner, can you torture him for information?' Philokles asked.

The boys wriggled, and Eumenes paid too much attention to his food.

Kineas kicked Philokles in the knee without getting up. 'Odysseus tortures a prisoner,' he said. 'It's in the *Iliad*. I remember it.'

'Would you?' Philokles asked.

Kineas rubbed his beard and looked at his food – much like Eumenes. Then he raised his head. 'No. Not without some compelling reason, and even then – that's filthy. Not for men.'

Sophokles glanced up from his bread. 'Are you saying that rules are foolish?'

Philokles shook his head. 'I'm not saying anything. I'm asking questions, and you are answering them.'

'The captain says that war is to the death. So why have rules?' Sophokles glanced at Kineas, looking for approval. 'Anything that wins is good. Isn't it?'

Philokles leaned forward. 'So – would you attack an enemy during a truce? Perhaps while he is collecting his dead?'

Sophokles sat back, and his face displayed outrage, but with the tenacity of the young, he stuck to his argument. 'Yes,' he said. 'Yes, if it would give me victory.'

Philokles looked at Kineas and Kineas shook his head. 'Never,' he said.

Sophokles' cheeks developed two bright red spots, and his throat blotched, and he hung his head.

Kineas fingered his beard again, rubbing in the oil from his lunch. 'Rules in war have purpose,' he said. 'Every broken rule deepens the hate between the enemies. Every rule preserved keeps hate at bay. If two cities fight, and both abide by their oaths, follow the rules, and fear the gods – then when they have settled the dispute, they can return to trade. But if one side violates a truce, or murders women, or tortures a prisoner – then hatred rules the day, and war becomes a way of life.'

Philokles nodded. And he added, 'War is the greatest of tyrants, once fully unleashed. Men make rules to keep the tyrant bound, just as they use the assembly to keep the over-powerful citizens from dominating other men. Fools speak of "getting serious", or of making "real" war. They are invariably amateurs and cowards, who have never stood in the line with a spear in their hands. In the phalanx, where you smell the breath of your enemy and feel the wind when he farts – war is *always* real. Real enough, when death awaits every misstep. But when the tyrant is fully unleashed – when cities fight to the death, as Athens and Sparta did a hundred years ago – when all the rules are forgotten, and every man seeks only the destruction of his enemy, then reason is fled, and we become mad beasts. And then there is neither honour nor victory.'

The boys nodded solemnly, and Kineas was left with the feeling that he and Philokles could as easily have proclaimed the utility of torture and rapine and convinced them.

After lunch, Kineas had them throw javelins at a tree on foot, and he watched them mount their horses and commented on how that could be improved. While they threw, he said to Philokles, 'That was quite a speech. You are against war?'

Philokles frowned. 'I am Spartan,' he said, as if that answered Kineas. 'That Kyros has a good arm.'

Kineas let the subject drop.

'In combat, you'll be unhorsed,' Kineas said. 'It'll happen several times. Every time you are on foot in a cavalry fight, you are very nearly a dead man. Being able to remount is the most important skill you can master. Practise mounting your own horse, if you can, practise mounting other men's horses – because the usual reason for finding yourself on foot is because some bastard has killed your horse.'

When they were all riding into the afternoon, passing the very last walled field and the last deep ditch and dyke that marked the very edge of the town's property, he said, 'In wrestling, were you taught first how to fall?'

Ajax smiled, because he'd heard this speech so many times already.

'Practise coming off your horse, recovering, and getting back on. Practise it at a walk, at a trot, even at a canter. Ajax, here, was barely able to ride a few weeks ago.' Kineas spared him a good-natured glance. 'Now he can come off at a canter and remount in a flash.'

Ajax did it on cue, without warning, taking his horse a few steps away into a field, rolling from the saddle and landing on his side. He looked winded, but he bounced to his feet and his horse had already stopped. He ran to her and vaulted into the saddle, his back straight and his leg thrown clear of her back. He looked like an athlete.

Several of the young men thought he looked more like a god. Then they all had to do it, their fine cloaks and armour getting an array of dirt and dents as they threw themselves to the ground and remounted. Several of them lost their horses entirely – Eumenes, a competent young man, rolled out of the saddle and his horse bolted, and had to be run down by Kineas himself. After that, Kineas curtailed their enthusiasm. 'We have miles to ride today,' he said.

Ajax rubbed his hip. 'That hurt.'

Kineas smiled at him. 'You did it very well.'

Ajax beamed. If he still held an opinion on Kineas's actions in the fight with the Getae, it had been dulled by time and the routine of the unit. Kineas felt some awkwardness in having Ajax as his second in command with all these raw youths, but Ajax took to it immediately, tacitly appointing Eumenes his own second man. Only when Kineas and Philokles had spoken about war had there been something in Ajax's look – some hesitation perhaps, or disagreement.

The sun was slipping down in the west when Ataelus, his red hood brilliant in the dying sun, came back. Kineas had his cloak tight around him, the bulk of his horse warming his lower half and the icy wind cutting through his helmet.

'Well?' asked Kineas.

'Easy,' said Ataelus. 'For me, yes? Tracks and hooves, tracks and hooves. For me I find it. Tomorrow night, we for they camp. Yes? They camp?' He gestured.

'You saw their camp, and we'll be there tomorrow night?' asked Kineas.

'See? No. See with eyes? Not for me. See with this!' and the Scyth pointed at his head. 'Tracks and hooves – for knowing where, not for seeing where, yes?'

Kineas lost the thread of this, especially as the Scyth tried to introduce details – and barbarian words. 'So you went out, saw tracks – and we'll be there tomorrow night?'

'Yes!' The Scyth was happy to be understood. 'Tomorrow, maybe night. Yes. Food?'

Kineas offered him a loaf of bread from lunch and a clay flagon of wine – good wine. The Scyth rode away chuckling.

They continued until near dark with the river flowing dark and cold on their right. On a deep, sandy curve they stopped, and the slaves made camp. The boys were amateurs and insisted on having their own tents, their own bedding, and consequently were too cold to sleep. Kineas slept in a huddle with Philokles, Arni and Ajax, while Ataelus, more private or perhaps more practised still, pulled his horse down and slept against it.

In the morning the boys were drawn. They stood and shivered, waiting for their horses, waiting for the food to be prepared. Kineas set them to throwing javelins. His throat hurt, and he rubbed at it. Arni brought him a tisane and he drank it with honey. It helped for a while.

The sun was a bright orange ball against a dark sky. Arni came over to Kineas with a cloth in his hand, rubbing Kineas's silver wine cup clean. 'That's heavy weather,' he said, pointing his chin at the sun. Kineas nodded absently.

The boys warmed up quickly and in a few minutes they were again abuzz with questions, most of which were directed at Ajax, who handled them well enough. All of the boys were curious about the Scyth and most wondered aloud if he was some sort of privileged slave. If Ataelus understood any of it before he rode away, he gave no sign and left Ajax to explain his status.

It took more than two hours to get all of the boys packed and mounted – their slaves, while patient and capable, were not used to moving quickly and none of them was used to any discipline beyond the rods of their tutors. Ajax had to raise his voice, and Kineas enjoyed the spectacle of Ajax shouting down an embarrassed Eumenes when the boy wanted the fire to stay lit.

'But I'm cold!' said the boy. He sounded horrified that anyone could fail to see this as a crisis.

'So am I. So are the slaves. Get mounted.' Ajax sounded so much like Niceas that Kineas turned away to smile.

That second day they played at being a patrol. Kineas didn't insist on any real degree of skill, but he sent the boys out to scout and report and he went out a few times with them, listened with patience to their reports of deer or cattle tracks, dead sheep, marshland to the west. He instructed. He kept them busy. By noon, he had started to cough in earnest. He didn't feel bad – in fact, he was enjoying himself – but the coughs got longer. They ate in the saddle when the sun was high, because the boys were tired and Ataelus had returned to report that there were groups of Sakje ahead of them and they could expect to meet a hunting party any time. Kineas had long since admitted to himself that he liked what he had seen of the Sakje, barbarians that they were, and he didn't expect any hostility from them – but professional caution and a certain desire to impress made him unwilling to be caught with a fire at a meal by one of their patrols. Besides, the sky was dark and it had grown curiously warm. Kineas didn't know the plains, but he knew the sea. Weather was coming. From the saddle he said a prayer and poured a libation.

After lunch, it began to snow. Kineas had seen snow in Persia, but not like this – big, heavy flakes like the down from a goose. He pulled his cloak around himself and started to cough again, finally leaning over in his saddle and coughing until his chest ached. He noticed that Philokles was supporting his weight in the saddle.

'You're scaring the boys,' Philokles said. 'And we can't see the river any more.'

Kineas raised his head and realized that he could scarcely see the head of his horse. His helmet sat on his brow like a block of ice. His brain began to function again. 'Ataelus!'

The Scyth appeared out of the swirling snow. 'Here I am!' he shouted.

'Go fetch in the two boys who are out. We'll stay right here.' He coughed again. 'Hermes, protect us.'

Ataelus vanished into the snow. The horses crowded together, which suited their riders. Greek gentlemen rode in tunics and boots, armour if the occasion demanded, but fashionable gentlemen did not wear trousers. All of the boys were in their best tunics and their armour, to awe the barbarians. Now they were very cold indeed.

'Philokles? Pick your way along the river and find us some trees. Better yet, find a house.'

'Or a tavern?'

'You understand. Don't go far and don't risk getting lost. We won't move until Ataelus comes back, and then we'll ride upstream. Take Clio.'

Philokles collected the boy and trotted off into the white curtain. Kineas thought the stuff was letting up; man and boy remained visible to him several horse lengths away.

Eumenes pressed his horse against Kineas's mare. 'Are we – lost?' he asked. *Are we in real trouble?*

'This'll pass soon enough,' said Kineas, and coughed again. 'I'm going to get us together and then find some cover. We may be cold …' He lost the ability to speak, coughed and coughed, then felt better. He spat some phlegm and was relieved to see there was no blood in it. *I made my sacrifice to You, lord of contagion. I helped a horse race for your glory, Lord Apollo.* But, he remembered he had not offered a sacrifice, being busy with his own affairs. A white lamb on your altar when I return, he vowed. And coughed again.

Eumenes watched him, his clear brow furrowed with worry under the bronze brim of his helmet. Kineas got himself erect in the saddle. 'How do you keep a company moving in heavy weather?' he asked.

'Uh,' murmured Eumenes. Kineas looked around. The snow was lighter, but the boys were huddled together and their faces were pale, their mouths thin. They were on the edge of panic.

'You find a mark you can see and move to it. Then you find

another mark and you move to that. It's slow, but it beats getting lost. If you can't see far enough to find a mark, you stop and wait for the weather to clear.'

Kyros, the one who threw the best javelin, said, 'I'm cold.' He said it softly, but his words carried real conviction and his cheeks had bright red spots.

Kineas knew that he was on the edge of real difficulty, but he had already made a hard choice – to stay put until the Scyth returned. He stuck to it. 'Push in closer to Ajax. By Ares, young gentlemen, you should all learn to love one another a little more. Ajax is a particularly elegant specimen – no one should mind cuddling with him.' Several of the youths glanced at Ajax and most of them chuckled, and he seized on this slight thaw in the tension. 'How many of you were cold last night? Everyone? Learn to be comrades! Tonight, you are going to have mess groups – you'll eat and sleep in sections, like Spartans. It works. Don't blush, Kyros. No one is threatening your virtue. It's too cold.' He was holding back a cough, trying to get them in hand before he made a spectacle of himself, but the urge to cough overpowered him. The snow in the air seemed to trigger the coughing. He tried to keep his back straight and cough into his hands. It was shorter, but the coughs seemed deeper in his chest, harsher. His hands were shaking.

Ataelus's red hood appeared over Eumenes's shoulder. 'They here for me!' called the Scyth. 'Good boys, off horse, wait. No problem for me, yes!'

'Well—' *Hack, hack, cough, cough.* 'Well done.' Ataelus's success gave him hope. In fact, it turned the situation around. He wished his head were clearer. 'North along the river bank. Look for Philokles. Understand?'

'Sure. No problem. Heya, Kineax – you for *Baqcas*?' Ataelus asked.

'What?' asked Kineas. The Scyth seemed to be using more and more barbarian words, as if getting closer to his people freed his tongue from the fetters of Greek. 'What is a *baxstak*?'

Ataelus shook his head. 'Bacqca soon!' he called, and waved. Then he led the way. The two boys he'd been speaking with followed him and Kineas encouraged them. They were taking their role as scouts seriously. He liked that. He didn't like that he was beginning to feel distant from the situation. He had a fever – he'd had one before, at the siege of Gaza, and he knew the signs. The distance would serve him for an hour or so, but then he would be useless to command.

'Ajax!' he called, a pure order. Ajax trotted to his side – or rather, his horse tried to trot, snow billowing from her hooves. Already, the stuff was a hand deep on the ground.

'Sir!' Ajax actually saluted. *If this boy lives, he'll be a fine soldier.*

Kineas leaned over. 'I'm sick,' he said quietly. His voice rasped in his throat, and his nose was full. 'Sick and gedding sicker. If I can'd command, you keep dese lads moving until you meed Philokles or you meed the Sakje. Understaaad me?' Hermes, he sounded like he was seventy years old.

'Yes, sir.' Ajax nodded.

Kineas pushed his horse into a canter, and she flailed her way back to the head of the boys. Behind him, Ajax called out, 'Two files! We're not on a hunting party!'

Kineas wanted to smile, but things were getting farther and farther away.

An hour later, he was still in command of himself and the group, but only just. Twice he had snapped to – not asleep, perhaps, but drifting. Both times he'd recovered to see the Scyth's red cap bouncing along ahead of him.

The snow almost stopped, and then came on full force again, and Kineas began to fear that they might pass Philokles and the boy Clio in the snow. He became sleepy, and he knew that wasn't good. Behind him, Ajax continued to heckle his charges, demanding that they sit straight, stop wiping their noses, an endless litany of little faults that, under other circumstances, would have seemed ridiculous.

The coughing grew worse, which, at each bout, didn't seem possible – until the next. And then Philokles was there with him, and the boy Clio. He sat up straight.

'Cleared the ground under the trees,' said Philokles. His nose was as red as wine.

'I started a fire!' said Clio. 'Myself!'

'Well done, boy. Right.' Cough. 'How far?'

'Half a stade. Ataelus has the two boys at the fire.'

'Go. Ged these boys under cover.' He blew his nose in his hand and coughed. 'Two tents – slaves in one, cavalry in the other. Get the slaves on food. Hot drink – you know?'

'I'm a fucking Spartan!' said Philokles. 'I've been out in a storm before. You look like Apollo put an arrow in you. Hermes send we get you to the fire. Hades, you're burning up.'

The sight of Philokles eased Kineas more than medicine. He felt better – he brushed the snow off the plume in his helmet and led the way to camp. When they followed the tracks down to the fire, he halted them and made them wheel their horses into line.

'Listen to me! You behaved like soldiers. That was dangerous and we did it.' He blew his nose on his fingers again and wiped it off on his thigh, coughed, and straightened. 'We're not done yet. Every man gathers wood. I want a pile of wood as big as a house. Don't leave it to the slaves – it's your life as well as theirs. Horses curried and blankets on.' He coughed again. They sat like statues – either inured to discipline in one day or too miserable to twitch. 'Arni – slaves to boil water and make food. Let them get warm first. Masters – to work.'

None of them rebelled. None of them went to the fire. They started to get wood – pitiful, snowy branches at first, but Ajax and Philokles led them and suddenly it was a contest, a feat worthy of Achilles, and they fought to get more of the stuff, driftwood from the river beach, downed branches from the stand of woods that filled the bend in the river. Even Kineas, who could not entirely control his body, felt drawn to participate.

Soon he was drinking from a hot bronze beaker that burned his hands even as the mulled wine burned away the pain in his throat. His hands were bright red. The others were standing around a huge fire, a fire that was itself as big as a house, and the heat blasted their clothes dry.

And then he was in a tent, and coughing.

He is hot, and the spirits of the dead gather around him with tongues of fire – Aristophanes, who died screaming with an arrow

*in his belly on the Euphrates, bellows fire so that a cloud of it bil-
lows around his head like a shroud of flame. A Persian – suddenly
he's sure it is a man he killed himself – has no face, just bone, but
his hands make precise signals, and then ...*

*He is cold, and the bodies of the dead are frozen. Amyntas has ice
in his beard on his cheeks and when he smiles, his cheeks develop
little fissures like the crows' feet at the edge of a matron's eyes.*

'I didn't think you were dead.'

Amyntas has no eyes, no voice and no response.

*Artemis's hands are cold as clay and wet with something, and his
manhood shivels away from her touch, and her eyes glitter – there
is frost on her lashes and a dagger in her neck, and he flinches
away*

*The moon rises like an accusing goddess over the battlefield at
Guagemela, and he walks alone among the dead. Mostly Persians,
they lie in sad little heaps where the Macedonians reaped them
when they broke, or windrows where they were cut if they stood.
And he thinks,* This is real, *because he was there in that moonlight,
but then the dead begin to stir, rising like cold men who have had a
hard sleep on the ground, one patting about him for something lost
(his intestines, at his feet), another holding his back and groaning
– but no sounds come, only a stream of black bile.*

*Artemis takes his hand and he is on the bank of the Euphrates
with her, or perhaps the Pinarus – perhaps both at once. The cold
moon gives no real light. And he looks at Artemis.*

'I didn't think you were dead.'

*'Am I dead?' She raises her hand, beautiful as it always was,
even when red from work, the hand of Aphrodite, and points across
the river at the cloud of dust raised by the Persian cavalry – or the
snow. He can't remember what made the cloud. It smells like smoke
– like burning rope, or pine needles. He can't remember his own
name, although he knows hers.*

*He longs for her, longs to take the slim dagger from her neck. He
even knows the dagger, but he can't put a name to it. Somewhere,
a strong voice is singing, but if there are words, they mean nothing.
It is not the voice of a man or a woman.*

*He stumbles down the gravel bank to the river because he
is so thirsty, and tries to drink. She smells – not of rot – earthy.*

Unwashed. She has smelled this way before, in the field. Her hair is full of dirt.

Perhaps he could wash it for her.

The singing is very attractive. Was there ever anything to be seen on the other side of the river? He can't remember – now there is nothing, but he is sure that he had fought his way there once, and lived. Surely that is true. Was there smoke?

He needs a horse. He is dismounted and needs a horse. And Artemis is gone, but he doesn't care, so great is the urgency to find a horse – he is dead if he doesn't find one and get mounted and he rises through the water and pushes with his legs, but the water must have been deeper than he expected, there is nothing under him and his armour is dragging at him, dragging him down, and he will sink, and it is dark and cold, so cold he cannot move, and only seeks to sleep ...

The urge to find a horse survives and he pushes up on the water, but it is more like dust and his mouth is full of the stuff, and he coughs, and coughs.

His head comes clear of the water-dust, and the horse above him is huge – so tall that its legs rise above him like the pillars of a temple, but desperation drives him, terror – he takes hold of the hair at its hocks, and it drags him from the river and there is singing, barbarian singing all around him, and the smell of unwashed hair in his nose, and smoke everywhere, something is burning. He is on the sand in the desert – no, he is on the snow, and Darius is dead – begging in the agora – he is on the horse, his first, and he cannot control it and it canters and then gallops and he cannot get off, the horse ownshimandhecannotridecannotridecannotride.

The singing is loud and he is on the horse, riding at night on the open plain, but the plain is dark and sparks fly when the horse's feet touch the ground, which is seldom. He is flying. And he is flying down a mountain, or up – there are flashes of lightning but they linger, so that each overlays the last until the sky is white with a single Levin bolt in Zeus's hand – the mountain and the light around the mountain, and the singing – nasal, dull, barbaric – smell of unwashed hair – water in his mouth – arms around his waist. Artemis is holding him on the horse, and she is hot – her touch is like fire, and not for the first time – he smiles, but the light *is everywhere now and the only darkness is like a tunnel ahead of him, and at the end of it waits a Persian in full armour, on an armoured horse, and he has no spear of his own, no sword, and he does not trust this barbarian horse between his knees – her hands – the dagger – the light – the rhythm of the horse – singing – water – warmth – fur against his head and warm light around him and the smell of fire ...*

'Kineas?'

Kineas could see him, but he had no place in the world with the horse and Artemis and all the dead. And then he smiled, or tried to. He had fur under his head. 'Philokles?' he said.

'Gods be praised.' Philokles held a cup of water to his mouth. The air tasted of smoke and something barbaric.

He slept.

He woke, and a barbarian loomed over him with a woman's voice and a man's stubble on his cheek, singing. The singing seemed familiar. He slept again.

He woke, and the barbarian was still singing, her voice soft, and she played with a man's hands on a drum, and Philokles sat across the fire – a fire in a tent. Taste of water – taste of wine. He slept.

He woke, and Ajax stood in the door, and a great gust of wind came in, snow against his face, never penetrating the pile of skins atop him. Ajax gave him soup – good soup – and cleaned him where he had fouled himself, so that he was ashamed, and Ajax laughed. 'You will recover and humiliate me again,' he said. 'No, no – I didn't mean you to take that so harshly, Kineas. Rest easy. We are all well. We are with the Sakje.'

And he dreamed, and words tumbled in his dreams, because Philokles was speaking them, hearing them, from the man who was a woman – *amavaithyå, gaêthanãm, mîzhdem* – Philokles repeated them, over and over when the woman said them, and the drum beat. He was awake, but they didn't know it, and the language was like Persian, which he knew a little, and then it wasn't – the woman was called Kam, or perhaps Baqca.

And then he was awake, and the thin layer through which he had watched the world was stripped away and he was himself. He struggled to sit up, and Philokles came and the whole embarrassing business of stripping him and washing him happened – but he knew it for what it was.

'Who is that?' he asked quietly, pointing at the woman. He could see her more clearly now, and she was clearly a man – but he had known her voice so long that her gender remained with the voice.

'That is Kam Baqca, who cured you.' Philokles had some message in his words – he was always like that, but Kineas's grasp on the world, while strong, was still not clear.

'She – he? Is Sakje?' Kineas croaked out the words, regretting them – so much else he'd like to ask. Where were the men – the boys, really? Was anyone else sick?

'She is very much Sakje. And everyone is well, or well enough. I would have gone back to the city, but the snow is high and the Sakje themselves are staying in their camp. Are you still with me?'

'Very much so,' Kineas managed a laugh. He was very happy. He was alive.

'This is a small part of their nation. Three hundred or so. But an important one. Kam Baqca serves the king – the most senior king of the Sakje, I think. The *Ghan*. As does Srayanka. They have come to Olbia on embassy. Are you ready to hear this?' Philokles stopped because Kineas was coughing.

It was a pale shadow of his former cough, but it still hurt his chest. His chest had exactly the feeling of having been struck repeatedly while wearing armour – the same deep pain, as if bruised under the skin. 'Ready enough. How long?'

'Seven days since we arrived. We carried you here from the tent camp – I thought you were dead.'

Kineas could remember snatches of his dreams. He shook his head to drive them away and didn't comment. 'You can talk to them?'

'Eumenes had a Sakje nurse – he can speak. And Ataelus has never slept – without him I wonder if we would be alive. And now I have learned a little. And the Lady Srayanka speaks a very little Greek, and the king speaks a good deal, I think, although he seldom speaks to us.'

Kineas looked around him. He was in a round tent, or hut

– it was open to the air at the top, where the smoke billowed out and had a central pole, but it felt solid under his hands and he reached up and touched it – felt. Thick felt. The floor was covered in closely woven reed mats and rugs and skins – the rugs were violent, colourful, and barbaric. He had seen them in Persia. A fire burned in the centre, and there were chests of wood with heavy iron corners and designs. Savage beasts lurked in the iron and the rugs and the gold of a lamp above him. He lay back, already exhausted.

Philokles said, 'Listen. I'm tiring you, but I have to share this with someone before I burst. They will not meet me formally – they are waiting to see if you live and they gave their best to save you. But Diodorus is right. They say that Antipater is coming in the spring, with a vast army and they are here to make an alliance.'

Kineas shook his head. 'Fuck,' he murmured. And went to sleep.

When he woke again, it was dark. Ataelus was sitting by the fire, playing with it, and Kineas watched him for what seemed a long time, as he collected chips of bark and wood from the carpets and fed them into the flames, absorbed by the flickers of light and the process of burning. Then he slipped out through the door and returned with an armload of small stuff, carefully broken to length. He placed it neatly atop the remnants of an older stack and built the fire up until it roared. In the new light of the high flames, Kineas could see that Kam Baqca was sitting across the fire – had been sitting the whole time. She wore a long coat of skin, covered in minute symbols carefully worked in dyed deer hair. Hundreds of small gold plates covered the sleeves and breast, so that she glittered in the new light. Her feet were clad in tight-fitting shoes and stockings of skin – the shoes were little more than socks of leather – also covered in minute decoration. Kineas could see horses and antelope and stranger animals, especially gryphons, repeated in endless variety, no two the same.

She saw that he was awake and came around the fire to him. Her face was middle-aged, handsome and dignified, with a long straight nose and high plucked brows – but the eyes were a man's eyes, and the throat was a man's throat. And her hands, when she lifted a cup for him to drink – the cup was solid gold – were a man's hands, heavy with calluses and broken skin.

Ataelus was still toying with the fire. Kam Baqca spoke, her voice low, and Ataelus came and joined her.

'Kam Baqca asks, how is it for you, this night?' Ataelus enunciated more clearly than he usually did.

Kineas shook his head to be rid of the gold cup. 'I'm better. Yes? Good? Can you give her my thanks? She is a doctor?'

Ataelus cocked his head to one side like a very smart dog. 'You better?' he said and then repeated himself in his barbarian tongue.

'Can you tell her "Thank you",' Kineas asked again. He spaced his words carefully.

Ataelus spoke more in his other language, and then turned back to Kineas. 'I say thank you, for you. Good? Good. Speak so much Greek, for me.' He laughed. 'Maybe learn more Greek for me, yes?'

Kineas nodded and lay back on the pile of furs beneath his head. Just raising his head took too much effort.

Kam Baqca began to speak. The longer she spoke, the more familiar her words seemed – so like Persian. She said *xshathrâ Ghân*, the Great King – he knew that word. It wore him out, listening, so near to understanding.

Ataelus began to translate. 'She say, for you important seek the king, soon. But sooner for you talk to her. More important, most important thing talk to her. She say, for you almost die. Then she say, yes, do you remember for almost die?'

Kineas nodded. 'Tell yes. Yes, I remember.'

She nodded at his response and went on. Ataelus said, 'She say, did you go into the river?'

And Kineas was afraid. She was very barbarous and her male/female role was alien, and now she was asking him a question about his dream. He didn't answer.

She shook her head violently. A hand shot out of her cuffs and gestured at him, and when she spoke, her Greek, while Ionian, was clear enough. 'Be not afraid! But only speak the truth. Did you go into the river?'

Kineas nodded. He could see it – could taste the dust. 'Yes.'

She nodded. From behind her she produced a drum, covered in more little animals – mostly reindeer. She produced a small whip, like a children's toy riding whip, except that the handle was iron and the whip was made of hair, and with the whip she began to play the drum and sing.

Kineas wanted to go. He wanted free of the alien tent and the alien he-woman and he wanted to be spoken to in proper Greek. He was very near the edge of panic. He stared at Ataelus – familiar Ataelus, his *prokusatore*, searching for stability.

She snapped the drum up into the air and said a long sentence. Ataelus said, 'She says, I find you in the river, I bring you home. Only for you. Only for Baqcas. No warrior is – was – will ...' Ataelus sat and struggled with language, and suddenly smiled: '*Should* be alive. She say, this for most important thing. Yes? You know what I say?'

Kineas turned away, unable to understand past the sheer barbarity. 'Tell her I thank her,' he said and pretended to fall asleep. Soon, he was.

9

The next day he was stronger and they moved him. The move cleared his head and his glimpse of the outside world, even amidst the snow, cheered him; there were dogs and horses and men wearing skins and fur, women in trousers and heavy fur jackets, gold rings and gold decorations everywhere. He had been in the tent of the Kam Baqca, he now understood, and now they took him to a tent set aside for him. He had piles of furs and two gold lamps, rugs and mats and several Thracian cloaks for good measure. Philokles led the move and all of the boys were there, fighting for a place in carrying his litter, arranging his furs, his blankets, getting him hot wine.

It was deeply touching and he enjoyed it. And the conversation with Kam Baqca seemed less alien. Perhaps he had still had a touch of fever, but it was gone now.

'I take it you are all waiting for me to recover,' he said to Philokles. The rest of the boys had cleared out, led by Ajax, to join hunters from the Sakje.

'Yes. The king wants to speak to you before he moves. To be frank, I suggested we leave you with his people and I lead the escort back to Olbia, but he thinks that you are a person of consequence.'

'Ares' balls. Why?' Kineas snorted. Many things had gone below the threshold of worry during the last days, but they were all back now – his alienated employer, the factions, the city.

'Lady Srayanka – I mentioned her. The king's niece, I think, although they have a different word for every degree of relative.'

'Like the Persians.'

'Just so. She's a niece, or maybe a sister's adopted child, but she's someone with power and she's our girl from the plains. She claims you are a man of importance. Ataelus says it's a warrior thing.' Philokles shrugged. 'I gather you killed someone important – or perhaps just at the right time? Or – Eumenes says this – avenged somebody here by your act and that gives you status.'

Kineas shook his head. 'We're a long way from home.' He felt an excitement – *our girl from the plains. Now I've learned her name. Srayanka.* It seemed an absurd thing for a grown man to be so pleased by, but he was pleased. He repeated it over and over, like a prayer.

Philokles sat on a pile of furs. Kineas realized with a start that Philokles was wearing leather trousers. It was so un-Greek; so unlike a Spartan, however exiled. Philokles followed his gaze and smiled. 'It's cold. And someone made them for me – Eumenes said it would be rude to refuse. They are warm. They rub the parts.'

'If the Ephors could see you now, you'd be an exile for ever.' Kineas began to laugh. It hurt his chest, but it felt good. He was speaking Greek to a Greek. The world would be right soon enough.

Philokles laughed with him and then leaned over. 'Listen to me, Kineas. There's more to this than you know.'

Kineas nodded.

'No, listen! These people – they hold the military power on the plains. They don't need hoplites or walls. They're nomads – they just move when they want. *They* hold the power here. *They* have the ability to stop Macedon on the plains. Or not.'

Kineas sat up. 'Since when do you care so deeply what Macedon does?'

Philokles stood up. 'This is not about me.'

Kineas lay back. 'It is. It is about you.' There was something nagging at the edge of his thoughts, some connection. 'You wanted to be here. Here you are. Macedon? Are they really coming here? Do I care? I'll get the company clear before—'

'NO!' Philokles leaned over him. 'No, Kineas. Stay and fight! All these people need to hear is that Olbia and Pantecapaeum will stand and fight beside them, and they will assemble an army. Srayanka says so.'

Kineas shook his head and said slowly, 'This means a great deal to you, Spartan. Is this why you came? To make an alliance against Macedon?'

'I came to see the world. I am an exile and a philosopher.'

'Bastard! You are an agent of the kings and Ephors, and a spy.'

'You lie!' Philokles snapped up his cloak. 'Rot in hell, Athenian. You have it in your power to do good, to hold the line and save something – bah. Like an Athenian – save your skin and let the others rot. No wonder the Macedonians own us.' He pushed out through the flap, bruising snow off the roof and leaving a gap where an icy wind crept in. The fire began to smoke.

Kineas climbed out from underneath his furs and made his way to the door. It wasn't as bad as he had feared – just cold. He tugged at the heavy felt flap until it fell into place across the door, and he pushed on a stick sewn into the felt until it closed just right – sealing the door. An inner curtain fell over the whole. He was warmer immediately. He found dried meat and apple cider by his bed and tore into them – the meat was softly seasoned, almost tart, and the cider smelled of Ecbatana. He drank it all.

Then he had to piss. He was naked in his tent, and there was nothing like a jar or a chamber pot.

He wondered what had led him to accuse Philokles and he shook his head at the hypocrisy of his accusation. He had to piss and he needed someone to help him. That revealed to him how foolish he had been to antagonize the Spartan – and for what? He was suspicious of the Spartan's motives – he always had been.

'Who cares?' he asked the tent flap. He had no clothes and it would be cold as hell outside, and he needed to piss. 'Who gives a shit?' which under the circumstances, seemed funny.

The flap rustled and Philokles's head appeared.

Kineas smiled in relief. 'I apologize.'

'Me, too.' Philokles came in. 'I antagonized a very sick man. What are you doing out of your blankets?'

'I have to piss like a warhorse.'

Philokles wrapped him in two Thracian cloaks and led him out in the snow. His feet hurt from the cold, but the relief of emptying his bladder trumped the pain of his feet and in seconds he was back in the furs.

Philokles watched him intently. 'You are better.'

Kineas nodded. 'I am.'

'Good. I have found someone more persuasive to make my argument. Lady Srayanka will be here when the hunt ends. She will make the case herself.'

Kineas cast about the tent again. 'Where are my clothes?'

'Don't be a fool. This is not a mating ritual – I imagine the lady is well wed. This is diplomacy and you have the advantage of illness. Sit and look pale. Besides, you've seldom been lovelier. Eumenes pines for you when he isn't pining for Ajax.'

Kineas glanced at him and realized that he was being teased. 'Cut my beard.'

'An hour ago I was a coward and a liar.'

'No, a spy. You said liar.'

The possibility of real enmity hung in the air between them, just a few words away from the raillery. Kineas made a sign of aversion in the air, a peasant sign from the hills of Attica. 'I have apologized, and I will again.'

'No need. I'm a touchy bastard.' Philokles looked away. 'I am a bastard, Kineas. Do you know what that means in Sparta?'

Kineas shook his head. He knew what it meant in Athens.

'It means you are never a Spartiate. Win at games, triumph in lessons and still no mess group will welcome you. I thought that I had escaped from the weight of the shame – but apparently I brought it here with me.'

Kineas thought for a moment, sipping more cider. And then he said, 'You are not a bastard here. I'm sorry for the word. I use it too often. It is easy – I'm well born, whatever I am now. But I say again – you are no bastard here, or in Olbia. Or in Tomis, for that matter. Please forgive me.'

Philokles smiled. It was a rare kind of smile for him, free of sarcasm or doubt – just a smile. 'The Philosopher forgave you when I walked out the tent.' He laughed. 'The Spartan needed a little more combat.'

Kineas rubbed his face. 'Now trim my beard and comb my hair.'

And Philokles said, 'You bastard.'

*

It was long after dark when she came. Kineas and Philokles had spent the afternoon talking, first in a gush and then comfortably, by topics, with silences. Twice, Kineas went to sleep and awoke to find him still there.

The snow had finally ceased. Eumenes said so when he came back with an antelope he'd knocked over with his own spear, proud as a boy reciting his first lines of Homer, 'These barbarians can ride! My father calls them bandits, but they are like centaurs. I'd only seen them drunk in the town – and my nurse, of course. Not like they are here at all!'

Philokles smiled. 'I fancy you are seeing a different type of Sakje altogether.'

'Noble ones. I know. The lady – she rides like Artemis herself.'

Kineas started before he realized the boy must mean the goddess. He made the avert sign – women who rivalled Artemis seldom came to a good end. But his Artemis had been a fine rider, in many different ways. He smiled to himself. He was becoming an old fool.

Eumenes continued. 'She killed twice, once with a bow and once with her spear. A woman, sirs, imagine? And the men – so courteous. They found my buck. I was nervous – what if I failed my throw right there, surrounded by barbarians?'

Kineas laughed aloud. 'I know that feeling, young man.'

Eumenes looked hurt. 'You, sir? I saw you throw in the hippodrome, sir. But anyway – I'll never let my father call them bandits again.' Philokles ushered him out.

'I gather Lady Srayanka has gone to dinner.'

Kineas was disappointed. He was shaved and under the furs he had a good linen tunic, now somewhat creased from being napped in. But he smiled. 'You are good company, sir.'

Philokles flushed like a young man. 'You please me.'

'Socrates said there was no higher compliment. Or maybe Xenophon. One of them anyway. For a soldier – but why hector you about what soldiers think? Have you made a campaign? Is it not something about which you will speak? I mean no insult.'

'I made a campaign with the men of Molyvos against Mytilene. It was my first, for all my training.'

'Why did you leave?'

Philokles looked into the fire. 'Many reasons,' he began, and there was a stir at the door cloth.

Lady Srayanka entered alone and without fuss, sweeping the door aside and closing it with a single sweep of her arm. Having entered, she walked around the fire, brushed her long doeskin coat under her knees and sat in one fluid motion. She flashed a brief smile at Philokles. 'Greetings, Greek men. May the gods look favourably upon you.'

It was delivered so well, so fluently, that only later did Kineas realize it was a practised phrase learned off by heart.

Philokles nodded gravely, as if to a Greek matron in a well-ordered house. 'Greetings, Despoina.'

Kineas couldn't help but smile. The head was the same, although the face was less severe. Still the same clear blue eyes and her ludicrous, heavy brows that nearly met in the middle of her face. He was being rude, staring into her eyes – and she was looking back at him. The corner of her mouth curled.

'Greetings, lady,' he said. It didn't sound as stumbling as he had feared.

'I desire – to send – for Ataelax. Yes?' Her voice was low, but very much a woman's.

'Ataelax?' asked Kineas.

'Ataelus. His name as it is said here, I gather,' Philokles explained as he opened the flap and called.

Ataelus came in so quickly it was obvious he had been waiting nearby. The moment he entered, something changed. Until then, her eyes were mostly on Kineas. Once he was through the flap, they were everywhere else.

'For speaking,' he said.

Kineas decided that he would pay some teacher in Olbia to improve on the cases of the Scyth's nouns as soon as possible.

Lady Srayanka spoke softly and at length. Ataelus waited until she was completely finished and then asked her several questions, then she asked him a question. Finally, he turned to Kineas. 'She says many fine things for you, you birth, and how to say? Hearting? Brave. She say you kill a very big man Getae. Man kill her – for special friend, and for dear man. Yes? And other thing.

166

For other thing, all good. Then this – sorry she take tax on plain for her, from us. Make trouble with stone houses; make trouble for horse people Sakje. She say, "You never say Olbia!" and I say, "You never ask!" but truth for truth, you never tell me, or maybe I for understand. Or not. Yes?'

Philokles leaned over. 'I've heard this before, Kineas. This Getae you killed – he had killed someone important to her. Not a relative. Not a husband. A lover? I don't think we'll get to know.'

Kineas nodded. Praise was praise when you valued the giver. 'Tell her I am sorry for the loss of her friend.'

Ataelus nodded and spoke to the lady, who nodded too. She spoke, tugging one of her heavy black braids. 'She say, "I cut these for loss." So not now, but long ago, I think.'

She went on, gesturing with her hands. She was wearing a different coat and her golden breastplate was not in evidence, but this coat was also decorated in dark blue lines, abstract patterns from the middle of the sleeve to her wrist, and it had the same cones of gold foil wrapped around hair that tinkled and whispered as she moved.

'Now she say other thing. She say you *airyanām*. Yes? You know this word?'

Kineas nodded, flattered. The Persian word for aristocrat, old noble, and also for good behaviour. 'I know it.'

'So she say, you this airyanām, you big man for Olbia. She say, Macedon walks here. She say, Macedon kill father, brother. I say this – big battle, ten turns of the moon. Years. Ten years. Yes? In the summer. Sakje fight Macedon. Many kill, many die, no win. But king, he killed. Me, far away on the plains, care nothing for this king, nothing for Macedon, but I hear this, too. Big battle. Big. Yes? So – so. Her father this king, So I say, not she – she big woman, big she, like I think first time. Yes?'

Philokles glanced at her and said, 'You think her father was the king who died fighting Macedon? In a big battle ten years back. You weren't there, but you heard a lot about it. And you think she is very important?'

'Good for you,' said Ataelus. 'For me, she big. Yes? And she say, Macedon walks. She say, hands of hands of hands of men walk for Macedon, like grass, like water in river. She say, new king good man, but not fight. Or maybe fight. But if Olbia fight, king fight. Otherwise, not. King go off into plains, Macedon walks to Olbia.'

Kineas nodded that he understood what had been said. He was sitting up, watching her. She ignored his regard, concentrating on Ataelus. Now, she was passionate, her hands flashing in front of her as if she urged on a horse by pumping the reins. She was loud.

Ataelus continued. 'She say, you big man for Olbia, you man airyanām, you make for her.' Although Ataelus was just starting to translate her most impassioned speech, she was finished, and she sank back with her head against the tent's central pole, her face turned up to the smoke hole, her heavy lashes covering her eyes – as if she couldn't bear to watch the result of her words. Kineas realized that he was watching her so intently he was missing the translation of her speech.

'You go, bring Olbia, make Olbia fight. War down Macedon. Make Sakje great, make Olbia great, break Macedon, everybody free. She say more – all word talk. And Kineax – she like you. That she not say, yes? I say it. Little childrens ouside yurt say it. Yes? Everybody say it. King poke her with it. So you knowing this, I say it.' Ataelus was smiling, but he had forgotten that the lady spoke some Greek. Like an arrow from a bow, she rose to her feet, glared at him, struck him with her riding whip – a substantial blow that knocked him flat – and vanished through the door flap.

'Uh oh,' said Ataelus. He got to his feet unsteadily, holding his shoulder. Then he pushed through the flap and called out. A steady stream of obvious invective greeted him. It was quite loud, fluent, and went on for long enough that Kineas and Philokles exchanged glances.

Kineas winced. 'Very like a Persian. I think she just said that he could eat shit. And die.'

Philokles poured himself wine. 'I'm happy that your romance is flourishing, but I need your brain. You understand her words about Macedon?'

Kineas was still listening to her. She was running down,

using words that he didn't know. They all seemed to end in -ax. 'Macedon? Yes, Philokles. Yes, I was listening. Macedon is coming. Listen, Philokles – I've made seven campaigns. I've been in two great battles. I know what Macedon brings. Listen to me. If Antipater comes here, he'll have two or three *Taxies* of foot – half as many as Alexander has in Asia. He'll have as many Thracians as he can pay and two thousand *Heterae*, the best cavalry in the world; he'll have Thessalians and Greeks and artillery. Even if he only sends a tithe of his strength, these noble savages and our city hoplites wouldn't last an hour.'

Philokles looked at his wine cup and then held it up. It was solid gold. 'You've been sick a week. I've been talking to people. Mostly to Kam Baqca. She is their closest approach to a philosopher.'

'The witch doctor?' Kineas said with a smile. 'She scared me last night.'

'She is a great deal more than a witch doctor. In fact, she is so great that her presence here is probably more important than the king's. She speaks some Greek but – for her own reasons – seldom uses it. I wish I spoke this language – everything I think I know comes through the sieve of other men's thoughts. Kam Baqca scares Ataelus so badly he can barely keep his thoughts in order to translate for me.'

Kineas was losing hope that Srayanka would come back. 'Why? I admit she has tremendous presence—'

'Have you ever been to Delphi?' Philokles interrupted. 'No? The priestesses of Apollo are like her. She combines in herself two sacred functions. She is *Enareis* – you remember your Herodotus? She has sacrificed her manhood to function as a seer. And she is Baqca – the most powerful baqca anyone can remember, according to Ataelus.'

Kineas tried to remember what had been said in her tent. 'What is baqca?'

'I have no idea – Ataelus keeps telling me things, and Lady Srayanka – they speak of her with reverence, but they don't speak of baqca in detail. It is a barbarian concept.' Philokles shook his head. 'I'm losing my thread in a maze of details. Kineas, there are thousands of these people. Tens of thousands.'

'And their king is wandering around with a witch doctor and a handful of retainers, looking for support from a little town on the Euxine? Tell me another one.'

Philokles tossed off the rest of his wine. 'You're pissing me off. They are barbarians, Kineas. I don't understand the role of their king, but he's neither figurehead nor Asian tyrant. The best I've been able to understand, he's only king when there is something "kingly" to do. Otherwise, he's a major chief ruling his tribe – and this is only a fraction of his tribe. His escort, if you like.'

Kineas lay back. 'Tell me all this in the morning. I'm better. In the morning, I intend to see if I can ride.'

'And Srayanka wants it,' said Philokles. He smiled nastily. 'Whichever head you want to think with, I have an argument.'

As soon as it was known that Kineas was up and dressed, he was summoned to meet the king. He was prepared, dressed in his best tunic and sandals. He left his armour off, as he was still too weak to bear the weight for any time. Outside the tent his escort waited, his eight men from Olbia in their cloaks and armour, looking like statues. They faced together like professionals and marched him to the king's yurt, flanked by a crowd of curious Sakje. Dogs barked, children pointed, and they crossed a few yards of muddy snow. The king's yurt was by far the largest and the entrance had two layers of doors that had to be thrown back by his escort.

Inside, it was so warm that he shed his cloak as soon as dignity permitted. A dozen Sakje sat in a semicircle around the fire. They sat cross-legged on the ground, chatting easily and as Kineas entered the yurt, they all rose to their feet. In the centre of them stood a boy, or perhaps a very young man, with heavy blond hair and a short blond beard. His position marked him as the king, but for the splendour of dress and the quantity of gold, any one of the dozen Sakje might have been royal.

Srayanka stood at his right hand. Her face was closed and cold and her glance flicked over him, rested briefly on Philokles, and returned to the king next to her.

Kam Baqca stood behind the king, dressed simply in a long

coat of white, with her hair coiled atop her head. She inclined her head in greeting.

The king smiled. 'Welcome, Kineas. I am Satrax, king of the Assagatje. Please sit, and let us serve you.' At his words, all of the people in the tent sat together and Kineas tried, and failed, to match their grace. Philokles and Eumenes had entered with him and sat on either side by prior arrangement, and Ataelus sat a little to his right in a sort of no-man's-land between the groups.

Kineas spoke once he had settled. 'I thank you for your welcome, O King. Your hospitality has been gracious. Indeed, I was sick and your doctor healed me.' He watched the king carefully. The boy was younger than Alexander had been when they crossed the Hellespont, his face still soft and unmarked with harsh experience. His wide eyes spoke well of his good nature, and his gestures had a fledgling dignity. Kineas liked what he saw.

Greek wine was brought in deep vases and poured into a huge bowl of solid gold. The king dipped cups of wine in the bowl and handed them to his guests, blessing each one. When he filled Kineas's cup, he carried it to where Kineas sat.

Kineas rose, unsure of the protocol and unused to be being waited on by any but slaves.

The king pressed him back down. 'The blessings of the nine gods of the heavens attend you, Kineas,' he said in Greek. He had an accent, but his Greek was pure, if Ionic.

Kineas took his cup and drank, as he had seen others do. It was unwatered, pure Chian straight from the vase. He swallowed carefully and a small fire was lit in his stomach.

When the king was seated with a cup in his own hand, he poured a libation and spoke a prayer. Then he leaned forward.

'To business,' he said. He was aggressive, in the half-timorous way of the young. 'Will Olbia fight against Macedon, or submit?'

Kineas was astonished at the speed with which the king moved to the issue at hand. He had made the mistake of finding similarities between the Sakje and the Persians and had therefore expected ceremony and lengthy conversation about trivialities. No answer came to him.

171

'Come, Kineas, several of my friends have already broached this topic with you.' The king leaned forward, clearly enjoying his advantage. 'What will Olbia do?'

Kineas noted that the boy's eyes flicked to Srayanka's for approval. *So.* 'I cannot speak for Olbia, sir.' Kineas met the king's eye. Close up, he could see the young king was handsome – almost as handsome as Ajax, with a snub barbarian nose the only jarring feature on his face. Kineas toyed with his wine to give himself time to think. 'I think the archon will first have to be convinced that the threat of Macedon is real.'

The king nodded and exchanged a glance with a big, bearded man at his left. 'I expected as much and I have no proof to offer. Let me ask a better question. If Macedon marches, will Olbia submit?'

Kineas suspected that the boy was giving memorized questions. He shrugged. 'Again, you must ask the archon. I cannot speak for Olbia.' He squirmed as Srayanka glanced at him with indifference and turned back to smile at the king.

The king played with his beard. After a short silence, he nodded. 'This is as I expected and that is why I must go and see your archon myself.' He paused. 'Will you advise me?'

Kineas nodded slowly. 'As far as I am able. I command the archon's cavalry. I am not his confidant.'

The king smiled. 'If you were, I should hardly ask you to advise me.' He suddenly seemed very mature for his years – it occurred to Kineas that the boy might be asking his own questions, after all – and his sarcasm was as Greek as his language. 'Many of my nobles feel we should fight. Kam Baqca says we should fight only if Olbia and Pantecapaeum intend to fight. What do *you* say?'

Easy to be derisory when facing Philokles. More difficult when facing this direct young man. 'I would hesitate to fight Macedon.'

Srayanka's head snapped in his direction. Her eyes narrowed. He noted how dark her lips were and how, when she turned her head away, they turned down.

Kam Baqca spoke a few words. The king smiled. 'Kam Baqca

says that you have served the monster and you know more of him than any man here.'

'The monster?' asked Kineas.

'Alexander. Kam Baqca calls him the Monster.' The king poured himself more wine.

'I served Alexander,' Kineas admitted. They all looked at him and he wondered if he was in danger here. None of the looks were friendly; only Kam Baqca regarded him with a smile. And Srayanka busied herself with her riding whip rather than meet his eye.

And he thought, I served him. I loved him. And now I begin to suspect that Kam Baqca is right. He is a monster. He was confused, and the confusion fed his tone. 'The army of Macedon is the finest in the world. If Antipater sends Zopryon here, he will bring thousands of pikemen, Thracians, archers – probably fifteen thousand men on foot. And cavalry from Macedon and Thessaly, the best in the Greek world. Against that, the men of Olbia and Pantecapaeum, plus a few hundred Scythians, were every one of them Achilles come back from the Elysian Fields, would not be enough.'

The king fingered his beard again, and then played with a ring – embarrassed. 'How many riders do you think I can put in the field, Kineas?'

Kineas was at a loss how to answer, since barbarian kings inevitably exaggerated the numbers of their men. If he flattered and guessed too high, he robbed his own argument of validity. Too low and he insulted the king.

'I do not know, O King. I see a few hundred here. I'm sure there are more.'

The king laughed. As Kineas's words were translated, more and more of the Sakje laughed. Even Srayanka laughed.

'Listen, Kineas. It is winter. The grass is under the snow and there is little wood out on the plains for fires. In winter, every band from every tribe goes its own way, to find food, to get shelter and to cut wood. If we all stayed together, the horses would starve and the animals would all stay away from our bows. I have seen the cities of the Greeks – I was a hostage in Pantecapaeum. I have seen how many people you can put inside a stone wall, with slaves to till the land and slaves to cook it. We have no slaves. We have no walls. But in the spring, if my chief war leaders agree that we must fight, I can call tens of thousands of horsemen here. Perhaps three tens of thousands. Perhaps more.'

Philokles put a hand on Kineas's knee. 'Ataelus says this is so. I think it is true. Think before you speak.'

Kineas tried to imagine three tens of thousands of horsemen in a single army. 'Can you feed them?' he asked.

The king nodded. 'For a while. And for a longer while, with the cities at my side. Let me be straight with you, Kineas. I can also simply ride away north into the plains and leave you to the Macedonians. They can march until the snow falls next year and never find me. The plains are vast – greater than all the rest of the world.'

Kineas took a deep breath, shutting out the hand on his knee and the blue eyes under the dark brows across the tent. 'If you wish to sway the archon, you must convince him that you have such force.' With three tens of thousands of men and women who rode like Artemis ...

The king pointed the toe of his boot at the great golden bowl at his feet. 'I cannot show him the riders on the great plain, Kineas. But I can show him an enormous amount of gold. And gold is the way to the heart of a Greek, or so I have observed. And your archon might ask himself this. If the bandit king has a mountain of gold, why should he not have thirty thousand riders?'

Kineas winced at the words 'bandit king', and the king laughed again. 'Isn't that what he calls us? Bandits? Horse thieves? Worse? I heard them all when I was a hostage.'

Kineas said, 'Then why would you fight at all? Why not retreat into the plains?'

The king sat back until his shoulders rested against a wall hanging. He looked comfortable. 'Your cities are our riches. We sell our grain there, and we buy goods we love. We can lose these things – we are not bound by them. But we might fight to keep them, too.' He raised his hand and rocked it to and fro. 'It balances like this. Fight for our treasure, or leave it?'

He smiled wryly. 'If I decide rightly, I will be a good king. If I decide poorly, I will be a bad king.' He stood. 'You are tired. I will have more questions as we ride. Will you be prepared to depart tomorrow?'

Kineas stood as well, Philokles rising impatiently by his side. 'O King, I will. By your leave, I will escort you to Olbia.'

'Let it be so.'

The next day, Kineas still felt light-headed when he moved too fast and the effort of wearing armour was at first too much for him, but he was soon accustomed to it. The snow lay in deep drifts around the camp, tramped flat where the tracks of hunters or wood gatherers left the circle of wagons. Away to the south he could see a great black curve of the river. There was no sign of the track they had followed this far.

'We will have to go slowly,' Kineas said to Ajax and Eumenes. Philokles was avoiding him.

'The Sakje will all have changes of horses.' Eumenes pointed to where the travelling party was preparing; the king and ten mounted companions. They were all dressed like kings, heavy with gold ornaments. All of them wore red cloaks, although no two cloaks were dyed to exactly the same hue.

Kineas looked for Srayanka, but she was not there. She would not be accompanying the royal party. He wondered if she would have come had he spoken as she desired. He wondered what, exactly, she and Philokles had wanted him to say. He thought about the reception waiting for him in Olbia and a winter training rich men and their sons to be cavalrymen, and for the first time the prospect seemed empty and worthless. He thought about the proposition he had been made after being exiled, and what it might now mean.

He thought about her, and the way the king had looked at her. Royal mistress? Fiancée? Sour thoughts – the kind of jealous thoughts that first inform a man that he's in love – were filling his mind when Philokles appeared at his elbow.

'You look as if a dog ate your breakfast,' Philokles said. He looked happy, fit, and ready for anything.

'Is she actually well wed, brother?' Kineas asked.

Philokles grinned – Kineas seldom referred to him as brother, and he enjoyed the compliment. 'She is not. Something told me that you might enquire.' He laughed aloud.

Kineas could feel the flush rolling down his cheeks to his neck. 'Laugh all you want,' he said tersely.

Philokles held up a hand. 'My pardon,' he said. 'Unfair to laugh, who has so often felt the sting of Aphrodite himself. She is unwed – and, as Ataelus thought, the lord of a great tribe of these barbarians. And a famous warrior.'

Kineas rubbed his beard, watching the king and his mount and avoiding Philokles's eyes. 'Is she the king's ... concubine?'

Philokles put his hands on his hips. 'Can you imagine that girl as anyone's concubine?' He grinned. 'I have half a mind to tell her you asked.' Kineas whirled around, and Philokles laughed again. 'You have it bad!' he said.

Kineas grunted. Then he turned away from Philokles, grabbed Eumenes by the shoulder, and strode to the king's side.

The king was checking the hooves of his mount. He had a forefoot between his knees and a crooked knife in his teeth. 'Good morning,' he said around the knife.

Kineas bowed stiffly, the weight of his breastplate making him clumsy. 'I don't want to slow you, sir. But we have only a few remounts and we won't be able to travel quickly.'

The king put the horse's foot back on the ground, gave the beast a friendly pat, and began tightening the girth. Kineas still had difficulty watching a king tighten his own girth. It rendered him unable to believe that the same king might have thirty thousand horsemen.

Sure that his girth was adequate, the king waved his whip at a tall man with white–blond hair and an enormous beard, dressed from head to foot in red. At the council, he had sat at the king's left side. 'Marthax! I need you.'

Marthax rode over on a tall roan stallion. He was a heavy man, with a paunch that spilled over his belt, but he had arms like small trees and his legs were enormous. His red pointed hat was trimmed in white fur and he had a set of gold plaques modelled as kissing Aphrodites that ran around the top of each bicep. He and the king exchanged a few words. Kineas was sure that they said 'horse' and 'snow'. Then they both looked at him. Marthax grinned widely.

'You friend king!' he said. 'Some friend. King give horses. Come! See horses, take.'

Kineas shouted for Ataelus and said to Eumenes, 'I don't want to be beholden for these horses. Just tell him to loan us a few so that we have remounts.'

Eumenes began to hem and haw, interjecting a few tentative words of Sakje, but the king shook his head. 'Just take them. I have a few thousand more. I want to go fast and get this over with. My people here will be waiting and we have a long, long ride north across the plains when this is done.' His words were friendly, but the tone was pre-emptory. The gift was not a request; it was an order.

Kineas pointed to Ataelus, already mounted, to follow Marthax. He returned with a string of sturdy plains ponies and two tall chargers. They were both pale grey like new iron, with black stripes running down their spines.

Kineas watched them go by, scrutinizing their size and strength. He was so absorbed with the chargers that he almost walked into Kam Baqca. She held his shoulders firmly and looked into his eyes. Her own were dark, so brown as to be almost black even in the glare of the snow. She began to speak, almost to sing, and the king came and stood beside her.

'She says, "Do not try to cross the river again without my help."' The king raised his eyebrows. The seer smiled, still holding his shoulders, and he looked into her deep brown eyes: *All the way down to where the dreams waited, and a tree grew in the dark ...*

And then he was standing in the snow, and she said, 'You must not leave without speaking to my niece,' in clear Greek.

The king turned to look at her – the sudden turn and glare of an eagle. Kineas noted it. The seer ignored her king. Instead, she reached up and attached a charm to Kineas's horse's bridle. The bridle was plain, just a loop of leather with a bronze bit. His good bridle was with his charger, safely back in Olbia. The charm was of iron, a bow and an arrow.

'Will that keep me warm?' he asked lightly.

The king frowned. 'Do not joke about Kam Baqca. She does not sell her charms, but we are greatly favoured if we wear them. What river can you not cross without her?'

'I dreamed a river,' Kineas said. His eyes were on Lady Srayanka, who stood in the muddy snow by the king's yurt, giving orders to men loading a wagon. He looked back at the king, and his eyes were wary and his face closed.

'She says, "Next time you will dream a tree. Do not climb it without me."' The king rubbed his beard. He was too young to hide his anger, and Kineas had no idea what the king might be angry about. 'This is seer talk, Kineas. Are you, too, a baqca?'

Kineas made the sign of aversion. 'No. I am a simple cavalry-man. Philokles is the philosopher.'

His aside was apparently translated, because Kam Baqca spat an answer back and then, as if relenting, gave him a pat on the head as if he were a good child. 'She says, the one who says poems is a fine man, but she has never seen him and he did not go alone to the river. And she says,' the king paused, his eyes narrowed, 'she says this decision will come down to you, however you twist and turn. I think she speaks of the war with Macedon.' Kam Baqca hit the king lightly on the shoulder. 'And she tells me this is not for me to think on, that I am only her mouth.' The king frowned again, adolescent petulance warring with natural humour. 'What satrap, what great king can be ordered around in this way by his people?' The king began to collect his arms; a heavy quiver that held both bow and arrows, called a *gorytos*; a short sword on an elaborately decorated belt with a heavy scabbard, and a bucket of javelins that attached to his saddle.

Kam Baqca patted Kineas on the head again, and then turned him by his shoulders so he faced Lady Srayanka. Srayanka caught his eye and then looked away. Her indifference was a little too studied; a younger man would have read her motion as a direct rejection, but Kineas had seen some of the world and recognized that she wanted his attention. He couldn't help but smile as he walked to her. He had no translator, which, given the last occasion but one, seemed just as well.

And, as he came close to her, she extended a hand in greeting.

On a whim, he reached up and took the gorgon's head clasp off his cloak and put it in her hand. Her hand was warmer than his, with heavy calluses on the top of the palm and a velvety smoothness on the back he hadn't remembered, and the contrast – the hard sword hand and the soft back – went through him like poetry, or the sight of the first flower of spring – recognition, wonder, awe.

At first she didn't meet his eyes – but neither did she reject his touch. She shouted a command over her shoulder and then flicked her eyes over the brooch, smiled, and looked at him. She was taller than he had imagined. Her eyes had flecks of brown amidst the blue, and were very nearly level with his own.

'Go with the gods, Kin-y-aas,' she said. She looked at the gorgon's head again – decent work from an Athenian shop – and smiled. He could smell her – woodsmoke and leather. Her hair needed washing. He wanted to kiss her and he didn't think that was a good idea, but the urge was so strong that he stepped back to avoid having his body betray him.

She put her whip in his hand. 'Go with the gods,' she said again. And turned on her heel, already calling to a mounted man carrying a bundle of fleeces.

Kineas looked at the whip after he mounted. He had never carried one, despising them as a tool for poor riders. This one had a handle made of something very heavy, yet pliable. He could feel it moving under his hands. Alternating bands of worked leather and solid gold were wrapped over a pliable core. The worked leather showed a scene of men and women hunting together on horseback that wound up the handle from an agate stone in the pommel to the stiff horsehair of the whip. It was a beautiful thing, too heavy to hit a horse, but a useful pointer and a pretty fair weapon. He flexed it a few times. His young men were mounting behind him. They looked better for a week riding with the Sakje and today they all had their armour, helmets and cloaks. He took his place at their head, still playing with his whip.

Ajax saluted. He was already a competent hyperetes – the men were formed neatly, and Kineas saluted back. 'You're a fine soldier, Ajax,' he said. 'I'll be sorry when you go back to marry your rich girl and trade your cargoes.'

Ajax flashed him his beautiful smile. 'Sir, do you ever pay a compliment without a sting in the tail?'

Kineas flexed the whip again. 'Yes.' He smiled at Clio, the nearest trooper. 'Clio, you look like an adult this morning.' and to all of them: 'You gentlemen ready for a hard ride? The king intends to do this in two days. That's going to be ten hours in the saddle. I can't let anyone drop out. Are you ready?'

'Yes!' they shouted.

The Sakje stopped whatever they were doing to watch them for a moment. Then they went back to their preparations.

Philokles came up, mounted on one of the Sakje chargers – a fine animal, with heavy muscles. 'The king gave me this horse. I must say, he's a generous fellow.' He looked around and then whispered, 'Not your greatest fan, Kineas.'

Kineas raised an eyebrow.

Philokles spread his hands and bowed his head, a gesture universal among Greeks – *I'll say no more on the subject.*

Kineas shook his head and returned his mind to the matter at hand. 'I couldn't find a horse your size. That's a superb animal, Philokles. Don't waste him in the snow.'

'Bah, you've made a centaur of me, Kineas. With this beast between my legs, I could ride anywhere.' Philokles gave him a broad smile. 'If you don't wipe that grin off your face, Kineas, people might mistake you for a happy man.'

Kineas glanced at the Spartan, ran his eyes over his horse. 'You might want to get your girth tight first.' Kineas slid down, got under the Spartan's leg, and heaved. 'And roll your cloak tight. Here, give it to me.'

Philokles shrugged. 'Niceas always does it for me.'

'Shame on him. Shame on you.' Kineas flipped the cloak open over the broad back of the charger, who shied a little when he saw the flapping cloak in the corner of his black eye. Then Kineas folded it, rolled it tight and hard, and buckled it to the high-backed Sakje saddle.

'In the infantry, we just wear the damn things,' Philokles said.

'Tie it like this, behind your saddle and you have something to lean your ass on when you're tired.' Kineas was looking at the

Sakje saddle that Philokles had acquired. It had a much higher back than any Greek tack. Most Greeks were content with a blanket. He remounted and gathered his reins.

'Nice whip,' Philokles said. 'That didn't come from the king.' He flashed a wicked smile.

'Philokles,' Kineas said, putting his hand on the Spartan's rein.

The king rode up on his other side and interrupted him. 'We're ready if you are,' he said curtly.

'In what order would you like us to ride?' Kineas looked at his own disciplined Greeks and the milling Sakje nobles. They were showing off for women, or men, performing curvets and rearing their horses. Two were already off, having a race, and the snow erupted from under their hooves in the early sun.

The young king shrugged. 'I thought that I would send out a pair in front, like any decent commander. And then, since this is a peaceful mission, I thought you and I could ride abreast, perhaps with this talkative Spartan for company. I shall practise my Greek, Philokles shall learn more of my land, and I can teach you how to use the Sakje whip.' The king indicated the whip in Kineas's hand. 'That looks familiar to me,' he said with Greek sarcasm.

'At your command, sir,' Kineas said. He raised his hand.

'Forward,' said the king in Greek, and then: '*Ferâ!*'

10

The sickness was almost gone from his body, praise to the deadly archer Apollo for passing him by and to Kam Baqca for saving him – and the coughs scarcely troubled him. The journey back to the city was pleasant despite the chill and the deep snow on the plains, because the king's men were good companions, and because his Olbian boys were becoming something like soldiers. For two days, Kineas had nothing to worry about. The king's men chose camps and erected felt tents from the two heavy wagons that carried all of the party's baggage. Kineas rode and talked, and in brief intervals alone, thought of Srayanka. Whatever coldness was between him and the king, it disappeared soon after they left the camp.

The holiday ended forty stades from Olbia.

'We spotted a patrol!' young Kyros shouted, as soon as he was close enough to be heard. He slowed his horse, sweeping in a wide arc in front of the king, and gave a belated salute.

Kineas waited with apparent indifference until the young man brought his horse to a stand in front of them.

'Four men, all well mounted. Ataelus says they are your men from the city.' Kyros looked a trifle downcast. 'I didn't see them. Ataelus did. He's watching them.'

Kineas turned to the king. 'If Ataelus saw them, they'll have seen him and they'll be with us shortly.' Even as he spoke, two riders crested the next ridge and began a rapid descent.

Kineas knew Niceas by the set of his shoulders and the way he rode, even on the horizon of a snowy plain, and as soon as he spotted his hyperetes cantering down the ridge towards the Sakje king's party, he began to worry.

'That man rides well,' said the king at his side.

'He's been in the saddle all his life,' Kineas said. He gave a cough.

'To keep watch on the roads in winter is no easy task,' the king said. He tugged his beard thoughtfully.

Niceas rode up at a fast trot, and saluted. 'Hipparch, I greet you,' he said formally.

Kineas returned his salute and then embraced him. 'You are better,' he said.

Niceas smiled. 'By the grace of all the gods, and despite the meddling of Diodorus with various potions, I'm a new man.' Then he seemed to recollect the company he was in. 'Pardon, sir.'

Kineas, used to the rampant informalities of the Sakje, had to make himself think like a Greek. 'The King of the Sakje – my friend and hyperetes, Niceas. Like me, an Athenian.'

The king held out his right hand, and Niceas took it. 'I'm honoured, Great King.'

'I'm not a great king,' Satrax said, 'I am king of the Assagatje.' He narrowed his eyes. 'I do intend to be a great king, in time.'

Niceas looked back and forth between his commander and the barbarian king. Kineas read his hesitancy and motioned to the king with his whip, already a part of him. 'Niceas has private news for me, O King. May I have your permission to ride aside with him for a little space?'

Satrax waved his riding whip in return. It was a Sakje habit – they talked with their whips. 'Be my guest,' he said.

'I like him,' said Niceas as soon as they were out of earshot. 'Nothing Persian about him. But Ares' frozen balls, he's young.'

'Not as young as he looks. What in Hades brought you out to freeze your hairy ass in the snow?' Kineas was taking both of them out of the column at a good standing trot, and his words were shaken by the motion of the horse.

Niceas was silent until they both reined in at the top of a low ridge. Below them the king's two heavy wagons toiled along, drawn by a double yoke of oxen. 'You were supposed to be back in three days – a week at longest.' He looked around. 'The assembly didn't accept the archon's taxes. Now there's trouble. Nothing solid – yet. But when you didn't show, people started to talk. Trouble that will be solved the hour you ride in the gate. A lot of rich fathers are missing their sons – led by Cleomenes. So Diodorus and I decided we'd send out patrols to look for you. That was three days back.' Niceas looked like a man ridding himself of the weight of the world. 'Why are you so late? There's men in the city saying you were killed by the barbarians. And others saying the archon won't let you bring back the boys until the taxes are voted.'

'What men?' asked Kineas. 'Who said so?'

'Coenus was off to find that out when I took the patrol out.' Niceas shrugged. 'Even money says it's the archon.'

'Did you have his permission to look for me?' Kineas waved to get the king's attention.

'Somehow, that slipped my mind.' Niceas pantomimed repentance.

Kineas sighed. He had enjoyed days on the plains without any burden of command beyond his handful of promising boys. He felt as if all of Niceas's burdens had shifted squarely on to his own shoulders. He kicked his heels and his sturdy pony, one of the king's gifts, trotted back down the hill towards the column.

'How are the rest?' Kineas asked.

'Pretty fair. Bored. This patrol had everyone volunteering. Diodorus put everything off limits except the gymnasium and the hippodrome until your return.' Niceas chuckled. 'We've acquired some whores. Diodorus bought the services of a hetaera.'

Kineas congratulated Diodorus in his mind. 'Where'd they come from?' he asked. They were approaching the king and Marthax, who were laughing with Ajax and Eumenes.

Niceas glanced away. 'Oh – here and there, I guess,' he said evasively.

Kineas made a note to himself to find out, and then saluted the king. 'O King – I am required in the city.' Ajax made room, and Kineas brought his horse alongside the king's.

Satrax nodded. 'Then let us go faster,' he said, and set his horse to a gallop. Every Sakje in the party did the same, and the Greeks had to scramble to keep up.

For the first time, Kineas saw the full measure of the Sakje as horsemen. They galloped their horses for an hour, halted, and every man switched horses, and they were off again. It was a pace that would have broken a troop of Greek cavalry in two hours, but with their herd of remounts and their unflagging energy, the Sakje rode at a gallop for three hours, pausing once to drink unwatered wine and piss in the snow. They left their wagons and half their party to come along at the pace of the oxen. Before the sun was three fists from the horizon, the whole party was passing over the city's boundary ditch and through the outer fields of the Greek and Sindi farmers.

'Fast enough for you, Kineas?' asked the king, reining in. 'I'd prefer to arrive without all my horses blown.'

Kineas's legs felt as if hot lead had been poured down his thighs. His Olbian boys were all still with them, but the moment the cavalcade stopped, every one of them dismounted and began to rub his thighs. The horses steamed.

The Sakje merely pulled out their wineskins and drank. Next to the king, Marthax opened his barbarian trousers and pissed in the snow without dismounting. His horse did the same.

Kineas rode back to his own men. 'Ten stades, my friends. Let's finish with the same spirit we had at the start. Backs straight, good seat, and a javelin in your fist. Niceas?'

Even the hyperetes looked tired from the last three hours. 'Sir?'

'Check their gear. Helmets, I think. Look sharp!' Kineas rode back to the horses and exchanged his pony for his warhorse, who seemed happy to see him. He didn't feel too sharp himself, but as he rode he pulled his freezing helmet off his pack and pushed it on to the back of his head. Eumenes rode up and handed him a javelin.

Marthax rode up beside him. 'King says – fear what?'

Kineas had gotten to know a little of Marthax on the ride. He was a relation to Srayanka, and he had a little Greek. He seemed to be the king's steward, or his closest companion, despite the age difference. Marthax was a warrior in his prime, or perhaps past it. Kineas suspected he was the King's warlord.

'I'll tell the king. Let's go.' Kineas hadn't mastered much of the Sakje tongue beyond simple cognates of Persian he already knew, but he had gotten the knack of speaking simple Greek to the Greek speakers and to Hades with subtlety.

Ataelus was sitting on his horse beside the king. 'I have for the town gate. And back,' he said. He held up an arrow. 'Got this for greeting.'

Kineas pushed his horse into the king's group. 'I can explain, O King. The town is in some turmoil. I am overdue, and Niceas had told me a rumour was spread that – that we were killed. On the plain.'

Satrax gave him a level look. 'But all of your men are arming.'

'For show, sir. Only for the show.'

Marthax spoke quickly in Sakje, and there were grunts from the other warriors. Ataelus pushed his horse to Kineas's side. 'For going home. For not trust city. Trust you, he says, trust not city. For telling king he told all this before.'

Kineas raised his voice over the murmurs of the Sakje nobles. 'If we move now, Satrax, we will be in the city before dark and we'll quell these rumors. If we wait a day ...' He shrugged.

Satrax nodded. He spoke in Sakje, and Dikarxes, a noble of the king's age, spoke, and then Marthax spoke, clearly in agreement. The king nodded, and turned to Kineas. 'We'll wait here for the wagons. If you'll be so kind as to send one of your men to get permission from the farmer. We'll make our camp by the first bend in the river – where the horse market is held.'

Kineas glanced at the rapidly setting sun. 'I had thought to take you to the city.'

'Best you go ahead. Dikarxes and Marthax agree – a horde of bandits like ourselves might get a grim reception.' He extended his hand and clasped Kineas's hand. 'You look worried, my friend. Go attend to this, and come fetch us in the morning. In truth, your city makes us nervous. I think we will be happier to camp in the snow.'

Kineas shook his head. 'You shame me, O King. And yet I fear that your decision is a wise one. Look for me in the morning.' He rode back to his own men. 'Gather round,' he said, and they pressed close. 'The king will camp here. The city is nervous – some fool has spread a rumour we're all dead. We'll go to the city, but the king needs a man to guarantee the good behaviour of the farmers. Remember that to them, he's a dangerous bandit.'

He could see at a glance that they'd taken it in. They were good boys, and every one of them had matured in two weeks on the plains. He went on, 'I need a volunteer to spend another night in the snow with them.' Ataelus immediately waved his hand, but Kineas continued, 'I'd prefer one of the citizens.'

They all clamoured to volunteer. He was impressed. 'Eumenes. And Clio. My thanks to both of you. I want you to ride around to every farmer in ten stades, tell them who is camping at the bend in the river, and why. Take all your slaves – make a show, and don't take any crap from the farmers.'

Eumenes seemed to grow a hand span. 'Yes, sir. Clio's father owns this farm and the next. I don't expect we'll have much trouble.'

Clio, who had matured the most of all the boys, saluted. 'No problem at all, sir. Please tell my father I'm at Gade's Farm.'

Kineas pointed his heavy whip at Ataelus. 'You stay with them. Help them translate. Make sure anything taken is paid for. And stay sober. If I don't come back in the morning, stay sharp. I'll return as soon as I can.' He shook hands with all three of them. Finally he said to Eumenes, 'You are in charge.'

Eumenes glowed. 'Thank you, sir.'

'Thank me when you see me again.'

Behind him, Ajax was forming the rest of the Greeks. Niceas formed as a simple trooper, allowing Ajax to be the hyperetes, just as the younger man had done for the past two weeks. The two Syracusans, Antigonus and Andronicus, had come out with Niceas, and they formed the next file, equally willing to allow Ajax to command.

Kineas pulled up beside Philokles while Ajax checked equipment and inspected.

'You're leaving the two boys as hostages,' Philokles said.

'Nothing so brutal,' Kineas said. 'They'll have a fine time, and the king and his men won't feel that we abandoned them amidst a horde of terrified Sindi farmers.'

The Spartan shrugged. 'You are worried about what the archon intends.' Kineas nodded. Philokles spat in the snow. 'Ajax makes a good hyperetes.'

'He's had good teachers.' Kineas worried that all of them in armour would frighten the city watch into some action, but it was too late, and the die was cast. 'Ajax, are we ready to ride?'

Ajax raised his fist to his breastplate. 'At your command, sir.'

Kineas took the lead spot, and waved his whip. 'Let's ride,' he said.

He prayed to Hermes and to Apollo as he rode, asking that they preserve the peace. He worried that the tyrant had done something, said something, to provoke so much anguish and fear that a city man had fired an arrow at Ataelus. And he worried what the archon intended for the Sakje. And for his men.

He had lots to worry about.

The sun set red on the city, and their jingling column rode down out of the hills of the isthmus. Peasants, slaves and farmers came out to the edge of their fields despite the cold, and word spread like lightning, so that by the time they approached the suburb beyond the city's fortifications, the streets were lined with people bundled in cloaks and blankets.

Kineas feared mischief, feared an accident – considered assassination, cursed his imagination. He wasn't sure what he was afraid of, but he was afraid. He turned to Niceas. 'You have the best lungs. Ride ahead and announce us – first to the crowd, then at the gate. The hipparch and hippeis of the city return from an embassy to the king of the Assagatje. Got it?'

Niceas nodded once, and kneed his horse into motion.

Kineas turned to Ajax at his side. 'Let us walk our horses slowly, as if in a temple procession. But Ajax – tell your men to watch the crowd and watch the roofs. Antigonus – watch the rear.'

Slowly, they walked through the suburb. In the distance, he could hear Niceas's voice roaring at the gate.

'Do you know the Paean of Apollo?' he asked. The five boys all nodded. 'Sing it!' he said.

There were only a dozen of them all told, but they made a good show, and the young voices carried, so that before they entered the last narrow, muddy street, the crowd had taken up the Paean. There was cheering.

The main gate was open, and Kineas offered thanks to Zeus. Two files of Memnon's mercenaries lined the road inside the gate, and his second officer, Licurgus, saluted with his spear. Kineas's fears began to calm. He returned the salute.

Niceas fell in by his side. 'Memnon wants to speak to you at your earliest convenience. In secret.'

Kineas kept his eyes on the crowd, which was even thicker inside the city walls. 'That can't be good.'

'I laid out a few obols to send boys to the homes of your lads. So their fathers would know,' Niceas said.

'Thanks,' Kineas said. The crowd was thick, and the street narrow at the best of times. The little column had to ride single file, and they had to be attentive to avoid trampling children under their hooves. It was the largest crowd Kineas had seen since the festival of Apollo, made ominous by the loom of night and the narrow streets.

Kineas scanned the rooftops again. There were people on the flatter roofs, but they seemed to be watching the spectacle. 'Why are we getting this hero's welcome?' he asked.

Niceas grunted and shrugged. 'There's a rumour on the streets that you're going to overthrow the archon,' he said. When Kineas whirled on him, he shrugged again. 'Don't blame the messenger – but I've heard it often enough. It makes you quite popular.'

'Athena protect me,' Kineas muttered.

They tried to watch the crowd and the roofs as they picked their way through the streets. They were careful.

Nothing untoward occurred. They rode through the gates of the hippodrome to find a smaller assembly – gentlemen of the city, many mounted and in armour. And the rest of Kineas's men, also mounted and armed, with Cleitus and Diodorus at their head.

Diodorus looked as relieved as Kineas felt. They clasped hands, and Diodorus waved to his little troop to dismount. Cleitus smiled ruefully. 'I guess we're a bunch of worried hens,' he said. He took off his helmet and gave it to his son, Leucon.

Fathers were embracing their sons. Young Kyros dismounted to regale a circle of family retainers with his adventures. Sophokles was embracing his father, and the word 'Amazon' carried clearly and echoed off the stone seats above them.

Nicomedes was there, mounted on a magnificent horse and

wearing a breastplate worth more than all of Kineas's possessions. He gave Kineas a wry smile.

Kineas could feel that something – *something* was right on the edge of explosion. All these men – mounted and armed, with full night just moments away.

'What in Hades is going on here?' Kineas said to Diodorus.

Diodorus unbuckled his chinstrap. 'Hades is about it, Kineas. The archon didn't get his taxes – at least, not yet. The assembly did some business without the archon's approval.'

'Like what?' Kineas asked. He was watching the cavalryman. Their assembly was probably illegal, and such things could have serious repercussions. It occurred to him that the muster he had appointed was tomorrow. He almost missed Diodorus's answer. 'Say that again?'

'The assembly appointed you hipparch,' Diodorus said. 'Cleitus made the motion. It didn't go by without argument, but it did pass. I need to talk to you.'

'Later,' Kineas said. He smiled. He was quite happy to be the legally appointed hipparch. 'I need to make this assembly of armed men legal. Before the archon gets the wrong idea.' Eighty years ago, in Athens, the cavalry class had seized power in the city. It had started with a muster of the mounted gentlemen. The scars of the aristocratic revolt were still visible in every Athenian assembly.

'Or the right one,' said Diodorus. He knew the history of Athens as well as Kineas – or better. His grandfather had been one of the ringleaders.

Kineas glared at him. 'Don't even *suggest* it, friend.'

Diodorus held his hands up, disclaiming responsibility. 'People are talking,' he said.

Kineas rode to the front of the gathered horsemen. 'Since we're all together, and since I see so many faces from the muster, perhaps we could have a quick inspection. Niceas?' Kineas waved with his whip. Niceas looked hesitant. Kineas's voice hardened. 'Do the thing,' he said.

Niceas took a deep breath and bellowed. His voice rang like a trumpet, and the hippodrome fell silent. 'Assemble the hippeis!' he bellowed.

The boys who had made the trek out to the plains groaned, but as one they left their fathers and their friends standing on the sand and went back to their weary horses. Young Kyros had a little trouble mounting.

Nicomedes raised an eyebrow and shook his head, but he pulled his helmet on over his carefully oiled locks and fell in where he was told. So did the others. Leucon handed his father the helmet he was holding and, brandishing his baton, joined Niceas in pushing the gentlemen of the city into their ranks. At the edge of the muster Kineas saw Cleomenes, Eumenes' father, take his helmet from a big blond slave – the gesture was an angry one.

Out on the sand, Ajax began to help Leucon and Niceas, and as fast as the city slaves lit the torches by the gates, the whole troop was assembled and mounted. There were almost a hundred of them.

Kineas looked at them and thought, Too few to have a chance of taking the city, but enough to think about it. Trouble indeed – and power. He rode to face them and raised his voice. 'I seem to remember appointing tomorrow as the day of exercise, but I thank every one of you who turned out this evening for your display of spirit. To the men who rode with me on the plains – well done, every one of you. Your fathers should be proud men. And despite all your pains, gentlemen, tomorrow is the day of exercise, and muster will be in the third hour after the sun rises. Dismissed!'

They sat still for a moment. Then someone gave a cheer and it was taken up. The moment passed, and the assembly began to disperse. Several fathers stopped to take his hand, and a dozen men congratulated him on his appointment. It seemed normal enough. He saw Cleomenes with his Gaulic slave and he rode over to tell the man where his son was.

Cleomenes had the heavy beard of the older generation. That and the darkness made it difficult to read his expression. 'You were gone longer than we expected,' he said carefully.

'All my fault. I was quite ill. Thanks to Apollo, none of the boys was struck by such an arrow. And the Sakje were very good to us.' Kineas raised his voice so that it would carry to the other fathers. He could see Petrocolus, Clio's father, at the edge of the torchlight. To him, Kineas said, 'Your son sends his greetings, and says they are at Gade's Farm. I took the liberty of placing the Sakje king there with his men.'

Petrocolus's relief was evident. 'Thanks for your words, Hipparch. I'll send a slave to make sure the bandits – that is, the Sakje – get a good reception.'

Cleomenes nodded up at him tersely. 'So you chose to leave *my* son with the barbarians. Very nice.' He unbuckled his breastplate and handed it to his blond slave, who stood impassively, apparently untroubled by the weight of the armour. Even in the flickering torchlight, Kineas could see that the man's face was lined with tattoos.

'Your son volunteered,' Kineas said, keeping his temper on a tight rein.

'Oh, of course,' Cleomenes replied. Diodorus was still by Kineas's shoulder, but Kineas rode away from him when he saw that there was a palace slave by the main gate of the hippodrome, flanked by two torchbearers. Kineas recognized him as the archon's Persian steward, Cyrus. He had intended to try to win Cleomenes over, but the man's face in the light looked closed and angry. Kineas shrugged and rode over toward Cyrus, despite the complaints from his thighs and knees.

'Cyrus, I greet you,' Kineas said.

'My master wishes to have you attend him,' Cyrus said. He did not raise his eyes.

Kineas was tired, and it was hard to see in the shifting light of the torches, but it appeared to him that all three slaves were afraid.

Kineas dismounted. 'Cyrus – tell the archon I will be with him directly. He must understand – I have been on the plains, and I rode at dawn this morning. I ask his leave to have a bath.'

Cyrus glanced up. 'You *will* come?'

Kineas raised an eyebrow. 'Of course I'll come. What foolishness is this?'

Cyrus stepped away from the other two slaves. 'There are rumours abroad – rumours that you intend ... to take the city.' His eyes flickered to the horsemen still milling about at the far end of the hippodrome, and rested on the one on the best horse, wearing the most expensive cloak. 'Or that Nicomedes intends it,' he said, meeting Kineas's eyes.

'You heard me dismiss them with your own ears,' Kineas said. What in all the Stygian flood is going on here? Kineas thought, but even as he did so, a great deal was slipping into place. In fact, it was just as he had feared it might be. The tyrant feared the hippeis. The tyrant feared *him*. That was the root of the thing.

He sighed for the wasted time and his own fatigue. 'I'll come immediately. Lest your master think I'm busy plotting.'

Cyrus gave him a long look. 'The archon prizes loyalty above all things, Hipparch. In your place, I would hurry. Or not come at all.' He turned quickly, leaving the scent of something spicy in the wake of the swirl of his cloak.

Kineas dismounted and handed his horse to Diodorus. 'I'll be back soon,' he said.

'Don't go,' Diodorus said. 'Or go in the morning with some witnesses. When the streets are full.' He looked around as if fearing to be overheard. 'Cleomenes voted against you in the assembly, and he thinks you left his son with the barbarians as a hostage as retribution.'

'I heard that in his voice,' Kineas replied. 'I swear by Zeus, the father of all the gods, the man is a fool!' Kineas stopped and cursed. He gave the stallion a slap on the rump. 'That bad?'

'Worse. Since the assembly met, the archon sees everyone as a plotter. Even Memnon.' Diodorus grabbed Kineas by the shoulder. 'I'm in earnest. Go in the morning. Even that perfumed Mede said as much, if you read his words the way I do.' Diodorus looked around, and said, 'Nicomedes has a slave – Leon. You've seen him?' Kineas nodded. 'Men attacked him. He says they were Kelts – perhaps from the archon's bodyguard. He escaped. Nicomedes has been pressing for action ever since.'

'Hades,' Kineas said. 'I'm not afraid of the archon, and there's too much going on right now for me to wait for morning. You don't know *my* news, and I haven't time to tell it all. Macedon is marching – and they are coming here. Antipater wants to control the grain – he wants Pantecapeum and Olbia. The king of the Sakje is outside the suburbs, waiting to negotiate with the archon. He won't wait long.'

Diodorus let go of Kineas's shoulder. 'The archon could kill you tonight, from pure fear.' He pulled his helmet off, rubbed his hair, and sighed. 'What a stew of crap.'

Kineas laughed. 'I don't think I'll die tonight.' He felt the weight of his cavalry breastplate on his shoulders. 'I want to go to bed. But I'm better off seeing him tonight.'

'Let me send one of the men.' Diodorus tucked his helmet under his arm. 'I'll come myself.'

Kineas shook his head. 'Thanks, but no. I don't want to spook him. I think I have his measure, now. I'm betting that a quick display of loyalty right now will go a long way. If I'm wrong, and some god moves his hand to strike me, take the company out the gates to the Sakje, winter over with them, and go south in the spring.'

Diodorus shook his head. 'I don't know why he fears you so. In his place it would be Memnon I'd watch.'

Kineas pulled his cloak around his shoulders. He'd given the clasp to Srayanka, and he hadn't replaced it. 'That reminds me. Send a boy to Memnon and tell him I'll speak to him in the morning.'

'You are set on this course.'

'I am.' Kineas took the other man's hand. 'Trust the gods.'

Diodorus shook his head. 'I don't.'

Then, ignoring his friend's protestations, Kineas walked off to the palace.

Kineas hurried. His confidence in his course of action, so high in the hippodrome, ebbed in the dark streets outside. Four streets from the palace, he wished he had a pair of torchbearers, or even a file of cavalry as escort. Twice he heard motion on rooftops, and a flash of bronze drew his eye in the alley that ran parallel to the main street.

He quickened his pace, hoping to catch sight of Cyrus and his torchbearers. He decided that his virtue would not be injured by running to catch the Persian. Even the main street was empty. There was not so much as a beggar under the eaves.

Speed, and his cavalry breastplate, saved his life. He saw, too late, the blur of motion at the alley corner by a closed wine shop. He planted a foot to turn and something hit him, hard, right in the side where the bronze was thickest over his belly.

There were at least two of them. One he'd seen – and the other who hit him.

He pushed through the attack, took another step, two, and threw himself against the sidewall of another wine shop. He had his arms free of his cloak and Srayanka's whip in his hand. He flicked it as the king had taught him – straight into the eyes of one of them.

The man gave a choked scream and fell back. But the other man bore straight in like a wrestler, determined to knock him off his feet and finish him.

Kineas sidestepped. It wasn't his first alley fight. He wanted room to shed his cloak and draw his sword. He knew he had room to his right, but he had to wonder if there were only two of them.

And then the time for thinking was past, and he was fighting for his life.

The first man landed a blow that rang his back plate like a gong. The man's fist caught his cloak, seeking to unbalance him or choke him, and the whole heavy garment came away – no cloak pin.

Kineas flipped the riding whip from his right to left hand, catching the whip by the tail, and drew his sword. He lunged towards the man in front of him, holding the Sakje whip by the fronds of horsehair rather than by the handle.

The handle snapped up and took the barbarian in the side of the head and he fell as if his head had been severed.

His mate leaped forward with a bellow, but he had to get around the falling body. The two collided.

Kineas stepped back again, clear of the collision, and flipped the whip in his hand. He slashed it across the other man's face. The fight was over, barring fresh attackers or the will of some god, and Kineas wanted the second man to run.

The second man didn't run. He was tall and heavily built, and his big hand held a heavy club – clearly the weapon that had struck Kineas in the first seconds of the fight – and he swung it.

It whistled in the air as Kineas retreated, his booted feet clumsy on refuse. Bad footing.

Kineas swung the whip at the man's hands – once, twice, three times in a rhythm that put the bigger man on the defensive and drove him back into the centre of the street as he tried to protect his hands.

Kineas let him gain a step. He still believed that the man would bolt as soon as he came to his senses.

The step gave the big man time to recover. With both hands on the haft of his club, he leaped to the attack, swinging the club faster than Kineas thought possible. Kineas scrambled, ducked, and slashed with both whip and sword, but he was parried. The lash landed twice, but the big man showed no effect.

His assailant was a skilled fighter, not a thug. Big, skilled, and brave.

Kineas was driven back by a flurry of blows he could neither parry nor fully avoid without retreat. Suddenly his back foot was stopped by the stucco of the wine shop and he had no place to move to the right due to the presence of a huge urn by the door.

The big man paused. He hadn't said a word, except to grunt when the lash went home. Both of them were breathing hard.

Kineas began to be afraid – not the normal fear of every warrior, but the fear that he might be outmatched. Might die, in the old vomit at the door to a wretched wine shop. His assailant was very skilled. Not a common hired killer.

He feinted movement towards the open ground to his left, and at the same time, feinted an underhand sword cut at the clubman's hands. The big man changed his guard, shifted, and Kineas gave him the whole lash of the whip across his face. The man screamed and swung his club, and Kineas tripped and fell in attempting to avoid the blow, and his head hit the shop front hard enough that he smelled blood in his nostrils. He pushed himself on his heels, rolled to avoid a second blow, and got his legs under himself despite the weight of the breastplate and the fog in his mind. He staggered.

The clubman wasn't blind, but he was in pain. He swung the club. The swing was wild, and lacked the full power of the man's arms, but it almost ended the fight, glancing off Kineas's left shoulder. Even so, the blow numbed his left arm and he dropped the whip.

Kineas moved in, despite his body's urge to run while the other man was hurt. He got in close, punched with his left hand against the big man's head and cut with his sword at the man's fingers, several of which fell in the street. The big man's blood steamed as it sprayed.

'Ungggh!' screamed the clubman, more in rage than fear – his first loud noise. With his one good hand, he brought his club down on Kineas's sword. It wasn't a heavy blow, but it knocked the weapon clear and left Kineas's hand numb.

Kineas was disarmed.

His enemy had trouble recovering the club.

Kineas threw himself on the bigger man. He got his arms around him and threw him, a simple wrestling move that his assailant didn't know, and then Kineas was atop his foe, kneeing him in the groin.

The man thrashed, trying to break his hold, and he bit into Kineas's arm, so that Kineas had to move his arm. He smashed his right fist into the man's face and his flailing left hand found the pliable fronds of his Sakje whip. Without conscious thought, he snapped it up and rammed the haft of the whip into his opponent's belly, kneed him again in the groin, grappled him close so that he could smell the garlic and the pork on the man's breath. The big man tried to squeeze him but the breastplate stopped him.

Even with the damage Kineas had just wreaked at close quarters, his assailant managed to break his remaining hold and started to struggle to his feet.

Kineas twisted, placed a leg behind the other man's thigh and levered him over. The bigger man was unprepared – or had never wrestled – the whole sequence surprised him again, and in three heartbeats he was face down in the icy mud with Kineas's foot on the back of his neck. Kineas was too afraid of the clubman to let him up. So he reversed the whip again and hit him, hard, on the head.

The giant lay still. His back rose and fell to show that he was alive. Kineas lifted his head by the hair and then let it down, so the man didn't drown in the mud – and so he knew the man was out.

He couldn't remember fighting hand to hand with an opponent so dangerous. 'Ares and Aphrodite,' he breathed. His lungs were eager for air, any air, and his throat felt like a narrow funnel through which molten bronze had to pass. He bent to retrieve his sword and felt light-headed. His whole body shook in reaction, and he sat down in the mud suddenly, his knees too weak to support him. But the mud was as cold as the Styx, and it got him to his feet again quickly.

He went back to the smaller man, counting himself lucky that he had landed so heavy a blow at the very outset – two men as well trained as the giant clubman would have had him down in seconds. He whispered a prayer of thanks to Athena and bent by the body. He turned aside to vomit as the reaction hit him again, and then he shook again.

It was all right. He was alive.

The smaller man was oiled like a wrestler – good olive oil. He was almost naked, despite the cold. Close up, he looked like a barbarian – close examination showed that he had yellow hair. The oil made it lank and dark.

The big man wasn't oiled, but he, too, had blond hair. The smaller man had tattoos on his face.

Kineas wanted them both alive, but the streets remained obstinately empty, and Kineas knew from experience that the sound of a fight late at night would drive any sober slave or decent citizen to shutter their windows. His limbs ached and his breastplate weighed more than the Atlas mountains.

He looked at his sword. It was badly bent where the club had hit it, and the iron was notched. He straightened it against the ground and felt the slight give in the weak point. The sword would break soon.

'Aphrodite and Ares,' he said again. Then he set his shoulders, gathered his cloak from the mud, and started for the palace.

Night or day, the gloom in the palace was the same, and the opulence. Memnon's men were on duty on the porch of the megaron, but inside at the door to the archon's sanctum were two of the archon's giants in their lion skins. They relieved him of his sword without a word spoken.

Looking at their blond hair and oiled skin, Kineas smiled grimly. Neither of them reacted in any way.

Two more stood flanking the man himself. Cyrus stood behind the archon, a tablet in his hand.

'I'm surprised you came,' said the archon. He looked Kineas up and down. 'You look a little the worse for wear.' He grinned at his own witticism.

'Cyrus told me you suspected me of plotting revolt.' Kineas didn't like the look of the two barbarians any more than he had the first time he had visited the archon. 'I'm not. I hope my presence here demonstrates as much, because we have more important matters to discuss.' He could smell the garbage, and more, on his sandals and feet. His tunic was foul with mud and the backs of his legs were worse. 'I was attacked on my way here.'

The archon held out a gold goblet, and a slave hurried to fill it. Otherwise, he didn't react, although Cyrus, behind him, gave a start. 'There is no matter more important than the obedience of my men. I ordered you out to the plains—'

'And I went.' Kineas was tired, in pain, and suffering the bleakness that the gods send to men after they fight. He was impatient with the tyrant's games.

'You returned without permission.' The archon was drunk. The words were slurred. It didn't shock Kineas – Alexander had ruled the world through a haze of wine, but he was never drunk in a crisis.

'What permission?' Kineas demanded. 'You sent me on a mission. I accomplished it. I have a report to make.'

'You also arranged to be appointed hipparch in your own absence. It makes me wonder who is ruling this city.' The archon sat up. 'You were a fool to come here alone.'

Kineas flicked a glance at the two big barbarians. Probably Kelts. Kineas had heard a great deal about the Kelts. He readied himself. 'Macedon is marching, and Antipater intends to take this city,' Kineas said.

The archon didn't seem to be listening. 'They could kill you right now.'

Kineas took this for an admission – not that he needed one. 'Their two comrades failed. And if these two try, and fail, I'll kill you.'

Kineas still had his Sakje whip – Srayanka's whip. His wrists trembled a little with fear and fatigue. All bluff, now. He didn't think he could muster the virtue for another fight. But his threat got through to the archon. His head snapped around, and for the first time, he seemed to give Kineas his full attention.

'You think you could best them?' Then more slowly, he said. 'Their comrades attacked you? Where?'

Kineas shrugged. 'In the street. Does it matter? Can we move from these threats to the war that is coming? I serve you and this city. I have come – despite the attack – to prove my words are true.'

The archon appeared moved – even shocked. 'You were attacked. And yet you came?' He looked at Cyrus.

Cyrus gave a small fraction of a nod.

The archon looked at him carefully. 'I appear to have been mistaken in my estimation of you,' he said. 'Tell me of this war. Apollo be my witness, these last days have been unkind enough. More bad news may send me mad.'

'Macedon is marching here. The king of the Sakje is waiting to speak to you of alliance. And Apollo and Athena be my witnesses, I am *not* plotting to take this city.'

Kineas felt the reaction from the fight. Just six days ago he had argued against war with Macedon. Something in his head had changed during the fight in the alley, or perhaps here in this room that choked him with riches and incense.

The archon held out his hand and Cyrus put another cup of wine in it. Then he looked up. 'Where is this bandit king?'

Kineas met the tyrant's eyes. 'Hard by the city ditch, at Gade's farm.'

The archon put forth his arm in a dramatic gesture of negation and shook his head. 'Why? Why is Macedon marching to take *my* city? I already paid a hefty bribe to send them elsewhere.' He looked up and met Kineas's eye. 'We can't fight Macedon.'

Kineas stood unmoving. Did he agree? He had already begun to plan his campaign on the endless grass. With tens of thousands of Sakje horsemen, one of whom had dark blue eyes … Suddenly he realized that his thoughts had been fully changed, as if by one of the gods. His pulse raced. It was like insanity. 'Talk to the king,' he said carefully.

'Do you know that the assembly used to meet at my whim and vote anything I asked?' The archon looked into his wine cup, and then at Kineas. 'They loved me, Kineas. I protected them from the bandits on the plains, and they grew rich in peace, and they loved me. Now they simmer to revolt – for what? That fop Nicomedes could no more protect them from the bandits than a whore in the agora. And *you*, with your talk of Macedon and war – what can some bandit from the grass tell me of Macedon?' he said. 'Perhaps it doesn't matter, anyway.' He sounded drunk, and maudlin, and tired. 'I've ridden this horse too long, I think, Athenian. I can no longer remember how to get their agreement.' He waved out the doors of the megaron at the city beyond, and laughed bitterly. 'Antipater can come and depose the assembly, perhaps. And set up a new tyrant. Nicomedes, perhaps.'

Kineas approached the ivory stool, words coming unbidden to his head as he saw both of his campaigns form in his thoughts; the one to defeat Antipater, and the other to push this tyrant to make a stand. He thought of Achilles on the beach, his rage at Agamemnon, and then his acceptance of the council of the Goddess, so that he spoke in honeyed words.

Because, like it or not, Athens had hired him from exile for this very task. They'd lied about it, of course. But it was clear to him – as clear as if Athena had just whispered it in his ear – that Licurgus and his party had sent him to Olbia to stop Antipater.

Aye. Honeyed words. They came to him as if on a whisper, and he used them. 'The threat of Macedon should serve to unite your city,' he said, and he saw on the archon's face that his arrow had struck home. 'And the king could be a better friend than you think, Archon. Peace on the plains, and more grain in our ships.'

The archon grunted. 'I doubt that my city will be saved by the bandits,' he said, but he had his chin in his hand and he was looking thoughtful. 'But as soon as it is known that Antipater is marching, this city will empty.'

'Not in winter, it won't,' Kineas said. 'and by spring, with a little effort, we can build an alliance and a force to stop Macedon on the plains of the Sakje.' Plans trembled at the edge of his thoughts, ready to tumble out in speech if he let them, but he held his tongue.

The archon shook his head. 'You're drunker than I am.' He drained his glass. 'Nothing can stop Macedon. No one should know that better than you. It is a pretty dream you spin, and I'll grant you that the threat of Macedon would bring the city to heel as if by magic, but – no. No, I'll send you to Antipater – overland – immediately. If you are loyal, you can buy me peace. You know these people. You can get them to listen.'

'I doubt it,' Kineas said. I hate them, he suddenly thought. All the slights of being a Greek in the army of Macedon – passed over for promotion, dismissed by Alexander. It was as if every scab had been ripped off every wound ever inflicted on him. *I hate them.*

'I will make you a rich man. They made you a citizen – you know that? And *elected* you hipparch. You've only been here a month! Of course, I thought you were having a shot at my diadem.' The archon held out his cup again. Cyrus hurried to get more wine. No other slave appeared. 'My father was a mercenary. I know just how the thing is done. You won't find me sleeping!' The archon bellowed the last, and sprung to his feet, glaring at Kineas.

Kineas ignored the tyrant's fears. 'No matter what you offer Macedon, they will march,' he said with a patience he didn't feel. 'Antipater needs money and he needs a war to keep the nobles from coming after him. He still fears Sparta. That leaves us. We look easy. And control of the Euxine will strengthen Antipater's hold on Athens – on the whole of Greece.'

The archon rubbed his face with both hands like a mime removing face paint. 'Athens – aye, Athens, from which you are supposedly an exile. Athens, which probably sent you here. To replace me? I've always been loyal to Athens.'

Kineas paused like a man crossing a swamp, who suddenly finds the going treacherous. 'I swear by Zeus I am not here to replace you!'

The archon ignored him. 'I'll offer to become the client of Macedon – to rule in their name. Pay taxes – the same contribution Athens levied. More.'

Kineas looked at him with disgust. 'Archon, Macedon can have all that if they come and take the city. And my sources say that Antipater *wants* a war. Are you listening to me?'

The archon tossed his wine cup on the floor, and the gold rang as it hit the stone. 'I'm fucked,' he said. 'No one defeats Macedon.'

It sounded craven to Kineas, even though it was the very same argument he had used to the king. Coming from the mouth of the archon, the drunk and despondent, murderous archon, it disgusted him.

In that hour, he had become a convert. Srayanka wanted war with Macedon. The archon feared it. He wondered what god had whispered in his ear, seized his tongue. He had become an advocate of the war.

'Talk to the king,' he said. 'He knows much.'

'Bloody brigand,' said the archon. But his tone had changed. 'When?'

'Tomorrow. The king has to ride for the high plains before the snow comes in earnest. But he wants an alliance, and he has much to offer.'

The archon sat up. 'I'm drunk.' He rose. 'I was right about you – you are a dangerous man.' He settled the diadem more exactly on his head. 'What do you want, anyway? Money? Power? Restoration to Athens?' He gave Kineas a look. If the effect was supposed to be menacing, his drunken stagger and the skewed diadem on his brow ruined it. 'Is this Athens' doing, horse master?' And then he slumped a little. 'Never mind. Whatever you want, you'll grab at in time. You're that kind. Right now, you don't seem to want my little crown.' He smiled. 'I still do. And I suppose your barbarian bandit is my best chance to keep it. I'll see him. Bring him in the morning.'

Kineas felt bold. 'You promise his life is safe?'

The archon raised an eyebrow, looking like an old satyr eyeing a young maiden in the theatre. 'You think I threaten his life?' He passed Kineas on his way to his own chamber. 'Or yours?' His voice trailed back into the throne room. 'You have a lot to learn about my city, Athenian.'

11

There were bruises on his ribs in the morning, and a long red welt on his left leg where skin had been ripped away, and the joints in his fingers were swollen and prickly. He couldn't remember how some of the injuries had happened.

Sitalkes tended them with oil and herbs and got him dressed and armoured while Philokles and Diodorus argued.

'We're not leaving,' he said. 'Get it through your heads. He's a tyrant. Tyrants fear every man's hand. I lived. Let's move on.'

'He'll kill you. He'll kill us.' Diodorus stood with his hands on his hips. 'Macedon is coming, and we can't trust our employer. Get us out.'

Philokles shook his head. 'He'll trust Kineas now.'

Diodorus raised his hands in frustration, as if invoking the gods. 'He doesn't trust anyone. He's a tyrant! And it doesn't matter, because *we can't trust him*. Get us out!'

Kineas got to his feet slowly, and took the weight of his armour on his shoulders. The shoulder straps were resting on last night's bruises. 'The king of the Assagatje is waiting at Gade's farm. Two hundred gentlemen of the city will be mustering in an hour. A hint of any of this will be like sparks on tinder. Let me be clear. We are staying. We are going to prepare this city to fight. If you can't stomach it, you have my leave to depart.'

Diodorus let his hands fall by his sides. 'You know I won't leave you,' he said. He sounded as tired as Kineas felt. He took a deep breath, and said, 'Kineas, can you tell me why? Why you are hazarding our lives to fight Macedon?'

Philokles stood very still. Quietly, he said, 'That is the question, isn't it? A few days ago, you told the king that we should *not* fight. What changed your mind?'

Kineas picked his Sakje whip off the oak table and rubbed his thumb across the gold decoration. 'Last night, while I argued with the archon, it came to me, as if a god had spoken in my ear. Friends, I cannot explain better than that. In one moment, my mind was set. It is not so much a matter for rational argument as a – a revelation.' He tucked the whip into the sash he wore over his breastplate. 'My mind is clear. I intend to do this thing.'

Diodorus sighed. 'The men will not be happy.'

Kineas nodded. 'Any who wish to leave will be allowed to go.'

Diodorus shook his head. 'None of them will leave. But they will not be happy.'

Kineas nodded again. 'That is in the hands of the gods. For now, we have a great deal of work to do. Philokles, you will take Sitalkes and ride to the king, telling him we will attend him with all of the gentlemen of the city in the second hour after noon. Diodorus, the rest of us shall spend the morning throwing javelins and practising the cavalry at riding in formation. After noon, we will ride in a column out to the king and fetch him to the archon in style.'

Philokles said, 'Someone had best warn the archon. And don't forget that you were to speak with Memnon.'

'Send Crax to the palace and ask Cyrus the steward if the archon will be available at the second hour after noon. Send a slave to Memnon to ask him if he can attend me here. Explain the need.'

Diodorus saluted. 'Yes, Hipparch.' He smiled.

Kineas smiled back. 'Despite everything, I like the sound of that.'

The muster started well. There were more men missing – making their last trading trips of the year, or home sick, or making excuses. On the other hand, there were far more men mounted and armed. Niceas, Ajax and Leucon had them in their ranks in a few minutes. The rolls were called and the absent noted.

Kineas rode to the head of the troop. There were almost two hundred men mounted. They filled the east side of the hippodrome in four sloppy ranks. Horses moved back and forth, or shifted, and in the second rank, a stallion nipped a mare.

'Welcome, gentlemen of Olbia!' Kineas called across the turmoil. He sat straight, trying to ignore the fatigue of the last day's ride, the scars of the fight by the wine shop. 'I thank you for the honour you have done me in granting me this office, and further in making me a citizen of this city. I will not waste further words when none can express my feelings.' He looked back and forth under his helmet. 'This morning we will have our first drill. Every man will present himself, his horse, and his armour to my hyperetes, Niceas, who will advise you on how to better them. As soon as a man passes Niceas, he will join Diodorus in practising the throwing of javelins, and from there pass to Ajax, who will instruct on remounting in combat. At noon, we will take some bread and oil while we hold our mounts, like cavalrymen should. Then we will practise various formations. This afternoon, the full troop of the city will do its first duty in many years – we will ride to escort the king of the Sakje.' A buzz of talk from the ranks. 'Silence, please, gentlemen. During the whole of a muster, you are no longer free to chatter. Do the citizens who serve on foot chatter in the phalanx? No. They listen for orders. So you must. Any questions?'

A plaintive voice from the fourth ranks called, 'I have an appointment to buy linen seed in the afternoon.'

Kineas smiled under the cold cheek pieces of his helmet. 'You will miss it.'

'I didn't bring food,' said another.

'When I dismiss you, you may send your slaves for food. Next time you will know better – a muster is for the whole day.'

'Are we all to have blue cloaks?' asked another.

'Niceas will inform you. Anything else?' He looked at them.

They sat on their horses in silence. As a group, they were better disciplined than their Athenian counterparts, but they looked like what they were – rich men playing soldiers. Kineas sighed.

'Hippeis!' He called. He glanced around. Niceas, Ajax and Leucon were all together by the stadium seats, with horses hard by and equipment laid out on blankets as examples. Diodorus and the two Gauls had paced out a run for javelin practice, and Antigonus was propping a heavy shield against a pair of spears as a target. As ready as they were likely to be. 'Dismissed to your posts!' he said.

The whole mass surged into motion. A quarter of them rode straight to him with complaints, demands and suggestions.

He'd expected as much. They weren't soldiers – they were rich men, and Greeks.

Kineas knew how to make short work of them. Lykeles helped him – another veteran of the Athenian hippeis musters. Lykeles rode among them, hearing their complaints and dealing with the easiest himself. Kineas was patient but firm with the rest. Half an hour sufficed to see every one of them off to one of the stations.

Against the tiered seats, Niceas could be heard urging the purchase of cornell-wood javelins. He had done his research, and already knew which merchants in the town could get the wood from Persia and which smiths made the best heads. He and Leucon, ably supported by Coenus, reviewed the quality and training of the men's horses.

Coenus walked across the sand to Kineas and waited to speak. When Kineas glanced at him, he said, 'We have a horse problem.'

Kineas grunted and pushed his helmet back on his head. 'Mares and stallions?'

Coenus nodded. 'Horses are cheap here. We should have a standard sex. Otherwise, when the mares come into season, we'll have chaos.'

Kineas tugged at his beard. 'What would Xenophon say?'

Coenus smiled. 'Geldings.'

Kineas felt as if he had to sleep or die. He leaned down. 'Geldings it is, then. Exempt the hyperetes and the officers.' Having said so, he rode off to watch the first group of riders tackle the javelin throwing. They were all the young men who had ridden to the Sakje, and they made a creditable showing. Watching them gave him an idea – that he should form troops of fifty within the hippeis. All of the best men would just make one company of fifty.

Kyros galloped down the sand, his bay horse stretching to the task, hooves flashing. His throw was hard and true, and the shield fell with a crack like thunder.

'That boy throws like the hand of Zeus,' Philokles said at Kineas's shoulder. 'The king sends his regards. He will be waiting for you at the second hour.'

The boys were competent, but the rest of them were not.

Nicomedes set the standard by falling during his first remount and missing the shield every time he rode by it. He affected an air of humorous disdain, but he hid his irritation poorly. Kineas guessed he was unused to failing at anything.

Like every other gentleman on the sand.

Ajax rode up alongside the city's fashion leader and twirled a javelin in his fist. He shouted – Kineas couldn't hear the words, but it was a tease – and rode at the target, scattering slaves who had intended to help their master. Nicomedes cursed, pulled himself up with a fist in his horse's mane, and followed, and Ajax threw true. Nicomedes' throw was wide by a hand's breadth. His curses flowed across the arena.

'The old men ride like sacks of goat shit and the middle-aged men are so afraid to get themselves dirty they remind me of fucking priestesses,' said Niceas. 'And that's *before* we try riding in formations.'

Kineas tried not to smile. 'The boys aren't bad. I want to put all the best men in one company of fifty. Make me a list. Let it be known, so that men will struggle to be in that company.'

'Think of that yourself, did you?' Niceas said with a hard smile. The six Athenian companies of horse were rivals in every kind of procession and game. He pointed with his chin at Eumenes' father, Cleomenes, who sat quietly with a group of his friends. They were not participating. 'Not quite mutiny,' he said. 'But he's half the problem.'

'I'll see to it,' Kineas answered, turning his horse.

An older man threw a leg over his horse and fell straight off the far side. 'You intend to fight Macedon with this lot?' Niceas asked.

'You too?'

'Me first. I'm told that the gods themselves have told you to fight Macedon. Did they send you that whip, too?' Niceas pointed at the heavy whip in Kineas's sash. 'A troop of companions would scatter these like dandruff at the first charge. Leave 'em for the peltasts to clean up. Half of them will fall off and stay down until their throats are slit. Tell me if I lie.'

Kineas wheeled his horse. 'Sounds like you have a lot of work to do, then.'

Niceas's ferret face wrinkled in a rueful smile. 'That's what I knew you'd say.'

Kineas rode over to where Cleomenes and his twenty friends and allies sat. 'Which station would you prefer to go to first, sir?' he asked.

Cleomenes ignored him. One of his friends laughed. 'We're gentlemen, not soldiers. Don't include us in this farce.'

Kineas looked at the man who had spoken. 'You lack a breast-plate. Your horse is too small. Please report to my hyperetes.'

The man shrugged. 'And if I say no?' he said.

Kineas didn't raise his voice. 'I might fine you,' he said. 'I might report you to the archon.'

The man grinned, as if that was not a threat he feared.

'I might beat you to a bloody pulp right here on the sand,' Kineas added. 'Any of the three are within my legal right as hipparch.'

The man flinched.

Kineas turned to Cleomenes. 'I am a gentleman of Athens,' he said. 'I hold no grudge that you voted against me as a citizen and again as hipparch. That is how democracy functions. But if you fail to do your duty, we will very soon come to a test that cannot benefit anyone.'

Cleomenes never met his eye. He was looking at someone else – probably Nicomedes, his principal rival in the city. 'Very well,' he said tersely. 'I feel a sudden need to throw a javelin.'

It was a curiously empty victory. Cleomenes walked over to the butts, mounted his horse, and threw – competently – and then sat down again.

Kineas tried a different tack. He waved at Coenus to join him, and indicated Cleomenes. 'There sits one of the city's principal gentlemen. He dislikes me. He's behaving like an arrogant fool and I can't figure him out. Befriend him.'

Coenus chuckled. 'As one arrogant fool to another, you mean?'

'Something like that,' Kineas agreed.

The close order drill was terrible. The first attempt to form the rhomboid formation that Kineas preferred was hampered by the size of the hippodrome and the numbers involved, but it would have been horrible nonetheless. It took them half an hour to get every man to see his place in the formation, and they couldn't ride ten strides without becoming a mob.

Kineas sighed and gave it up. Instead, he formed them into a column of fours and rode them in circles until most of them learned to keep their intervals – a full hour.

He was hoarse from shouting. All the professionals were hoarse, and so were some of the boys who had ridden the plains. He shook his head and rode over to Cleitus. 'I'm losing my voice. Would you order them to disperse and take their lunch?'

'With pleasure,' Cleitus said. And when he had fetched his own bread, he returned and said, 'I knew you were the right man for the job. Look at them!'

Kineas took some sausage from Sitalkes. 'Why? They look like dog shit.'

Cleitus frowned. 'No, they don't. They look like they are trying. If they stop trying, we lose. So far, we're winning. Get them through three of these, and they'll feel the difference. Could set quite a fashion. Can I have some of that sausage? The garlic is making my stomach rumble.'

Kineas handed over a chunk of sausage. Cleitus cut off a piece with a knife and tossed it to his son, who was eating with Ajax and Kyros. They were sitting on their horses to eat, like Sakje. In fact, all the young men who had gone with Kineas were sitting mounted to eat.

Cleitus offered a skin of wine to Kineas. 'Rotten stuff. Perfect for soldiers. So – we're fighting Macedon?'

'News travels around here.' Kineas took a pull at the wineskin. They were going to be late fetching the king.

'Is it different in Athens? The way I heard it, you killed a squad of murderous Persian assassins – or perhaps they were Kelts – and then thrashed the archon with your big whip and told him to behave, and then your eyes rolled back in your head and you prophesied that we would defeat Antipater.' Cleitus's light tone didn't cover the anxiety on his face.

Kineas handed back the wineskin. 'That's pretty much how it was,' he said.

'My first rhetoric tutor told me that my facetious ways would get me in trouble, and look, he was right. Kineas, I proposed you for citizenship. My friends made you hipparch. Don't get us all killed.' Cleitus grimaced and took more sausage.

Kineas pulled off his helmet and scratched his head vigorously. Then he met Cleitus's eye. 'I don't have a place to invite gentlemen to dinner. Will you host for me? I'll explain to your guests why I think we have to fight, and what they stand to lose if we don't.'

Cleitus grunted. 'I was hoping you'd just say the rumour was wrong,' he said.

'Macedon is coming here,' Kineas said.

The king was waiting. He and his men sat like gold-armoured centaurs. The column of city cavalry rode up and halted, more like a mob than Kineas liked, and Petrocolus and Cleomenes rushing to embrace their sons ruined any pretence to military discipline.

The Sakje didn't seem to mind. The king pushed through the throng of Greek horsemen to reach Kineas. 'You're late!' he said, smiling.

'I offer profound apology, O King. The archon awaits us.' Kineas motioned with his whip at Niceas, who raised his voice, and the city troop began to reform.

Satrax shook his head. 'I'm teasing you. What is time to us? But it seems to mean so much to you Greeks – the second hour after noon!' The young king laughed. 'Try getting the Sakje to assemble within a single moon!'

'Yet you would fight Macedon,' Kineas said.

'Oh, it's easier to assemble them for war,' Satrax said. He narrowed his eyes. 'You've changed your mind. I can see it on your face.'

'I have, too,' Kineas said. He shrugged. 'The gods spoke to me.'

The king shrugged. 'Kam Baqca assured me that this would happen. I am not surprised she is right. She is nearly always right.'

Kineas watched both hyperetes pushing the column into some form of order. He had a few minutes. 'I have spoken to the archon.' Satrax nodded. 'I think he will support the war,' Kineas said. 'At least, for now.'

'This, too, is as Kam Baqca said it would be.' The king smiled, showing his even teeth and the full lips that hid under his moustache and beard. 'So – I will lead my clans to war against Macedon.' He didn't sound excited. More resigned.

Kineas nodded. The day's muster had taken the eagerness out of him. He was going to lead these enthusiastic amateurs against the veterans of fifty years of war. 'Gods send us victory,' he said.

'The gods send victories to those who earn them,' said the king.

Kineas attended the meeting between the archon and the king on the porch of the temple of Apollo, but he didn't speak. The archon was a different man – direct, sober, blunt – a commander of men. He changed faster than an actor who took multiple roles in the theatre. Kineas had seen it done in *Oedipus* – the king was also the messenger. In Olbia, the drunken tyrant could also be the philosopher king.

Cyrus stood at his right hand and wrote the terms of the treaty. The king and the archon drafted it in an hour and clasped hands, each swearing by Apollo and by their own gods to support the other in war, should Macedon march in the spring. They did not pledge eternal friendship. The king did not agree that Olbians were free to travel the plains without hindrance, but he did agree to forbear taxing them for as long as the treaty was in effect.

After they clasped hands, the archon mounted a horse and escorted the king to the walls of the city, and the two men chatted as they rode. Kineas, directly behind the archon, heard more silence than chatter. In the arch of the gate, the archon drew rein.

'We will need to meet in the spring to discuss strategy,' he said.

The king looked out over the city's fields and nodded. 'I will need time – and space – to muster my people.'

The archon was an excellent rider. Kineas hadn't had an opportunity to note it before. He surprised Kineas by backing his horse a few steps and catching Kineas's bridle. 'My hipparch pressed me to make this war, O King. So I'll send him to you in the spring.'

Satrax nodded. 'I will look forward to that,' he said.

The archon nodded. 'I thought you might. We'll know for sure about what Antipater plans when the Athenian grain fleet comes in the spring.'

The king's horse was restive. He calmed it with a hand on its neck and some words in Sakje, and then he reached for Kineas's hand. 'In the spring, when the ground sets hard and the grass is green, I will send you an escort.'

The streets were crowded, and the gate was almost surrounded by the people of the town and the suburb. The king waved in farewell, and then he made his horse rear and leap, so that it almost seemed that the two would gallop across the sky, instead of merely riding along the road.

At his side, the archon said, 'You enjoyed your time among these barbarians?'

And Kineas, who could dissemble when need required, said, 'I befriended one of their war leaders. I had this whip as a guest gift.'

The archon nodded slowly. 'Your friendship with these bandits may be more of a boon than I thought, Athenian. They like you.' He nodded again. 'Their king is not a simple man. He has education.' He gave a nasty grin. 'He is young and arrogant.'

'He was a hostage in Pantecapaeum,' Kineas said.

'Why did I never meet him?' the archon asked. He shrugged. 'Or perhaps I did. They breed like maggots. And their women are so unchaste – hard to know which little bastard is the get of which sire. Still, they'll make good fodder if we must fight this war.' Kineas stiffened but said nothing. 'Which I will now work like a slave to prevent.' The archon turned his horse. 'Back to the palace!'

Cleitus gave a dinner in his honour on the night when Athens honoured her dead and her heroes, and he drank too deep of too much wine. He drank too much wine because he was called to speak in public. At Cleitus's urging, and with help from Diodorus and Philokles, he prepared an oration, and after dinner, when urged by Cleitus and all the guests, he rose from his couch and went to the centre of the room like the politicians who had attended his father's dinners in Athens. He had never thought to use such tactics himself, and his hands shook so that he had to thrust them into his tunic.

'Gentlemen of Olbia,' he began formally. But that wasn't the tone he wanted at all, especially with the quaver in his voice and he smiled, shrugged, rubbed his beard. 'Friends and sponsors.' Better. 'It has been said – indeed, it's being said right now, somewhere not far from here – that having been sponsored as a citizen and then raised to hipparch, I have repaid your kindness by plunging you into desperate war.'

They looked interested, but no more. The younger men – Eumenes, for instance – had no idea what a war would mean. They were excited by it. The older men had the means to board their ships and vanish around the coast, to Heraclea or Tomis or even to Athens.

Kineas took a deep breath. 'The war is none of our making. Alexander – the boy king who I served – is now a man. More than a man, he has declared himself a god. He marches to conquer, not just the Medes, but the whole world.' Kineas spread his arms like an actor. Funny how these things came back to you. Kineas hadn't practised rhetoric in ten years, at least.

'But,' he continued, 'one of the ways we can tell that Alexander is not so much of a god as he would like to be, is that his wars still require men, and money. The gods, I think, could conquer the world with their own power. Alexander does it with the treasury of Persopolis and the manpower of the whole Greek world. And this hunger for treasure to fight his wars has cost Macedon dearly. None of the gold of Persopolis went home. None of the spoil of Babylon waits in chests of cedar in Phillip's treasury. Olympia does not bathe in the pearls of the Nile. Alexander burns gold as other men burn wood.' He took watered wine from a servant and sipped. 'Antipater needs money. He needs to put his boot on the necks of the cities of Attica and the Peloponnese. He needs our grain and our gold, and he needs a war to toughen his levies before he sends them to his master, the god.'

He paused a moment to let that sink in. Then he began to pace around the circle of couches, speaking directly to them, first one and then another. 'This will not be a simple war between cities, where hoplites clash and the winner dictates the terms to the loser or burns his fields. If Antipater takes this city, he will keep it. He will appoint a satrap to rule – one of his own men from Macedon.' Kineas said the last directly to Nicomedes. It was done as if by chance, and Nicomedes' smooth face didn't betray whether the shot went home or not.

'There will be a garrison of Macedonians and heavy taxes. No assembly, and no men of property. You might ask me how I know all this, and I will say that I know because I watched it done from Granicus to the Nile. You think the archon is a tyrant?' Kineas looked around at the little starts – that had them awake. 'The archon is the purest democrat next to a garrison of Macedon. You think that Antipater might benefit the city? Or perhaps that you can slip away and return in a few years when the business opportunities are better?' Kineas stopped again and pointed at Lykeles. 'Lykeles was a gentleman of Thebes. Ask him what the occupation of Macedon meant.'

They were restless, fidgeting on their couches, the older ones refusing to meet his eye. Like most rich men, they heard him, but they doubted that his words would apply – they'd find a way to bribe their way free, they were sure. But again, his argument hit home – every man present knew that Thebes had been utterly destroyed, the walls cast down, most of the citizens sold into slavery for attacking their Macedonian garrison. And that was Thebes, a pillar of the Greek world, the city of Oedipus and Epaminondas.

Kineas sipped more wine. 'I will not tell you that we can defeat the might of Macedon. If Alexander came here, with seven taxeis of his veterans and four regiments of companions, with all this Thessalian horse and all his psiloi and his peltasts and the guard – then I would say that, despite our alliances and our own strength, we would be broken in an hour.

'But it is *not* Alexander who marches. It will probably not even be Antipater – no mean general, let me tell you. It will be one of the junior generals who stayed home from the Persian wars, and are now eager for fame – eager to make a name on a march to the sea. That general will have two taxeis of Macedonians, and one of those will be raw. He will have one regiment of companions – every troublemaker that Antipater wants out of the country. He will have Thracians, Getae and Bastarnae. And that army, gentlemen, we can defeat. Or, even if we fail to defeat it, we can keep it on the plains so long that it will have no time to lay siege to this city.'

They lay quietly on their couches, listening and drinking wine. He made it clear that he was finished by sitting on his couch. He felt empty. He felt like a schoolboy who had given a speech and forgotten some part of it. He shrugged – oh, the birching that gesture would have gotten him from his rhetoric tutor. 'That is the way I see it,' he said, and felt the poverty of his summation.

Cleomenes rose in turn. He lay by himself – he had brought his son, but Eumenes had gone off to share the couch of Kyros. Most of the other men present either ignored him or fawned on him. Unlike Nicomedes and Cleitus, who were bitter rivals in trade and politics but appeared to enjoy each other's company, Cleomenes was aloof, as if he didn't want to be caught associating with his rivals.

'The hipparch speaks well – for a mercenary.' He looked around the room with patrician disdain. 'Just as well might I visit another man's city and tell him how he can, with enormous risk, win through to a little gain. But despite the fact that you, Cleitus, and you, Nicomedes, conspired to give this man the vote, I say he is a foreigner, a man with little stake in our city – surely not the same stake as I have. Why would a man of my accomplishments wish to provoke a war with Macedon? Our mercenary thinks so highly of his profession that he desires for us all to take part in it. I say that it is the business of his sort to make war. I have neither skill nor appetite for it. Men of property have no need to do such things. When I need them done, I can hire – a mercenary.' He looked around. 'You are a pack of fools if you think that your little squadron of horse will last a minute against the force of Macedon. Men like you have no business fighting – your business is business. Achilles was a fool, and Odysseus not much better. Grow up. Accept the coming changes. Let this city grow and prosper as it is meant to, regardless of who claims to rule it. And leave fighting to mercenaries.'

He gave Kineas half a smile. 'Although when I hire one, I'll try to find one with less arrogance, less pretension, and superior skill at fighting – not a wine-sack blow-hard who was dismissed by Alexander.'

He sat down, and the room erupted. Men were watching Kineas. He was acutely aware of how deeply Cleomenes' speech had cut him – both in his own pride and in the eyes of some of his most prominent supporters.

But despite the instant rise of rage in his heart, and the double grip of fear and anger in his gut, Kineas was a veteran of many years of Athenian politics – in his father's house, and in the hippeis. He refilled his cup, spilled a libation with a prayer to Athena, and rose again, outwardly calm – inwardly both enraged, and hurt, even saddened. His stomach seemed to rise to fill his throat. In some ways, it was worse than a fight – in a fight, the daemon came to hold you up, to stiffen your sinews, but in debate, a man who was a friend, or at least sometimes an ally, suddenly turned on you and spoke insults.

Face to face. Like battle.

Kineas took a breath to steady himself. 'I'm sure Cleomenes speaks with the best of intentions,' he said. His mild sarcasm, so at odds with what the room expected from him, silenced the babble. 'Cleomenes, am I the wine-sack blow-hard to whom you refer?'

Cleomenes glared at him like Medusa, but Kineas pinned him with his own gaze.

'Come, we're all friends here – you must have had someone in mind.' Kineas's raillery was still light.

Cleomenes wasn't fooled. He wriggled on his couch like a bug on a pin.

Kineas raised an eyebrow. 'So, you don't mean me?' He took a step forward, and Cleomenes wriggled again. 'Perhaps you mean Memnon? Or perhaps Licurgus? Perhaps my friend Diodorus? Or perhaps young Ajax, Isokles son of Tomis – is that who you mean?'

Kineas took another step towards the man. He had the feeling that Cleomenes would make a bad enemy – but that enmity was already there. He was not going to win the man to his side – so he had to be defeated. 'Except none of them served Alexander. Only I.' He stepped closer. 'Or were you speaking generally, of wine-sacks and blow-hards you've known in your wide experience of the world?'

Cleomenes leaned back. 'You know who I meant!' he said, his face red.

Kineas shrugged. 'I'm a poor mercenary, slow of intellect. Tell me.'

Cleomenes spat, 'Figure it out.'

Kineas spread his hands. 'I am a simple soldier. I admire those men to whom you referred – Achilles and Odysseus. They may not have been good men of business – but they were not afraid to speak their minds.'

Cleomenes rolled off his couch, his face purple. 'Damn you, you insolent—'

Cleitus rushed to intervene – both men had their hands balled into fists. 'Gentlemen – I think we have left reasoned debate and good feeling at the bottom of the last wine bowl. This is mere argument – there is bad feeling. Cleomenes did not mean the insult he implied, I'm sure – and neither would Kineas mean to call Cleomenes a coward, would you, Kineas?'

Kineas nodded – and let his next words drawl out with all the Athenian arrogance he could muster – which was considerable. 'I didn't say that Cleomenes was a coward,' he said with a mocking smile. 'Indeed, I spoke generally, about the long-haired Argives who fought for Helen on the windy plains of Illios.'

Several guests applauded. Kineas's rhetorical tricks had the elegance of an Athenian gentleman's education. Cleomenes looked rude by comparison, and he'd lost his temper entirely. Without another word, he picked up a scroll bag he had brought and walked to the door. 'You will all rue the day you brought this man into our city,' he said, and left.

Despite the lazy smile pasted to his face, Kineas felt weak at the knees, as if he had fought a combat. He felt as if he needed more wine. When he reached the couch he shared with Philokles, the Spartan smiled at him. Other men asked a few questions, but most chose to change the subject. He drank a great deal, Cleomenes' insults still rankling, and went to bed drunk.

The tree was bigger than the world, and its trunk was like a city wall rising from a rocky plain. The lowest branches hung to the ground. It was a cedar – no, it was a black pine from the mountains of Attica.

Closer, it seemed that it was not one tree, but all trees. And the fallen leaves and needles littered the ground, so that every step he took, he sank to his ankles, and when he looked down to watch his footing, he saw that the leaves were mixed with bones. And under the leaves and bones were corpses – strange that the bones lay over the corpses, he thought, with the clarity of dream thought.

He felt strangely in control of his dream, and he made his body turn and look away from the tree, but there was nothing to see except the branches hanging to the ground, and the near dark beyond the tree, and the leaves and bones, and all the dead.

He turned back and set his hand against the trunk, and it was warm and smooth like the back of Srayanka's hands, and he ...

Awoke. Troubled because of the dream's clarity and because it was alien. While he dreamed the tree, he was another man. A man who didn't think like a Hellene. And that was terrifying.

He covered his terror in work, training the hippeis, which he did despite the first serious winter storm. The sailing season closed. The threat of Antipater became known throughout the city. No one could flee, so rich and poor alike settled in for months of cold, telling each other that there would be time to flee in the spring if Antipater really did come.

In the next week, Memnon called a muster of the city's hoplites. It was the first muster held in four years. The archon had restricted such musters because he feared the power of the hoplites all together and under arms as much as he feared everything else, but Memnon insisted and he had his way.

The city hoplites looked better than the cavalry. They wore more armour than their compatriots in Athens or Sparta. The thirty years' war in Attica and the Peloponnese had taught Greeks to wear less armour and move faster, but the hoplite class of the Euxine had missed those bloody wars and they came to muster in the bronze cuirass, greaves, and heavy helmets of their fathers.

They mustered in the open fields north of the suburbs and trampled the snow and the grain stubble for three hours. Despite the four-year hiatus and the presence of a new generation who had never been trained, they looked competent. They had three hundred mercenaries to provide file-closers, and they had seasoned men in their ranks who had served in the war with Heraclea.

Kineas watched them drill with Cleitus and half a dozen city gentlemen. He was unstinting in his praise, whether to his own men or to Memnon and the city officers when they approached at the end of the drill.

Memnon stopped and leaned on his spear. He had been charging about the field, black cloak flapping behind him, correcting faults and praising virtue, and now he panted like a dog. 'I've got to get them out of all that armour,' he said. He pointed to a group of young men at drill. 'They keep all the old traditions here – the youngest, best fighters make a select company to cover the flank. I'll try to keep them from wearing it.'

Kineas watched the older men standing in glittering ranks. 'Depends on what we think they're for,' he said.

Nicomedes stopped flirting with Ajax and pushed his horse forward. 'Surely we all know what hoplites are for,' he said. 'I used to serve as one myself, you may recall. Before the hipparch forced me to serve on horseback.'

Kineas smiled. 'I gave you the excuse to buy that beautiful blue cloak and that exciting breastplate,' he said. Then he turned back to Memnon. 'For dash – or to chase down Thracians – our light-armed hoplites are the thing. But here on the plain ...' Here Kineas raised his head to gaze across the snow. He didn't even know exactly where she was, but she was somewhere out in the endless white. He caught himself. 'Here it is cavalry country. Armour makes a man braver, and steadies him, and keeps him safe from the javelins and bows.'

Memnon rubbed his jaw, which was as black as his cloak. 'By Zeus, Hipparch, let us never have to face the bandits out in open country. I stood against the boy king at Issus, when his horse came against us. If they'd had bows, none of us would have escaped.'

'Armour might stop the first push of a Macedonian taxeis,' Kineas said.

Memnon curled his lip. 'Keep my flanks secure, and I'll stop them dead. These lads may hate the archon like fire hates water – many of them hate me, I dare say, and they'll hate me worse before spring. But they're good lads, and every man and boy has done his years in the gymnasium and in the field – real hoplites. Not so many of those left in Greece – most left their bones at Chaeronea. I hear you boned Cleomenes up the arse.'

Nicomedes snorted aloud. Cleitus looked away, embarrassed.

Memnon winked. 'Cleomenes is one of the many men in this city who think they would make a good archon.' He glared at Nicomedes. 'But he's more of a boil on the arse than his rivals, and no mistake.' Memnon nodded to Kineas. 'If you survive the winter, you'll know 'em like I do. How'd you arrange for the assembly to make you a citizen? And hipparch?'

Kineas shook his head. 'Cleitus did it. I was as surprised as any.'

'The endless advantages of birth,' Memnon spat. His face was unreadable behind the shape of his helmet. 'Antipater is really marching here in the spring?'

Kineas nodded. 'Yes, it is true.'

'This isn't some trick of the archon's to keep us all biddable for another season? This is real? And you will fight him?' Most of the hoplites were watching them.

'Yes,' Kineas said.

'Why? You were one of the boy king's men.' Memnon took Kineas by the hand. His hand was hard as iron, and it held Kineas's tight, as if to read him for truth.

'I think a god told me to fight.' *Or a woman. Perhaps the gods spoke through her. Or Athena. Or all together.* Kineas knew he had to fight Macedon as clearly as he had ever known anything in his life. Such revelations were divine.

Memnon relinquished his hand. 'I do not honour the gods as much as I should,' he said. 'But I would like to fight Macedon again.' He turned on his heel and walked away across the last blades of autumn grass where it waved above the snow.

PART III

THE TASTE OF BRONZE

'... but come, he shall taste the bronze at the point of our spears ...'

Iliad, Book 21

12

The sun shone on the first blades of spring grass that waved in the north wind, so that they rocked back and forth like a thousand beckoning fingers. Kineas pulled on his reins and looked back over the column toiling up the ridge that lined the riverbank, following it with his eye down the steep road, past the last files of the column and past the two baggage carts and the donkeys to fields by the city walls, where the whole force of the city's hoplites could be seen marching. Memnon's black cloak was a speck in the front rank. Beyond the fields and the mass of men stood the city on the river. The spring sun was warm and the clear yellow light gilded the marble of the temple of Apollo and lit the gold dolphins at the edge of the port with fire. From here, the archon's citadel stood clear of the walls like an island in a pond.

At the boundary ditch, Kineas halted the column and waved to Niceas, who raised a trumpet to his lips. The shrill notes rang clear in the wind, and the long column bunched, heaved, and then formed itself into a compact rhomboid, with Kineas at the tip.

Kineas didn't hide his grin of satisfaction.

Kineas trotted the formation across fields that belonged to Nicomedes and then ordered an abrupt change of direction, and the formation obliged – the turn was sloppy, but the rhomboid reformed quickly because, despite confusion, every man knew his place. Kineas raised his hand and Niceas blew the halt.

Kineas gave his warhorse a hard pressure with his knees and heels, and the big animal surged out of the formation. Under gentler pressure, the horse turned in a long curve as he accelerated to the gallop, so that Kineas was riding out to the left of his rhomboid and around it, looking for confusion, for error, for fatal weakness.

He rode all the way around, and then halted facing them. 'Sound: Form Line by Troop!' he called.

Many men were moving before Niceas could raise the heavy trumpet to his lips. It was a bad habit – something that needed to be worked on – but the performance of the manoeuvre was adequate. The four troops, each separated by an interval the width of four riders, formed along the edge of the road running north.

Again, Kineas didn't disguise his pleasure. He rode to Diodorus, sitting at the head of his troop, and clasped his hand. 'Well done,' he said loudly.

Diodorus wasn't much given to broad grins, but he looked as if his lips might split.

While the hoplites marched solidly up the ridge and began to deploy from column into their deep phalanx along the road, Kineas rode along the ranks of the hippeis as if inspecting, but his ride was more a long string of congratulations – troop commanders, hyperetes, individual troopers who had either shown great improvement or had natural skill. The third troop had most of Niceas's new recruits from Heraclea, and Kineas saluted them as he went by – only six men, but their combined experience had already shown its effect.

Then he rode back to the centre of the line and knelt on his stallion's back – a boy's trick, but useful when you needed to address troops. The hoplites took the heavy shields off their shoulders and set the rims on the ground, planted the spikes of their spears and leaned on them for comfort.

'Gentlemen of Olbia!' he called.

Horses moved and made sounds, and a few pulled at their reins to be allowed to crop grass, but the men of the city were silent and still. The wind blew warm from the south, drying the ground, and the sun sparkled on bronze and silver and gilt along the ranks.

The quiet grew. It wrapped itself around them, a palpable thing, as if they sat in the midst of a bubble of eternity. It was one of those moments men recall by their firesides in old age – the whole scene seemed to be set in crystal.

Suddenly, nothing in Kineas's prepared rhetoric was sufficient to the day. They were magnificent – the hoplites and the hippeis together. He said a prayer to Athena in his heart, and raised his hand, pointing at Olbia.

'There is your city. Here beside you are your fellow citizens, hoplites and hippeis together. Here are your comrades. Look at them! Look to the left, to the right. These are your brothers.' The words came to him from the air, and his voice carried in the unnatural calm.

'War is coming,' he said. He looked across the plain to the west, as if Zopryon's army would appear on cue. 'The fate of the city is in the hands of the gods. But it is also in your hands – in the hands of every man here.'

He looked up and down the ranks, and found that he didn't have control of his voice. His throat was sore, and his eyes burned, and the image before him wavered and flowed, so that great gaps appeared in the lines of men where they blurred to his tear-filled eyes. He sat quietly, waiting for the moment to pass.

'Zopryon believes that he will have a quick campaign – an easy conquest. I believe that with the help of the gods, we will stop him on the plain of grass and send him back to Macedon. That is why you have given your winter to training. That is why you are standing here rather than tilling your fields.'

The silence was still there, and the stillness. It was daunting. The wind from the plain of grass ruffled his horse's mane, and he could hear the hairs move against each other.

'I have served Macedon,' he said at last. 'In Macedon they say that Greece is done. That we love beauty more than war. That we are soft. That our only place is in their empire.' He raised his voice. 'But I say, what is more beautiful than this – to serve with your comrades, to stand beside them when the shields ring?' And quoting the Poet, he said, '"My friends, Argives one and all – good, bad and indifferent, for there was never a fight yet, in which all were of equal prowess – there is now work enough, as you very well know, for all of you. See that you none of you turn in flight, daunted by the shouting of the foe, but press forward and keep one another in heart, if it may so be that Olympian Zeus the lord of lightning will grant us to repel our foes, and drive them away from our city."'

The sound of the familiar words, Ajax's famous speech that schoolboys learned by heart, drew a response, and they cheered – first the hoplites, and then all of them, so that the hoplites banged their shields with their spears and the horsemen's swords rang against their breastplates – an ominous sound, the cheer of Ares.

Kineas wasn't used to being cheered. He felt the daimon that infected him in combat, so that his chest was full and he felt more alive and he wondered if this was the feeling Alexander had every day.

Then he turned his head, embarrassed, and called to Niceas who trotted out of the ranks to him. 'Sound: All Captains.'

Niceas blew the trumpet. The troop commanders and their hyperetes trotted out of the cheering ranks and halted in a neat line.

'Gentlemen,' Kineas began. He pulled his helmet off and wiped his eyes. Several of the officers did the same.

Nicomedes looked around him dry-eyed and said, 'No wonder they call Greeks emotional.'

Memnon walked up in his big black cloak. 'Good speech. *Fucking* good speech. Let's go kill something.'

Kineas cleared his throat while the other men chuckled. 'I'm off for the sea of grass. Memnon has the command while I'm away – Diodorus has the command of the hippeis.' He looked them over. 'Listen to me, gentlemen. The archon is now a desperate man – he fears this war just about as much as he fears you. I ask you to be careful in what you say or do in the assembly. I ask you not to provoke him in my absence – indeed, I ask you not to provoke him until we've seen the back of Zopryon.'

Memnon spat. Cleitus nodded. Nicomedes made a face. He shrugged and said, 'But that's my hobby!'

Kineas met his gaze and stared him down. 'Make the command of your troop your hobby.' He collected their eyes and went on. 'Don't fool yourselves that because we have a competent troop of horse and some good hoplites we have an army. Zopryon has an army. We have a tithe of his strength. Only if the Sakje agree to our plan will we have the power to face Zopryon. Even with the Sakje – even if the king sends all his strength – we will be hard pressed to save our city.'

Ajax coloured, but his voice carried conviction. 'I felt a god at my shoulder while you spoke,' he said.

Kineas shrugged. 'I cannot speak of gods, though I revere them. But I can say that I have known a handful of good men to shatter an army of multitudes. Your men look good. Make them better. Don't let them forget what is coming – neither make them fear it so that they take a ship and sail away. That is what I had planned to say this morning but other words were set in my throat.' He didn't say that the small army had been Macedonian, and the multitudes had been the Medes.

Kineas turned to Diodorus. 'I'll take the first troop, as we discussed. Will you continue without us?'

'I have a long day planned,' Diodorus said with a wicked smile. 'I'm sure that most of them will wish they were crossing the sea of grass with you by the time the sun is setting. Travel well!'

They told each other to go with the gods, and they clasped hands. And then Kineas and all of the first troop changed from their warhorses to their lighter mounts, formed a column, and rode off on the track north to the waiting grass.

Kineas had all the younger men, with Leucon in command and a sober Eumenes as his hyperetes. Cleomenes had taken ship and deserted, leaving his son an empty house and a ruined reputation. Eumenes bore it. In fact, he seemed happier – or freer.

Kineas told them that they would live rough, and he meant it. They had just ten slaves for fifty men. Kineas had arranged that all the slaves were mounted.

Like the first trip to find the Sakje, he kept them busy from the moment they left Diodorus, sending parties of scouts out into the grass, making mock attacks on empty sheepfolds, skirmishing against a bank of earth that rose from the plain, the soil visible as a black line, until the dirt was full of javelins and Eumenes made the required joke about sowing dragon's teeth and reaping spears.

Kineas was eager to go forward to the great bend, eager to meet Srayanka, and yet hesitant, as all his doubts of the winter flooded him. Would the city hold behind him? Would the archon stay steady? Would the citizens desert?

Had his anticipations of meeting the Lady Srayanka exceeded the reality?

Fifty young men with a hundred times as many questions did a great deal to distract him, as did Philokles, whose questions rivalled the whole multitude of the rest. By the end of the first day, Kineas felt like a boxer who had spent a whole day parrying blows.

'You ask too many questions,' Kineas growled at the Spartan.

'You know, you are not the first man to say as much,' Philokles said with a laugh. 'But I'm doing you a service, and you should thank me.'

'Bah – service.' Kineas watched his scouts moving a few stades in advance of the column – a passable skirmish line.

'If it weren't for me, you'd do nothing but moon for your amazon.' Philokles laughed. 'Not bad – I hadn't even intended the pun.'

Kineas was watching the scouts. Beyond them, there was a flash of red – Ataelus's cap? He summoned Leucon and ordered him to pull the column together – the boys had a natural tendency to straggle. Then he turned back to Philokles. 'Did you say something?'

The big man shook his head. 'Only the best joke I've made in ... never mind.'

Kineas reined in and looked out under his hand. It was Ataelus for sure. 'Tell me again?'

Philokles pursed his lips and shook his head. 'You know, some things have to be taken on the bound or not at all.'

Kineas narrowed his eyes. 'What are you talking about? Hunting?'

Philokles raised his hands, as if demanding the intercession of the gods, and then turned his horse and went back to the column.

They camped in the open, where a small brook had cut a deep gully across the plain. The miniature valley was full of small trees and bigger game, and Eumenes led three of his friends in cutting down a big doe. Like gentlemen, they made sure she was barren before they killed her – killing a gravid doe in spring would be a bad omen, or worse, an offence. The doe didn't feed seventy men, but the fresh meat served to season their rations. The evening had more the air of a festival than a training camp.

'Too many fucking slaves, and the boys are already up too late,' Niceas said. His recruiting trip to Heraclea hadn't mellowed him.

'I have known you to stay up too late and drink too much, the first night of a campaign.' Kineas passed a cup of wine to his hyperetes.

'I'm a veteran,' said the older man. He reached up and pinched the muscles where his neck met his shoulders. 'An old veteran. Hades, the straps on my breastplate cut like knives.' He was watching Eumenes, who was regaling the younger men with the tale of their winter ride together. 'I doubt he even notices.'

'You aren't smitten, are you?' Kineas asked. He meant the comment in jest and cursed inwardly when he saw that it had hit home. 'Of all the old ... Niceas, he's young enough to be your son.'

Niceas shrugged and said, 'No fool like an old fool.' He looked at the fire, but soon his gaze was back on Eumenes, still posturing to his friends. Like Ajax, he was beautiful – graceful, manly, brave.

'Keep your thoughts on the war,' Kineas said. He tried to make the comment light.

Niceas gave a lopsided grin. 'Fine talk from you. You'll see your filly tomorrow, and then you won't notice the rest of us exist for – I don't know, until we're all dead.'

Kineas stiffened. 'I'll try to spare some time for other thoughts,' he said, still trying for a light tone.

Niceas shook his head. 'Don't be a prick. I don't mean to offend – not much, anyway. But some of the boys think we're in this fucking war so that you can mount this girl, and for all that the Poet is full of such stuff, it's thin enough if we're all dead.' The lopsided grin was back. 'I liked your speech today. Hades, *I* felt the touch – whatever it was. I won't say gods – I won't say it weren't.' He took Kineas's cup and refilled it.

Philokles spread his cloak and fell on it with a thud. 'Private conversation?' he asked when it was too late for them to evict him.

'No,' said Kineas. Curious how little of his authority seemed to carry over to the campfire. 'That is to say, yes, but you're as welcome as my other friends to be critical of my love life.'

A look passed between the Spartan and the older man. They both smiled.

Kineas looked from one to the other and got to his feet. 'Aphrodite take you both,' he growled. 'I'm for bed.'

Philokles indicated his cloak with an expansive wave. 'I'm in mine.'

Kineas rolled his cloak out, and slept between them by the fire. No more was said, but he lay awake for a long time.

There was an owl, and he was determined to catch it, though he couldn't think why. He rode his horse – a great rough beast that he didn't want to look at – across the endless rolling plain of ash. The ash was everywhere, and devoured all the colour, so that he felt as if he was riding in a dark summer twilight, with all the colours robbed by the loom of night. And still the horse – if horse it was – galloped on across the plain.

When he saw the river in the distance, he felt fear, as sharp and total as the first fear he'd ever felt. The beast between his legs cared nothing for his fears, and it ran on, straight for the sandy ford at the base of the slope.

He lifted his head and saw the sea glimmering darkly, and knew that he was again on the field of Issus. There were bodies all around the ford, men and horses mixed, and the men had been mutilated.

His beast's hooves rattled on the gravel of the slope toward the river – still black water that reflected no stars.

He had been chasing an owl. Where was the owl? He turned and looked to the right, where the second taxeis should have broken through the wall of mercenaries, but there were only corpses and ash and the smell of smoke, and then he saw a winged shape rising against the high ground. He pulled at the beast's reins, sawing them back and forth, increasingly desperate as the thing crashed into the ford.

'Do not cross the river,' said Kam Baqca. The voice was clear and calm, and the beast turned, splashing along the margins of the river, and the black drops rose slowly through the air and burned like ice when they touched the skin, and then he was galloping free

of the water – if water it was – over the field of the dead, and the owl spiralled down towards him as if stooping on prey.

His beast shied – the first time it had missed a step in its mad career – and he looked down past its hideous hide to the ground, where Alexander's body lay broken, his face covered with a smiling golden mask. Around him lay the bodies of his companions.

That's not what happened, *complained some rational part of his mind. But the thought slipped away.*

The owl swooped out of the air. He saw it in the periphery of his vision and turned his head to see the claws sink into his face, through his face, the owl melting into his flesh like a sword thrust sinking home. He screamed ... and he was flying. He was the owl, the owl was him. The beast was gone – or the beast, too, was one with the bird and the man. The great brown wings beat, and he watched the earth below and knew where his prey lived, saw every mortal movement on the plain of ash. He rose with the world's wind under his wings, and then beat strongly, without fatigue, over the low hills that had lined the battlefield of Issus until he was clear of the plain of ash and flew over the world of men, and still he rose, until he could see the curve of the sea from Alexandria to Tyre, and then he fell with the long curve of an arrow past Tyre and Chios and Lesvos, past the ruins of Troy, past the Hellespont, until he slowed his descent and hovered over the sea of grass, and in the distance he saw the tree growing to shade the whole world, and yet it seemed to grow from a single tent on the plain. He soared to the tree and as his talons bit into the rich comfort of its bark ...

He awoke, missing the warmth of his hyperetes against his right side. He could hear Niceas berating someone, and young voices raised in laughter, and he thought, Time to get up. And then the enormity of the dream hit him, and he lay there, trying to see it all again. Terrified all over again at the alienness of his own thoughts. He shivered with more than just the cold of the morning, pushed himself to the fire, and one of Eumenes' young men brought him a cup of hot wine. 'Agathon,' he said, remembering the lad's name.

The boy beamed. 'Can I get you anything else? We slept in the open like real soldiers – I wasn't even cold!'

Kineas couldn't handle too much adolescent enthusiasm so

early in the morning. He drank off the rest of the hot wine and rolled his cloak tight. In the time it took the sun to get his ball of fire fully over the horizon, they were mounted, their breath streaming away like pale plumes in the cold spring air, and the dream with all of its bonds to the other was again banished by a counter spell of work.

Kineas waved for Ataelus to join him. With the exception of his abortive attempts to learn the Sakje tongue over the winter, Kineas hadn't seen much of the Scyth. He gave the man a smile.

Ataelus looked tense. Kineas couldn't remember seeing the man look so reserved. 'Will we find the Sakje camp today?' he asked the scout.

Ataelus made a face. 'Yes,' he said. 'Second hour after the sun is high, unless they were for moving.' He didn't look as if he relished the prospect.

Kineas rubbed his new beard. 'Well, then. Lead on.'

Ataelus looked back at him gravely. 'The lady – for waiting two weeks of you.' He sighed heavily.

'Do you mean she may have left?' Kineas said in alarm. Ataelus's Greek had improved considerably over the winter. His vocabulary was much bigger – his grammar was about the same. He could still be difficult to understand.

'Not for leaving,' Ataelus said heavily. 'For *waiting*.' He shook his reins and touched his riding whip to his pony's flanks, and he was gone over the grass, leaving Kineas to worry.

Philokles joined Kineas as the column started forward. 'What was that about?'

Kineas waved dismissively. 'Our Scyth is in a state because we're late.'

'Hmm,' said the Spartan. 'We are late. And the lady doesn't strike me as the sort of commander who likes to wait.'

Kineas rode out of the column, signalled to Leucon to join him, and barked out a string of commands that set the whole troop into an open skirmish line two stades wide. When the rough line was moving well, he rode back to Philokles, who as usual took no part in the manoeuvres.

'She'll understand that I was delayed,' Kineas said. 'So will the king.'

The Spartan pursed his lips. 'Listen, Hipparch. If you were waiting for her, and you'd sat for two weeks while she drilled her cavalry ...' He raised an eyebrow.

Kineas was watching the skirmish line, which was sticking together pretty well. 'I don't—'

'You don't think of her as another commander. You think of her as a Greek girl with some equine skills. Better get over that, brother. She's had to put up with two weeks of ribbing from her troopers about waiting like a mare in heat for her stallion – that's my guess. Look how well you handle *our* teasing.'

The left half of the skirmish line was bunching up as the young troopers chatted while they rode. Riding with a horse length between each file pair took practice, and the line was starting to fall apart.

'Sound HALT,' Kineas bellowed. To Philokles, he said, 'She may not even want me.'

The Spartan didn't blink. 'That's a whole different problem – but if she didn't want you, chances are Ataelus wouldn't be looking so worried.'

Kineas watched the outer arms of his skirmish line galloping to the centre to form on their commander. 'As always, I'd treasure your advice.'

Philokles nodded. 'Make the same apologies to her that you'd make to a man.'

Kineas scratched his beard. 'Kick me when I go wrong.' He cantered for the command group to discuss the skirmish line.

They saw the first scouts by mid-morning – dark centaurs on the horizon who vanished between hoof beats. They found the camp in the afternoon, as Ataelus had predicted. Kineas's stomach turned over at the sight of the wagons, and he clenched the barrel of his horse between his knees until the animal began to curvet and fidget. There were a few riders at the edge of the camp, and a mounted group was gathered at the edge of the river.

The riders came to them at a gallop – two young men resplendent in red leather and gold ornament flashing in the sun, who raced by the head of the column, waved, and raced off again yipping like dogs. They ran their horses right in among the crowd at the edge of the water.

Kineas led his column through the tall grass to the edge of the camp and ordered it to halt. He sat at the head of the column, feeling foolish because he didn't know what to do. He'd expected that she'd come out and meet him. Instead, he saw that there was some sort of archery contest going on.

'Shooting with bows,' Ataelus said at his side. 'Lady shoots next. See?'

Kineas saw. How had he missed her? Srayanka was seated on a grey mare at the edge of the water with a bow in her hand, her jacket half off so that one breast was bare in the warm spring sun, the sleeve falling free, one shoulder bare to the gold gorget at her neck. Her hair was bound in two heavy braids and as she turned her head, he saw her heavy brows and the focus of her expression.

That's what she looks like, he thought. Yes.

'Wait here,' he said to Niceas. He motioned to Ataelus to attend him and touched his horse with his whip – her whip – and cantered across the grass to her.

A man was shooting. As Kineas reined in, the man kneed his horse into motion, first a canter and then a gallop along the flat grass at the water's edge. He leaned out over his horse's neck and shot an arrow into a bundle of grass. A second arrow appeared in his fingers and he shot it point-blank, leaning so far down off his pony that the head of the arrow almost brushed the target as he released, and then he was past, turning in the saddle with a third arrow nocked, and he drew and released in one smooth motion. The last shot hung in the wind for a moment, the arrow visible as a black streak, before burying itself in the ground an arm's length beyond the target. The other Sakje hooted and cheered.

Kineas looked back to Srayanka, and she took a deep breath, her whole body focused on the target of grass the way a hunting dog would watch a wounded stag. Like a man, Philokles had said. Her visible breast and the line of her muscular shoulder to her neck were like a Phidian statue of Artemis, but the Athenian sculptor would never have known a woman's face to have such an expression – set and hard with purpose.

Kineas stayed silent.

Without another glance she tapped her heels against her mare, and the horse leaped straight from a stand into a gallop. Her first arrow was in the air with the horse's first full stride. She had three more in the fingers of her draw hand, and she flipped one like a conjuror, drew and shot, leaned out close to the target just as the man had done, her whole body at an impossible angle to the horse, her braided hair straight out behind her head, the muscles of her arm standing out with the strain of drawing the bow, her hips and legs one with her mount.

Kineas couldn't breathe.

She put the last arrow on her bow and turned back so fast that her body seemed to rotate free of her waist and shot again, her arrow invisible until it punched through the grass target. And then, as the horsemen began to cheer, she drew a fifth arrow from the *gorytos* at her waist, whirled again and loosed, her upper body straining to the heavens like a priestess offering a prayer to Apollo. The arrow lofted up and up into the blue sky and hung as if caught by the god's hand at the top of its arc before plummeting to the earth where it transfixed the bundle of grass. Before the arrow hit, she had slowed her horse as she turned to be greeted by the roars of all the warriors and the Greeks up the ridge.

The sound went on and on, though there were just fifty or so of them, with a high crescendo of screams – yeeyeeyee – from the women, and bass barking from the men. Several stepped forward, raising their hands in obvious congratulations, and an older woman – her trumpeter – rode up close and embraced her.

She handed the trumpeter her bow, turned and put her arm down into her sleeve and shrugged the jacket back over her naked shoulder. She walked her horse toward Kineas empty-handed. He was still bellowing his appreciation like a good guest at a symposium. Behind him, the other Olbians were cheering, too.

He fell silent as she rode closer. Her eyebrows were just as he remembered, her nose long and Greek, her forehead clear and high. How could he have forgotten how large her eyes were? Or their brown flecks within the dark blue?

He couldn't think of anything useful to say. He had to say something. 'Tell her that's the finest shooting I've ever seen,' he said. His voice came out clear and calm. He was surprised he got it out at all.

Ataelus spoke in Sakje. Kineas knew the words enough to know that his compliment was passed unadorned.

She raised an eyebrow and replied to Ataelus without taking her eyes off Kineas. 'She say she shoot bow much when she has long wait.' Ataelus sounded more nervous than Kineas. 'She say she packed wagons for leaving. Saw us coming. She say, are you ready to ride, or need more rest?'

Kineas didn't take his eyes off hers. 'Tell her I'm very sorry we are so late.'

Ataelus spoke. This time he spoke at some length. She raised a hand and silenced him. She pressed her mare forward.

Kineas's stallion rolled his lips back from his teeth and sniffed, his neck extended as far towards the mare as he could manage despite Kineas's rock hard hand at the reins.

The mare shied a step, and then, fast as thought, her head came round and she nipped Kineas's horse on the neck with her teeth and he shied, stepped back, and Kineas had to struggle to keep his seat.

Srayanka spoke. Kineas caught words he knew – mare and stallion.

The Sakje warriors laughed. One of them laughed so hard that he fell to the ground, and pointing at him led to more laughter.

Kineas got his stallion in hand and turned to Ataelus. He could feel the heat of his face. She was laughing too. 'What did she say?' he asked.

Ataelus was laughing so hard that his eyes were closed and both of his hands were wrapped in his horse's mane.

'What did she say?' Kineas demanded again, this time in his battlefield voice.

Ataelus wiped the grin off his face and sat straight. 'She made for joke,' he said after some hesitation.

The Sakje were still laughing. Worse yet, someone who had some Sakje had translated the joke to the Olbians. The older men were trying to hide their laughter, but the younger were unable to control themselves.

'I can see that,' Kineas snapped.

She turned away from him to her trumpeter and snapped a string of orders, and then she turned her head back to him and he caught the flash of deep blue as her eyes sought his and she smiled. Don't be an ass, he thought to himself. But he was boiling inside, and he couldn't manage to return her smile.

'Tell me this joke,' he said to Ataelus.

Ataelus was struggling to restrain laughter. He panted like a dog, slapped his horse, finally gave up the struggle and dissolved into laughter with his arms crossed over his chest.

Kineas glanced after Srayanka's retreating back – she was gathering riders and shouting orders, and a group of younger men were harnessing oxen to the wagons. Most of the laughter had stopped among the Sakje, but it was still spreading among the Olbians as the joke was translated and passed from file to file.

Kineas trotted over to Niceas, who sat on his charger fingering his amulet with a fixed and dutiful expression that Kineas knew all too well. Kineas spoke quietly, firmly, as if nothing untoward had happened. 'Get everyone off their warhorses and on their riding horses. Water all the animals at the river – bread and cheese in the saddle.'

Niceas nodded, as if he didn't dare speak.

Philokles had a broad grin on his face. He pulled out of the column as Niceas began to shout orders. Leucon rode by, red-faced, avoiding Kineas's eye. In fact, none of the men met Kineas's eye. Eumenes was still laughing.

Ataelus reached out and touched his elbow. He was smiling. 'She say – maybe mare ...' He began to laugh again. He managed to croak out, '... In heat – two weeks ago.'

Kineas had to work through the words in his mind, and then a slow smile punctured the grim mask of his face.

Before the sun had moved another hand across the sea of grass, the whole column, Sakje and Olbian, was mounted and heading north. Kineas changed horses and cantered up the column to where Srayanka rode with her trumpeter, a hard-eyed older woman with skin like leather and bright red hair like Diodorus, whom Kineas remembered from the summer before.

Srayanka smiled as he rode up – the best smile she had ever given him. She nudged her trumpeter and spoke to Ataelus. Behind him, the lead Sakje tittered.

'She say – where your stallion, Kineax?'

'Tell her my stallion is too sad to be ridden. In despair – can you say "in despair"?' Kineas was at a heavy disadvantage in translation.

Ataelus shook his head. 'What's despair? Something bad?'

'So sad you can't eat,' Kineas said.

'Ah. Lovesick!' Ataelus laughed, and then spoke quickly before Kineas could stop him.

The Sakje tittered again, and a big black-haired man behind Kineas leaned out and slapped his shoulder.

Srayanka turned and brushed a hand against Kineas's face. The motion took him by surprise – she was that fast – and he squirmed and almost missed her touch.

Ataelus laughed with the rest of the Sakje, and then said, 'She say – not worry. She say,' and he broke off a while to laugh again, 'she say – maybe mare in heat again – in about two weeks.'

Kineas felt his face grow hot. He grinned at her, and she grinned at him. The look went on too long. Kineas decided it was time to change the subject. 'Ask her if the king is ready to make war,' he said.

The laughter from the Sakje stopped. She replied in a few words. Her face changed, returning to the hard look she had worn while she shot her bow.

'She say – not for her to speak for king. She come to guide. She say – speak not for war until we come for king.' Ataelus had a look on his face that pleaded for understanding.

Kineas nodded. But he continued, 'I have heard of Zopryon's army. It is very great, and ready to march.' It was infuriating to have to listen to Ataelus's halting translation and her reply.

Ataelus turned back to him. 'She say the king is for having many things for talk. Much talk. Not for her to take the words for the king.'

'Tell her I understand.' Kineas pantomimed understanding

to her. She spoke directly to him. He understood *Getae* and *Zopryon* and the verb for riding.

'She say the grass already knocked down with hooves of the Getae. She say she know Zopryon ready to ride.' Ataelus wiped his forehead with his sleeve. 'I say for talking – *that* talking is hard work.' He laughed grimly.

Kineas took the hint and rode back to his own men.

The column moved fast, and the land became flat, the endless grass greener with each warm day, extending to the horizon on the left, and the river coiling like a snake. Sometimes it was at their feet, and sometimes it passed far away to their right in long curves. Those curves were the only marker of their progress, otherwise they might have been standing still for all the variation in the landscape. When the river passed out of sight, the plain of grass and the solid blue of the sky spread unchanged in every direction, like a blue bowl inverted over a green bowl. The immensity of it made the Greeks uncomfortable. Time seemed to stand still.

Yet by the second day the whole life of the column was routine – rising in pre-dawn cold, the welcome warmth of the horse at first mounting, a hasty meal with the first rays of the new sun, and then hours walking and trotting through the grass, the trampled line of their passage straight as the flight of an arrow behind them and the virgin grass before them as far as the eye could see.

Evening was different. Srayanka's scouts chose the halting place each night, always close to water and often shaded by trees at the river's edge, and fires were lit against the cold. The product of the day's hunt roasted on iron spits, and the warriors told stories or pushed each other to vicious competitions. Horse races, wrestling, archery, contests of strength and memory, wit and skill filled the evening from the last halt to the dying of the fires.

At first the Olbians hung back, but on the second night Niceas wrestled Parshtaevalt, the black-haired Scyth who had shown interest in everything Greek. Then Eumenes raced his best pony against Srayanka's trumpeter and lost the race and the pony.

The third evening became an equine Olympics, with mounted

races, a dozen wrestling matches, and new events – boxing and foot races. The Sakje were as poor on foot as they were gifted on horseback. Their notion of boxing was even stranger. The Sakje had a contest that appeared similar, where two champions would stand toe to toe and hit each other by turns until the weaker man fell or declared himself beaten. Leucon, a passable boxer, thought that he was seeing the Greek sport and proceeded to block blows, to the consternation of his opponent and half the audience, and Kineas had to explain boxing to Srayanka through Eumenes and Ataelus, and then he and Leucon gave a demonstration.

Leucon was a sturdy man, powerfully built and well trained, but he lacked the speed and grace of Ajax – or Kineas. Kineas drew the match out, both for Leucon's vanity and for the benefit of the audience, but when he parried Leucon's best punch and responded with a flurry of blows too fast to be counted in the dwindling light, the crowd, Sakje and Greek alike, roared approval. Leucon fell.

Then, by torchlight, Philokles and a score of other men threw stones from the river. They threw for distance and argued the rules – did a bounce count? – until Kineas feared violence would ensue, and ordered the Olbians to bed.

The fourth day passed like the others – the Olbian horse drilled and skirmished, formed and reformed, and the Sakje watched and hooted, or hunted, or rode in speculative silence. A week in the saddle, and all of Leucon's troopers were already hardened to the life – eating in the saddle, riding all day. Kineas reined in next to the young commander in the late afternoon. Leucon had a hard head from the boxing, but he kept his temper like a gentleman and everyone respected him the more.

'Your men are very good,' Kineas said. 'You're a good commander.'

Leucon smiled ruefully at the praise. 'Good thing,' he said. 'As my Olympic boxing career seems to be over.' Then he said, 'But thanks. I'm so proud of them I feel like I might burst, or start singing.'

Kineas rubbed his jaw, where his new beard was now

prominent. It barely itched any more. 'I know what you mean.' He glanced at Niceas. 'They're good, aren't they, old man?'

Niceas had Eumenes by his side in the column, and he glanced at the younger hyperetes before responding. 'Better than I expected,' he said. Then he broke into a smile. 'Of course, we'll see what they're really made of when we have to fight.'

'Don't stop drilling,' said Kineas. 'After *achieving* excellence comes *keeping* it.'

On the fourth evening, Kineas found himself throwing javelins against Niceas and Kyros and one of the more promising boys. The Sakje watched curiously as the men rode through the course, throwing to the right and left. Kineas was done, having struck all his targets, and was watching the boy intently when he saw that Srayanka had mounted her mare and was starting the course behind the boy. She had a bow, and shot twice for every javelin he had launched, and rode past the last target, flushed with triumph, to the cheers of her band.

Kineas rode back to the lists and retrieved all of his javelins, determined to answer her challenge. He took two more javelins from Niceas. His hyperetes shot him a look through the failing light at the crowd of Sakje. 'This is a good idea?' he asked.

'Ask me after I ride,' Kineas responded.

He halted his horse at the start line and cleared his mind. Srayanka was still receiving the applause of her warriors. He watched her for a moment, and then pressed his horse into motion.

The stallion hadn't been ridden all day, except for his first pass, and he was full of energy. Kineas threw his first javelin from well out – a difficult shot, but well placed, and the heavy dart sank into the rawhide of the target, a Sakje shield. He threw his second just before he passed the target and heard the *thunk* as the head bit home. Without looking at the result, he took his third javelin from his rein hand and threw for distance. It was one of Niceas's – lighter than his own – and it flew high, catching the top of the second target and knocking it flat. At a gallop, too fast to think, he took his fourth javelin and sent his horse over the shield rather than past it, raised the second javelin high as he gathered the horse to jump, and plunged it down with the whole weight of his arm. He heard a reaction from the crowd but he was already throwing his fifth, his whole being concentrated on the last target and his last javelin. He was a stride behind – he fumbled the grip change for a heartbeat – and the shield was past. He turned – if she could do it, he could – and threw side-armed at the last target. He felt a muscle pop in his neck as he released and felt the pain as he turned back to the course, but the sudden burst of sound from a hundred throats told him that the pain was well won.

He trotted his charger back to Niceas. Niceas was holding the second shield over his head and shouting his approval. His leaping throw had punched right through the rawhide and through the wood, so that the black spike of the head protruded the length of an arm from the back.

Parshtaevalt, Srayanka's second in command, reached up and embraced him, shouting in Sakje, and then Srayanka, still mounted, put her arms around his neck and pressed him close. The crowd shrieked approval. Then Eumenes was pushing a cup of wine into his hands. Unseen hands made wreaths, and Kineas found himself reclining on a carpet wearing his, while Srayanka sat with her back to a rolled cloak, wearing hers with her hair loose and looking like a muscular nymph.

They watched the rest of the competitions together. At some point he took her hand, and she turned to him and her eyes were wide, her pupils huge, and she moved her thumb across his palm. Despite the crowd around them, she continued to stroke his hand, turning it back and forth as she would, and he began to join her at the game – stroking the back of her hand, comparing the calluses on her palm to the warm softness on the back, daring to touch the inside of her wrist as if it were a much more private place.

It was the closest they had been to privacy. Neither said a word. Time passed, and then the competitions died away into drinking, and then the pressure of the wine on Kineas's bladder made him rise, much against his will. He looked down, aware that he was grinning like a fool or a love-struck boy with his first serving girl. They didn't even speak a common language.

She met his eyes and then looked down. She laughed.

'Srayanka,' he said.
'Kineax,' she said.
And that was the fourth night.

13

The next day, he was stiff and cold when he awoke, and his hands ached, every joint swollen. His right shoulder burned when he reached up to fasten his cloak, the trophy of last night's throw. He summoned Eumenes and Ataelus.

'I want to work on my Sakje as we ride,' he said.

Both of them looked away, smiling. But when they were all mounted, Eumenes and Ataelus joined him, and began to point around them – mare, stallion, sky and grass – and give him the words in Sakje. The roots of the words lurked at the edge of familiarity, like Persian, some like older Greek forms in the Poet, but the declensions were different and the end sounds were barbaric.

Kineas had started the process in the winter, but the press of politics and training had drowned his attempts at language lessons. Now, with the object of his lessons at hand and nothing to do but ride and watch Leucon handle his men, Kineas worked like a boy with a tutor.

Parshtaevalt joined them at the midday halt. He was a tall man, for a Sakje, with pale golden hair and a deep tan. Kineas had gathered that he was some relation to Srayanka, but the relationship was hard to define – a matrilineal cousin. He was also a successful war leader with the hair of a dozen enemies on his saddlecloth. He had a keen intelligence, and he took to the language lessons easily. He seemed to enjoy and admire Greek things.

He rode away after an hour and returned with Srayanka, who rode with them the rest of the day, naming things in Greek as Kineas named them in Sakje. She continued to command the column while she practised her Greek, and Kineas had an opportunity to observe her at work.

She was a fine commander. He watched her separate two men who were fighting over a haunch of venison, her eyes blazing in contrast to her calm, level voice. They shrank down as if struck.

She moved around the column, she knew the state of every horse in her considerable herd and her scouts were always alert. In the evening, she spoke to her people when they won contests and when they lost them. That much he gleaned just from watching her. But he learned more from watching her warriors – the respect, almost awe, with which they treated her could be seen in every interaction. She never shied from a contest, and although she didn't win them all, it was a matter for boasting for the victor when she lost *any* of them. She was first in the saddle at the start of the day and last in the saddle when the column halted. She had a different face and a different voice for every warrior in her band, man or woman – to some, she explained using her hands to emphasize a point, whereas to others she simply directed.

And all her people loved her.

He talked to Parshtaevalt through Eumenes on the sixth day, when she had ridden away from the language lessons to question a scout. Parshtaevalt now rode with Niceas and Eumenes most of the time, asking questions of the younger man as quickly as he could think of them. When Parshtaevalt mentioned a raid he had been on the year before, Kineas asked, 'Did Srayanka lead the raid? Against the Getae?'

Ataelus passed the question and then rolled his eyes at the answer. 'He say – fucking Getae. They burning towns – three towns. For killing every man they found.'

Kineas nodded to indicate he understood. 'How many actions has she fought?' he asked, pointing at Srayanka. 'Raids? Battles?'

Eumenes phrased the question. His Sakje was better every day.

The black-haired man looked down at his reins and then up at the sun, as if looking for inspiration. 'As many as the days of the moon,' he said, through Eumenes.

'Thirty?' Kineas said aloud. 'Thirty actions!'

Philokles, who always rode to the sound of a good conversation, appeared from the Sakje part of the column. 'More than Leonidas,' he said.

'More than me,' said Kineas.

'More than me,' said Niceas. He gave Kineas a grin. 'I'll be more respectful.'

On the seventh day, the scouts found a herd of deer, and a mixed group of hunters, Sakje and Olbian, rode away to procure fresh meat. They returned with six big carcasses, and Kineas stood beside Srayanka as they ordered the division of the meat. The youngest warriors of the Sakje were skinning the animals, and the Olbians' slaves were breaking the joints and butchering.

Srayanka watched two young women skinning the biggest buck. Kineas watched her. He could see her desire to say something, or perhaps take the chore herself, although he couldn't see that they were making any error.

A trio of Olbian cavalrymen, younger ones with no immediate duty, had gravitated to the sight because the two Sakje women had stripped naked to do the bloody work.

Srayanka glanced up from her own concerns when one of the Olbian men said 'barbarian' a little too aggressively. She turned to Kineas and raised an eyebrow.

Who needs language? he thought. He walked over to the knot of hippeis. 'If you gentlemen don't have anything better to do, I expect I could teach you to do some basic butchering.'

The mouthy one – Alcaeus – shook his head. 'That's slave's work,' he said. 'We're just watching the amazons bathe in blood.'

'They're skinning the buck to get the skin, not to impress you with their charms. Move along, or I'll put you to butchering.' Kineas kept his voice low. He didn't want to advertise the poor behaviour of his men. Out of the corner of his eye, he could see Srayanka's trumpeter and a half-dozen other Sakje, watching and flicking their riding whips.

Alcaeus put his hands on his hips. 'I'm not on duty.' He tossed his head arrogantly. 'I can watch the barbarians show their tits if I want.'

His companions both moved away from him as if he had the plague. Kineas glanced around for Niceas or Eumenes – he would have preferred that this obvious indiscipline be dealt with by someone else. But they were both busy.

Still keeping his voice low, Kineas said, 'No, you can't. Don't be a fool. Go to your horse and curry him. Then join the sentries until I order you in.'

The man looked affronted rather than sheepish. 'I take my orders from Leucon,' he said. 'And besides—'

'Silence!' Kineas said in his battlefield voice. 'Not another word.'

Alcaeus shifted his gaze to look past Kineas at the two women. He glanced at his two companions with all the arrogance of an adolescent assuring himself of an audience. He smirked. 'You're blocking my view,' he said lazily.

Kineas lost his temper. It happened in a moment – he felt the flood of anger and then he had knocked the stupid boy unconscious with a single blow. It hurt his shoulder and split a knuckle. He turned on one of the man's companions. 'Roll him in his cloak and put him by his horse. Both of you stay with him until he wakes, and then help him curry his horse, mount it, and the three of you go on sentry until I recall you. Do you understand?

They all nodded, their eyes as round as Athenian owls.

When he returned to Srayanka and Ataelus, she shook her head. 'For what you hit the man?' she asked in passable Greek.

Kineas turned to Ataelus. 'How do you say *disobey*?'

Ataelus shook his head. 'What is *disobey*?'

Kineas breathed out slowly. He was angry – too angry. 'When I give an order, I expect the man to obey. If he won't, he *disobeys*.'

Srayanka turned her head back and forth between them. Then she asked a short question in rapid Sakje. Kineas caught his own name and nothing more.

Ataelus shook his head, glanced at Kineas, and spoke at length, making gestures of riding and sleeping. To Kineas, he said. 'She ask me, for how long am I with you? And I tell her. And she ask how often you hit men, and I say not so much.'

Srayanka's eyes locked with his. They were like the blue of the Aegean when the sun returns after a squall. He was taller than her by half a head. She was standing quite close to him. She spoke directly to him, speaking slow, careful Sakje.

He didn't understand a word.

Ataelus said, 'She say – if I hit one man for hurt – if I hit one, I kill. Or he ride away or make for enemy.' He stopped, looked back and forth, like a trapped animal. Finally he said, 'Then she say – man watch girls. Men all fools when women show tits. So what? Why hit?'

Kineas was not used to having his judgement questioned in matters of command. He was not used to being questioned in public, through an interpreter, or by a woman.

Like a man, Philokles had said. But she could have had a man flayed to ribbons with a riding whip and he wouldn't have questioned her authority.

He could feel the red in his face, feel his temper, rarely unleashed, building. He could feel his mind in revolt against the unfairness of it, against the censure in her eyes. He breathed in and out several times. He counted to ten in Sakje. Then he gave her a nod. 'I will explain,' he said in Greek, 'when I am less angry.'

'Good,' she said, and walked away.

That night he related the incident to Leucon, Eumenes, Niceas and Philokles. They sat by a small fire, distant from the Sakje, who were quiet and kept to themselves.

'He's got a dick instead of a brain,' Niceas said. He glanced at Leucon. 'Sorry. I know he's your friend, but he's a fool. He had it coming.'

Leucon looked miserable. 'He's been my companion since we were boys. He always gets what he wants – hard to change that now.'

Niceas gave a nasty grin. 'Not that hard,' he said.

Leucon put his head in his hands. 'I feel that I've failed you, Hipparch. But also – I have to say this – I feel that ... that you didn't need to hit him. He's a gentleman. No one has hit him since his first tutor.'

Kineas bridled, trying not to react.

Philokles spoke. 'In Sparta, he could have been killed. On the spot.'

Leucon sat back on his stool, clearly shocked. 'For a little back-talk?'

Philokles shrugged. 'Indiscipline is poison.'

Leucon looked at Eumenes. Eumenes didn't meet his eye. 'He's the kind of bully who would draw a knife in a wine-shop brawl. I've seen him do it.' He looked at Niceas and then back at Leucon. 'I don't like him.'

Kineas leaned forward. 'That's not at issue. Like or dislike – a commander is above them. I don't dislike the boy – I hit him because he was disobedient. In my experience disobedience is a plague that starts slowly but spreads rapidly.' He spread his hands to catch more warmth from the fire, leaned forward so that his elbows could rest on his thighs. He was cold, his knuckle and his shoulder both hurt, and he didn't want to think of what damage he'd done to relations with Srayanka – or the Sakje. 'He was offending the Sakje. He offended me. And he disobeyed a direct order.' Kineas rubbed his beard. 'I am a hard man. A mercenary. Perhaps your men needed to remember that.' And then he sighed. 'I let myself grow angry.'

Leucon looked more bewildered than informed. 'What will I tell his father?' he asked, before he walked off into the dark.

Philokles watched him go. 'I take it Lady Srayanka was unimpressed.' Kineas nodded. Philokles shook his head. 'You did the right thing. What else could you do?'

Kineas rubbed his hands together. 'You're the philosopher. You tell me!'

Philokles shook his head. 'I'm a Spartan first and a philosopher second, I suppose. I might have killed him.'

Kineas nodded wearily. 'Odd. That's what Srayanka said. She said if she had to hit a man, she'd kill him. Rather than leave an enemy at her back – or at least, that's what I got from the whole thing.'

Eumenes said, 'They don't even strike their children.' He shrugged. 'I'm serious. I had a Sakje nanny. In war, or in a contest – no holds barred. But not for discipline.' He thought for as long as it took Niceas to put an armload of wood on the fire, and then said, 'I don't think they even have a *word* for discipline.'

'Now *that* is interesting,' Philokles said.

Kineas left them to it. He sent Niceas to recall the three

sentries before he went to roll in his cloak. Then he lay awake for a long time, thinking about women – his mother, his sisters, Artemis and Srayanka. He didn't reach any conclusion at all. Artemis and Srayanka were like a different sex from his mother and sisters. It was not that he thought that Artemis and Srayanka were really so alike. Artemis used her sex as a tool to get what she wanted from men. Srayanka was a commander. And yet there was some basic similarity.

He thought of Philokles, telling him to treat Srayanka as if she were a man. The thought made him frown, and he fell asleep.

They didn't ride together the next day. Kineas rode with his men, practising words with Ataelus as the grass vanished under their hooves. It wasn't that everything was the same, nor that anything was different.

The same could be said in the Olbian section of the column. Kineas couldn't define the problem, but something had changed. It confounded him – he had the ability to read his troops, and he knew that they agreed with him that Alcaeus deserved his punishment. In fact, from his demeanour, it appeared that Alcaeus himself felt he merited the blow. He looked sheepish now, rather than angry. And yet – something was different in the column, as if by demonstrating the force that underlay the discipline, Kineas had forfeited some of their goodwill.

Niceas added a barb to the situation when they were alone. 'The idiot was ogling the Sakje girls, right? And you spend all your waking hours with one. You know what soldiers say when one man has something the others can't have.'

Kineas had to admit the fairness of the point – at least, through the eyes of soldiers. He stroked his beard and blew on his cold hands. 'You know, if all these pampered gentlemen soldiers have to complain about is my love life, they're doing pretty well.' He looked off at the horizon. 'She won't speak to me today.'

Niceas gave him a half-grin in return. 'Exactly.' He raised an eyebrow. 'You worry too much, Hipparch.' He glanced at the sky, where a line of heavy dark clouds came at them like a phalanx. One corner of his mouth curled. 'The rich boys'll sing a different tune soon enough.'

After three days of rain everyone in the column had plenty to complain about.

The three days were miserable for the Greeks, who spent them learning to live like soldiers, rather than like rich men on an extended hunt. Their cloaks were wet through – some men found that the blue dye in their cloaks ran, staining their skins – and their fires were fitful and smoky. The nights were cold and wet, and the troopers from Olbia finally learned to huddle together for warmth. It wasn't really like sleeping – the best most men could manage was a troubled half-sleep as the pile of bodies moved, every man searching for warmth at the centre. By day they had their horses for warmth, and by the third day, most of them could sleep on horseback.

Kineas was just as miserable, because while he drilled his men and taught them to live in the rain, Srayanka eluded him. Worse, he sometimes caught her watching him, her face serious, her brows a single line across her face. She was judging him.

On the fourth day the sun shone, and towards evening they found the king.

The 'city' of the Sakje stretched for miles, and when he first saw the extent of the walls the size of it took Kineas's breath away. A temple stood on a high bluff over the river, and around it lay an acropolis of large log structures, brightly coloured, and smaller buildings built of hewn timber and earth. The acropolis itself was small enough, but the walls that surrounded it ran off to join earthworks three men tall that ran off almost to the horizon.

'It's not really a city,' Satrax said. They were standing together on the walls of the acropolis. 'It's really a big stock pen.'

Kineas had spent two days discussing plans with Marthax, the king's principal warlord, and other of his inner council – Kam Baqca, the king himself, and Srayanka. Eumenes and Ataelus were exhausted from constant translation, and even the king, the only man among them to speak Sakje and Greek with equal fluency, was showing the strain. When Kineas slept, he had dreams of languages, where Sakje dogs accosted him in broken

Greek, where objects named themselves in Sakje. He was learning the language, but his brain was tired all the time.

The king ordained a break, and dragged Kineas outside to see the sun. He was less distant, less aggressive, than he had been at their winter meeting.

Srayanka, who ignored Kineas as if he didn't exist, spent most of her time with the king. While they debated the conduct of the war, she opposed him, always seeking the rashest course. In this, he sided with the young king and caution. She didn't seem to hold the cautious policy against the king. She focused her discontent on just one man.

That morning, however, she was off with the other fighting women and Kam Baqca. Something about religion.

Kineas was heartsick, and only the loss of Srayanka's favour informed him fully of what she had come to mean to him over the winter. He chided himself for being a fool – he had help in this from Niceas – and tried to concentrate on the weighty matters at hand. Of course she, as the greatest magnate among the Assagatje, would favour the king, who doted on her.

Kineas realized that the king had been speaking for some time. He seemed to expect a response.

Kineas waved at the stock pens. With the exception of the acropolis, and a built-up stretch along the river where the Sindi farmers had a town and Greek merchants had their warehouses, the rest of the walls were empty.

'Who built the walls?' Kineas asked. 'They go on for what – forty stades?'

'Twice that, if you include all the tribal enclosures.' The king gave a proud smile. 'The Sindi did it. Many years ago, after the threat of Darius. The Sakje decided that we needed a safe place for all the herds in time of war, and the Sindi agreed to build the walls.'

'The Sindi are your peasants?' Kineas asked. There were Sindi farmers in Olbia, but there were also Sindi aristocrats. They were native to the Euxine, but many of them had assimilated so successfully with the Greeks that the only sign of them was their dark eyes and straight black hair. Eumenes had the hair, Kyros had the eyes, and young Clio had both.

The king shook his head. 'The Sindi love the dirt. The Sakje love the sky.' He shrugged. 'When first we came, so our legend says, we had contempt for the Sindi. We destroyed their army and took their women.' He glanced at Kineas and raised an eyebrow. 'All sounds likely enough. But they fought back in their own ways. They shot our men from behind trees. They fouled wells and killed men in their sleep.' The king shrugged. 'So the legend says. Myself, I think that the wiser Sakje knew from the first that without the grain raised by Sindi farmers, there would be no gold and no Greek wine. Does it matter? We are not really two peoples any longer. We are one people with two different faces.' He leaned out over the timber hoarding of the acropolis wall and pointed at a crowd of merchants arguing over grain prices at the base of the wall. 'Sometimes in the villages, there is a boy or a girl. They live in the dirt, but they want the sky, and one day, when a band of Sakje ride by, the boy or girl goes to the chief and says, "Take me." And in the same way, sometimes a rider, old or young, watches the grass grow and yearns for the earth, for something solid under his feet. Such a one goes to the chief of a village and says, "Take me." He turned to Kineas, his handsome face lit by the rising sun. 'I am the king of all of them. So I love the dirt and the sky.'

The wind was warmer and the grass was greener, but the north wind bit hard and Kineas pulled his cloak tight around his shoulders for warmth. He looked at the walls he could see, following them from west to east, right up to the river. Athens, Piraeus, Olbia and Tomis would fit inside those walls and still have room. But there weren't enough people to fill a small Greek town. 'Stock pens,' he said as a reminder.

'When the tribes come in for the festival, or in time of war, there is grazing for their herds – at least for a month. The walls serve to keep the animals in, and to keep raiders out.' He grinned. 'So we have a population higher than Athens – if you count goats.'

'I see a great many merchants.' Kineas could see further than usual over the plains. 'And villages on the river. We never saw a village in two weeks' travel.'

The king nodded. 'The merchants don't speak much about

this. It's a trade secret. This is where the grain is grown. Those warehouses are where the grain is stored. They ship it down the river in barges, spring and fall. Why tell other men?' He looked out over the wall. 'But neither is it a secret. I suspect most of your men could have told you.'

Kineas shook his head. 'I feel like a fool. I thought I was going to find a field of tents.'

'In a month, you would have. We don't live here – except for the Sindi, the merchants, and a handful of priests.'

'Not even for the winter?' Kineas asked.

The king nodded. 'I have wintered here. The hill is cold.' He looked north. 'I prefer to winter in the north, by the trees.'

The king began to walk back into the great hall at the top of the acropolis, opposite the temple. The great hall was a log version of a Greek megaron, with a central hearth. The fire blazed as high as a man. The warmth could be felt as soon as the two men pushed through the tapestries that covered the great door.

The tapestries were a shock of colour. They were as alien as the endless sky and the sea of grass. The pair that kept the cold at bay in the door were made from heavy felt in many layers, with figures of men and horses and fantastic beasts cut out or applied in bright colours and geometric patterns on a white ground. On the walls hung larger panels of heavy wool embroidered with griffons and horses, huge horned deer and hunting cats. The floor was deep in bright carpets such as Kineas had seen in Kam Baqca's tent. The dominant colour was red, and the warmth was palpable.

The king waved at Marthax, standing by the fire with Kam Baqca in a magnificent robe, and Philokles.

'What trees? How far are the trees?' Kineas asked. He was looking for Srayanka.

'A thousand stades, or more. I doubt it could be measured. The trees are like another world. A world of forests. The Sindi say that once, all the world was a single forest.' He shrugged. 'I have seen the sea, and I have seen the trees. Each is like another world.'

'Why winter there?' Kineas asked.

'More wood makes bigger fires,' Satrax said with the

adolescent sneer he'd avoided all morning. He grinned. 'It's not complicated.'

Kineas thought of the walls, the warehouses, and the grain. 'You don't need Olbia as a base to feed your army,' he said.

Satrax grinned. 'It wouldn't hurt to spread the cost. I don't own all that grain. But no. I lied. Kings do that, when they must. I don't need Olbia.'

Kineas grinned back, but then narrowed his eyes. 'But you do have something for the Macedonians to march against. A city to lose. You can't really just melt into the grass.' He stopped as if struck. 'You have to fight for your farmers.'

They joined the circle at the fire. The Sakje had little ceremony – the king came and went like any free man, and the respect accorded him was no more – or less – than that given by Greek soldiers to a commander they respected. The king took a cup of heated apple cider from the woman who was mulling it by the fire. Then he sat on a pile of carpets.

While Kineas got his own cider, the king answered. 'Yes and no, Kineas. I could still melt into the grass. Nothing here is built in stone. That's our law. Zopryon can burn the lot – we'll build it back in a season. Or move.' He waved at a group of merchants by the fire. 'And if we all agreed to it, the Sindi would come with us.'

Kineas sat – without the grace all the Sakje showed in descending to the carpets.

The king looked into the fire. 'But I don't want to build it again. I don't want the interruption in trade. In fact, I don't want this war at all.' He sighed. 'But it is coming here, and I'll fight it.'

Kineas drank some of the cider. He loved the stuff. 'Where does this come from?' he asked. 'Apples won't grow for two seasons.'

The king shrugged. 'Cold has its advantages. We make cider in the fall and freeze it in blocks for the winter.' He beckoned to the other people that Kineas had come to think of as the war council. To Kineas, he said, 'Drink up – spring is here, and soon all the cider will go bad.'

Kam Baqca sat next to Kineas in a rustle of silk. Kineas had seen silk before, but seldom worn so often and by so many. Most of the Sakje had a silk garment, even if worn to tatters. Kam Baqca had a robe, pale yellow, covered in pink flowers and curling griffons. It was so magnificent that Kineas kept looking at it despite himself.

'We have wrangled for days,' Kam Baqca said. 'Marthax says that you are ready. Tell us your plan.'

Kineas hesitated, his cup of cider to his lips.

Kam Baqca regarded him calmly, her large eyes relaxed, almost sleepy. 'You have a plan, Kineas of Athens. The king has an army, but he does not yet have a plan.' She nodded. 'The two fit together like a man and,' she smiled, 'a woman.' The shaman's eyes flicked to Srayanka, who joined the circle, also wearing a silk robe, and back to Kineas. Kam Baqca put a hand on Kineas's arm and said, 'You must come and visit my tent. You must face the tree.'

Kineas nodded politely, with no intention of passing under her hand again. The last two dreams of the tree had left marks on his mind, ruts into which the wheels of his thoughts fell and along which they travelled too often and too unpredictably.

As if reading his mind, Kam Baqca leaned close, so that he could smell the spice and resin of her magic. 'Without the tree, you will never win her,' she said.

Srayanka's robe was dark blue, and reached from her neck to her ankles, and under it she wore trousers of a rich red. She looked more like a woman – Kineas's native idea of a woman – than he had seen before. Kineas found it disconcerting. And distracting.

For two days he had fought her, tooth and nail, on the conduct of the war. No Greek woman would have faced him down, shouted him down, when he counselled caution. Of course, he thought with further heartache, no Greek woman would have been at a war council.

Aware of his regard, she turned her head away from him and sat, exchanging greetings with the king and with Marthax.

As she sat, other men and women gathered to them – Leucon and Eumenes and Niceas, Marthax and Ataelus and a dozen Sakje nobles. They sat in a circle. Some reclined. Srayanka lay on her stomach, kicking her slippered heels in the air, a posture that no Greek woman would ever have adopted out of her bedroom. Kineas felt like a besotted fool. But he couldn't take his eyes away.

They fell silent after a momentary babble of greetings.

'I, too, think it is time to speak of the whole plan,' said the king. He looked at Kineas.

'I am a mercenary,' Kineas said to the group. 'I have never commanded more than three hundred horse in action.' He pointed at Marthax. 'As the king's war leader, shouldn't Marthax present the plan?'

Behind him, Eumenes translated as quickly as he could into Sakje. Kineas was no longer surprised by how much the young man understood.

The king made a gesture with his hand. 'This is not a Greek council, and I am not a Greek king. I have translated for you for two days – I know the plan. But we all wish to hear it in its finished form.'

Kineas nodded, looked around the circle. 'Very well. The plan is simple. We never fight a battle.'

Niceas whistled. 'I like it already,' he said.

Marthax waited for the translation and then nodded. 'Exactly,' he said, in Greek.

Srayanka raised an eyebrow. She rolled over and sat up.

He looked at her too long. Again.

The king held out his cup for more cider. 'How?'

Kineas tore his eyes from the lady. 'It's a matter of timing and logistics.'

Marthax spoke in Sakje, and Eumenes translated. 'That's why you're the expert.'

Kineas held up his hand. 'Last year, I rode from Tomis to Olbia by the same route that Zopryon must use. It took me thirty days. It will take his army fifty. If he marches tomorrow, the best he can do is to reach Olbia at midsummer.' He paused to let Eumenes' translation catch up. 'If we destroy the ferry at Antiphilous, we add at least two weeks to his journey. If the men of Pantecapaeum stand with us, and their fleet will serve our need – then we will strip his triremes off his army,

259

and slow his march still further. He intends to build forts as he marches – he is wise enough to know that his road home needs protection – which will slow him longer.' Again he waited for Eumenes to catch him up. 'We will then be past the new year – past the month of games, past the summer festival, and we will not yet have shown our hand.' Kineas looked around the circle. 'You know why he is coming here?'

Srayanka answered, 'To conquer us.'

Satrax shook his head. 'In the long run, the result would be the same. But he seeks our submission to prove his worth. As a feat of arms.'

Srayanka's face at the translation of the word 'submission' had a look that Kineas hoped was never directed at him.

Kineas took a deep breath. 'When he is sixty days from home and not yet at the Borasthenes River, we have a choice.' He tried not to look at Srayanka. 'The simplest choice would be to offer submission.' He shrugged. 'He won't have time to press the siege of Olbia by that point. He won't have the time to march here, and it would be suicide to march to this place leaving Olbia in his rear, astride his road home. If we offer him the tokens of submission …' He paused again, and sighed, still avoiding Srayanka's eye.

Satrax nodded. 'You think like a king.'

Kineas glanced at Philokles, who gave a slight nod of recognition. Srayanka was boring holes in his head with her eyes. She sprang to her feet. 'This must be your Greek *discipline!*' She glared around the council. 'What are we – a nation of slaves?' she asked in Greek. To the king she said, 'Will we beat our warriors into submission for this Macedonian beast? Are we so afraid?'

Kineas dropped his eyes. He had hoped … it no longer mattered what he hoped.

Marthax spoke. 'The other choice?' said Ataelus.

Kineas breathed in again. 'We strike his march columns every day over the last hundred and fifty stades to the great river. The Sakje – who won't have shown themselves yet, except in handfuls, groups of scouts – appear as if by magic. They kill the stragglers and the foragers. A handful of warriors strike their camps at night.'

Marthax spoke again, as did most of the Sakje. Out of the babble, Ataelus translated. 'Marthax says that more for liking him.'

There was a brief silence, and Philokles leaned forward into it and said, 'But of course, each of those attacks will work just once.'

Kineas nodded.

Satrax leaned forward into the circle, pulling at his beard. 'Yesterday you sounded as if you could pick his army to pieces like a flock of vultures. Today you say every trick will work only once. Why will the attacks work only once?'

Kineas glanced at Philokles, but Philokles shook his head, declining to take up the argument. Kineas looked at Srayanka, who continued to avoid his eye. He determined not to look at her again. 'Macedon has good officers and excellent discipline. After we hit their column once, there won't be any stragglers the next day. After we kill their foragers, the next day they will forage by regiments, with the whole army standing to arms.' He looked around the circle, avoiding her but willing her to listen. 'With discipline, they can minimize our advantages of speed and stealth.' He gave a hard grin. 'Of course, every measure they take to minimize our advantages will slow them.' He finished the cider in his cup. 'And we will not take heavy losses to do it. The cost in money to Macedon will be staggering. And Zopryon will never have a chance to try again. He will be disgraced.'

Kam Baqca nodded slowly, and then shook her head. 'But of course, Lord Zopryon will know all this.'

Kineas nodded. 'Yes.'

'So that, as soon as the raids start, he will immediately recognize our strategy and he will react like a desperate, wounded animal.' She looked, not at Kineas, but at Philokles. And then at Srayanka.

Philokles met her eyes. 'Yes. It will perhaps take him a few days to pass his desperation to his officers. But yes.'

'So he will *not* retreat to disgrace. He will lash out. He will, if he can, force us to battle.' Kam Baqca sat up on her knees. 'Even if he must take reckless gambles with his men and his supplies.'

All the Greeks nodded.

She also nodded, as if to herself. 'It is the wounded boar who kills men. It is the boar with no hope who gores kings.'

'Ouch,' muttered Niceas.

Srayanka bowed her head to Kam Baqca. 'Honoured one, we need not fear him. With our full muster—'

Kam Baqca reached out and touched her face. 'We might still lose. Every person in this circle might lie broken under the long moon ...' She stopped and closed her eyes.

The king watched her closely. 'Do you prophesy?'

She opened her eyes. 'It is on a sword's edge. As I have said.'

Kineas spoke with all the conviction of a man forced to speak against his will. 'We will not win such a battle.'

Srayanka spoke – not angrily, but with great force, and the king translated for her. 'You sound as if he is Alexander!' he said, mimicking Srayanka's gesture. 'What if he makes the wrong choice? What if he retreats?' Kineas watched her face while the king translated her words. 'You have never seen us fight, Kineax. Do you think we are cowards?' She clenched her fist and held it up. 'Perhaps we lack the discipline you have, but we are strong.'

Kineas shook his head. He was not doing well at avoiding her eyes, but when he spoke, he was controlled. 'Zopryon is no Alexander. Praise the gods, he is an average commander with no particular gifts. But the worst commander in Macedon knows how to conduct this kind of campaign. In Greece, we have books to tell us even if we don't have veterans to tell us how to do it.' He frowned. 'I have never seen you fight, but I know you to be brave. But no amount of courage will break the front of a taxeis.'

The king translated his reply and then looked at both of them. 'Kineas, my father's sister's daughter has more merit in her argument than you might think. You have never seen us fight. You don't know what we can muster.' He turned to Srayanka. 'Yet as I first said, Kineas thinks like a king. Battle is a risk. War is a danger. Why chase fortune's tail?' He looked at Marthax, who nodded deeply, so that his grey and black beard rode up and down on his chest.

'I hadn't thought to destroy the ferry at Antiphilous,' the king continued. 'And I didn't know how great Zopryon's fleet might be. But in other respects, is this not the plan as we discussed it all winter? And you, my lady – did I not warn you that Kineas would bring even more reasons to be wary?'

Marthax drained his cup and belched. 'Better,' he said, and Kineas understood before Ataelus translated. He went on. 'When he reaches some agreed point we harry him. And then, unless he retreats, we offer submission.' He grinned. 'Only a fool would reject us.'

Kam Baqca sat back on her heels and sipped a cup of wine. 'He will reject us,' she said. 'I have seen it.'

Srayanka's head snapped around. She spoke at length, and with the kind of vehemence that Kineas associated with reprimands to errant troopers. She spoke quickly and her voice rose in pitch, so that he couldn't even pick out words.

Eumenes shook his head, lost by the fluidity of her speech. Even Ataelus hesitated. The king came to their rescue. 'She says that if Kam Baqca has already foreseen the rejection, we can save ourselves the shame of offering the submission and concentrate on proving Kineas to be a fool about the battle.' He avoided looking at Kineas. 'She said some other things best left between her and Kam Baqca. But I will answer her.' He spoke briefly in Sakje, and then said, in Greek, 'I am king. Kam Baqca is often correct, but she herself says that the future is like the wax of a candle, and the closer it gets to the flame, the more malleable it is. She has been surprised. I have been surprised.' He turned to Srayanka and spoke in Sakje, and she put her hands to her face – a girlish gesture Kineas had never seen her use.

In Greek, the king said, 'We will not have our full muster of strength. Many horses we should have counted from our cousins the Massakje. Many we should have counted from our cousins the Sauromatae.' He looked around the circle. 'This is not for every man to discuss. Alexander is beating at the eastern gates of the grass, just as Zopryon beats at the west gate. The monster is in Bactria, chasing a rebel satrap.' The king rolled his shoulders and looked very young. 'Or he has always planned the campaign this way – to have armies enter the plain of grass from either end. Kam Baqca says this is not true – that it is mere happenstance.

But it makes no difference to us. We will have only two thirds of our full muster. Perhaps less. The Getae are already marching east, and our easternmost clans will have to protect their farmers.' He shrugged, spoke a long sentence in Sakje. Kineas understood several words – *no horses* and *Macedon*. In Greek, the king said, 'Submission alone costs us nothing. There is no shame in it, because we have no intention to submit.'

Somewhere in his head, Kineas realized that *nothing* in Greek was indicated in Sakje by *no horses*. Surrender costs us no horses, the king said. Kineas nodded in satisfaction.

'The grass is growing,' Kam Baqca said. 'The ground is almost hard. In a week the last of the heavy rain will pass. In two weeks, he will march.'

Kineas nodded in agreement.

The king said, 'Where do we appoint the muster? Where do we assemble our army?'

Kineas shrugged. 'We need to cover Olbia. If Zopryon takes Olbia you will have no choices at all. And if the archon does not feel that you are willing to protect him, he will abandon the alliance and submit – really submit.' Privately, Kineas thought that the archon might be tempted to make such a submission anyway. 'The closer the main army is to Olbia, the more reliable will be your alliance with the Euxine cities.'

The king nodded while Kineas's words were translated for the Sakje. 'So that my army threatens even as it protects.' Satrax said. He put his chin on his hand. 'It will be a month before I have even half my army in hand.'

Marthax spoke. The king listened and nodded. Eumenes said, 'Marthax says that the ferry will have to be destroyed immediately – that the riders should be dispatched today.'

Kineas looked at Marthax and nodded emphatically. Then he said, 'Our camp should be on the other bank of the great river, near a ford. If a battle must be fought, we must seize every advantage. Make Zopryon cross the river, if we come to that extremity.'

Srayanka waited for his translation and then spoke, as did several of the other Sakje nobles.

The king said, 'All of them agree that if we need a ford and a place to camp, the best is the far side of the campsite at the Great Bend. There is water and forage for an army, and supplies can reach us easily on boats.' He paused, and then said, 'Let it be so. The muster is appointed for the summer solstice, at the Great Bend.' To Kineas, he said, 'You will bring the city troops? We have nothing like your hoplites – and few enough of our nobles have the armour of your cavalry.'

Kineas agreed. 'I will bring the troops of the Euxine cities to the Great Bend by the solstice,' he said. He hoped he was telling the truth.

They talked about the campaign for two more days. They planned the muster of the Sakje. Messengers were dispatched to the leading Sakje clans to appoint the muster. They drafted letters for Pantecapaeum and for Olbia. Marthax was to go with sixty warriors to destroy the ferry, a job he felt required his presence in person. Before he departed Kineas took him aside and asked him to spare the farm by the bay where Graccus was buried, and Marthax laughed.

'Many and many the wine I swill there, Kineax,' Ataelus translated. Marthax gave Kineas a hug, which he returned. 'Old man feel no fire from us.' He gave Kineas a squeeze that threatened his ribs. 'Worry for less, Kineas. Plan good.'

Kineas extricated himself from Marthax's hug. The trust that Marthax put in him unnerved him. 'I am not a commander of armies,' Kineas said.

The young king emerged from the door behind his warlord. He shrugged at Kineas. 'Nor am I. But if I intended to make shoes, I would go to a shoemaker.'

'Plato,' said Kineas with a sour smile.

'Socrates,' said Philokles. 'Plato would have tried to make the shoes all by himself.'

14

The Sakje town had a market as big as any on the Euxine. Twenty stalls competed to sell every edged implement from the simplest eating knife to the heavy *rhompheas*, the new, heavy swords favoured by the Thracian hillmen. Simple short swords were available at every booth, from plain iron weapons with serviceable bone hilts to fanciful examples decorated in Persian gold work.

Cavalry swords were less common because the Sakje didn't like them. Kineas walked from one booth to the next, comparing lengths and weights, price, ornamentation, and practicality. Kineas enjoyed shopping and hearing the talk of war. Sword merchants were notorious gossips, often spies. Most of the stalls were run by slaves, but one was held by its owner, a big Egyptian freedman with his own stall and a wagon.

After he'd examined every ware on the man's table, he was invited to drink wine. In half a cup, he heard professional gossip from Ecbatana and from Egypt and all the lands in between.

'You're the hipparch I've heard so much about?' the merchant asked. 'No offence, but you're in for it.'

Kineas shrugged and swirled the second cup of excellent wine in the plain horn cup he'd been offered. 'I gather Zopryon has quite an army,' he observed.

'Zopryon means to conquer these Sakje – all the Scyths,' the merchant replied. 'At least, that's what he says in his cups. Darius failed, Xerxes failed, Cyrus died fighting them – Zopryon figures that he can get a name up there.' The merchant took a sip of his own wine and gave a slight smile. 'All of them want to rival Alexander.' He made the lords of Macedon sound like foolish boys.

Kineas was sitting on a leather stool behind the man's stall, watching Laertes haggle for an expensive knife at the next stall. As he watched, Laertes' face went through a series of expressions like a comic mime – anger, irritation, puzzlement, pleasure – as the price dropped.

The merchant was watching the exchange as well. 'That man's good at haggling. One of your soldiers?'

'And an old family friend,' said Kineas. 'We grew up together.'

'In Athens,' the merchant said, and then paused, realizing that perhaps he'd said too much. 'Well – that's what I heard – and your accent.'

Kineas turned away to hide his smile. 'He helped save my life at Issus,' he said.

'Nice kind of friend,' the merchant said. 'The kind of friend the gods send to a man.' Both of them spilled wine on the ground. Then choosing his words carefully, the merchant said, 'That would be when you won the prize for bravery.'

Kineas nodded. 'Stupidity, more like.' He considered the merchant for a few breaths. 'You know too much about me.'

The merchant looked around and shrugged. 'I came here from Tomis,' he said. 'Where Zopryon is raising his army.'

'Ah,' Kineas replied, pleased at the man's calm. He was obviously a spy, but in some small way an honest one.

'Zopryon has heard all about you from the veterans on his staff. The hipparch of his regiment of companions – Phillip? They're all named Phillip, aren't they?'

'So they are,' Kineas agreed. He knew a Phillip who commanded companions. The dreaded Hetaerae – the finest heavy cavalry in the world.

'I gather this Phillip had a woman named Artemis.'

Kineas narrowed his eyes. 'Yes,' he said.

'She has a very high opinion of you,' said the Egyptian. 'I began to wonder if this campaign is as one-sided as people in Thrace claim it is.'

Kineas leaned forward. 'Zopryon may be surprised by the strength of the opposition,' he said carefully.

The merchant flicked his eyes around the Sakje and Sindi in the crowd and then let his gaze fall heavily on Kineas. 'Do tell,' he said.

Kineas smiled. 'Phillip barely scraped a victory out of his fight with the Scyths,' he said. 'Cyrus died. Darius ran home with his whiskers burned. What does that tell you?'

The Egyptian had a fur-lined Thracian cloak across his lap. He pulled it around his shoulders. 'You tell me,' he said slowly.

Kineas leaned back. 'I'm here to buy a good sword, not swap gossip.'

The merchant took his turn to shrug. 'I have a few good swords I save for special customers,' he said. 'The kind that bring me good gossip are my favourites.' He watched Laertes paying for his purchase. Kineas was glad to see the man happy.

Kineas got up and began to toy with one of the infantry short swords on the merchant's table. 'There are a lot of Scyths,' he said. He rolled his wrist, letting the sword fall into an imaginary victim under its own weight. Too light. He knew that.

The merchant looked bored. 'This is something about which I have wondered much,' he said. He poured more wine from a ewer and held it up for Kineas, who held out his horn cup.

'Think of it this way,' Kineas said. 'There are Scyths here, there are Scyths all around the Euxine. Scyths north of Bactria, and north of Persia, and everywhere in between.'

The Egyptian nodded. 'Just as Herodotus says.' He got up, shrugged the cloak into place on his shoulders, and took a heavy rug off the two-wheeled cart at the back of his stall.

Kineas had had all winter to read Herodotus. It had become one of his favourite pastimes. Especially the part about Amazons. 'He came to Olbia,' Kineas said. 'He knew what he was talking about.'

The merchant nodded. 'I expect he did,' he said. 'Will they fight?'

Kineas watched him unroll the rug. It had four swords in its folds. Two were short and two were long. The longest was shaped like a Greek cavalry sword, a true *machaira*, the weight near the tip of the blade, curved like a reversed sickle, but it had a wicked point. It felt curiously light in his hand, almost alive. The tang had a simple leather wrapping and no hilt. Kineas rolled it in his fist and let the point drop. It bit into the table with a soft *thunk*. 'Beautiful,' he said.

'Steel,' the merchant said. He flexed it in his hands and

handed it back. 'There's a priest in Alexandria who has the knack. He doesn't make many, but every one of them comes out right.' The merchant drank wine, put his cup down and rubbed his hands before blowing on them. Then he said, 'I've seen other men make steel blades – one in a dozen, or one in a hundred. This priest is the only man I know who makes them every time.'

The blade seemed to have a dozen colours trapped just under the surface, which was polished to a degree Kineas had not seen before. He made an overhand cut and the sword sang as it cut the air. Kineas realized that he had a broad smile on his face. He couldn't help it. 'How much?' he asked.

'How many Scyths are there?' the man asked again.

Kineas rubbed his thumb on the tang. 'Thousands,' he said, and sat back on his stool.

The Egyptian nodded. 'The Getae tell Lord Zopryon that there are only a few hundred warriors, the last remnant of a proud race, and that he can conquer them in a summer. Zopryon intends to take Olbia and Pantecapaeum to pay for the campaign and to serve as bases, and then march inland, building forts as he goes. I tell you nothing that is not common knowledge, yes?' He looked intently at Kineas for a reaction.

It wasn't common knowledge in Olbia. Kineas tried to keep his face blank. It must have been good enough, because the Egyptian continued. 'But some of the older officers ask questions about the numbers of the nomads. They say the old king brought ten thousand horsemen to fight Phillip.' He gestured with his chin at the sword blade across Kineas lap. 'Eight minae of silver.'

Kineas handed the sword back with regret. 'Too rich for me,' he said. 'I'm an officer, not a god.' He rose. 'Thanks for the wine.'

The Egyptian rose as well, and bowed. 'I could perhaps accept seven minae.'

Kineas shook his head. 'He must be a very rich priest, this fellow in Alexandria. Two minae would break me. I'd have to go sell my services to Zopryon.'

The merchant gave him an amused look. 'You are the hipparch

of the richest city on the Euxine. You plead poverty? I think rather that you are some hard-hearted rich man who seeks to beggar me and leave my wife and my two expensive daughters as paupers. That sword is a gift of the gods to a fighting man. Look – I didn't even bother to put a hilt on it, because only a rich fool or a swordsman would want the thing. The first would want a hilt I can't afford, and the second would want to hilt it himself. The sword was made for you. Make me an offer!'

Kineas found that he had picked the sword up again. Not his best bargaining technique. 'I might be able to find three minae.'

The Egyptian raised his hands to heaven and then pulled them abruptly down on his head. 'I'd have my slaves throw you in the mud, except you are a guest,' he said, and then he smiled. 'And, of course, none of my slaves are big enough to throw you in the mud, and your friend the king could have me executed.' He put his hands on his hips. 'Let us drop this haggling. You pleased me with your tidbits about the Scyth. You are the first man of sense I have met in this market. Make me a genuine offer and I will take it.'

Kineas leaned close, where he could smell the rose-scented perfume on the other man and the fish sauce he'd had with his lunch. 'The Sakje here will eat Zopryon for dinner.'

The Egyptian narrowed his eyes. 'And your alliance with him is firm?'

Kineas shrugged. 'I suspect Zopryon would like to know.' He grinned. 'Will he hear it from you?'

'Amon – do I look like a spy for Zopryon?' The Egyptian smiled. With a sleight of hand that Kineas had to admire, two small scrolls were pressed into Kineas's cloak.

To cover the movement, Kineas nodded. 'I might go to four minae,' he said.

The Egyptian shrugged. 'Now you offer some money. Still not enough.' He pulled his cloak tighter. 'When the assembly restores your father's property, you'll be so rich you can buy every sword in the market.'

Kineas raised an eyebrow. 'Your words to Zeus, Egyptian. Or do you know something?'

'I know many people,' the Egyptian said. 'Some live in Athens.' He made a face and pulled his cloak tighter yet. 'By Zeus-Amon, it's colder than Olbia.'

Kineas's eyebrows shot up. 'You were in Olbia?'

'I just missed you,' said the Egyptian. Raising his voice, he said, 'Perhaps I might let you keep this sword for six minae.'

Kineas was too eager to read the letters to wait and haggle over the sword blade. 'I don't have six minae,' Kineas said. He put the horn cup down on the table and laid the sword gently on the rug. 'I wish I did.' He gave the Egyptian a short bow. 'Thanks for the wine.'

'Any time,' said the merchant. 'Borrow the money!'

Kineas laughed and walked away. At a table in a tented wine shop, he read the two scrolls – letters from Athens. The letters were months behind. He rubbed his face, and then laughed.

Athens wanted him to stop Zopryon.

One thing the Sakje town boasted out of all proportion to its size were goldsmiths. Kineas walked among them with the king's companion Dikarxes, as well as Ataelus and Philokles. Gold was cheap here – not cheap, per se, but cheaper than in Athens – and the Sakje required it for every garment, every ornament. There were shops of craftsmen from Persia and from Athens and from as far afield as the Etruscan peninsula north of Syracuse. The crowds of goldsmiths made Kineas feel yet more foolish for imagining the town a secret.

A freedman from Athens ran a shop with six men of all races working. The bust of Athena in his shop window and the sound of his voice moved Kineas profoundly, and he entered to talk and stayed to buy. He presented the Egyptian sword blade to be hilted – purchased the day before for five minae.

'Quite a piece of iron,' said the Athenian. He made a face. 'Most of my customers want a horse or a griffon on their swords. What do you fancy?'

'A hilt that balances the blade,' Kineas said.

'How much can you pay?' asked the man, eyeing the blade with professional interest. He put it on a scale and weighed it, made notes on a wax tablet. 'Point heavy? Show me where you want the balance. Close enough.' He set some weights on the balance and then wrote the result, drew a line on the blade with a wax stylus.

Kineas looked around the shop. Parshtaevalt was admiring a gorytos cover – solid gold, with magnificent depictions of Olympus – surrounded by a score of Assagatje nobles. 'Not as much as they can pay,' he said. 'Two minae of silver?' he said. He'd have to borrow it – the sword had returned him to penury.

The goldsmith tilted his head. 'I suppose I could make it from lead,' he said.

Parshtaevalt leaned over. 'Listen – you big man. King pay for you, yes yes.'

'I don't want the king to pay,' Kineas said.

'Let me build you something as fine as the blade,' said the Athenian smith. 'You're the hipparch of Olbia – I've heard of you. Your credit is good with me.'

Kineas relinquished the blade with some hesitation.

Dikarxes, the king's friend, pushed past Philokles. The shop was growing crowded with Sakje nobles – almost every man and woman from the council. Parshtaevalt growled a greeting and Dikarxes replied at length. Ataelus translated. 'Trust you to find out all our secrets! Our own Athenian goldsmith!' Parshtaevalt slapped his back.

Dikarxes spoke again, and Ataelus said, 'Of course the king for pay. He for show favour you. He ask everyone what gift to give. What better gift than sword?'

Dikarxes interrupted to introduce the other nobles. 'Kaliax of the Standing Horse,' he said through Ataelus. And went on, 'Gaomavañt of the Patient Wolves. They are the most loyal – the core of the king's army – with the Cruel Hands, of course.' He grinned at Parshtaevalt. 'It is a very good sign that they are already come in, with most of their strength.'

Kineas clasped hands with each in turn.

Gaomavañt gave him a tight hug and spoke while slapping his back. Ataelus choked, and Eumenes translated, his face red as a flame. 'He says – you are the one that Srayanka fancies. It is good you are so tough, or she will swallow you.'

Dikarxes said a few words, and the others roared, and again Gaomavañt slapped his back.

Ataelus wiped his eyes. 'Lord Dikarxes say – good for everyone if she mate you – you Greek, and no clan suffer from the alliance. If Cruel Hands join Patient Wolves, blood on the grass – yes? Cruel Hands mate with king – king too powerful. But Cruel Hands—'

'Cruel Hands?' Kineas asked. 'Is that Srayanka's clan?'

Ataelus nodded. 'And lady's war name, too. Cruel Hands.'

Philokles patted his shoulder. 'Nice name. Perfect little Greek wife.'

Kineas made himself laugh, but for the rest of the afternoon he heard Ataelus's voice in his head – *Cruel Hands mate with king.*

Kineas tried to avoid Kam Baqca because the woman scared him. She was the personification of the dreams that troubled him, and in her presence, the dreams of the tree and the plain seemed more imminent – almost real. But on his fifth day in the city of the Sakje, Kam Baqca found him in the great hall and seized his arm in hers – strong as an iron blade – and walked him to a curtained alcove like a tent. She threw a handful of seeds on a brazier and a cloud of heavy smoke rose around them. The smoke smelled like cut grass. It made him cough.

'You dreamed the tree,' she said.

He nodded.

'You dreamed the tree twice. You touched the tree, and you are paying the price. But you waited for me to climb it, so you are not altogether a fool.'

Kineas bit his lips. There was a drug in the incense – he could feel it. 'I am a Greek man,' he said. 'Your tree is not for me.'

She seemed to move in the smoke like a snake, coiling, flowing easily from one place to another. 'You are a baqca born,' she said. 'You dream like a baqca. Are you ready for the tree? I must take you now, while I have you. Soon you will be gone, and the maw of war will devour you. It is a war I will not survive – and then there will be no one to take you to the tree. And without

273

the tree, you will neither survive, nor win the lady.' She was telling him too many things too fast.

'You will die?'

She was beside him. 'Listen to me.' She held his arm in a grip of iron. 'Listen. The first thing the tree shows you is the moment of your death. Are you ready for that?'

Kineas wasn't ready for any of it. 'I am a Greek man,' he said again, although it sounded like a poor excuse. Especially as the tree itself was growing before his eyes, rising from the smoke-dense tent, straight out of the charcoal of the brazier, its heavy branches just over his head and rising into the heavens above him.

'Take a branch and climb,' she said.

He reached up and took the first soft-backed branch over his head, threw a leg over it clumsily and pulled himself up. His arms were as full of the drug as his head. He found that he had closed his eyes and he opened them.

He was sitting on a horse in the middle of a river – a shallow river, with rocks under his horse's feet and pink water flowing over and around the rocks. The ford – it was a ford – was full of bodies. Men and horses, all dead, and the white water burbling over the rocks was stained with blood, the froth of the water pink in the sun.

The river was vast. Not Issus, then, some part of his mind said. He lifted his head and saw the far bank, and he rode towards it. There were other men behind him, all around him, and they were singing. He was astride a strange horse, tall and dark, and he felt the weight of strange armour.

He felt the power of a god.

He knew that feeling – the feeling of a battle won.

He gestured, and his cavalry gathered speed, crossing the ford faster. On the far bank a thin line of archers began to form and fire, but behind them was the chaos of defeat and rout – a whole army breaking into fragments.

A Macedonian army.

A half-stade from the archers, he raised his hands, his gold-hilted sword of Egyptian steel like a rainbow of death in his hand. He half turned to Niceas – it wasn't Niceas, but a woman – the woman raised the trumpet to her lips, and the call rang like a clarion, and they charged.

The day was won. It was his last thought as the arrow knocked him from the saddle into the water. He was deep in the water, and he had been here before, and he pushed himself to his feet, but the arrow dragged him down.

He sat – alive – astride a branch of the tree, and it was as soft as a woman's leg against his groin.

Kam Baqca spoke. 'You have seen your death?'

Kineas was lying flat, holding someone's hand, his death scream still raw in his throat. 'Yes,' he whispered.

He opened his eyes and found that he was holding Kam Baqca's hand. Not a bad death, he thought.

Niceas had not been beside him when he fell. Had Philokles been there? Hard to tell in the chaos of a few seconds – all the men at his back had worn closed helmets, and most had been in coats of scale – Sakje armour, in fact.

Kam Baqca spoke again. 'Do not dare to interpret what you have seen. You may be sure of what it means and you can still be surprised. You have begun to climb the tree – I have climbed it all my life. I gave my sex to the gods to help me climb faster. You do not even believe in the climb. Beware of hubris.'

'What?' He coughed, as if he still had water in his lungs. His mind was clear, but his body was sluggish.

'There are no rules for Greeks,' she replied. 'But I think you will find it unwise to speak of it – especially in a few weeks, when you decide that I am a bent she-man who uses drugs to manipulate.' She shrugged. 'Perhaps I wrong you. You and Philokles – I have never met, nor seen in any dream, Greek men more open to new things.'

Kam Baqca rose on her haunches and threw another herb on the fire – this one redolent of pine. 'That will clear your head and take death from your spirit,' she said. She stood. 'It is a week for hard news, Kineas the Athenian. Here is mine for you. You watch Srayanka like the stallion watches the mare. I tell you, and I speak for the king – we will not allow stallions and mares to serve in the same company, because they disturb all the horses. So with you. You will not mate until this war is over.

Already Srayanka thinks more of you than of her duty. Already you fear to offend her rather than offering the king your best counsel.' She put a hand on his shoulder. 'Who cannot see that you are for each other, although you share no tongue? But not yet, and not now.'

Kineas spoke, and he couldn't hide the anguish in his voice. 'She hasn't spoken to me in a week!'

'Has she not?' Kam Baqca seemed unperturbed by his tone. 'You are blind, deaf, and stupid, then.' She gave him a small smile. 'When you grow less stupid, I ask that you have a care.'

'It's a care I would like to have,' Kineas said.

Kam Baqca reached out and touched his cheek. 'Everything – *everything* – is balanced in the blade of a sharp sword. One word, one act, and the balance tilts.'

Kineas thought less of the balance than of the fact that he was doomed to die – and soon.

15

They rode like Sakje on the road home, trotting for miles, changing horses, and moving again. They had no escort this time, just Parshtaevalt and a second Cruel Hand called Gavan as guides and messengers.

Through the entire trip, Kineas felt the press of urgency on his shoulders. The ground was hard enough. Zopryon could march at any time, and the campaign, for so long in abeyance, was suddenly upon him and he felt unprepared. He worried about the archon's treachery, and about the morale of the city, about the lives of his troops and about the alliance of the Sakje, their numbers, their quality.

And having foreseen his own death, he struggled to understand what it meant – or whether he accepted it as genuine prophecy, or merely the result of the smoke. The Sakje used a drug of smoke for many things, including recreation. He'd experienced it more than once now, when visiting Dikarxes, when sitting in the great hall while the drug was cast in braziers. He'd smelled it in Kam Baqca's tent in the snow. It was possible that the drug was the root of all the dreams. And if the dream was real – it was a two-edged sword. No man wanted to know he had just sixty days to live. But there was comfort, too – to fall at the hour of victory had at least the virtue of predicting victory.

Of all the things he had ever wanted to discuss with Philokles, this – the dreams, the prophecy, oracular powers, dreams of death and of the future – pressed on him every time they spoke, and yet some reserve, some caution about making it more real by discussing it aloud, kept him from it.

And, of course, the Baqca had forbidden it.

On the last day, when the outriders had already seen the walls of Olbia, exchanged shouts with the sentries on the walls, and relieved Kineas's mind of half its illogical worries by reporting all was well, Philokles rode up next to Kineas. He rode well enough now to be accounted a horseman. He required larger horses than any other man, and he tired them more quickly, but he was tireless in the saddle.

Kineas glanced at him with affection. Philokles was a big man, but he was now a tower of muscle. The fat he had worn when they first met was gone, burned away by almost a year of constant exercise. He was handsome, heavily bearded, and he smiled more often than had been his wont.

'All is well in the city?' he asked as he rode up.

'That's what the scouts say.' Kineas was still smiling to himself.

'You seem happier today,' Philokles said.

Kineas raised an eyebrow.

'You have been a silent man for six days, brother. You're putting the troops off their feed and Niceas is so worried he put me up to this. You are a worrier, but not usually a brooder. Did your amazon play you false? I confess that I heard much speculation about her relations with the king.'

Kineas fidgeted with his reins, which his riding horse resented. The horse showed his resentment by shying at a passing bee and then kicking his rear hooves until Kineas squeezed his thighs and stopped playing with the reins.

'I have a great deal to think about.' Kineas didn't meet his friend's eye.

'Doubtless. The man of the moment – the warlord of the alliance.' Philokles paused, and then said, 'May I tell you something I know about you?'

'Of course.'

'You worry all the time. You worry about many things – some of them very profound, like good and evil, and some of them very practical, like where we'll camp, and some of them quite silly, like the archon's potential for treason. It's all that worrying that makes you a good commander.'

'This is not news to me, my friend.' Kineas growled. 'Why is the archon's potential for treason silly?'

Philokles said, 'If he chooses to betray the alliance, you will take action – you and Memnon, and Cleitus, and Nicomedes. If he doesn't, then no action need be taken. The decision to betray us is in the mind of the archon, and you cannot affect it. So your worry is wasted.'

'Nonsense,' Kineas said. 'I worry at the effect his betrayal might have on the trust of the Sakje. And I plan for contingencies – what if he does thus and such?'

'Sometimes your worry touches on hubris. But I have strayed from the straight road of my intention. I have seen you worry since the first hour I knew you – sitting on your bench in that cursed pentekonter and worrying at what the helmsman's intention might be. It is your nature.'

'Again, this is not news to me.' Kineas shrugged. 'I am familiar with what happens inside my head.'

'So you are. But since we left that Sakje town, you are closed. Nothing moves in your face, and your eyes seldom light. This is not worry. This is more like fear. What do you fear?' Philokles spoke softly. 'Tell me, brother. A burden shared is a heart eased.'

Kineas made a motion to Niceas, who had allowed himself to fall behind, and the hyperetes sounded the halt. The column halted immediately, and every man dismounted. Wineskins were passed, and now that the heat of the sun was full in the sky, men rolled their cloaks and fastened them to their saddles.

Kineas dismounted, took wine from Philokles' skin, and stood at his horse's head. The horse pressed his nose into Kineas's hand, and he scratched the gelding's head. 'I cannot,' he said, at length. The desire to speak of his dream of death was so powerful that he didn't trust himself to speak more. The desire to speak of his feelings for Srayanka was equally strong.

Philokles spoke slowly. 'We have shared our secrets. You make me afraid that – shall I say it? That you know something from Athens that threatens us all. Or from the king.'

'You miss the mark entirely,' Kineas said, stung. 'If I knew some doom hanging over us, don't you think I'd speak of it?'

Philokles stood by his own horse. He took his wineskin, and shook his head. 'In one thing, you and the tyrant are like brothers. You would not tell us, if you thought we would be better off not knowing. You feel that your will is superior to that of most men.'

'No commander worth an obol shares all his thoughts with his men,' Kineas snapped.

'The tyrant lives in every commander,' Philokles agreed.

'Yet you supported my views on discipline,' Kineas said.

'Discipline is not secrecy. Every man in the phalanx knows that his survival depends on the actions of all. No deviation can be allowed. That discipline is a public thing. The rules are available to all.'

Kineas's heart was thudding, and his breathing was fast. He took a deep breath and counted to ten in Sakje – an exercise that was coming more and more easily. 'You provoke me more easily than any man on earth.'

'You are not the first man to tell me that,' Philokles replied.

'I am not ready to discuss the thing that I fear. Yes. You are right, of course. I am afraid. Yet – and I ask you to trust me on this – it is not a matter that need concern you.' *I am afraid of death.* Somehow, just admitting the fear to himself had lightened the load.

Philokles glanced at him sharply, and then held his eye. 'When you are ready, you should talk about it. I am a spy – I learn things. I know that you saw Kam Baqca. I suspect she told you something.' He looked hard at Kineas. 'And I guess she told you some ill news.' Kineas's face must have betrayed his inner anguish, because Philokles raised his hand. 'Your pardon. I see on your face that I am on poor ground. I know you love the lady. If she treats you ill, I'm sorry.'

Kineas nodded. 'I am *not* ready to discuss it.' Yet his friend's concern touched him, and he had to smile – confronted with the loss of a woman he'd scarcely touched, and his imminent death, which was more important? Men were idiots. His sisters had said as much, many times, and Artemis had concurred.

Philokles slung his wineskin. 'You're smiling. I have achieved something! Shall we ride to Olbia, then?'

Kineas managed another smile. 'Where the worst thing to face is the archon?' He waved to Niceas to sound the *mount* order. 'Who said that war makes things simple?'

Philokles grunted. 'Someone who had never planned a war.'

*

'Once again, I confess that I have underestimated you, my dear Hipparch.' The archon beamed with satisfaction.

Kineas was growing used to the archon's abrupt swings of mood and favour. Instead of betraying surprise, or giving an answer, he merely inclined his head.

'You have lured the bandit king to do his all in our protection – and then, before anyone is committed to a policy of war, we are allowed to negotiate a settlement? Brilliant! And Zopryon, out on the plains with bands of barbarians harrying him ...' The archon, who had been rubbing his chin, now clapped his hands together. 'He'll negotiate, all right. Hipparch, I appoint you our commander. I put in your hands the forces of the state. Please do your best to avoid using them.'

Kineas found that he was pleased, despite everything, to be appointed commander. He had thought that, on balance, he would get the post – Memnon, though older, hadn't seen nearly as much fighting as he – but these things were political and often unpredictable. 'I will, Archon.'

'Good.' The archon signalled his Nubian slave for wine and indicated that he wanted three cups.

Kineas glanced at Memnon, whose dark face was thunderous.

'You aren't pleased?' the archon said to Memnon.

Memnon's voice was flat. 'Very pleased.'

The archon's voice was all honey. 'You do not sound pleased. Are you slighted? Should you have had the command?'

Memnon glanced at Kineas. Shrugged. 'Perhaps.' He hesitated, but anger got the better of him. 'I want to push my spear into Macedon, not hide behind walls and then feign submission! What kind of plan is that?'

The archon put his chin on his hand, one finger pointing up along his temple towards heaven. His hair was cut in the latest mode, with a fringe of ringlets around the crown which accentuated the golden wreath he affected. 'The plan of a realist, Memnon. Kineas's plan's greatest elegance is that the Macedonians can spend all the money and do all the dying, and then at the end we have a full range of political options. We can, if I desire it, *rescue* poor Zopryon – supplies, a base of operations – and use him to rid us of the bandits for ever.' While he pronounced these words, the archon glanced at Kineas. He had a wicked smile on his face – the sort of smile a little boy wears when he knows that he does wrong.

Kineas maintained his impassivity. He was finding that the knowledge of his own death had gifted him with as much calm as fear. In fact, the fear was fading with acceptance. He had two months to live. The archon's desire to manipulate and disconcert was of little moment.

These musings kept him silent too long, and the archon snapped. 'Well? Hipparch? Why shouldn't I help Zopryon?'

Kineas wrapped his left hand around the pommel of his old sword. 'Because he would seize your city at the first pretext,' he said carefully.

The archon slumped. 'There must be a way to use him against the bandits.'

Kineas said nothing. The archon's desires were now of little importance to him.

The archon brightened. 'We must have a ceremony,' he said. 'At the temple. I will vest you with the command in public.'

Kineas's fingers betrayed his impatience with their rapid drumming at his pommel. 'We must get our citizens prepared. The hippeis, at least, must be ready to move to the camp.'

Memnon grunted.

'I believe we can find time for a ceremony that will have important repercussions,' said the archon. He motioned to a slave who stood behind his stool. 'See to it. All the priests – perhaps some token of benevolence for the people.'

The slave – another Persian – spoke for the first time. 'That will take some days to prepare, Archon.'

The archon's face set. 'You haven't heard. Zopryon executed Cyrus – my emissary – on the pretext that as a slave, he was unworthy of serving as ambassador. This is Amarayan.'

Kineas looked carefully at Amarayan, a bronze-coloured man with a rich black beard and a face that betrayed nothing.

'We will need cooperation from Pantecapaeum,' Kineas said. 'We will need their fleet.'

The archon shook his head. 'There, I must disagree. Any action by their fleet would commit us, I fear.'

Kineas sighed. 'If the Macedonian fleet is not kept in check, we will not have any options at midsummer.'

The archon tapped his fingers against his face. 'Oh, very well. I will ask that they bring their ships here.'

Kineas shook his head. 'They must do more than that, Archon. They must patrol south around the coast, seek out the Macedonian squadron, and destroy it. In addition, I'd like you to close the port.' He continued to watch Amarayan. 'There are, no doubt, spies here. I don't want them to communicate with Tomis.'

The archon spoke slowly, as if humouring a child. 'Closing our port would be ruinous to trade.'

'With respect, Archon, we are at war.' Kineas willed his hand to stop playing with his sword. 'If all goes well, the grain can be shipped in the autumn.'

'Athens will not be pleased if we hold their grain ships all summer.' The archon looked at Amarayan, who nodded.

'None of the autumn wheat will be coming down the river anyway,' Kineas countered. 'The king of the Sakje is holding the grain to supply his army.'

'Army?' spat the archon. 'Bands of savages on the grass are not an army!'

Kineas remained silent.

Memnon stifled a laugh. 'Archon, you cannot pretend that all is normal. Zopryon is marching here with the intention of taking the city.'

Kineas added, 'Athens would rather miss a season of grain than lose us to Macedon for ever.'

Amarayan leaned forward and whispered to the archon. The archon nodded. 'I will think on it,' he said. 'You are dismissed. You may inform our citizens to prepare themselves to take the field. In five days,' he glanced at Amarayan, who nodded, 'we will celebrate the spring festival by appointing you formally to lead the allied army. Perhaps after that I will close the port.'

Five days. By then the three ships in port would have loaded and gone, carrying whatever messages they had.

Kineas gave a salute and withdrew. In the citadel's courtyard, under the eyes of a dozen of the archon's Kelts, Kineas caught

Memnon by the shoulder. 'There will be a battle,' he said.

Memnon stopped. He was armoured and held his helmet under his arm, his curly black hair was cropped short and his black cloak flapped in the wind. His eyes searched Kineas's face. 'You plan to force one?'

Kineas shook his head. 'I would avoid battle with Zopryon if I could. But the gods—' Kineas stopped himself, unsure what to reveal. But he needed Memnon, and Memnon needed to know. Kineas couldn't endure a summer of open hostility with the man. 'The gods sent me a dream. A very vivid dream, Memnon. There will be a battle. I have seen it.'

Memnon continued to watch him warily. 'I am not one for gods and dreams,' he said. 'You are a strange man. You puzzle me.' He stuck his thumbs in his sash. 'But you are not a liar, I think. Do we win this battle?'

Kineas feared to say too much – feared that by saying something, he might change it. 'I – think so.'

Memnon stepped closer. 'You dreamed of it, but you only *think* you know the result? How can this be?'

Kineas let out his breath and shook his head. 'Ask me no more. I don't want to discuss it. I only wanted to say that, for all the archon's prevarications, we will fight. When midsummer comes, we will not submit.' Kineas glanced over his shoulder. 'Where did the new Persian come from?'

Memnon smiled briefly, showing his teeth, two of which were broken, and then he spat on the paving stones of the courtyard. 'Cleomenes gave him to the archon – a fully trained Persian steward. This one was born a slave. He will become very dangerous,' Memnon said, flicking his eyes towards the citadel. Then he gave Kineas a hard grin. 'As will the archon, if he finds that he's not actually at the helm.'

Kineas shrugged. 'I think that events will take the decisions out of his hands.'

'I want a battle. I don't much care how we come to it. All this skirmishing on the grass is well enough for the horse boys, but my lads need a flat field and a long day. We won't be raiding camps.'

Kineas nodded. 'Your men are the heart of the city's citizens.

Every week we keep them in the field is a week in which Olbia has no blacksmiths and no farmers. I think,' Kineas hesitated, wondering for the hundredth time how accurate his numbers were, 'I think that you can wait a month to follow me. Ten days to march to the camp – you should still be there twenty days ahead of Zopryon.'

Memnon fingered his beard. 'Twenty days, plus a ten-day march – that's a good amount of time. Enough to harden them, train every day – not so much that they'll be worn down.' He nodded. 'What if Zopryon doesn't keep your timetable?'

Kineas started to walk to the gate. He didn't want all of his thoughts reported back to the archon – although he doubted the Kelts knew much Greek. 'He hasn't much choice. An army his size, horse and foot – you know as well as I how slowly he'll move. If he bides his time then he won't get here in time to even *threaten* a siege. If he rushes, men will starve.'

Memnon walked with him, out through the citadel gate and down the walls to the town. 'Your reasoning sounds excellent.' He laughed mirthlessly. 'Alexander would take his time coming and to Hades with the consequences. He'd assume that he could take this city – even in late autumn – and that he could use it to feed his troops even if he had to put the people to the sword.'

Kineas nodded as he walked. 'Yes.'

Memnon stopped in the agora and turned to face Kineas. 'So why won't Zopryon do the same?'

Kineas pursed his lips, rubbed his beard. 'Perhaps he will,' he said. 'Perhaps that's why we'll fight a battle.'

Memnon shook his head. 'You sound like a priest. I have no fondness for priests. Dream or no dream – this will be a hard campaign. Mark my words – I'm an oracle of war.' He laughed. 'Thus speaks Memnon the oracle – Zopryon will do something we haven't considered, and all your timetables will be buggered.'

Kineas was stung – Memnon's dismissal of his calculations annoyed him – but he had to admit the truth of the man's assertions. 'Perhaps,' he growled.

'Perhaps nothing. You're a professional soldier – you know it as well as I. Plan all you like – Zopryon will win or lose at the point of the spear.' Memnon seemed to grow in size as he spoke. He was passionate. 'And all the horse boys in the world can't stop a Macedonian *taxeis*. When push comes to shove, it's my hoplites and those from Pantecapaeum who will stand or not stand.' The thought seemed to delight him. 'I'll need to arrange a muster for the Pantecapaeum troops – meet their commander, plan some drills, and see if they have some iron in their bellies.'

Kineas was pleased that Memnon was engaged. He slapped the man on the shoulder. 'You're a good man, Memnon.'

Memnon nodded. 'Hah! I am. They made me a citizen – can you believe it? I may yet die in a bed.'

For a few moments Kineas the commander had forgotten the imminence of his own mortality. Memnon's words brought it straight back. He sobered. 'I hope you do,' he said.

'Bah! I'm a spear child. Ares rules me, if there are any gods and if any of them care an obol for men – which I doubt. Why die in bed?' He chuckled, waved, and walked off into the market.

Pantecapaeum was very much in Kineas's thoughts the next few days. He sent a letter with Niceas as the herald, addressed to the hipparch of the city, requesting that the man meet him to plan the campaign and suggesting a tentative schedule of marches. He told Niceas to bring him a report on the city's preparedness.

Niceas returned the same day that the three ships sailed. Kineas was on the walls, watching Memnon drill the hoplites in opening gaps in their ranks to permit the passage of Diodorus with the horse.

Philokles came up behind him. 'Athens will be pleased to get the last of the winter wheat.'

Kineas grunted. 'Zopryon will be pleased to get a spy report from here outlining every aspect of our plans.'

Philokles yawned. 'Somebody here is. Two Macedonian merchants came in on the last ship – the pentekonter on the beach.'

Kineas sighed. 'We are a sieve.'

Philokles laughed. 'Don't despair, brother. I took some precautions.'

Kineas looked out over the walls. The hoplites had been too

slow in opening their files, and Diodorus's troop was caught against the face of the phalanx, dreadfully exposed. In a battle, that small error of marching would have meant disaster. Memnon and Diodorus were shouting themselves hoarse.

Kineas looked back at the Spartan. 'Precautions?'

Philokles twitched the corners of his mouth. 'I have allowed the archon's new factor – another perfumed Mede – to receive some reports that you have deceived the archon – that you intend to take the army and march south with the Sakje. In fact, he was surprised to learn that Sindi farmers have been paid to prepare a battlefield along the Agathes River, digging trenches and preparing traps.'

Kineas raised an eyebrow.

Philokles shrugged. 'Rumour – all rumour.' He sneered. 'Zopryon is more likely to believe a rumour his spies gleaned in the wine shops than a plan spoken before his face. It is a fault all spies share.'

Kineas wrapped his arms around the Spartan. 'Well done!'

Philokles shrugged again. 'It was nothing.' He was pleased by the praise, however. A flush crept up his cheeks.

'The Macedonian merchants – they'll know better in a few weeks,' Kineas said.

'Hmm.' Philokles nodded. 'Too true. However, Nicomedes and Leon have them in hand. That is to say – perhaps it is best if I say no more.'

Kineas shook his head. 'Nicomedes?'

Philokles nodded. 'Surely, having seen the ease with which he commands his troop, you no longer believe in his pose as a useless fop?'

Kineas shook his head. 'I think that I must, despite his obvious skills and authority. I find it difficult to take him seriously.'

Philokles nodded, as if a theory had been confirmed. 'That is why the Nicomedes of this world are so successful in the long run. At any rate, the merchants are similarly dismissive. They sit in his home, eating his bread, sneering at his effeminate ways, and chasing his slaves and his wife.' The Spartan looked into the distance. 'It will be a pity when an outraged freedman kills them both.'

Kineas's bark of shock caused the big man to look back at him.

'It's a rough game, Hipparch. Those men want our blood, as surely as a screaming Getae waving a spear.'

Kineas relaxed, watching the hoplites reforming for a second try at the manoeuvre. He nodded. 'Thanks. More than thanks. I had assumed there was nothing to be done – and you have done so much.'

Philokles grinned. 'You are unsparing with praise. Very un-Spartan.' But then his grin faded. 'The two merchants will be the first two dead in this war. And so it begins.'

'I know you hate war,' Kineas said. He reached out to take Philokles's shoulder, but Philokles moved away.

'What makes you think that?' he asked.

The spring festival of Apollo drew every man and woman in the city and most of the populations of the farms for stades around the walls. The streets of the city were packed with people in their best clothes, and it was warm enough to cast cloaks aside, for men to be abroad in fine linen and for women, those who chose to appear in public, to look their best.

The full force of the hippeis now filled the hippodrome – two hundred and thirty horsemen, resplendent in blue and polished bronze and brilliant gold. Kineas could see the difference among the cloaks and armour – the cloaks of the men who had gone to the Sakje had already faded by some shades from the royal blue of the first cloth, and their armour had deeper shades of red from long days in the rain. But the appearance of the whole body was magnificent.

Kineas felt oddly nervous at their head. He was wearing his best armour, mounted on his tallest charger, and he knew he looked the part. He couldn't explain it. His skills with men came from the gods, and he seldom doubted them, but today he felt as if he was an actor assigned a role, and the adulation of the crowds along the route to the temple increased his sense of unreality. To be appointed the commander of a city's forces – short of leading the army of his own Athens in the field, he was at the summit of any soldier's ambition.

His imminent death and all it would mean – the loss of worldly power, friends, love – was never far from his thoughts. He found that he could spare no time for trifles, that every moment mattered, and that he wanted to take his forces out to the camp on the Great Bend as soon as possible, to live his last campaign to the fullest.

To see Srayanka. Even if he could not have her.

He thought all these things, but on this day, he rode to the temple of Apollo like a bridegroom, eager, despite himself, for the honour that the archon intended to bestow.

Philokles rode at his side. 'You have a certain vanity, I find,' he said between plaudits from the crowd.

Kineas waved at a group of Sindi who were pointing at him. 'Most soldiers are vain, don't you think?' he asked.

Philokles smiled. 'Your love of finery is carefully hidden. You parade your poverty and your old, tattered cloak, the better to show the contrast to your magnificence.'

'If you say so,' Kineas answered.

'I do. Or are you, perhaps, afraid to show so much finery every day, for fear someone would take you for Nicomedes?' Philokles' last words were almost drowned by renewed cheers. He nodded to Ataelus, who rode forward. He had a linen wrapped bundle, which he passed over to Philokles.

'We swore an oath,' Philokles said, 'not to give this to you until the feast of Apollo.'

Kineas unwrapped the linen. Inside the bundle was his new sword, scabbarded in red leather and hilted with gold – an elegant, sweeping hilt decorated with a pair of flying Pegasuses. The pommel was cast and worked like the head of a woman.

The first squadron had begun to sing the Paean.

In the next quiet interval, Kineas said, 'It is magnificent. But I sought no gift from the king.'

'The king sent it nonetheless,' Philokles said with a mirthless grin. 'You might note the pommel. Do you see a resemblance?'

Kineas closed his hand on the hilt. 'You are like a bluebottle fly – no matter how often I swat you, you just come and settle to sting again.' His intended severity was ruined by his broad grin. He loved it. It fit his hand. Srayanka gleamed in heavy gold from the pommel. *Srayanka – Medea*. 'He sent this? Really?'

Philokles grinned. 'Really.' He shook his head. 'Stop grinning like that – you might hurt your face.' He pulled his horse out of the column, and fell back to his place.

Kineas didn't stop grinning. The king of the Assagatje had sent him a message. Or a challenge.

The ceremony was long, but pleasant, full of music and bright colour. It raised the spirits of the city and of the hippeis and the hoplites, and when the archon tied the magenta sash around his breastplate, Kineas, too, felt a thrill of joy.

After the last procession through the town, Kineas took the hippeis back to the hippodrome and dismissed them with his thanks and praise – and with orders to assemble in two days, ready to march. He listened to the sounds they made as they departed – the gossip, the tone of their grumbles, the taunts and the teasing.

Morale was good.

As if by prior arrangement, the old soldiers – the mercenaries who had come to the city just eight months before – met in the barracks rather than go off to the torch-lit races and the public feast. They were all there – Antigonus, Coenus, Diodorus, Crax and Sitalkes, Ajax, Niceas, fresh back from Pantecapaeum, Laertes and Lykeles, Agis and Andronicus and Ataelus, the last in because it was their turn to curry horses, and Philokles, who appeared with two town slaves and a big amphora of wine. The shape of the amphora revealed it to be from Chios, and they all applauded.

Philokles produced a wine bowl from under a blanket and everyone else fetched cups, laid pillows and cloaks on benches for couches.

'We thought we should drink some wine together, one last time before we take the field,' Philokles said.

'While we're still your friends – before we become your soldiers,' said Niceas, one hand on the owl at his neck.

They were all stiff at first – Sitalkes and Crax were utterly silent except for nervous giggles as they prodded each other on their shared couch. Ataelus, who rarely shared their revelry, seemed uncomfortable on a couch and moved to the floor, where he sat cross-legged.

Philokles rose. 'In Sparta, we have two customs on the eve of war. One is that we sing a hymn to Ares. The other is that in our mess, every man takes a turn at the bowl. He raises his cup, pours a libation to the gods, and toasts every one of his comrades.' He grinned. 'It's a good way to get drunk very quickly.' Then he raised his voice. He had no sense of a tune, but others did – Kineas and Coenus.

Ares, exceeding in strength, chariot-rider,
Golden-helmed, doughty in heart, shield-bearer, saviour
    of cities,
Harnessed in bronze, strong of arm, unwearying,
    mighty with the spear,
O defence of Olympus, father of warlike Victory, ally
    of Themis,
Stern governor of the rebellious, leader of righteous
    men,
Sceptred king of manliness, who whirl your fiery sphere
Among the planets in their sevenfold courses through
    the ether
Wherein your blazing steeds ever bear you above the
    third firmament of heaven;
Hear me, helper of men, giver of dauntless youth!
Shed down a kindly ray from above upon my life, and
    strength of war,
That I may be able to drive away bitter cowardice from
    my head
And crush down the deceitful impulses of my soul.
Restrain also the keen fury of my heart which provokes
    me to tread
The ways of blood-curdling strife.
Rather, O blessed one, give you me boldness to abide
    within the harmless laws of peace, avoiding strife and
    hatred and the violent fiends of death.

Andronicus got to his feet. 'Good song!' he shouted. 'Too seldom do you Greeks praise the lord of strife.'

Philokles shook his head. 'We are no friends to the lord of strife.'

But Andronicus was not in a mood for argument. 'Good custom!' He walked straight to the bowl, and dipped his cup full. He sloshed a libation on the floor, and raised his cup. 'To us. Comrades.' One by one, he said their names, raised his cup, and drank, until he came to Kineas. 'To you, Hipparch,' he said, and drained his cup.

One by one, they did it. Lykeles made jokes about each of them. Philokles imitated their voices as he toasted them. Agis spoke well, and Laertes had a compliment for every man.

Sitalkes drank in silence, meeting each man's eye in turn and drinking to him until he got to Kineas. To him, he raised his cup. 'I was Getae,' he said. 'Now I am yours.' He drank, and the others cheered and stamped their feet as they had not for Laertes' pretty rhetoric.

Crax took his stand at the bowl with a belligerent stare. 'When we fight, I will kill more than any of you,' he said. And drank.

Ajax took the cup and wept. Then he wiped his eyes. 'Every man here has my love. You are the comrades I dreamed of as a child, when I lay on my father's arm and he read to me how Achilles sulked in his tent, how Diomedes led the army of the Hellenes, and all the other stories of the war with Troy.'

Ataelus insisted on having pure wine in his cup. He stood by the bowl for some time. Finally, he said, 'My Greek is better. So I am not for fear speaking to you. All you – like good clan – you take me from city, give horse. Give *honour*.' He raised his cup. 'Too much talk-talk to toast every one. I toast all. *Akinje Craje*. The Flying Horse clan – what the Sakje call you. Good name.' He drank. Then he dipped and drank again, and again, saluting each one in turn in unwatered wine. He walked back to his place on the floor without a tremor, and sat with the same grace as all the Sakje.

Last was Kineas. He waved to Philokles, the acting host. 'By all the gods – put some water in it, or I won't live to reach the camp.' He stood by the bowl. He found that he had a smile across his face so firm that he couldn't crack it even to speak. He was silent – as silent at Sitalkes or Ataelus had been. Then he raised his cup on the tips of his fingers and tipped it to spill a libation.

'The gods honour those who strive the hardest,' he said. 'I doubt any group of men have worked harder in the last six months than you. I ask that the gods take notice. We came here as strangers, and have been made citizens. We came here as mercenaries. Now, I think most of us go to fight for our city, as men of virtue do.' He looked around. 'Like Ajax, I love every one of you, and like Ataelus, I know you for my own clan. For myself, I swear by the gods to do my best to bring you back safe. But I also say this. We go to a hard campaign.' He looked around. 'If we fall, let us do it so that some Olbian poet will sing of us, the way the Spartans sing of Leonidas, or the way every Hellene sings of Peleas's son.'

They cheered him, even hard-eyed Niceas. He drank to them. They raised their cups with a roar.

Much later, a very drunk Kineas slapped Philokles' shoulder. 'You're a good man,' he said.

Philokles smiled. 'I can't hear you say that too often.'

'I'm for bed. I'll have a head like an anvil come the dawn.' Kineas stood unsteadily. Crax was retching outside the barracks' main door. He sounded like a man on the edge of death.

Philokles pushed himself to his feet. 'I think you'll find that dawn is close,' he said. 'It's good to see you happy.'

Kineas hung on to the doorframe as he passed it. 'I'm happy enough, brother. Better to die happy than ...' He managed to shut his mouth.

'Die?' said Philokles. He sounded more sober. 'Who said anything about death?'

Kineas waved his hands unsteadily. 'Nothing. Shouldn't have said anything of the sort. My mouth runs away with me when I'm drunk. Like a diarrhoea of words.'

Philokles grabbed him and spun him around. He rested his forehead against Kineas, which steadied them both. He put a hand behind Kineas's neck like a wrestler going for a hold. 'Die happy, you said. Where's that come from?'

'Nowhere. Just a phrase.'

'Donkey shit. Piles of it.' Philokles sounded harsh.

Kineas rolled his eyes. He couldn't remember why he had to hide all this from the Spartan, anyway. 'Gonna die,' he said. 'In the battle.'

Philokles ground his forehead against Kineas. It hurt. 'Says who?'

'Dream. Kam Baqca. Tree.' Saying it aloud made it seem a little silly.

Philokles pushed him away, and started laughing. 'Ares' swelling member. You poor bastard. Kam Baqca thinks *she* is going to die in this battle. She's just spreading the misery.'

Kineas shrugged. 'Maybe. Knows a lot.'

Philokles nodded. 'So she does. So walk away. Board a ship. Go to Sparta.'

Kineas shook his head. The myths of his youth were full of men who fled fate to die foolishly. 'Achilles' choice,' he said.

Philokles shook his head angrily. 'You're too old for that shit. You aren't Achilles. The gods don't whisper in your ear.'

Kineas sat on a table. He'd made it to his room. He kicked off his sandals. 'Bed,' he said, and fell on his.

He was asleep before Philokles could muster an argument.

16

Kineas was the last man of the hippeis to reach the camp at Great Bend. He sent the squadrons off, one each day, while he continued to wrangle with the hipparch of Pantecapaeum and wrote detailed orders for the city allies.

Leucon took the elite first troop on the day after the festival. They were ready, still hard from the visit to the Sakje, and eager for it. Kineas sent Niceas to keep an eye on them – and to make sure that their camp was well sited and well built.

On the second day, when Diodorus's squadron was clear of the gates, six light triremes arrived from their fellow city, the first concrete sign that the assembly of Pantecapaeum intended to honour its pledge. Kineas went down to see them and to discuss strategy with their navarch, Demostrate, a short, fat man with a nose like a pig. Despite his looks – ugly as Hephaestes – he was cheerful, even comic, and his ships were in good order, from the lustiness of their rowers, citizens all, to their sails, painted with a seated Athena twice as tall as a man, floating over the black-hulled ships like banners to the goddess.

Demostrate immediately agreed to hunt down the Macedonian triremes. 'He'll get more as the summer wears on, mark my words,' said the fat man. 'I'd just as soon wreck those he's got as soon as they come under my hand.'

'Go with the gods,' Kineas said. 'The tide's on the make. I won't hold you.'

'Good to meet a general who knows the sea. Is it true you're a citizen? Will you stay? You've become quite the famous figure in Pantecapaeum.'

Kineas shrugged. 'I think I'm here to stay,' he said.

'That's good to hear. Hard to trust a mercenary – no offence intended.'

Kineas stood up on the oar rail and leaped to the wharf. 'Send me word if you have an action.'

Demostrate waved. 'I've played this game before. I can get

three more hulls in the water by midsummer – if I get them, and I've cleared his squadron, I may just cruise the Bosporus.' He leered. 'My lads would love to take a few merchantmen.'

Kineas turned to Nicomedes, who had accompanied him down to make an introduction. 'He looks more like a pirate than a merchant.'

Nicomedes laughed. 'He was a pirate. Pantecapaeum made him navarch to stop his predatory ways.' He laughed.

Kineas realized that he had been expected to know as much – that the fat man had been making fun of both of them with his comment about mercenaries. 'I assume he's as competent as he appears?'

Nicomedes nodded. 'He's a terror. He used to prey on my ships.'

'How'd you stop him?' Kineas asked.

Nicomedes made a moue and winked. 'It would be indelicate to relate,' he said. Then his voice changed – all business. 'I'm off with my squadron tomorrow. I want to voice a concern – a real concern. Come to my house.'

Kineas followed him up the hill from the port. Nicomedes was an important man, and walking to his house involved running a gauntlet of requests, factors, beggars of various degrees and stations – it took an hour he could ill spare.

Once seated in a room full of beautiful, if salacious, mosaic and marble, Kineas lay on a couch with a cup of excellent wine. He kept his patience – Nicomedes was not just one of his officers, but, next to the archon and perhaps Cleitus, the city's most powerful man. Probably as rich as any man in Athens.

'What's on your mind?' Kineas asked.

Nicomedes was admiring the goldwork on Kineas's sword. 'This is superb! You'll pardon me if I say I had not expected to envy you the ownership of an object – although I had heard of the wonders of the blade.' Nicomedes shrugged, made a wry face. 'Swords don't move me much – I like one that's sharp and stays in my hand. But the hilt – masterwork. From Athens?'

Kineas shook his head. 'An Athenian master – living with the Sakje.'

'The style – like great Athenian work, but all these outré animals – and the Medusa! Or is that Medea?'

Kineas smiled. 'I suspect it to be Medea.'

'Medea? She killed her children, didn't she?' Nicomedes raised an eyebrow. 'That face – I can imagine her killing a few children. Beautiful – but fierce. Why Medea?'

Kineas shook his head. 'Private joke, I think. What's on your mind?' he asked again.

Nicomedes continued to admire the sword. Then he straightened. 'Cleomenes has reappeared,' he said.

'Zeus, lord of all,' Kineas swore. 'Heraclea?'

'Worse. Tomis. He's gone over to the Macedonians. I found out this morning. The archon won't know yet.'

Kineas rubbed his jaw. Cleomenes, for all his party enmity, knew all of their plans – every nuance. He'd attended every meeting of the city's magnates – he was, after all, one of the leading men. 'That could be a heavy blow,' he said.

Nicomedes nodded. 'I respect your command – but you are sending every leader in the assembly out of the city. There will be no one left with the balls to contest the archon – or Cleomenes, if he comes here. And he will.'

Kineas rubbed his beard and made a face. He took a deep breath and then said, 'You're right.'

'He could murder some of the popular leaders among the people, and close the gates.' Nicomedes drank his wine. 'The archon has spent five years improving the defences – I'd hate to try and take this place.'

Kineas shook his head. 'We'd have it in our hands in three days.'

Nicomedes looked surprised – not an expression his smooth features often wore. 'How?'

Kineas raised an eyebrow to indicate that he wanted Nicomedes to guess.

'Treason?' asked Nicomedes, but as soon as he said it, he laughed. 'Of course. We're the army. All our people are in the city.'

Kineas nodded. 'I like to think of it as an exercise in military democracy. Well-governed cities can stand a siege for ever, unless they are unlucky. But an unpopular government will only last until someone opens a gate. Not usually a long wait. Tyrannies ...' Kineas smiled a wolfish smile. 'They fall easily.'

Nicomedes leaned forward on his couch. 'By the gods, you are tempting him.'

Kineas shook his head. 'I don't play those games. I need the soldiers in the field – if for no other reason, to show the Sakje that we are with them. But if the archon is tempted to be foolish, and he acts,' Kineas shrugged, 'I am not responsible for the evil actions of other men. My tutor taught me that.'

Nicomedes nodded, his eyes alight – but then he shook his head. 'He could still damage our property. He might attack families – he might even hand the citadel to Macedon, if he thought it was his only hope of survival.'

Kineas nodded. 'I believe that he is a rational man, despite his burst of temper. You think worse of him.'

'He is more stable with you and Memnon than he was last year. I fear that when you are gone – I fear many things.'

Kineas rubbed his beard. 'What do you want me to do?'

'Leave my squadron here.' Nicomedes shrugged. 'I can watch the archon. And I can deal with Cleomenes.' His voice hardened.

Kineas shook his head. 'Ah, Nicomedes – you have worked yourself too hard. Yours is the best of the four squadrons. On the day of battle, I need *you*.'

Nicomedes shrugged. 'I thought you'd say that. Very well, then – leave Cleitus here.'

Kineas rubbed his cheeks thoughtfully. 'The older men – the worst riders, but on the best horses and with the best equipment.'

Nicomedes leaned across the space between the couches, handing Kineas back his sword, hilt first. 'Most of them are old for a real campaign – but young enough to wear armour and stare down a tyrant.'

'You and Cleitus are rivals,' Kineas said carefully.

Nicomedes got up from his couch and walked to the table where a dozen scrolls were open. 'Not in this. I'd rather it was me – Cleitus has a lingering respect for the archon, and he's clay in Cleomenes's hands – but he'll hold the line.'

'All the more reason for it to be him. The archon remains my employer. He is autocratic, but as far as I can tell, he has acted within the laws of the city. You empowered him. He's your monster.' Kineas rubbed his beard. 'And I fear that you and Cleomenes – that it's too personal.'

Nicomedes looked bitter. 'It is. I'll kill him when I can.'

Kineas stood up. 'When the Athenian assembly voted for war with Macedon, many were against it, and some of them lie dead at Chaeronea. That's democracy.'

Nicomedes came and walked Kineas to his door. 'You'll do it, though – leave Cleitus's squadron?'

Kineas nodded sharply. 'Yes.'

Nicomedes smiled, and Kineas wondered if he'd just been out-manoeuvred. 'Good. It would kill Ajax to stay. And I've never seen war on land. It looks very safe compared to war at sea.'

Kineas didn't know whether this was humour or not. It was always hard to tell with Nicomedes. So he clasped the man's hand in his doorway, amidst a crowd of hangers-on, and went back to the barracks.

The third day, Nicomedes' squadron rode forth with more baggage and more slaves then the other two combined – but his squadron had the best discipline of the four. Kineas watched them go with a heavy heart – he wanted to go, but he had to finish his work with the allies.

Philokles, Memnon and Cleitus stood with him until the last spare horse and the last mule cart passed through the gates.

Memnon continued to appear a foot taller. He turned to Kineas and saluted – without a trace of sarcasm – and said, 'I'll just take my lads out for an hour, with your permission?'

Kineas returned his salute, hand on chest. 'Memnon, you do not need my permission to drill the hoplites.'

Memnon grinned. 'I know that. God help you if you thought otherwise.' He pointed at the waiting men, formed in long files in the streets of the town. 'But it's a good game for them.'

Philokles agreed. 'Those who obey will be obeyed,' he said.

Memnon pointed at him. 'Right! Just what I mean. Socrates?'

Philokles shook his head. 'Lykeurgos of Sparta.'

Memnon walked off, still laughing.

Memnon found much to admire in the hoplites of Pantecapeum – their phalanx he accounted very good, and their elite young men, two hundred athletes in top shape – the *epilektoi* – made him grin. 'Of course, their officers are a bunch of pompous twits,' he said through his snaggle teeth.

The hipparch of Pantecapaeum was about the same. He was a tall, thin, very young man with a dour face and a large forehead – usually a sign of immense intelligence.

'My troops will remain exclusively under my command,' he said. 'You may communicate your orders to me, and if I feel that they are appropriate, I will pass them to my men. We are gentlemen, not mercenaries. I have heard a great many things about you – that you force the gentlemen of Olbia to curry their own horses, for instance. None of that foolishness will apply to my men.'

Kineas had expected as much from their exchange of letters. 'I will discuss all of these points with you, of course. In the meantime, may I inspect your men?'

The allied hipparch – Heron – gave a thin smile. 'If you wish to view them, you may. Only I inspect them. Only I speak to them. I hope I've made myself clear.' Kineas knew him instantly – a man for whom intelligence replaced sense, and whose fear of failure made him distant and arrogant. All too common in small armies. Kineas had known from the first how lucky he was with Nicomedes and Cleitus – and Heron was the proof.

Kineas nodded. His mind was refreshingly clear of anger – and long years with the arrogance of Macedonian officers had accustomed him to this sort of thing. Instead of a reaction, he turned his horse and began to walk it down the front rank of the hippeis of Pantecapaeum.

The hippeis of Pantecapaeum were fifty years out of date in their equipment. Like the hoplites of Olbia, they were wearing equipment that their grandfathers would have used – light linen armour or no armour, small horses, light javelins. Most of the riders were overweight, and at least a dozen were sitting back on their horses' haunches – what Athenians called 'chair seat', a posture that was easier on untrained riders but hard on the horse. Kineas noted that they had no cloaks at their saddlecloths, and that the squadron, just seventy men, had a surprising mix of horses.

He smiled, because he suspected that if he had seen the hippeis of Olbia a year ago, the few who turned out might have looked like this. He reined up and turned to Heron.

'We'll train you. You'll have to work on your equipment. I'll treat you as one of my troop commanders for as long as you deserve it.' He rode up close to the man. 'I've seen years and years of mounted warfare, and this is going to be a hard campaign. Obey me, and you'll keep most of your men alive. Go your own way, and you are of no use to me.'

Heron stared to the front for a few seconds. 'I will consult with my men,' he said stiffly.

Kineas nodded. 'Be quick, then.'

Kineas sent a slave for Cleitus, and spent an ugly half-hour on the sand with an angry troop of allied horsemen. He gave them orders and they were sullen, or simply ignorant. Their hyperetes – Dion – seemed willing enough. Heron retreated – first to the far edge of the sand and then to the gate.

Cleitus appeared at the head of his squadron, it being an appointed drill day for the cavalry left in the city. They filed into the hippodrome, making it look empty compared to full muster days, but the fifty of them made a superb contrast to the men of Pantecapaeum.

'Thank the gods,' Kineas said. He was somewhere between frustration and rage. He had Niceas to do this kind of work, and always had. Kineas pointed at the allied horse. 'Can you train them for me? Two weeks?'

'Surely you can train them faster – and better – in camp.' Cleitus looked around. 'Where's Heron? Did you kill him?'

'No. He's brave enough – just pig-ignorant.'

Cleitus shook his head. 'He's the son of an old rival of mine. He grew up soft. Too soft.'

Kineas shrugged. 'So did I. Listen – they need armour, and they need the same big geldings we have. You can do all that here – I can't. I'll get them remounts at the camp, but the armour has to come from here.'

Cleitus scratched his chin. 'Who's paying?'

Kineas grinned. 'Let me guess. The thin kid – Heron – is rich?'

Cleitus laughed. 'Rich as Croesus.'

Kineas shook his head. 'I wish all my problems had such easy answers. Tell him I'll keep him as hipparch – even apologize – if he pays. Otherwise, send him home and pick a new one. Dias looks competent.'

Cleitus nodded. 'Dion. Dias is the trumpeter. He is. He's just dishonest.' He waved to his friend Petrocolus, who trotted up, looking a decade younger.

'What's up?'

Cleitus pointed at the men of Pantecapaeum. 'I knew we were getting off too easily when we were left as the garrison. Now we get to train *them*.'

Petrocolus eyed them with the disdain of the veteran for the amateur. The sight made Kineas smile. 'I'll do my best,' he said.

Kineas saw the archon one more time before he left. The archon refused to be serious, mocking Macedon and Kineas by turns. He was drunk. He accused Kineas of wanting to take the city and made him swear he'd defend it. And then he demanded Kineas's oath that he would not try to overthrow him.

Kineas swore and was eventually dismissed.

'You can be so naive,' Philokles said, when he heard the whole story. They were finally riding out, just the two of them with Ataelus for a scout.

'He was pitiful,' Kineas said.

Philokles shook his head. 'Note how he put you on the defensive. He made *you* swear a vow. He swore none.'

Kineas rode in silence for a stade. Then he shook his head. 'You're right.'

'I am,' Philokles said. He grinned. 'Nevertheless, you can't have hurt things. Perhaps you purchased a few more weeks of trust. My people in the citadel say that he fears an assassin – Persian courts are full of them.'

Kineas rode in silence again, and then said, 'I fear the archon and I fear *for* him.'

'He's useless and self-destructive and he will betray us. Are you ready for it?' Philokles asked.

'We'll have the army. Let's beat Zopryon. Worry about the archon later. Wasn't that your advice?' Kineas drank some water. He looked out at the sea of grass. Somewhere, around the curve of the Euxine, Zopryon was coming – forty to fifty days away. Imagine – every day that he kept Zopryon at bay was another day of life. It was almost funny.

'Does Medea know?' Philokles asked.

'What?' asked Kineas, startled out of his reverie.

'The Lady Srayanka. We call her Medea. Does she know about your dream?'

Kineas shook his head. 'I thought it was you lot. You got the goldsmith to take her as a model?'

Philokles grinned. 'I'll never tell.'

'Bastards, the lot of you. No, she doesn't know, at least from me.' Kineas watched the horizon. He ached to ride to her – day and night, until he got to the camp. Good, mature behaviour from a commander. He reached out a hand for the water skin and said, 'Kam Baqca and the king have forbidden us to – be together.'

Philokles turned his head away, obviously embarrassed. 'I know.'

'You know?' Kineas spluttered on his water.

'It was discussed,' Philokles said. He made a series of fidgets and motions indicating extreme embarrassment. 'I was consulted.'

'Ares and Aphrodite!' Kineas said.

Philokles hung his head. 'You had eyes for no one else.' Philokles looked out over the plain. 'She refused to speak to you. The king is mad with love for her. The three of you ...' He sighed. 'The three of you threaten the whole war with your lovesickness.'

With the clear head of a man who had forty days to live, Kineas did not succumb to rage. 'You may be right.'

Philokles glanced at him, searched for signs of anger. 'You see that?'

303

'I suppose. Solon had a rhyme – I don't remember it, but it was about a man who thought that he was right and every other citizen in the city was wrong.' Kineas gave a fleeting smile. 'You, Niceas, Kam Baqca – I doubt that you are all wrong.' His smile brightened. 'Even now, I consider touching my heels to this horse and riding hard to her camp. Just a stade back I was thinking of it.'

Philokles grinned. 'Her barb's sunk deep. I can see why – she's more like a Spartan woman than any barbarian I've ever seen.' He took the water back. 'Is it *eros*, or *agape*? Have you lain with her?'

'You are like some pimply boyhood friend asking after my first conquest!'

'No – I'm a philosopher studying my current subject.'

'The girl in the golden sandals has, indeed, smacked me with the big fat grape of love,' Kineas said, quoting a popular song from the Athens of his youth. 'When, exactly, can two cavalry commanders find private time to make love?' He rubbed the hilt of his new sword with his left hand.

Philokles smiled. He looked away. 'Spartans manage such things pretty well on campaign. Even Spartiates.'

'Bah, you're all men. You just pick your cloak mate.' Kineas raised an eyebrow.

The Spartan answered it. 'Is your amazon a woman? I mean, besides the anatomy – she's no more a woman than Kam Baqca is a man.'

Kineas felt his face grow hot. 'I think she is,' he said.

'Going to settle her down in the top floor of your house and raise babies?' Philokles said. 'From what I've seen of Sakje women, I understand Medea all the better. Bred to freedom – life as a woman in Thebes would be slavery. Cruel Hands. You know why they call her that?'

'Clan name,' said Kineas.

'In her case, she used to take heads from her kills – without a mercy blow.' Philokles slung his water skin. 'I'm not against her. I just want you to see that she will never be a wife – a Greek wife.'

'Do I want a Greek wife?' Kineas said.

'Perhaps not,' Philokles said. 'But if you change your mind, she will be a fearsome foe. Medea indeed.'

Kineas turned away, waved to Ataelus, and choked, somewhere between laughter and tears. 'Luckily,' he said finally, 'I'll be dead.'

His first sight of the allied camp made him stop his horse and stare. Across the river, as far as he could see, from the low hill to the north of the ford in a great curve away to the south, there were herds of horses. He did as his tutor had taught him. He took a deep breath, kneed his own horse forward, and divided the vast expanse into a grid of manageable squares. He estimated the size of one square and began to count the animals in it, arrived at a reasonable answer, and multiplied by his approximate number of squares, adding the columns as he moved, until his horse was splashing across the ford and he was shaking his head at the impossibility of the figure he'd calculated.

Ataelus led them to the king's wagon. The king's household, his personal clan, had their camp on the hilltop north of the ford, with fifty heavy wagons parked in a circle like a wooden fort. The king's wagon was in the centre. At the base of the hill herds of horses, flocks of goats, and dozens of oxen milled in promiscuous confusion.

Kineas greeted Marthax, who stood within a ring of other nobles. 'The raid?' Kineas called out in Sakje.

Marthax waddled over with the rolling gait of a man who scarcely ever walked when he could ride. He spoke rapidly – too rapidly for Kineas to follow, although by now his Sakje was sufficient to register the raid's success.

'Ferry destroyed,' Ataelus said. 'All boats burned, and town for burning. No horse lost.'

Kineas winced. Despite the ill treatment of his column at Antiphilous the summer before, he hadn't expected the whole town to be sacrificed to the war.

Marthax grinned. He said something, and all Kineas caught was a phrase about 'baby shit'.

Ataelus said, 'Lord say, I burned towns when you were baby.'

Kineas frowned at what he suspected the man had actually said, and Marthax grinned back.

Behind him, Philokles grunted. 'The tyrant rears his head,' he said.

Kineas looked back at him as he dismounted. 'Tyrant?'

The Spartan also dismounted and rubbed his thighs. 'Haven't I said it a dozen times? War is the ultimate tyrant, and every concession you make him leads only to further demands. How many died at Antiphilous?'

Kineas sighed. 'That's war.'

Philokles nodded. 'Yes. It is. And this is just the beginning.'

Kineas made the king laugh when he asked if the full muster was present.

'A tenth of my strength, at most. I, too, have my stronger and my weaker chiefs. My Olbia and my Pantecapaeum, if you like.'

Kineas waved at the plain below the hill. 'I counted ten thousand horses.'

Satrax nodded. 'At least. Those are the royal herds. I am not the greatest of the Sakje kings but neither am I the least. They are also the herds of the Standing Horse, Patient Wolves, and Man Under Tree clans.' He gazed out over the plain. 'By midsummer we will have eaten the grass from here to the water god's shrine upriver, and we will have to move.' He shrugged. 'But the grain is starting to come.'

Kineas shook his head. 'So many horses.'

'Kineas,' said the king. 'A poor Sakje, a man with no skills at the hunt and no reputation in battle, owns four horses. A poor woman has the same. A man with less than four horses isn't welcome with his clan, because he can't keep up with the hunt or the treks. Every man and every woman has at least four – most have ten. A rich warrior has a hundred horses. A king has a thousand horses.'

Kineas, who owned four horses himself, whistled.

The king turned to Ataelus. 'And you? How many horses have you?'

Ataelus spoke with obvious pride. 'I have six horses with me, and two more in the stables of Olbia. I will take more from Macedon, and then I will have a wife.'

Satrax turned to Kineas. 'When you met him, he had no horses – am I right?'

Kineas smiled at Ataelus. 'I take your point.'

The king said, 'You are a good chief to him. He has horses now. Greedy chiefs keep spoils for themselves. Good ones make sure every man has his due.'

Kineas nodded. 'It is the same with us. You know the *Iliad*?'

'I've heard it. An odd story – I was never sure who I was supposed to like. Achilles struck me as a monster. But I take your point – the whole story is about unfair division of spoils.'

Kineas, who had been taught from childhood to see in Achilles the embodiment of every manly virtue, had to choke back an exposition on Achilles. The king could be very Greek, despite his trousers and his hood-like hats, but then, in flawless Greek, he would render an opinion that showed just how alien he was.

The king saw his confusion and laughed. 'I know – you worship him. But you Greeks spend a lot of time being angry, so perhaps Achilles is your model. Why so much anger? Now come and tell me what your archon is going to do.'

'He was all compliance, my lord. The hoplites will march with the new moon. Diodorus will have explained about the troop of horse left behind.'

'He did indeed. He also chose your camp. Go to it, and we will talk later.' War had made the king more autocratic. Kineas noted that he had a larger court, and that he had more men and more women in attendance. He wondered what that might portend.

Diodorus met him with a hug and a cup of wine. 'I hope you like our camp,' he said.

He had taken the spur of ground immediately south of the king's camp, a spur that pushed out into the deeper water north of the ford as a rocky peninsula. The tents of the Olbians were arranged in a neat square, with a line for the horses and another line for fires, and beyond the fires, a line of pits – latrines. It was straight from one of the manuals, like a mathematics exercise transformed into hard reality. To the north of the hill he pointed out another square, a stade on a side, marked with heavy pegs and almost clear of Sakje animals. 'For the hoplites, when they arrive.'

'Well done,' Kineas said.

He walked among the fires, greeting men he knew, clasping hands and basking in their joy at seeing him. At the centre of the camp stood a wagon.

'The king presented it to you,' Diodorus said.

The wagon was painted blue from its wheels to the heavy boards of the sides. The felt tent that covered the roof was a dark blue, and the yokes for four oxen were blue. Steps led from the ground to the back flap of the felt cover.

Kineas handed his horse to a slave and leaned in. The box was small – just a little wider than the height of a man and twice as long. Inside was a bed, set into the wagon's wall and protected by hangings – felt, figured with deer and horses and griffons – and a low table. The floor was thick with Sakje rugs and cushions.

'I took the liberty of testing the bed for a few nights,' Diodorus said. He grinned. 'Just to make sure it worked.'

'And?'

'It does. It makes you want to stay in it. By the gods, Kineas, I am glad you are here. If ever I thought I could do your job, I was mistaken. A thousand crises a day—'

He was interrupted by Eumenes, who clasped Kineas by the hand and then turned to Diodorus. 'We were told there would be grain for the chargers today. Where will we get that?'

Diodorus pointed at Kineas with both hands. 'Welcome to Great Bend, Hipparch,' he said. 'You are in command.' He mimed lifting a great weight off his back and placing it on Kineas. Eumenes, Philokles and Ataelus all laughed.

Kineas smiled at all of them. 'Diodorus, where is this grain dole?'

'No idea,' he replied.

'Go find out,' Kineas said with the same smile.

Diodorus shook his head. 'Why didn't I think of that?'

Kineas's first week in the camp at Great Bend was a constant exercise in humility. His men – trained to near perfection by a hard winter and now being carefully tempered in the camp – were as good as any Greek cavalry he'd ever seen. The Sakje were an order of magnitude better.

Kineas had seen the Sakje in sport and contest, riding over the grass, racing, shooting for pleasure. But he had never seen a hundred warriors lying in the grass with their ponies lying beside them, invisible in a fold of the ground until their chief blew a bone whistle and, before the shriek died away on the air, every man rolled his pony upright and was mounted. It was one of a hundred tricks they had that used their god-like riding skills, and Kineas understood exactly why the earliest poets had thought them to be centaurs.

On the second day, Srayanka and a dozen of her warriors returned from a hunt. She eyed him coolly and challenged him to shoot a course with her, javelin against javelin.

'I have practised,' she said in Greek.

He rode almost as well as he had in the first contest, landing five of six javelins in the shields, the last one a hand's breadth too high. Srayanka raced through the shields faster, and missed none. Her eyes sparkled when she slid off her mare. 'So?' she said.

I practised five years to throw that well, he thought. But he mastered his disappointment and praised her.

She smiled up at him. 'Loser give winner gift,' she said.

Kineas went to his wagon and emerged with his first sword, the plunder of Ecbatana, the blade long since repaired. He handed it to her.

Ataelus spoke, and Srayanka replied. They shot back and forth several times as she turned the weapon in her hands.

'You give gift like chief,' she said in Greek. 'Like king. I dream of you, Kineax.'

'And I of you. I carry your gift,' Kineas said, and her eyes strayed to his whip.

'Good!' she said. She waved her whip at her companions, and they mounted and raced off across the grass, hooting and shouting.

'Nice little wife,' Philokles said.

'Why didn't I ever think of using swords as courtship gifts?' Niceas asked the air.

'Don't you people have work to do?' Kineas asked.

The Black Horse clan came into the camp on the fourth day – a thousand warriors and another eight thousand animals. They arrived in full panoply and Kineas had his first sight of Sakje nobles dressed for war.

The first hundred riders – the chief's companions – wore scale armour from shoulder to knee, heavy coats of leather with bronze and iron scales attached like the scales on a fish, or like tiles on a roof. The richest men on the biggest horses had the same armour on the chests of their horses, as well as full-face Greek helmets with enormous plumes.

And every man of the chief's companions rode a black horse. They were magnificent, and as well armoured and mounted as the cream of a Persian host. They each carried a bow in a gorytos, and a heavy lance, as well as a brace of javelins.

Niceas, watching at Kineas's side, said bitterly, 'What in Hades do they need us for?'

Srayanka was impatient for the rest of her Cruel Hands to ride in from her pastureland to the west. They were late, and she was losing prestige every day they delayed. Her retinue said as much, and so did Ataelus.

They came on the sixth day after Kineas's arrival. They did not make much of a show – the herds were as large as any other tribe, but the warriors looked tired, and a convoy of travois carrying wounded men and women led the herds.

She was gone among her people for an hour, and then the king summoned all the chiefs to meet in his laager.

'Zopryon has sent the Getae to burn the Sindi,' Srayanka said. 'My people were hard pressed to hold them, and my tanist chose to come to the rendezvous rather than fight alone.'

The king nodded grimly. 'Kairax is a good man. But your people are tired, and you have many wounded.'

Srayanka frowned. 'We can ride back tonight,' she said.

Marthax shook his head. 'If your people had been on time

for the muster, we'd never have known,' he said. 'As it is, your people took the brunt of the raid and your farmers are paying in blood and fire – but we're warned.' Eumenes translated as fast as Marthax could speak. Kineas, after a week in camp and more dreams of talking trees, understood Marthax before the translation was done. The army's language barrier was falling – slowly.

'We must strike back,' Srayanka said.

All of the Sakje were with her, even the king. Kineas let them talk, and then cut in. 'Zopryon is using the Getae to test your strength, and to see – if he's lucky, or you are foolish – if he can scare you into breaking up your army to protect your farmers.'

'Fucking Getae,' Ataelus said. A phrase that never needed to be translated.

'Fucking Getae indeed,' Kineas said. He ignored Srayanka's glare. 'They know where to find your farmers. They know just how to hurt you – yes? And if Zopryon sent them, they'll raid in a wide arc across the north – probably the whole of their strength – right to the walls of your town. How many of your chiefs will stay home to fight them rather than march through them to the muster? And Zopryon won't have to feed them – while they cover his army against your raids.' Kineas paused. 'It's a good strategy.' Privately, Kineas knew it was the strategy of a man who was fully informed of the Sakje plan – by Cleomenes. His stomach bubbled.

Satrax rubbed his temples. 'Why didn't we foresee this?' he asked Kam Baqca.

She shook her head. 'As you know, more is hidden than is revealed.'

'Very well,' said the king. 'What do we do?'

Marthax and Srayanka spoke together. Both said the same thing. 'Fight.'

'You disagree?' the king said to Kineas.

Kineas stood silent a moment, gathering his thoughts. Kam Baqca's sentence lingered in his head, and his idea was born from it. 'I agree,' he said. 'Let's fight.' He took a deep breath. 'If we are swift, and decisive, the result will allow us to return to our original plan – with an advantage. Zopryon has been bold

– but he may also have made an error.'

He spoke rapidly, outlining his plan.

'Mmm,' said Marthax.

'He like for plan,' said Ataelus.

Kineas's plan carried the day. But he didn't like the king's hesitation, or his frequent exchanges with Srayanka. And over the next dozen days, he had many opportunities to ponder what those exchanges might have meant.

PART IV

THE BATTLE HAZE

'Footmen were ever slaying footmen as they fled perforce, and horsemen slew horsemen, and from beneath them rose from the plain the battle haze which the thundering hooves of horses stirred up – and they wrought havoc with the bronze …'

Iliad, Book 11

17

'Chargers!' Kineas shouted, cantering down the slope he had just ascended. His trio of Cruel Hand scouts remained on the bluff, looking down on a village of six log houses, four of which were aflame. The last two were still holding out.

Kineas hadn't needed his scouts to find the Getae. This was Srayanka's land, eight hundred stades north and west of the Great Bend camp, and the Getae were putting it to the torch, moving slowly east, their progress marked by the funeral pyres of a hundred villages.

As soon as Kineas called, his column began changing horses. Most of the men were already wearing armour. They had been close to the enemy for two days, riding carefully to avoid detection.

Kineas pulled up with Niceas, Leucon and Nicomedes at the head of the column. He held his palm flat and spoke rapidly, a clear picture of the town, the river and the surrounding terrain clear in his mind.

'Leucon, take your troop south around the bluff and ride like Pegasus – get in east of the town and then cut north.' He illustrated this with his right finger, drawing on his palm. 'Here's the village – here's our bluff. My thumb marks the river. See it?' He indicated on his hand where Leucon would go. 'You close off their retreat. We smash into their main body. Let a handful flee away – north. Understand? Leucon, this will depend on you.'

Leucon closed his eyes. 'I – I think so.' He was hesitant. And he didn't understand.

Kineas spared a moment for a new commander's fear. He knew them all intimately – *I'll get lost, I don't know the country, I won't be able to find the village, I'll be too slow.*

Kineas leaned forward. 'Ride up to the summit, dismount where the Sakje horses are, and take a quick look. Nicomedes, go with him. Quickly, and *don't* let yourself be seen. Go!'

They seemed to take for ever. When he had been atop the bluff, he had seen a woman being raped in the street. Leucon's inexperience would cost that woman her life.

Kineas sacrificed her, a woman he had never met, so that his officers would know their roles. Which might save lives.

'Zeus, they take their time,' he muttered.

Niceas refused to answer, knowing this mood of old, and busied himself checking the column. Kineas decided to join him. He rode along the ranks. Most of the troopers looked nervous.

'Let your horse do the work,' he heard Niceas saying to a group of Leucon's young men.

'No different from a hunt. Place your javelin and ride on,' Kineas said to the men behind Eumenes. Even Eumenes looked pale.

Nicomedes and Leucon came down the hill at a rush. Kineas met them at the head of the column. 'You see it?' he asked.

Leucon was paler than Eumenes. 'I – think so. South around the bluff here, and then along the river bank under what cover I can find, and then hard back into the town to cut their retreat and break their resistance.'

Kineas put a hand on the young man's shoulder. 'You have it well enough.' He wanted to get on with it but he took the time to say, 'This may not work. There may be an irrigation ditch or something that blocks your movement. Perhaps the Getae have scouts down that way.' He shrugged, despite the weight of his armour. 'From this moment – take it as it comes to you. You'll be fine.'

If his words had any good effect, Kineas couldn't see it. Leucon looked almost paralysed.

'On your way, Leucon,' Kineas said crisply.

Leucon saluted, arm across his chest, and waved to Eumenes. The first troop moved out at the trot, and Nicomedes' older troop watched them go, calling encouragement – sometimes, fathers encouraging sons.

'First action,' Kineas said. He had his own nerves.

'They ain't bad, for rich boys,' Niceas said. He was picking his teeth with a tough grass stem. 'They needed a speech – something about the gods and their city.'

'No, they didn't,' Kineas said. He put his horse to the slope, and Niceas followed him with Nicomedes just behind. 'Hold the horses,' he said to Niceas. He and Nicomedes crawled on their bellies the last few feet to the summit. The Sakje had pulled branches from weedy bushes to cover their hide.

From the bluff, Kineas could see ten stades in every direction. The Getae had been fools not to put a sentry here, but they really were barbarians, and they thought they were at liberty to loot in an undefended land.

To the south, Leucon's column was now in a file of twos, a blue and gold caterpillar crawling across a narrow ditch. Nonetheless, he was making good progress.

Kineas's own tensions shot up as he realized how close his timing would have to be.

The Getae in the village street were preparing to rush the last house. Five houses had their roofs afire. The body of the woman lay naked and unmoving in the street.

There were two hundred Getae, give or take a dozen. Most were gathered thick around the town, looting the houses or preparing to take the last one. A few were straggling to the north, chasing some goats. And a dozen more to the south.

'Fuck,' Kineas said. He leaped to his feet and ran for his horse, Nicomedes hard on his heels.

'They're going to see Leucon any second. We have to go.'

Nicomedes looked at him without comprehension, but he followed, leaping on to his horse's back like a professional. Niceas got up and raised an eyebrow.

Kineas got to the head of the column and waved to the right. 'Column until we round the bluff. We'll form line as soon as we're in the fields. Right through the town – kill anyone in your path and keep the line straight even if you have to go around buildings. This won't be like drill. And gentlemen – if all else fails, kill every Getae to come under your hand. They're the ones with tattoos.'

No one laughed. Veterans would have laughed.

'Walk,' Kineas called. Niceas's trumpet was out, but silent. Surprise was still possible.

Nicomedes said, 'I don't understand.'

Kineas turned on his mount. 'Trot!' he shouted. To Nicomedes, he said, 'There's Getae south of the village – they'll spot Leucon and call their friends. The whole fight will now happen down by the river, and if we're not quick, a lot of young men will die.'

Nicomedes shook his head. 'You *see* this?'

Kineas had lived his whole life as a soldier largely unable to communicate just how clearly he could read a battlefield. 'Yes,' he said.

The head of the column rounded the flank of the bluff, and the village was immediately visible.

'Form line!' Kineas called.

Now a winter's training told. Despite their fears, they responded crisply enough to the orders, and even the corner of a boundary hedge that blocked the last formation of the line didn't slow them – the end files fell back and the line advanced in good order.

'Ajax – collect the last four files and keep them as a reserve. Follow the main charge.' Kineas waved at them, and Ajax turned out of the line at a gallop.

Kineas took a javelin in his free hand and raised it so that inexperienced troopers could see that it was time to ready themselves.

Nicomedes had his in hand. His face was set, and he looked old.

'They still haven't seen us,' Kineas said. 'That won't last, and I want to get their minds off Leucon.'

Nicomedes shrugged. 'You are commanding my troop,' he said without bitterness. 'I'm a trooper. Command me.'

Kineas felt vaguely guilty that he had seized command – but he wanted this to go well. The future morale and quality of the whole would depend on this one action. Victory would build confidence. Defeat would shatter it.

At the edge of town, a man in a red cloak rode into view, turned, and shouted.

A stade to go.

'Shouldn't we charge?' Nicomedes asked, shouting to be heard.

'Still too far,' said Niceas. 'It all looks closer than it is, the first few times,' he said.

Kineas farted, and his hands began to shake. Red cloak was pointing urgently, and men were joining him. Kineas had time to wonder how a man fated to die at a different river weeks from now could be so afraid, and then he forced himself to turn his head, glanced north and south, and assured himself that he was not riding into the jaws of a trap.

'Now!' he said to Niceas.

Niceas's trumpet came up, catching the sun in a blinding dazzle as he settled it to his lips and the long call began.

Nicomedes sang.

> *Come, Apollo, now if ever!*
> *Let us now thy Glory see!*
> *Now, Lord of Light, we pray thee,*
> *Give thy servants victory!*

By the third word, the troop vented their fear in song, and the Paean rose to the heavens like the smoke of the vanquished towns, and their hooves pounded the earth like a tide of vengeance flowing from the east.

Kineas leaned low over the neck of his grey stallion and dug in his heels for a final burst of speed, throwing his javelin side-armed into red cloak – his throw was high, and the point took the man in the mouth. His head seemed to cave in and Kineas was past him, whirling his heavy javelin like a scythe, seeking only to widen the hole he had made, but Niceas had killed his man and suddenly they were in the streets of the village. The handful of dismounted Getae died against the log walls, or pinned to the mud of the street, or trampled to death by a hundred hooves, and then the line burst out of the village. To the south, Nicomedes had led the right of the line around the town and they were in good order. To the north, there was chaos – a fight around a barn, and a tangle of hedge, and no officer.

'Ajax!' Kineas called. 'Sort that out.' He waved his sword at the mêlée at the barn. Where was his good javelin? Why was his sword out?

With half the men, he started down the slope towards the river, where he could hear sounds of fighting. 'Line!' he shouted. He didn't slow down his canter, and they came on like veterans, galloping up to take their places in the line despite the many men missing. His horse was tired – almost blown, and the other horses would be worse. Too late for that. He pointed his line as best he could at where he imagined the fight to be, just past the crest of the low ridge that lined the river, waited a few strides of his stallion to let the line adjust, and raised his sword. Niceas put the trumpet to his lips, and the call rang out, and then they were over the rise – straight into the rear of the Getae, not a line but a series of knots of men facing Leucon's outnumbered line.

Kineas had no javelin. He rode straight into one of the knots, cutting with his Egyptian blade. His horse reared, shying from a corpse, and then struck with his hooves. A blow on his back plate, and a line of fire along the top of his bridle arm – he cut back on instinct and felt the blade hit home, his eyes only seeing the target after the sword had fully severed the man's hand above the wrist – Kineas's horse danced again, and Kineas cut back with the whole weight of his arm and severed the man's head, so that it rose a few inches and then fell, blood fountaining from the stump of the arm and neck and the trunk slipping from a now terrified horse. Kineas reined his stallion in a tight circle, looking for a new opponent. He saw Eumenes locked in a grapple with a Getae warrior, and even as he watched the two fell from their horses. Eumenes landed on top, and his opponent had the wind crushed out of him, and Eumenes' fevered hands found a rock and smashed the man's head.

A few strides away, Nicomedes killed carefully, fastidiously, like a cat, his javelin licking out into men's faces and necks. In fact, he fought like a hoplite mounted on a horse – Kineas had never seen a javelin used that way, like a six-foot sword.

Just beyond the last knot of barbarians still fighting, Kineas found Leucon, clear of the mêlée, restraining a few files from the slaughter. The Getae were broken, panicked, seeking only escape, and the Olbians were not giving any quarter – they had ridden through the village to reach the fight, and they were in an angry mood. And they were fresh troops in their first action

– all their fear was being vented on the beaten enemy.

'I thought I should keep a few men back,' Leucon shouted.

'Well done,' Kineas called, just as his stallion paused, and then, in a long, slow fall, collapsed and died, blood gushing from a wound in his neck.

The Getae had been surprised and disordered in each combat, and the Persian stallion was the only casualty among the Olbians. By the time the routed enemy were butchered, over a hundred Getae were dead, and the Olbians killed the seriously wounded barbarians at Niceas's order. Few enough of the Getae had died fighting – most had been hacked down after they broke, pinned against the swollen waters of the river. More had drowned trying to swim to safety.

'No prisoners, the way we're moving. And no soldier worth a fuck leaves a man to die like that,' Niceas said to a group of red-faced Olbians. They were cooling down. Now was the time to give quarter. 'If they can walk, let them go.' To Kineas, he said, 'What do we do with all these corpses? Our rich boys won't want to bury them.'

'They seem quick enough to loot them,' Kineas said. Even the most starry-eyed, Achilles-loving stripling among the cavalry was taking his turn cutting gold and silver rings from the fallen Getae.

'How do you think they got to be rich boys?' Niceas sneered.

'Leave the dead for the crows,' Kineas said. 'I want to move as soon as we can. Make that Sindi farmer see sense – him and his fellows.' Kineas turned to Ataelus, who had missed the action scouting north of the village but had managed to acquire four new horses anyway. 'Ataelus – make him see sense. They have to come with us.'

'Column of refugees will only slow us down,' Niceas said.

Kineas smiled grimly. 'I want to be slowed down,' he said.

Ataelus shook his head. 'Men stay to bury,' he said.

'Take me to him,' Kineas said. He had to walk – his riding horse was lame and his stallion dead – the finest horse he had ever owned. To Niceas, he said, 'Get the best horse available – get two or three.'

Niceas shook his head. 'Sorry the grey bastard died. I'll miss him. Like an old friend.'

'Better a horse than a man,' Kineas said, but he had kept that stallion alive for three years, and the grey bastard had done the same for him. He followed the Sakje to a group of Sindi men – heavily built, squat, with broad faces and red hair, most of them. They were burying children, and the woman who had been raped and killed. Kineas tried not to look at her – wondered if he could have saved her by a simple charge into the town.

Then he made himself look at her. Simple courtesy, really. She was young, and she had died an awful death. He made himself breathe in and out. Next to her was an older woman – perhaps forty – with long blond braids and a small knife still stuck in her throat. 'Tell them I can take them – all of them – with me.' Kineas gestured.

Ataelus spoke to the broadest man – obviously a smith. Kineas understood all that he said.

The man shook his head and pointed at the row of little bodies with his shovel, and the blonde woman. All of the Sindi men were weeping.

Ataelus turned back to Kineas. 'Very bad thing. When house took fire, mother killed childs. Then kill her with own knife – brave. And men vow fight to death – and then we come. So wife, all children dead. Men want die.'

'Athena protect us,' Kineas said in horror. 'The mother killed her own children?'

Ataelus looked at him like an alien building. 'No Sakje – dirt people or sky people – go as slave. Mother brave. Brave brave.' The Sakje reached in his belt pouch and took out a pinch of seeds – the same seeds that Kam Baqca burned on her brazier. He threw the seeds into the grave, and threw a small, ornate knife from his boot beside it.

'I honour her brave.'

Kineas heart seemed to swell to fill his chest, and he thought he might choke, and his eyes burned. He turned away, walked back to where Ajax and Eumenes were telling of their exploits, watched with some amusement by Nicomedes and Niceas.

'Thirty men to help the townspeople dig graves for their

fallen. Right now.' Kineas's voice broke as he said it, and he turned so that his officers wouldn't see him unmanned. He was an old hand, and he had seen quite a few dead children, but this affected him so deeply that he was shaking.

He thought of Medea, killing her children at the end of the play, and he wondered what the playwright had missed. Or known.

The Olbians, aware of some change in their hipparch, dug without a grumble. The women and children were buried in an hour. The men gathered flowers to put on the graves, and Kineas threw a brooch in, as did many of the soldiers, so that the mother's grave was heaped with things she might have counted as treasures if she had lived.

By the time the last flower was placed on the last child's grave, Kineas had listened to all Ataelus had to tell him of the Getae to the north and west. When his column mounted, the Sindi men had Getae horses and a good wagon of their own. The Sindi men all had bows like Sakje bows, and every man had a heavy axe, and death in their faces.

'North and east, right across the front of the Getae advance,' Kineas said.

Ataelus smiled grimly.

After three days, Kineas had a hundred Sindi refugees, men and women and children, and his column was slowed to the speed of a walking man. And the Getae had taken notice. Three times he'd fallen on their raiders. Three times he'd destroyed the band he'd met. Every man in the Olbian column was a killer, now – there had been hard fighting in the last town, fighting inside the houses.

And with killing, death. Young Kyros, the brilliant javelineer, was dead, a Getae knife in his neck, and Nicomedes' business partner, Theo, lay on a cart breathing as best he could with a punctured lung, waiting to die, and Sophokles, whose contempt for the rules of war had entertained them on the first trip to the Sakje, took a sword cut to his arm and bled out before his comrades could save him. Luck, good armour, and barbarian indiscipline had kept the rest of them alive, but they were exhausted in body and in spirit, and many of them had wounds – wounds they would survive, but which sapped their strength and their will to fight.

Kineas and Niceas bore down, becoming monsters of discipline. No shortcoming was tolerated. Niceas struck two young troopers in a single morning. Kineas wondered what Srayanka would think – or what she would do.

So it was a silent, sullen column that moved through a steady drizzle on the fourth morning, the tired men riding tired beasts, man and horse alike with their heads down. Niceas and Nicomedes were both out with the scouts, because the scouts required the immediate presence of their officers to keep them alert. Kineas blessed the handful of Sakje every hour. They were doing most of the work.

Ajax and Eumenes rode with a silent Kineas. Both glanced at him from time to time, but neither spoke.

Ataelus returned from his latest scout by midday.

'Fuck-their-mothers Getae gather behind us,' he said. 'Three big bands. See them when night comes, if we camp.'

Kineas cursed and wiped water off his face. 'I don't want to lose them and I don't want my camp stormed in the night,' he said. 'How many?'

Ataelus shrugged. 'Many many. Ten hands and ten hands and ten hands and ten hands, in each group – and more. Too many to fight.'

Kineas nodded and waved to one of the Cruel Hand scouts, who cantered up. Like Ataelus, he didn't look tired, depressed, or unhappy, and Kineas wished he had a hundred veterans. The advantages of taking his Olbian horse for this part of his plan against the raiders was now balanced by how brittle their spirit was. They'd recover – and be better soldiers for it – but not for some days.

'Can you find the king?' Kineas said.

The Sakje nodded.

'Go find him. Tell him it will be tomorrow, just after dawn. I'll make for the big hill.'

The Sakje turned his horse. He raised his whip to his forehead. 'You good chief,' he said in Greek. He waved at Ataelus, gave

324

a loud *yip* in the direction of the other Cruel Hands, and rode off at a gallop.

Kineas watched him go, wondering if the king would come. Kineas had begun to distrust the king. Perhaps distrust is too strong a word, he thought. But the king, despite his youth, wanted Srayanka. And when Kineas had proposed to use his own men as bait, he'd seen something pass over the young man's face.

The rest of the day was brutal. Kineas kept the column moving by force of will, the fear he could inspire, and force. He terrified women, he ripped children from their mother's arms to put them on wagons, he struck Srayanka's whip at the slowest oxen.

Towards evening, they came to a stream. He'd been here before, en route to the first action. Then they'd crossed easily, but now it was swollen with a day's rain.

'Athena protect us,' he said grimly. He rode back to his officers. 'Go among your men. Select all the veterans and send them to me.'

'You'll weaken the files,' Niceas said.

'I don't think the files will fight. I need to survive the next hour.' Kineas was looking through the rain at the last hill, where he hoped his scouts were watching his back trail.

Niceas shook his head. 'Don't do it.'

A day of absolute authority had its cost. 'Obey!' Kineas demanded.

Leucon shook his head – sombre, but sure. 'They'll fight, Hipparch. You just have to say something – they're scared. Ares' balls, sir, I'm scared too. I – I thought we'd have a rest.'

Kineas mastered his anger and turned his attention to Niceas. 'Speak your mind, hyperetes.'

'Don't pull the veterans. Give 'em a talk, we lighten up a little, show them some respect, and they'll fight like heroes.'

Kineas rubbed his jaw, watching a cart begin to cross, pulled with ropes by men waist deep in muddy water. 'Think that'll work?'

'Worked on you, once or twice,' Niceas said. 'Pull the veterans and they'll think you don't trust them.'

Kineas smiled – his first smile in a day. 'I'll try it,' he said. 'Sound: Form line.'

Despite fatigue and rain, the two troops formed line on their tired horses like soldiers. Some men did it without raising their heads.

Kineas rode out to the front of the line. 'I'm tired,' he said. 'So I'm pretty sure you're all tired. I've driven you like a coach drives athletes, and you've come up to the mark every day. And now we're at this Hades-damned stream, and I have to ask you for more.'

He pointed at their back trail. 'There are two thousand Getae behind us, about an hour's march away.' He swung Srayanka's whip over his head and pointed past them. 'A day's march that way is the king of the Sakje.' *I hope.* 'One more fight, and one more day on the trail, moving fast, and you can rest. And before you despair, gentlemen – you've fought three actions in three days. None of you are boys any more. Now you know what the animal looks like. Any man worthy of his father can stand in a big field on a sunny day and hold his piece of ground for an hour. But to be a real soldier, you have to find it in yourself to do it day after day, in the rain, in the desert, when you are tired and sore and when your dinner runs down your legs or when you have no food to eat at all.' He pulled his helmet off and rode closer to the line. 'We can get across this stream and back to the king – if you have the spirit to do it.'

Ajax raised his sword. 'Apollo!' he shouted.

The answering shout was not deafening – but neither was it hopeless. The troops gave three Apollos.

Kineas summoned his officers. 'Have the men dismount and stand by their horses. Send the most junior files of each troop to help move the wagons. Let's do this thing!' He spoke in a different tone than he'd used all day – like an officer commanding veterans. He turned to Niceas. 'You were right,' he said.

Niceas shrugged. 'It happens,' he said. He watched young Clio leading two younger men in pushing at a wagon wheel, up to their waists in freezing water. 'They don't look so much like rich boys now.'

Twenty minutes later the last wagon was across and Ataelus

returned at a gallop to report that the lead Getae band was in sight. Kineas looked at the sky – more rain – and the crossing. To Niceas, he said, 'I think we're going to do this.'

Niceas huddled in his cloak. 'Did you doubt it, Hipparch?'

Kineas shook his head. 'I did.' He waved to Leucon. 'Get your men across. Nicomedes, mount and cover them. The Getae are coming.' Something tugged at his right foot, and he saw the blacksmith. 'What?' he said in Sakje.

The blacksmith pointed at the stand of small trees by the swollen river. 'Die here,' he said, pointing at himself. 'You cross.'

Kineas wiped the water off his face. 'No. No one will die here. Too much rain. Get across.'

The man planted his feet. 'Die here.'

Kineas shook his head. He called for Ataelus. 'Tell him it's raining,' he said. 'Tell him that his bowstrings are wet, and he'll be lucky to kill one Getae – and that it'll be for nothing, because the Getae won't want to push across against us. Not enough light left.'

Ataelus translated, speaking rapidly, using his hands more than he was wont, speaking, Kineas thought, with great emotion. Ataelus thought highly of the blacksmith.

The blacksmith finally nodded. He put his axe over his shoulder and walked to the ford, his friends falling in around him, and they followed Leucon's men through the rising water.

Kineas rode up to Nicomedes. The Getae were still well distant, and the ford was clear. 'Better cross,' he said.

Nicomedes gave a tired smile. 'You won't have to tell me twice.'

The two Cruel Hand scouts were coming in, one galloping far to the north, the other far to the south. Both turned periodically and shot from the saddle, and Ataelus gave a *yip* and rode out to the front.

Nicomedes shook his head. 'Does that change our plans?'

'No,' Kineas said. 'Get across.'

He sat in the rain, watching the Sakje – just three of them – harrying the advancing Getae, who had few bows and none that would fire in the rain. One by one, the Sakje bowstrings became wet through, despite the best efforts of the Sakje warriors to keep them dry, but they each hit two or three men, slowing all the Getae for a few more minutes as the precious grey light slipped away to night. All three rode to the ford untouched. The Getae were just two stades away, clear despite the heavier rain and gathering gloom.

The four of them pushed into the heavy water. After ten steps, Kineas put his arms around his horse's neck and allowed himself to float free from his saddle cloth, and then his horse – an ugly Getae beast, but strong as an ox – pushed up the far bank of earth, showering both of them in mud in the process of shaking like a dog.

The Sindi men were cutting poles – stakes, it turned out, and as Kineas wrung the water from his cloak and tried to get warm, he watched them pound the stakes into the soft earth at the side of the stream so that the ford was blocked with man-high spikes pointed at horse-chest height.

Kineas rode up to the officers. 'The Getae are mad – they may try it anyway. If not, they'll come an hour after the rain stops. We'll hold them here. We won't get better ground.' To the blacksmith, he said, 'Tell the people in the wagons that we move before dawn. We will abandon the wagons – every man and woman is to ride on the spare horses. No unloading, and leave the fires lit when we go.' He looked at Ataelus. 'Will the Getae fight at night?'

Ataelus shrugged with a sneer, as if the petty superstitions of the Getae were beneath his consideration.

Kineas looked around. 'I want our scouts up and downstream ten stades, looking for another ford – if they find one, we leave. Half a troop on duty every watch – two hours a trick. Get a hot meal in them and then we'll sleep in the open.'

'In the mud?' asked Eumenes.

'That's right. If you aren't tired enough to sleep in the mud, you aren't really tired. Leucon's boys know how to huddle up. Tell them to teach their fathers. Right – we move before dawn. Any questions?'

There were none. Nicomedes was almost asleep in his saddle.

The slaves and the Sindi cooked faster and better than the Olbians, and they had hot food – mostly a thin soup of roots and some meat, but as good as ambrosia after their day – and heavy bread nine days old. Kineas ate his and handed his bowl to Niceas to use. 'Wake me if the rain stops,' he said. He lay down with Eumenes and Leucon, and the soggy ground met him with an icy embrace. It was horrible, and then it was merely uncomfortable, and then he was asleep.

He woke from a dream of being trapped in a cave full of water to find Leucon's cloak over his head, and he was blind. He threw it off, reaching for his sword, and Niceas, silhouetted by a fire that burned as high as a man, jumped back.

'Rain stopped. Sky is clearing,' he said. He was munching something, and he pointed. 'Stars,' he said through the bread in his mouth.

Kineas ached, and he shivered, his whole body moving as if he was going to vomit. His fingers were swollen and their joints burned. The wound he had taken on his left bicep in the first fight was hot and tender. He didn't know where he was for a few heartbeats, and then he did.

'Get everybody up,' he said. 'What're the Getae doing?'

'Huddling around their fires,' Niceas said. 'There's quite a pack of them – fires all the way back to the hills.'

Kineas's brain began to function. He squelched over to the fire and its warmth began to soak into his joints. 'Get everyone in the saddle.'

A Sindi woman pushed something hot into his hand – a clay cup full of herb tea. It tasted bitter, but it was warm. He drained it, burning his tongue. The cut on his arm ached.

'Mount all the Sindi on the spare horses and leave the wagons,' Kineas said.

'Heard you last night.' Niceas said. 'Done. Had to use a stick on the refugees – they don't want to leave their little bits of things behind.' He gave a hard grin. 'I took care of it.'

'Athena's shield, Hipparch – we could have done that two days ago and left the Getae in our dust!' Eumenes spoke from the other side of the fire.

'We could have,' Kineas said. 'But that's not what I ordered. Now I have.'

Eumenes held his hands up like a boxer defending himself. 'I spoke hastily.'

Kineas ignored him, turning to Nicomedes. 'You are the rearguard. Try to keep the stragglers moving, but if you must, abandon them and push on. Don't be trapped into a fight – once we stop, the whole pack will be on us. Understand?'

Nicomedes drank some of the woman's tea and nodded. He had circles under his eyes, and he looked sixty years old. Ajax stood behind him, as beautiful as ever. 'If we aren't to fight, why are we the rear guard?' he asked.

Kineas shook his head. 'Don't be a fool – If I have to, I'll sacrifice you to get the rest away. But not without an order from me. If you see me form Leucon's troop in line, come and fall into your accustomed place.'

'For a last stand?' Ajax asked.

'For whatever I order,' Kineas said. He took a deep breath and drained the tea left in his cup, bowed to the woman and handed her back her cup, and then turned back to grin at his men. 'Trust me,' he said.

Again, he wondered if he could trust the king.

The Getae were as slow to rise as any barbarians, and they were two hours behind at mid-morning. Helios's winged chariot was climbing in the sky, and the Sakje rode with their bowstrings across their knees to dry the sinew in the sun.

An hour later, the men had passed from cold to heat, and the ground was already dry, rolling out to the horizon in waves of grass. A few stades to the east, a single tall ridge rose above the plain. Kineas had scouted it on the trip out, just ten days ago.

Behind them the Getae were less than three stades away, and their flank companies were beginning to press forward, extending to the right and left in the high grass, calling to each other as they came. They were beginning to encircle him, like good hunters. They were pressing on quickly, assured of their prey and embarrassed by so much defeat in the last few days.

Kineas rode to the head of the column. 'Straight up the ridge,' he said. 'At the gallop!'

The column was losing cohesion, the weary men showing a

tendency to lose control of their horses, but the gallop galvanized them again. The Sindi in the centre of the column were mostly accomplished riders, but not all. Kineas rode back down when he saw them slow. He and Ajax took children and mothers on their own jaded horses, and the Sindi men took others, and the little band of Sindi pressed on. Kineas saw the base of the hill rising between his horse's ugly ears, and prayed to Zeus. He looked back. The Getae were two stades back, forming a line, and their flanking bands were a stade distant to the right and left, but already level, pacing them. The Getae were calling back and forth, their war cries loud and shrill.

Kineas's tired horse grunted as he started up the ridge. The child in his arms was a girl, perhaps three years old, with blonde hair and deep blue eyes. She looked at him curiously.

'Horse is tired,' she said. She smiled. 'Are you tired?'

'Yes,' he said. 'What's your name?'

Leucon's company was at the crest, forming a line as they arrived. They weren't neat, but they were still under control, and he was proud of them.

'Alyet. I'm three years old.' The little girl held up three fingers, spread broadly. 'Are we going to die?' she asked with all the lack of understanding of the young. 'My mother said we might die.'

'No,' Kineas said. He was three quarters of the way up the slope, and his animal was making heavy work of it. He let her take the slope at an angle and she responded well. Leucon's men were formed, and Nicomedes' men were passing the refugees, just as he had ordered, scrambling up the face of the ridge to form alongside Leucon's company.

The Getae didn't pause. They were coming on; so close that Kineas could see the plaques they wore as decoration on their harness and the designs on their cloaks. The companies to the right and left were angling in, eager to be in at the kill, hill or no hill.

Kineas made it to the crest. He rode to the huddle of Sindi and swung the girl into her mother's arms. Mindful of the horror in the village, afraid that on the edge of victory they would despair, he patted the little girl's head and raised a hand for attention.

'Now we win,' he said loudly, in Sakje.

A hundred doubting faces looked back at him.

He smiled, all the cares of the last few days lifted by what he could see from the top of the ridge. 'Watch,' he said, and rode away to the centre of his line.

The Getae were at the base of the slope, calling and shouting. The bolder spirits had pushed their horses up the first part of the slope.

Far out on the sea of green, beyond the farthest horns of the Getae advance, the grass moved as if pushed by a wind, and lines of Sakje rolled their horses erect – lines that stretched for a stade each, hundreds of riders rising from the grass like warriors grown from dragon's teeth.

And from behind the ridge came the king and his nobles, riding easily on unwearied horses up the back of the ridge to form a compact line of armoured men to Kineas's left. And another company appeared on the right – more and more riders. The Olbians and the Sindi gave a cheer, and the Sakje crossed the crest to fall like the bolts of Zeus on the Getae.

The king had come. The king *had* come. Kineas felt the weight fall from his shoulders, and then the slaughter began.

The Olbians played no role in the fight. They watched the revenge of the Sakje with the weary joy of men who know that they have accomplished much and can now rest. Before the last Getae fell, where a knot of nobles gathered around their leader and died in a heap, Kineas led his column the last few stades to the king's camp, a great circle of wagons enclosing thousands of horses by yet another river, guarded by yet more Sakje deemed unnecessary for the massacre.

The Olbians were greeted as heroes. Kineas found that despite his weariness, he couldn't listen to too much praise. He rode from group to group, watching their faces, amused that his men, exhausted moments before, suddenly had the energy to drink wine and boast. There was food, and fire, and soon they were joined by the first Sakje returning from the rout of the Getae. Many had heads tied to their saddlecloths. Later, Kineas saw a man scraping carefully at a whole tattooed skin. Others had loot – a little gold, a great deal of silver, and horses.

Ataelus returned just before dark, riding in with Srayanka's

Cruel Hands. She was covered in blood, but before Kineas's fears could rise in his chest, she waved. He returned her wave, a broad smile across his face, and saw that his own skin was filthy, mud and blood and sweat fighting for possession of his wrists and hands. He hadn't bathed or strigilled in a week.

Ataelus rode up proudly, sitting on his tired pony like a king. 'I take ten horses!' he said. 'You great chief. All warriors say so.' He glanced at Srayanka, issuing orders to her inner circle. 'Lady say you hero. Say you *airyanām*.'

Kineas grinned again.

While Ataelus praised him, the king rode into the laager. His armour was gold, and it was blinding in the setting sun. He looked right and left, and finding Kineas, he rode up to him – a mass of gold from head to toe.

'It worked,' he said. He struggled with the chinstrap on his Corinthian helmet, got it, and lifted the whole gilt thing off his head. His hair was matted flat, and he had a trickle of blood running out of one nostril. 'By the gods, Kineas! The Getae will feel this for ten generations!'

'We were lucky,' Kineas said. 'I thought of all the things that could have gone wrong while we rode. A foolish plan, and far too ambitious.' He smiled wearily. 'And I seem to remember that you were to have no part in this fight. I seem to remember Kam Baqca extracting a promise.' You came! he wanted to say.

'I said I would not place myself in any danger,' the king grinned. 'Nor did I. They were broken before we rode down the hill.'

He dismounted and opened his arms in embrace, and Kineas hugged him, armoured chest to armoured chest. 'Oh, we pounded them!' the king boasted. 'The Cruel Hands lay so still that their scouts practically rode over their lines without seeing them. I must have killed six.' The boy ended the embrace. 'I feel foul. Tired. This is my first big fight – my first victory as king – and you gave it to me. I won't forget.' Satrax was stripping armour while he babbled. He was still fighting the laces on his scale vambrace. 'Marthax says I should stay out of the fight – but if I didn't fight, I would cease to be king. We are Sakje, not Greeks.' He grinned, the same relief from tension on his face that could be seen on every other leader's. 'Sometimes I think that Marthax wants to keep all the glory for himself. Or that he wants to be king in my place.' He seized a proffered cup of wine and drained it.

Kineas stepped up close and started on the other lace. Other men and women did the same, so that the king's disarming was itself a celebration. They babbled to each other, exalted by victory and survival.

When his scale breastplate was dragged over his head, the king stepped out of it and then embraced Kineas again. 'Smile,' he said. 'Laugh. We are alive. And now I believe we will defeat Zopryon. I believe we could defeat Alexander!'

The young king pounded his shoulders, and Kineas smiled at them, suddenly wanting to be free of their embraces and their praise, feeling dirty. He slipped away gradually, telling himself that he was as eager to be free of his armour as the king had been free of his. He went to a fire that the Olbians had appropriated and was greeted with a roar. Ajax helped him out of his breastplate, and Kineas felt lighter, if not younger.

Nicomedes came and placed an arm around Ajax's broad shoulders. The age had fallen away from his face, and he was a gentleman of forty again. 'We honour you, Hipparch,' he said. 'It is one thing to hear of your exploits, and another thing to see.'

Kineas looked at his legs, streaked with mud, and his arms, with blood and ordure mixed. All the rain had done was to streak it, and where he had lain in the mud, his tunic was soaked through and his side was itchy and his left arm was swollen. 'If you are quoting someone, I don't know it,' Kineas said.

Nicomedes said, 'I am a rich man, and I have been privileged to see many great craftsmen and artists at work. It is always the same – when you watch them work, you see the focus of their genius, and you know you have the real thing.'

Ajax laughed. 'I doubt Kineas wants to be in your collection, my friend.'

Kineas half grinned. 'Thanks – I think.' He pulled off his chiton. 'Can you get a slave to find my kit? I need to wear something else. In the meantime, I'm going to the river to bathe.'

Nicomedes made a show of sniffing his battered cloak. 'A splendid idea.'

Ajax produced a strigil as Niceas joined them with another. 'I have oil,' Niceas said.

Ajax cheered him as if he'd won a race. As they walked, a few other men joined them – Leucon and Eumenes, and several of their young men. They walked the stade to the river on sore legs, and Kineas was happy, as happy as a man who can foretell his own death can be. He had lost four men in a hard campaign. He regretted them – but he knew he, and they, had done well, and he knew that for a few hours he didn't have to worry about anything but the aches in his muscles and the fever in his wound. Death seemed very far away.

He listened to the younger men chatter, and he walked a little ahead of them, naked, with his filthy tunic over his shoulder. He heard the pounding of hooves and he turned.

Srayanka was behind him, with a few of her officers, all naked, covered as they all were in mud and filth, the horses as well as the riders. She saw him and he saw her, and she rode past him, her eyes flicking over his body even as he looked at hers. Then she was past, kicking her horse to a gallop, turning back to wave. She raced on, as beautiful as anything Kineas had ever seen despite the grime and the blood, her unbound black hair flying out behind her, her back straight as she gathered her horse for a jump and then leaped from the bank straight into the river with a splash like a leaping whale. All the rest of her warriors followed her.

The Olbians pointed and shouted and cheered. 'Like Artemis and her nymphs,' Nicomedes said. He appeared shocked. He took a breath. 'Who expected such beauty on a day like this? I wish I had a painter – a sculptor – anyone to make that for me.'

'I'll settle for a bath,' Niceas said.

'Let's run,' said Kineas. And the Olbians began to run. They ran like Olympians, squandering their last reserves in the setting sun. And as they came to the bank they made the leap into the cold water, and they shouted as they fell.

Kineas swam across the broadest pool. The water was deep but full of silt from the rain, or stirred up by the horses. He didn't care – it felt wonderful against his skin despite the cold. He swam with his tunic in his teeth, looking for her in the slowly falling dark.

He found her in the shallows under a tall tree. She was scrubbing her warhorse clean, scooping sand with her hands from the river bank and scrubbing at her horse's legs where the big beast appeared to have waded in blood.

She smiled at him. 'He bites,' she said in Greek. 'Not too close.'

Kineas stayed in the deep water. He was a practical man, and he was happy just to be with her, admiring her body – he began to wash his tunic as best he could. After a while, he passed behind her and went to the bank, where he collected a handful of her sand and began to grind away at the dried crud on his arms.

Down the pool, he could hear shrieks and shouts from the other Olbians. From the voices, it appeared that more and more were coming to bathe – more Olbians and more Sakje.

'You airyanăm,' she said, looking over her shoulder. She pushed a tail of black hair back over her naked shoulder. She glanced downstream, and back at him.

He stepped up to her and she entered his arms as though they had rehearsed the embrace a thousand times, and her mouth came under his as easily as the clasping of two hands.

They wrapped themselves into each other ...

For a few seconds, until Ataelus called, 'Here they are!' and they were surrounded, Cruel Hands and Olbians, laughing, jeering, with more than a few obscene suggestions.

Kineas slipped into deeper water to hide the truth of their assertions, still holding her hand, and she swam after him leaving her horse. And they swam together with their people until they were clean. They dried naked in the warm evening air, on the grass, and Agis the Megaran and Ajax both sang from the *Iliad* while the Greek men used olive oil and strigils on their skin, to the delight and amusement of all the Sakje. Then Marthax sang with Srayanka, turn and turn again, an endless ballad of love and revenge. Kineas found that the king had joined them, and he sat with the king while men fetched dry tunics and food, and then Srayanka finished singing and sat with her back against his as if they were old war companions. Her people had brought her clothes, and she was dressed, and she had given him a tunic of pale skin covered in embroidery like her own. It was barbaric. He put it on anyway.

The king sat stiffly with them, and then turned away, clearly angered, when Kineas donned the tunic. Later, when she kissed Kineas, an absent and affectionate peck as she reached past him for wine, the king rose to his feet. He spoke to her in rapid, angry Sakje.

She tossed her drying hair, flicked her eyes at Kineas and then nodded to the king. 'My mind knows,' she said clearly. 'And my mind rules my body.'

The king turned and strode off into the dark.

Srayanka's back remained warm against his, her iron and deerskin hand supple in his, and he was, again, as happy as a man could be who had only a few weeks to live.

In the morning, the army lay in a stupor of exhaustion and wine-sickness. A handful of Getae could have wrecked them. Kineas had never seen an army behave differently after a victory, but wondered if there might be a value in keeping a guard.

The swelling in his arm was less, and the heat from it almost gone, as if the river spirit had drawn away the poison. He was one of the first up, and having drunk some Sindi tea, he donned the leather tunic that Srayanka had given him. Despite its outré appearance, it was clean. His military chiton was damp, and despite his desultory washing while he watched Srayanka, it was still filthy, and the rest of his kit had vanished in the retreat – probably left at the last camp.

The king rode up to where Kineas was eyeing the Olbian's string of captured Getae mounts, working to select a decent riding horse. To his eye, they were all too small.

'I think it is time we spoke as men,' the king said, with an obvious attempt at dignity. 'You have given me a great victory. I would not be ungenerous.'

Kineas sighed and looked up at the king. 'I am at your service, Lord.' He looked at the ground, unused to discussing such matters. Then he looked back. 'Are we speaking of Srayanka?'

The king wouldn't meet his eye. 'After Zopryon is defeated – would you marry her?'

Kineas shrugged. 'Of course,' he said, because he had to say something. *Of course, if I were alive.*

The king leaned down. 'Perhaps the prospect is not as enticing – she is no Greek woman, and she is fierce. But she will not settle to be your leman – she is the chief of the Cruel Hands, too great a personage to be a trull. Perhaps you cannot wed her – perhaps you are already married, or promised?'

The king had mistaken his tone entirely. 'I would be proud to be wed to the lady,' Kineas said, and found that he meant it.

The king straightened in his saddle. 'Really?' He sounded surprised. 'She would never live in a city. It would kill her.' Now he met Kineas's eye. 'I have lived in a Greek city. I know the lady. She lives as a free spear maiden, and your city would kill her.'

Fantasizing aloud, Kineas said, 'Perhaps I could buy a farm north of Olbia – she could visit.' He laughed even as he spoke.

The king shook his head. 'I like you, Kineas. I liked you from the first. But you come like the doom of my happiness. You brought this war, and now you will take my cousin. I will try to speak as a man, and not an outraged youth. I wish her for myself – but she will have only you. Now I must endure not just the loss of her – a woman I have desired since I was old enough to feel a man's desire – but to know that my best warriors speak of you as airyanăm. If you wed her, you will be a potent ally – or a deadly rival. And I ask myself – is this what you desire? Will you leave your men to ride the plains? Or bring them, like a new clan?'

Kineas rubbed at his beard and felt old. 'Lord, I will serve you. Indeed, I had not thought on any of these matters. I can see that they prey on you. But ...' Kineas struggled for words. 'It is the lady herself that I value.'

'How will you live?' the king asked. 'Can you leave Niceas, or Diodorus, to be the consort of a barbarian girl?' He looked away over the grass. 'Or would she leave the Cruel Hands to grind flour and weave with Greek women? I think perhaps she would – until she hated you, or went mad.'

Kineas nodded, because he had thought these thoughts, and because the sentence of death hanging over him had saved him from having to decide. Except he felt – knew, in his heart – that they would have found a way.

Or would he have ended as Jason, and she as Medea?

But what could he say? Lord, I'll be dead, so it doesn't matter? 'I think we would – will find a way,' he said carefully.

The king was still watching the grass. He drew himself taller. 'I will try not to stand between you,' he said. The sentence cost him. And then he added, 'Kam Baqca says I must do this thing.'

Kineas wondered what it was like to have so much power at eighteen years. 'It is a noble thing to do, whether Kam Baqca recommended it or not.'

Satrax shrugged. Then he straightened and sought again for dignity. 'I hear you lost your warhorse,' he said. 'You lost that grey – which gives me a beautiful opportunity to show you how highly I value you.' He extended a hand, inviting Kineas to mount behind him.

Kineas mounted with the king. 'People will laugh,' he said.

'Unlikely,' the king answered. He kicked his horse into a trot and then a canter.

They were riding through the royal herd, or rather the abbreviated version that the king had brought on the pursuit of the Getae. Kineas knew the brands.

The king spoke suddenly, 'My other lords think you are the perfect choice – she will have a husband, and the Cruel Hands will have heirs, and you, of course, are already a war leader of repute.' The horse continued for a few strides. 'I am told I should pick a girl my own age, with better hips for childbearing – a Sauromatae princess is recommended.' Kineas was pressed against the king's back, and Satrax was stiff – angry. Angry that he had to bow to the wishes of his lords. Then he relaxed and pointed. 'There!' he said.

The stallion was not so much grey as silver, a dark silver the colour of polished iron, or steel. He had a heavy black line down his back – a marking Kineas had only seen among the heavy Sakje breed – and a pale mane and tale. He was tall, and self-possessed. In fact, he was twin to the king's war mount.

'He won't be as well trained as your Persian,' the king said – like all men giving a great gift, he had to decry its faults. 'But he's well broken to harness – my next warhorse. Yours, now. And a couple of riding horses – Marthax has them for you, but I wanted to talk.'

Kineas walked around the stallion, admiring his haunches. He had a short head, without the purity of line the Persian had, but he was big and the colour was either ugly or magnificent. It was certainly rare. 'Thank you, Lord. This is a kingly gift.'

The king grinned, embarrassed and looking very young indeed. 'He is, isn't he?' Satrax smiled, showing his essential good humour. 'There's the advantage of owning ten thousand horses,' he said after a moment.

'I am sorry,' Kineas said. He couldn't think of anything else to say.

The king grimaced. 'Kings have to think hard thoughts. If you are her husband, you will be a man of great power among my people. A baqca who was also a man with a wife who commanded a clan. A great soldier with Greek allies. You may be my rival.' He looked at the horse. 'As Marthax is.' He stared out over the plain. 'Or is this just my jealousy speaking?'

'You are blunt,' Kineas said. 'You think like a king.'

'I have to.' The king gestured at the horse. 'Give him a try,' he said.

Kineas caught the mane of the stallion in one hand and vaulted on to the beast's tall back. He almost missed his seat – this monster was a hand taller than the Persian – and he was thankful that the animal waited patiently while his feet scrambled.

Satrax restrained his laughter with difficulty, pleased to see the Greek discomfited by the horse. Kineas made a clucking sound, and the big animal flowed into a curve. 'What a gait!' Kineas crowed. The beast's easy flow of hooves was strangely familiar. He tried his knees alone, his hands free, and brought the stallion alongside the king's mount easily. The two horses sniffed at each other like stable mates – which they probably were. They were the same colour.

'Same dam?' he said.

Satrax grinned. 'Same dam and sire,' he said. 'Brothers.'

Kineas inclined his head. 'I am honoured.' He patted the horse's shoulder, thinking of his conversation with Philokles. 'I swear to you that no action of mine will harm your kingship. Nor will I wed Srayanka, or ask for her, without your permission.' He slapped the horse. 'This is a wonderful gift,' he repeated.

'Good,' said the king. He nodded, obviously relieved and just as obviously still troubled. And jealous. 'Good. Let's get the army moving.'

It was later in the day when Kineas, who was becoming more enamoured of his new horse by the hour, realized why his gait seemed so familiar.

The silver horse was the stallion from the dream of his death.

18

They crossed the plains from west to east at speed. The Sakje set their usual pace, and the Olbians, with remounts provided, kept up. They made a hundred stades a day, by Kineas's estimation, watering at rivers that crossed the plain at measured intervals, camping in established spots with fresh green grass for fodder and a few trees for firewood.

The level of organization was staggering, for barbarians. But Kineas no longer thought of them as barbarians.

Kineas had never seen an army of five thousand move so fast. If Zopryon pressed his men as hard as Alexander himself, he might make sixty stades, although patrols would go farther. And Kineas suspected he had not seen the fastest march of which the Sakje were capable.

Most of the campsites were shadowed by tall hills of turf that grew out of the plain, often the highest point for many hours riding. On the fourth evening, his muscles sore but his body clean, Kineas sat with his back against Niceas's, rubbing tallow into his bridle leather and then working carefully at the head-stall where it had begun to burst its stitches, making minute alterations in the fit as he went. The new horse had a big head.

Srayanka came with Parshtaevalt, and Hirene, her trumpeter. She had become less shy about seeking him out.

'Come walk, Kineax,' she said.

Kineas used the awl in his palm to punch two new holes, working carefully with the old leather. He needed the headstall to last until they were back at the camp at Great Bend, and no longer.

'Soon,' he said.

She sat down by him and pointed at his work to Hirene, who frowned. Niceas was cutting a Getae cloak to make a saddle blanket.

Hirene spoke quickly in Sakje. Her lip curled, whether in sneer or smile Kineas couldn't tell. Srayanka laughed, a lovely sound, and sat gracefully on Kineas's blanket.

'Hirene say – you have uses, after all,' Srayanka said. 'The great war leader sews leather!'

Kineas ran a stitch back through the last hole, and then again, and then a third time, and then bit the linen thread as close as he could to the leather. Kineas buffed the headstall with the palm of his hand and then laid it carefully atop the pile of his tack. Parshtaevalt knelt by the pile and began to examine the bit.

'Not good ours,' he said. 'But good.' His Greek, like their Sakje, was improving by the day.

Niceas tossed his blanket on his own tack and waved across the fire for Ataelus to translate. To Parshtaevalt, he said, 'You just show me, mate.' He gave Kineas a friendly wink.

Hirene looked torn – she wanted to follow her mistress, but Srayanka shook her head. Turning to Kineas, she said, 'Bring your sword.'

Kineas thought that he had the oddest courtship since Alexandros met Helen. But he fetched the Egyptian blade from his blanket, where the precious thing was rolled at the centre.

She took his hand, and they walked off into the red evening. By the camp, the turf was even and the grass bright green and short, but she led him out into the sea of grass, where hummocks made walking treacherous. They laughed together when their mutual refusal to relinquish the other's hand cost them their balance.

Kineas looked back over his shoulder to find that they were in full view of the camp, stretching out to the north and south along the stream, and that many heads were turned, watching them.

Reading his thoughts, she said, 'Let them watch. This hill is grave to the father of me. Here, we kill two hundred horses, send him to *Ghanam*. I *baqca* here.'

They came to the base of the mound. Closer up, it was clearer that the hill was made by the hands of men. Turfs were set like steps running up the barrow, and a deep trench, invisible from a stade away, ran clear around the base with a barrier of stone around the outside.

Srayanka led him around a quarter of the boundary ditch, and then they entered at a gate flanked by wild roses and began to climb the mound. She began to sing tonelessly.

The ball of the setting sun came to rest on the far horizon, bathing the green grass of the turf with red and orange and gold light, so that the hill appeared to be an amalgam of grass and gold and blood. Her singing increased in volume and tone.

'Hurry!' she said. She pulled at his hand, and they ran the last few steps to the top, where a stone sat in a slight depression. From the stone rose a bar of rusted iron. Closer up it proved to be the remnants of a sword, with the gold of the hilt still standing proud above the decay of the blade.

The sun was huge, a quarter gone beneath the curve of the world.

'Draw your sword,' she ordered.

Kineas drew his sword. She reached out and took the rusted sword reverentially by the hilt and drew it from the stone. She seized Kineas's sword from him, and as the last rays of the sun turned its hilt to fire, she plunged it straight into the stone – deeper, if anything, than the other sword had been.

As the sun vanished, leaving the sky like a dye shop, with vivid reds and pale pink contrasting to the growing purple and dark blue veil of night, she stopped singing. She knelt facing the stone.

Kineas stood by her, embarrassed at his own ignorance of her ways, equally embarrassed by the extent of her barbarism – but she was a priestess, and it was not the Greek way to ridicule any people's gods, so he knelt by her in the damp hollow. He could smell the moss on the stone, and the oil on his Egyptian blade, and the woodsmoke in her hair.

They knelt there until his knees burned and his back was a column of stone against his muscles. Darkness fell, complete, so that the plain beyond the hollow vanished, and there was only the sky and the stone, the smells of the hollow, and then the cry of an owl, and ... *he was flying over the plain of grass, looking for prey, the pinprick glow of uncountable stars sufficient light for him to see.*

He rose higher over the plain, in lazy circles, and when he saw a circle of fires – a dozen circles of fire, a hundred circles of fire

— then he descended again, watching the camp as he came down in spirals ...

As suddenly as she had knelt, Srayanka rose, took a pouch of seeds from her waist and scattered them in the hollow and on the stone.

Kineas got to his feet with considerable difficulty. One of his feet was asleep. But his mind was clear, part of it still high in the dark sky.

'You are *baqca*,' she said. 'You dream strong dream?'

He rubbed his face to clear his head. The inside of his mouth felt gummy, as if he'd eaten resin. 'I dreamed,' he said in Greek.

She put a hand on his face. 'I must sit in the,' she paused, seeking words, 'smoke tent – even here, under the *Guryama* of the father of me.' She rubbed his face affectionately. 'You dream free.'

He was still in the grip of the dream, and she took his hand and led him down the hill.

Halfway down, he began to recover. 'My sword!' he said.

She smiled, used her position higher on the turf hill to lean to him, eye to eye, and kiss him.

It was a long kiss, and he found that his hand quite naturally went to her right breast, and she bit his tongue and stepped back, laughing. 'Sword right here,' she said, slapping at his groin with a hard hand. Then she relented. 'Climb for sword with dawn. Baqca thing, yes?'

Kineas spoke hesitantly. 'You are putting the power of your father's sword into my sword?"

She considered him for a moment, with the look a mother gives when a child has asked a difficult question, or a question whose answer may itself cause harm. 'You marry me?' she asked.

Kineas's breath caught in his throat. But he didn't hesitate. 'Yes.'

She nodded, as if the answer was just as she expected. 'So we ride together, yes? And perhaps ...' She wore an open look, like a priestess at worship, a look that scared him to his bones and marrow. 'Perhaps we rule together?'

Kineas took a step back. 'The king rules,' he said.

Srayanka shrugged. 'Kings die.'

Kineas thought, You're backing the wrong horse, my love. I'm the one fated to die. He reached out his arms to her, and she came into them. When her head was against his shoulder, he said, 'Srayanka, I—'

She put a hand on his mouth. 'Shhh,' she said. 'Say nothing. Spirits walk. Say nothing.'

Kineas embraced her – almost a chaste embrace, and she stood with her head on his shoulder, her arms around his waist, for a long time, and then they walked back down the hill. Without discussion, they began to separate at the edge of the short grass, she to her camp and he to his, but their hands stayed together too long, and they almost fell again.

They laughed, and walked away.

She came for him in the morning, dressed in white skins with gold plaques and gold embroidery, crowned with a headdress of gold that towered above her. The king was with her, and Marthax, and twenty other chiefs and warriors. Kineas waved to Leucon and Nicomedes to attend him, and the group repeated the journey, climbing through the last of the dark to the hollow at the summit. All the Sakje began to sing, even the king.

The first ray of the sun licked over the dark line of the world's edge like a flame rising from a new fire. The sun picked out the gorgon's head – Medea's head, Srayanka's head – on the hilt of his machaira, so that it seemed to draw colour from the rising run, and the line of flame crept down the blade, faster and faster, so that in a few heartbeats, the sword seemed to have drawn the sun down into the stone.

All the Sakje shouted, and Srayanka's hand took the hilt and she sang a high, pure note, and motioned with her other hand at Kineas. Kineas took the sword hilt in his right hand, and just for an instant it seemed to pull him down.

Srayanka released the hilt, and Kineas's hand shot aloft, pulling the sword clear of the stone.

Kineas had been so drawn into the effect of the ceremony that for a moment he expected something – a tide of energy, perhaps, or the words of a god. Instead, he saw the look on the king's face – jealousy and envy naked to his glance. When their eyes met, the king flinched.

Marthax frowned and then slapped him on the back. 'Good sword,' he said. And they all walked down the hill.

'What was that about?' Nicomedes asked. 'Beautiful light effect.'

Kineas shrugged. 'Srayanka's father's barrow,' he said quietly, and Leucon and Nicomedes both nodded.

After they reached the short grass, Marthax began to bellow orders. Kineas took the king by the elbow. 'I dreamed up on the barrow.'

The king pulled away. 'That is as it should be,' he said after a moment.

'I saw the army of Zopryon – camped in good order. Perhaps two hundred stades south of here – perhaps more.'

Satrax rubbed his beard and made a face. 'He makes good time.'

Kineas said, 'Can we trust this dream?' He thought of the details – the hobbled horses, the pickets, the circles of fire. But his mind could supply all of those.

The king stared at Kineas. 'Kam Baqca sees nothing – she is closing her mind to the visions, as they show her nothing but her own death. So I must rely on yours. As much as any dream. I will send scouts. Then we will know.'

'If it is a true dream,' Kineas said, and his voice trembled. He wanted it to be a false dream. He wanted the scouts to place Zopryon another two hundred stades to the west, because that would mean that he dreamed falsely, that these barbarians, however much he loved them, were superstitious like all barbarians, and he was not fated to die in a few short weeks at the crossing of a river. He took a breath and released it. 'If this is a true dream, then it is almost time to begin harrying his army.'

One of the king's companions came up with a cup of tea, and the king took it eagerly. 'Our hooves are hard. The horses are conditioned.' He nodded. 'If the scouts confirm your dream, then yes. We will begin.'

The king sent twenty riders, one of whom was Ataelus. Three days later, when they were a short morning's march from the camp at Great Bend, they returned in a group. The king summoned all of the chiefs and officers.

It had been a true dream.

To the Greeks, Ataelus said, 'Zopryon's army is not for big so rumour make. Has many, many, many hands of men, not so many of horses.' Ataelus grinned his horrible grin. 'Send Getae – no Getae come back. Oops.'

Kineas's stomach twisted and turned, and his blood ran riot in his veins. He had, at most, two weeks to live.

Srayanka spoke in Sakje. 'Now we harry him,' she said, and the look in her eyes was disturbingly like the look in her eyes when he had come up behind her, the night of the victory over the Getae. Or when she spoke of how they might rule together. Like lust.

Satrax spoke carefully. 'Tonight I ride for our camp. Marthax will bring in the column. The rest of you – Sakje and Olbians – must be ready to ride with me. We will see what clans have come in, and what the rumour of our victory has done for numbers. We will see if the Sauromatae have come. And the rest of the Greeks.' He looked around. 'And then, we will let Zopryon feel the weight of our hooves.'

The party with the king comprised most of the officers and nobles of the allied army – twenty clan leaders, the king's bodyguard of nobles' sons, Kineas, Nicomedes, Leucon and Niceas. They rode through the soft summer evening, without herds, without wagons, and they rode fast.

Kineas rode by the king, but they exchanged few words, and Kineas felt that there was still a barrier between them. Whether the barrier was of his own construction or of the king's was the sort of question Philokles might have answered, but Kineas couldn't see the answer himself.

Just as full darkness rolled over the plains, they saw the great bend of the river in the east, a greater darkness and a hint of moist air, and then a thousand points of fire burning on the far side of the ford. The camp had doubled or tripled in size. The smell of burning wood carried almost as far as the sight of so many fires.

All of the horses gave voice, and the herds responded.

The king paused, turning his head from the last glow of ruddy light in the west behind him to the sparkle of campfires beyond the great river. 'When I was a boy,' he said to Kineas, 'I loved boats. Every spring, I would go and ride the boats of the merchants going down the river to Olbia. I remember how one of the wisest of them, an old Sindi called Bion, would judge the spring rush of waters, stopping frequently, because, as he said, when the river swelled past a certain point, then no effort of man could beach a boat, and that boat would either rush down the river to its destination, or would be swept up on a rock or a log and utterly destroyed.' The king pointed at the camp, oblivious to the crowd of nobles pressing around them.

Kineas nodded. 'It is much the same at sea, Lord. You can feel your way along a coast to a certain point, but when Poseidon wills it, you must chance to the wine-dark sea and ride the waves or perish.'

In the last light, the king's smile was grim. 'My meaning was a little different, Kineas. On the river, Bion would *stop*. He would stop to rest, stop to prove that he still could stop, to delay that moment when he committed to everything to that last rush to success or destruction.' He shrugged, the motion almost lost in the darkness. 'In an hour, I will give the order, and my people will fall on Zopryon. And from that moment, I am on the river, and it is in full spate.'

Kineas kneed his horse closer to the king's, and put his hand on the other man's. 'And you wish to stop?' he asked.

The king put his whip hand over Kineas's hand. 'You, too, are a commander. You, too, know the terror – the weight of other men's hopes, and other men's fears. I wish to stop – or to have it done.'

'I know it,' said Kineas, voicing his own fears.

They sat together for a few more seconds, watching the fall of darkness out to the west. And for that night at least, they were friends.

'Come,' said the king. 'Let's board the boat.'

Philokles and Diodorus were waiting with a group of strangers at the edge of the camp. The king had already appointed the place and time for the meeting of his council – the hour after dawn, in his wagon laager. Kineas, Nicomedes, Leucon and Niceas rode along the river to the encampment of the Greeks, now full of tents and wagons stretching off into the darkness.

'Congratulations are in order?' Diodorus said, clasping Kineas's hand as soon as he slid from his horse.

Niceas laughed, touched his amulet as if to avoid hubris, and said, 'You missed some good fighting.' He grinned. 'As good as anything against the Medes. The Getae don't even know our tricks – it was grand.'

Philokles stood a little apart, although he greeted each of the commanders warmly enough. Kineas clasped his hand. 'I missed you,' he said.

Philokles' look of reserve melted away. 'And I you,' he said. Then, after casting a glance toward the Olbian officers, he said, 'I have news, most of it bad.'

Kineas took a deep breath. 'Tell me.'

'It should be told in private,' Philokles said. 'It isn't known in camp.'

'Are the hoplites here?' Kineas asked.

'Two or three days away, and marching hard. The Pantecapaeum horse is in camp, and the Sauromatae.'

'That will please the king,' Kineas said. 'What's so bad?'

Other men were coming up from the darkness. Antigonus cast his arms around Kineas and they embraced. 'We heard you were close,' he said. 'And that you won.'

Niceas was already regaling a crowd of the older hands with war stories. Wineskins appeared, with strong country wine that tasted of goat and pine pitch. Kineas stood with Leucon and Nicomedes and told the basic story of the campaign while most of the men in the Greek camp came up to listen.

'So the Getae are smashed,' Philokles said.

'The king thought they had been destroyed for a generation – perhaps longer,' Leucon said.

Philokles winced, his eyes flicking to Sitalkes, who was

laughing with the men of his troop. Kineas took him by the elbow and led him a little apart. 'You are behaving like a fury at a feast,' he said.

Philokles glanced around the crowd and lowered his voice. 'I have a man in my tent,' he said. 'Pelagius, a man of Pantecapaeum. He came north in a boat from the fleet, and he reported things in Olbia from just five days back.'

Kineas nodded.

'According to Pelagius, Demostrate found the Macedonian squadron thirty days back, caught it on the beach and burned two ships. Then he dispatched messengers to tell us the job was done and went south to the Bosporus to prey on Macedonian shipping.'

Kineas nodded. 'That's what he said all along,' he said.

'Pelagius arrived in Olbia in a small boat with a handful of crewmen. He intended to find the archon and tell him of developments at sea, but what he saw caused him to take his boat upriver instead.'

'What did he see?' Kineas asked.

'A Macedonian garrison in the citadel,' Philokles said. 'That was five days ago. He arrived today and I sat on him.'

Kineas shook his head. 'Hades. Hades! We're fucked.' Kineas felt as if he had been kicked by a stallion – he was having trouble breathing. 'Hades, Philokles – is he *sure*?'

'Sure enough to come pelting upriver to us without putting in.'

'If Demostrate burned the Macedonian triremes, how in Hades did it happen?' Kineas smacked a fist into his palm. All his plans were rising away, like the smoke of an altar fire in a breeze.

'I can only speculate. A merchantman with a hold crammed with soldiers? And the archon in it to the hilt?' Philokles shook his head angrily. 'I don't *know*.'

Kineas hung his head. 'Ares' balls. Our asses are going to be in the air. We need to know what's happening.' He looked back at the crowd by the fire. Men were watching him. 'We can't hide this. Better if I put it to the officers immediately.'

Philokles pulled on his beard. 'You know what this may mean?

Your men – all your men – may go home. Can you hold them if the archon orders them home?'

'Is the archon the voice of the city?' Kineas asked.

Philokles crossed his arms. 'Memnon is two days away with the hoplites.'

Kineas nodded. 'So we have the assembly here.'

Philokles took his arm. 'You expected this.'

Kineas was looking out into the dark, thinking of the king and his image of a boat swept down the river. 'Yes,' he said. 'I expected betrayal from the archon.' He made a motion as if throwing a handful of dice on the ground. 'The game is well under way, my friend. Too late to walk away and save our cloaks.'

Philokles laughed bitterly. 'It seems to me that in one throw, the archon has already triumphed,' he said. 'He has the city.'

Nicomedes obviously felt the same when he was told an hour later. His ruddy face went white in the firelight. Leucon was similar, except that he cried out, 'My father!' Eumenes became silent, his jaw set. All of the Olbians were moved. Some wept.

Kineas stood on the tongue of a wagon. He had taken the time to go to Philokles' camp and hear the sailor speak. The man was a gentleman, a citizen of Pantecapaeum, a veteran trader who knew the coast and knew the politics. His account was reliable. When Kineas left the man he ordered Niceas to gather all the men of Olbia in the camp. And he sent Philokles to tell the king.

Nicomedes shook his head. He stood just below Kineas and when he spoke, his voice carried. 'We left men as a precaution against something like this. Is there any news?' His voice cracked from emotion. 'Has the archon ordered us home?'

Kineas spoke loudly into the crowd of men around his wagon. 'This war was voted by the assembly of the citizens of Olbia,' he said. 'The archon and his – extraordinary powers were voted by the assembly of the citizens of Olbia.' He paused, and received silence, the best accolade of any assembly of Greek men. 'In two days, the hoplites will be here. I propose that we then hold an assembly of the city – here in camp. Perhaps we will choose to agree with the action that the archon has taken. Or perhaps,' he made his voice loud, and hard, a trick of rhetoric and one of command, 'perhaps we will find that the archon has betrayed the city.'

'The archon holds the city,' Leucon said. His voice was flat.

Kineas had no response to that. He dismissed them to go to bed. They moved off, grumbling.

Philokles stood by his shoulder when they were gone. 'You are a surprising man, Kineas. I think perhaps you would have been a dangerous opponent in the law courts, if you had not taken to the cavalry. You will argue that the army, and not the archon, is the voice of Olbia?'

'I will,' Kineas said. 'I would lie if I said that I expected this, but by Zeus, I feared it, and I thought about it. And now all I can do is to ask them – they are men – let them act like men.'

Philokles shrugged. 'Sparta has no walls,' he said.

In the morning, the men were calm and obedient, which was as much as Kineas had hoped for. He attended the king's council with his own officers. When called on, he rose and addressed them.

'King Satrax, noble Sakje, men of Pantecapaeum. I wish to speak before rumour exaggerates. It appears to us from a report that the archon of Olbia has allowed a garrison of Macedon into the city's citadel – or perhaps it has taken by surprise.'

A murmur rose, first from the officers of the Pantecapaeum horse, and then from the Sakje. Kineas raised his voice and continued.

'It is possible that, even now, there is an order en route to this camp from the archon, ordering this part of the army home.' He caught Srayanka's eye unwittingly. Her dark brows were drawn together as one.

The king flicked his whip. 'And what will the men of Olbia do?' he asked.

Kineas bowed. 'We must have a few days to decide.' He had explained in private, as soon as the king was up, and again to Srayanka, choosing his words carefully, but none of them smiled at him. The atmosphere of the council was heavy and cold. Many new men and some new women sat there now – the war leaders of the western clans, and the alien Sauromatae, handsome, tall men and women from the east with closed faces, who wore their armour to the council.

Kam Baqca spoke carefully. Her eyes were wide and her pupils enormous, as if she had received a blow to the head, or recently awakened. She seemed to have trouble focusing, and her body writhed from minute to minute, as if inhabited by a giant snake. 'Do you think,' she asked carefully, into a dead silence, 'that the Sakje should allow you to ride away, if your archon intends to make war on us?' Her head sunk suddenly to her chest and then snapped back erect, and her eyes were locked on the king. 'I never saw this,' she said.

Kineas spoke over the first angry response from his own officers to Kam Baqca's threat. 'I ask for time to deal with this crisis in our own way. Threats, promises, censure – none of them will help the men of Olbia deal with their own sense of betrayal and their own very deep fears for their city. I beg this council and the king to exercise patience, lest our alliance, already touched with victory, dissolve.'

The king made a sharp notion for Kineas to desist. Before he could speak, the best armoured of the Sauromatae rose from his seat and spoke. He spoke rapidly, in the Sakje tongue with a strong accent, and Kineas could catch little more than his anger.

The king listened attentively and then said to the council, 'Prince Lot speaks for the Sauromatae. He says they have come far – far from their tents on the great sea of grass, and farther from the queen of the Massagetae, who also carved their lances in Bactria. He says they come to find a handful of foreign allies preparing to desert to Macedon, and he wonders aloud if I am a strong king.'

The king rose to his feet. The campaign against the Getae had hardened him. There was no adolescent rage – just a cold focus. He spoke in Sakje, and Kineas understood him well enough, and then he spoke again in Greek. 'I *am* a strong king. I have crushed the Getae, who preyed on my people for ten generations of men. I won this victory with the help of the men of Olbia, and such brotherhood is not lightly set aside.' He looked at Kineas. Kineas read a great deal from that look. The boy was putting his kingship above his desire for Srayanka – again.

He continued. 'I give the Olbians five days to make their decision, and then we will take council again. In the meantime, I command that the harrying of the army of Macedon begin. Zopryon is two hundred stades distant. He will take at least a week to reach the bank of the great river. By then, all questions of Olbia and its archon will have been resolved.'

The king sat. He had never looked less young, or more fully a king. Srayanka smiled at him, and Kineas felt the bile in his gut. It occurred to him to wonder what, exactly, Srayanka wanted in a man. Was it power?

The thought was black with jealousy, and unworthy of her.

But the barb stuck.

Marthax's army returned, with the rest of the Olbians, and all the other veterans of the campaign against the Getae. Srayanka's Cruel Hands came into camp with a whoop of victory. Kineas saw them at a distance; he saw Srayanka greet Parshtaevalt, just as he saw the king welcome Marthax, and he saw the subdued celebrations among the Sakje. For the first time that summer, however, he was separate, distant, and not welcome. And as soon as they came and celebrated, they rode away again. Kineas watched Srayanka lead the Cruel Hands out of the camp on the third day after their return.

She rode up to him. He hadn't touched her in days – hadn't spoken to her, except at the council. She gestured with her whip at the knots of Olbian men gathered by their fires. 'Fix this – it is between us.'

Kineas tried to grab her hand. She frowned, shook her head, turned her horse, and galloped back to the head of her column, and Kineas felt a hot jab of rejection – and rage.

Behind Kineas, there was a great deal of comment – the veterans of the Getae campaign filling in their mates on just how the ground lay between their commander and the Lady Srayanka. Kineas whirled on them, savage, and a great many punishments were handed out.

It was ruinous for morale. By the time Memnon's spears

marched into sight on the east bank of the river, those who remained, Sakje and Greek alike, were waiting to hear the news like men waiting for a bolt of lightning.

Memnon arrived at the head of the phalanx of Pantecapaeum, with the phalanx of Olbia a few stades behind. Kineas rode out to him as soon as the glitter of his spears was identified. It was obvious from their first exchange that Memnon's news of the city was out of date – he had left a city dedicated to the war.

Kineas took Memnon aside as soon as he could, pressed a cup of wine into his hands, and sat him on a stool. 'We have reason to believe that the archon sold the city to Macedon a day or two after you went out the gates,' he said.

Memnon took a gulp of wine, spat it in the fire, and then drank some. 'Bastard. Whoreson. Dickless catamite.' He drank off the wine. 'We're fucked. They'll all go home.'

Kineas shook his head. 'Let them hear the news tonight. Tomorrow, all the men of Olbia will gather in assembly.'

'Ares, it'll be chaos, Kineas. And there'll be desertions. I hate to say it – I love the whoresons, but I know them.' Memnon shook his head. 'Bastard – boyfucker. He just waited for us to march out, and then he handed the citadel to Zopryon.'

Kineas raised an eyebrow. 'Did you expect anything else? I didn't. Now we'll see what we've made.'

Memnon shook his head. 'Listen, comrade. We're old soldiers – mercenaries, masterless men, exiles. We know that the loss of your city is a bitter pill, but in the end – nothing. A city is a city. Yes? They don't know. They will feel as if their gods have died. And they'll crawl back to the archon and swear whatever he requires to have their city back.'

Kineas looked at the marching column. 'They look good,' he said.

'They are good, fuck your mother!' Memnon spoke with angry pride. 'They trained all winter and they marched here like – like Spartiates. They've trowelled off a lot of weight and they like it. Most of them are middle-aged men who just won themselves a last summer of youth. They'll fight like heroes,' he said glumly, 'if they choose to fight.'

Kineas slapped the dark man's shoulder. 'Isn't that the way it ought to be?' he said. 'Men ought to fight only if they vote it.'

'You spend too much time with that fucking Spartan,' Memnon grumbled. 'If somebody pays me to fight, I fight. I don't ask a lot of questions.'

Kineas met his eye. 'That's how we both came to work for the archon,' he said. 'From now on, I think I'll ask more questions.'

In the night, Leon the slave of Nicomedes came into camp, having run day and night from the city. He brought news.

Kineas, summoned from a dream full of smoke and monsters, was muddled when he made his way to Nicomedes' tent. Leon looked like a literal man of clay – he was coated in pale river mud, and he stank of it.

Nicomedes handed Kineas and Philokles a cup of wine. 'It's bad,' he said. 'Tell him, Leon.'

Leon drank from his own wine cup. 'Cleomenes had Cleitus murdered by the Kelts day before yesterday,' he said. He rubbed his face with his hands as a man does when he tries to stay awake, and flakes of mud came away from his face, as if he was literally falling to pieces. 'He has seized command of the rest of the hippeis.'

Kineas pounded his right fist into his left hand. 'Zeus! Of all the base acts ...' He drained his wine. 'What of the archon?' Thoughts and images boiled in his mind. The archon's treason came as a shock, for all of his preparation.

Leon shook his head. Nicomedes swirled some more wine – unwatered – in his cup. 'It's always worse than you think. No one has seen the archon. Cleomenes has seized power and turned the citadel over to a garrison from Thrace.'

'Amarayan gives the orders in the citadel,' Leon said. 'No one has seen the archon in ten days, since the garrison came. They came out of a big merchant ship, and by the time Cleitus had heard and mustered the hippeis, they were installed in the citadel.'

'How many?' asked Kineas.

'Two hundred?' Leon speculated. 'Hard to know – they haven't come down into the town. Indeed, they only hold the gates and the citadel – they don't patrol the walls.' He hung his head. 'Cleitus was going to try ejecting them with his hippeis and some citizens who remained behind. That's when Cleomenes showed his hand and had Cleitus killed.' He looked at Nicomedes. 'You are exiled. Kineas and Memnon have their citizenship revoked. The army of the city is recalled. All our goods have been seized.'

'How'd you come free?' Kineas asked. It was harsher than he meant, but he was not in a trusting mood.

Leon met his eye. 'I'm a slave,' he said. 'I walked through the gates with the market crowd, took a horse from the Gamelios farm, and rode hard.' He shrugged heavily. 'When I saw the Macedonians, I got down in the riverbed and walked.'

Nicomedes put his hand on the seated man's neck. 'Now you are a free man,' he said.

Leon glanced up – taken aback. 'Can you afford to free me?' he asked. 'I'm quite valuable.' Then he laughed, despite everything. 'By all the gods – you mean it, sir?'

Nicomedes tossed his cloak off his shoulder and curled his beard with his fingers. 'Why not? I used to be the richest man in Olbia. Get some sleep.' He glanced at Kineas. 'I thought you should know first.'

Kineas mutely held his cup out for more unwatered wine. Philokles shook his head. 'I thought it would be the archon,' he said blearily. 'Or – or you, Nicomedes.'

Nicomedes shrugged with a pained look. 'It might have been me – after we dealt with Zopryon.'

Philokles nodded. 'We're in deep trouble. Cleomenes – he knows exactly how to hurt us.'

Kineas nodded. 'Yes,' he said, and rubbed his jaw like a boxer who had taken a heavy blow.

19

The next day dawned red, with a promise of heavy weather later in the day. Kineas gathered all the men of Olbia in a great half-circle, a conscious recreation of the place of assembly in the city. Kineas and Nicomedes had worked to make the assembly ground as familiar as possible.

It was an odd assembly, because, for whatever reason, all the men, hoplites and hippeis, brought their spears, and stood leaning on them, so that the assembly was a forest of bright spear points in the red morning light.

First came Helladius, a priest of Apollo, who made a sacrifice in the name of the god and declared the day favourable, just as he would have in Olbia. He was solemn, and the steam that rose from the blood of his slaughtered lamb in the red light of dawn seemed to waft the sacrifice straight to the gods.

After Helladius, Nicomedes strode to the centre of the assembly and spoke. He stood in the centre of the half-circle, holding his spear like every other man present. He didn't look like a fop this morning.

'Men of Olbia,' he said. 'Fellow citizens!' He proceeded to tell the story of the war, from its inception to the demands made by Zopryon. He rehearsed for them every vote they had made – the grants of citizenship to the mercenaries, the subsidies of money to the archon for more men, more arms, armour, horses, more mercenaries. The treaty with the king of the Sakje, and the treaty with the city of Pantecapaeum. If it was dry, or boring, no one showed it. They stood leaning on their spears, grumbling when they didn't like his point, or speaking up with shouts of 'That's right', and 'There's the thing!' when they felt that Nicomedes had the right of it.

Nicomedes took them right through to the end. When he came to the presence of the new garrison in the citadel, they groaned, and the spear points moved as if they were blades of grass in the wind. And then he spoke to them of the proclamation, and the threat of exile, and their voices rose around him until he could not make himself heard. He glanced at Kineas, shrugged, and stepped down.

Kineas motioned to Niceas, and the hyperetes drew a breath and blew a single note on his cavalry trumpet. Then he walked forward into the empty ground at the centre of the crowd.

His appearance was greeted with a grumble. Nicomedes was what they were used to; Nicomedes addressed the assembly on every issue that appeared. Kineas was a mercenary whom they had voted to citizenship. A foreigner from Athens. And, as hipparch, the captain of the city's financial and social elite. But his military reputation stood him in good stead, and he received a silence punctuated only by a handful of complaints, imprecations and conversations.

'Men of Olbia,' he began. 'I stand before you, almost a stranger, and yet your captain in war. I have appeared in your assembly only a handful of times, and yet I will dare to address this one as if I were an old citizen – as if I were Cleitus, or Nicomedes or some other voice to whom you are accustomed. According to the tyrant of Olbia, whoever that is today, I am no longer a citizen.'

Kineas gestured at the camp, the horses and wagons and herds of the Sakje. 'Learn the lesson of Anarchises the Scyth,' Kineas said. 'You are the city. You, the citizens, are the city. The walls and the citadel are nothing. They hold no vote in the assembly. Not one stone will speak to defend the archon or Cleomenes. Not one house will proclaim him as king, or as tyrant. No roof will speak to vote a law in his favour. No statue will rise to defend the archon. Do not be slaves to your walls, men of Olbia. You are the city. Will you vote to continue what you have started?

'You, not the archon, hold the city in your hands – you have the power to make war, or peace. The presence of a garrison in our citadel is of as much moment to you, men of Olbia, as would be the presence this moment of a thief in your shop, or rats in your granary. It is something we will have to deal with when we return from this war.'

Silence. The hillside was quiet enough that horses in the king's herds could be heard whickering to one another.

'Nicomedes has related how this assembly voted on each step of this war. You are not the aggressors. You have not marched with fire and spear to burn the lands of Macedon, or sent mighty fleets to raid their shores and take their women!' His mock-Homeric language and the absurdity of the image – Olbia launching aggressive war against Macedon – got him a laugh. 'You sought peace, and only sanctioned war when Zopryon made clear that he would not accept peace.'

Kineas paused, took a breath, and when he spoke, his voice was level, quiet, but assured. 'Zopryon is losing this war,' he said.

A hundred voices – the men who had ridden north and west to fight the Getae – were raised. Kineas lifted a hand.

'Enough of you rode north to speak here, or anywhere, of how badly we defeated Zopryon's barbarian allies. But there have been other conflicts. The men of Pantecapaeum met the Macedonian squadron and destroyed it. Even now, they cruise the Hellespont, taking a toll from any Macedonian ship bold enough to venture north of Byzantium. Even now, our allies, the Sakje, are harrying Zopryon's advance, killing his foragers, riding in close at night and shooting arrows into their campfires, or killing men who go beyond the circle of fires to have a piss.

'Zopryon has garrisoned a dozen forts between here and Tomis. He has divided his force and divided it again to force a passage over the sea of grass, and now, when his doom is close and the hooves of the Sakje echo in his dreams, the Tyrant of Olbia declares that we should put our spears on our shoulders and slink home or face exile. The Tyrant has betrayed us. Like tyrants everywhere, he thinks that his word can order the will of all men, and like a tyrant, he gives orders without consulting you.'

Kineas found it difficult to decide how this was going down. His eyes strayed to familiar faces – Ajax and Leucon, and the young men of their generation, who stood closest to him, were already in full agreement – but what of the older men who stood farther back? And Eumenes stood alone, his eyes red. Today, for all his beauty and his heroism, he had no friends.

Too late to worry over it. 'Today, we, here, are the city of

Olbia. The archon, or Cleomenes, or whoever holds power today in the city has revealed by his proclamation that he is a tyrant.' Kineas raised an arm and shouted, 'He is a tyrant!' and the assembly responded with shouts and calls. He began to feel that he had them. 'His laws are not valid! His proclamation is worthless! The Tyrant of Olbia can sit in his citadel with his Macedonian garrison and proclaim himself the Great King of the Medes and the absolute Lord of the Moon. Here, right here, are the bones and sinews of Olbia! If we stand with the Sakje, we can destroy Zopryon – and then we can march home and deal with the rats in our manger at leisure. Or we can tuck our spears between our legs and drag our asses home to Olbia and proclaim ourselves slaves. Have it as you will – you are free men.'

There was a silence, and then Eumenes came forward, leaning on his spear like an older man. The crowd parted for him as if he had a disease. Kineas stepped aside for him, and the young man raised his voice.

'My father,' he said, 'is a traitor. The archon is a traitor. And I will remain to fight beside the Sakje, whatever you vote.'

He turned away. Kineas reached out to him, but he turned his face away and walked through the crowd. Kineas was glad when he saw that Ajax was following him.

Other men spoke. No man spoke directly for the archon, but there were those who questioned their right to assemble and vote, barracks lawyers of the commonest sort, and more who wanted to march on the city immediately and seize it back from the archon.

Kineas stood with his hand clenched on the bronze socket of his spear. He could smell the rain in the air and feel the throb of distant summer lightning. He ceased to listen to the men who spoke, because ... *he was an owl, flying out over the sea of grass, flying out of the sun towards the clouds that rose like pillars over the advancing Macedonian host, and their dust rose like another pillar, an ugly brown one.*

At the feet of the monster of dust and men, the Sakje toiled, knots and bunches of them riding close and then riding away. He looked for Srayanka, but from this height, the riders were dots in the sea of green.

They were close, though. Close, and the storm was getting ready to break.

Cheers brought him back. Nicomedes greeted Kineas by clasping his hands – both of them – and embracing him. Leucon and Ajax, and men he didn't know as well crowded around. Many of them were deeply moved – one tall man wept openly, and others were close to tears, or hoarse from shouting. Even Memnon was moved. He grunted and smiled before he caught himself.

Kineas and Nicomedes were in the middle of more than a thousand men, buffeted to and fro by the storm of congratulations.

'I take it we carried the day,' Kineas said. As he looked about, he felt that the emotion of these men was affecting him – his throat was closing, his eyes hot.

Nicomedes rolled his eyes. 'My dear Hipparch,' he said. 'You may be the man for an ambush or a cavalry charge – but you don't know much about managing an assembly. If you had spoken last, you might have seen – but you didn't. As it was,' Nicomedes shrugged, 'I was only worried once.'

'When was that?' Kineas asked, shouting.

'The sacrifice,' Nicomedes shouted. 'Helladius cannot be bribed, the old fool. A bad omen might have sunk us. Other than that – you were right, Hipparch, to tell them early and often. Had this treason taken us by surprise – suddenly – I shudder to think. But prepared, with time to grumble and drink some wine – they never hesitated.'

'Thank the gods,' Kineas said. 'I must go to the king.'

Nicomedes nodded. 'Certainly. But Kineas – may I advise you? When this war is over, our world will change. The Tyrant will have to be deposed. And we will have to have new ways of doing things. The way you act with the king – all of our relations – will set the path for the next generation of men who rule in the Euxine cities. Don't rush to him as if he was our patron. Act his equal. Don't appear like an eager supplicant to him – send him a message declaring our whole support – tell him that we carried the assembly without a count – put his mind at ease. But do it with a message, so that the Olbians see that we don't dance to their tune – we are allies, not subjects.'

Kineas gave Nicomedes a hard look – thinking that way could sink an alliance.

The man shook his head. 'Glare at me all you like. An empowered assembly – an assembly that has just rejected tyranny – is a dangerous, powerful animal.'

Kineas made a face. 'I don't like it,' he said. *There is already too much between me and the king.* But he waved to Ajax.

Ajax went to the king and returned. A band of Patient Wolves came into camp with empty saddles and many wounded. A troop of Sauromatae nobles, armoured from head to foot, rode off to the west in close order.

Kineas found that he was standing in the flap of his wagon, watching the king's laager and trying to will the man to send for him. He was starved for news. And his dream – his waking dream – told him that the danger was close.

Philokles came up, rubbing his hands on a piece of linen. His hair was clean and his skin newly oiled. 'I have made sacrifice to all the gods,' Philokles said.

Kineas nodded. 'It is a good day to greet the gods,' he said, his eyes still on the king's camp. 'I believe Diodorus is doing the same?'

Philokles sat on the wagon step, using a small knife to get sacrificial blood out from under his nails. He nodded absently at the mention of Diodorus, and said, 'When we get to this battle?'

'Yes?' Kineas asked. He misunderstood Philokles' purpose. 'It'll be different in battle. The Sakje have some heavy cavalry – I was surprised by how well armoured the nobles are, and you saw the Sauromatae – they're like brick ovens on horses. But they can't manoeuvre like us.' He glanced at Philokles and saw that he had missed his mark. 'That's not what you wanted to know, is it?' he said with some embarrassment.

Philokles shook his head. 'No. Interesting enough, but no. Where do you die? Do you mind if I do something to prevent it?'

Kineas frowned, then smiled. 'I think I'm too used to it. It has become the central fact of my existence, and yet it is like a burden released. I know the hour of my death – I know we will triumph. It seems almost a fair exchange.' He shrugged, because there was no explaining how he felt about it – the fatalism. 'I don't worry as much as I used to,' he said, hoping that this would sound like a joke.

Philokles' face grew red, and his eyes sparkled, and he smacked the wagon bed with his fist so that the whole wagon moved. 'Bullshit! Bullshit, Hipparch! You do not need to die. I have great respect for Kam Baqca. But her trances come from drugs – from the seeds they all carry. I say it again – she has foreseen her death, and it colours all her dreams.' He paused, took a breath. 'Tell me where you die?'

Kineas sighed. He pointed out at the ford. 'It is not here – but it is very like. There should be a huge tree on the far bank, and driftwood on a beach – also on the far side. Big driftwood – whole tree trunks. That's what I remember.' He shrugged. 'I haven't really looked.'

Philokles stood like a bull, breathing through his nose – angry, or frustrated, or both. 'You haven't looked. Do you think the battle will be here?'

Looking out the flap in the wagon tent, Kineas could see Eumenes and Niceas standing with a third man – a big man. Niceas gestured toward Kineas. Kineas saw that the third man was the Sindi smith. He poured himself a cup of wine. He gestured silently at Philokles, who nodded, and he poured wine for the Spartan while he responded.

'I think it will be here – yes. The road runs to this ford, and this is the best ford for stades – dozens, even hundreds of stades. The king assures me this is true.' Even as Kineas said this, he considered the assertion. It was untested. He should be exploring himself. The Sakje were superb horsemen, but they were not professional soldiers, and he'd already seen the difference between their observational skills – excellent, and their scouting reports – pitiful. His own sense of fatalism was sapping his professional competence.

Philokles took the wine. 'So what – Zopryon will just march up to the river, see our camp, and force a crossing?'

Kineas could see Niceas and the smith walking up the hill

toward the wagon. 'It will depend on how badly the next week hurts him. On the spirit that motivates his army. I think he will march up to the ford, and camp, leaving a strong force to block the ford. This will free him from night raids and allow his men to sleep – and if the Sakje have harassed him for a week, that sleep will be valuable. After he's rested his men and horses for a day – perhaps two – he'll make his move.'

'Straight across the ford?' Philokles asked.

'Alexander – or rather Parmenion – had two ways to deal with this. One was to force a crossing with the cavalry, and then use them to cover the taxeis when they cross.' Kineas smiled wolfishly. 'That would not work against the Sakje. If Zopryon attempts it, he will be beaten swiftly. So rather, the second method – to send the taxeis across with shields locked, push up our bank, and then move cavalry across under cover of the pikes.' Kineas nodded to himself. 'I've seen it done. It has the added charm of demoralizing the foe – every unit you get across and formed in line seems like another stitch in his winding sheet.'

Philokles finished his wine. 'So, it will all hinge on Memnon holding the taxeis at the river?'

Kineas shook his head. 'No. If I have my way, we'll let him cross unopposed. We'll let him have our camp.'

Philokles nodded slowly. 'Are you perhaps more Sakje in your heart than Greek? Is not the loss of your camp the ultimate humiliation?'

Kineas shook his head. 'Slavery and defeat are the ultimate humiliation. But yes, in this, I am more Sakje than Greek.'

Philokles watched the three men coming. 'They want to speak to you. Listen, then – I want to fight on foot, with the phalanx. I'm wasted in the saddle, and if you are going to sacrifice yourself for glory, I refuse to watch it.' His voice was tight with emotion. He looked away, steadied himself, and his voice became lighter. 'Memnon seems to feel that he could use me to keep some youngsters in line.'

Kineas suspected it was all pre-battle jitters. Even Spartans succumbed. He rested a hand on the iron muscles of Philokles' shoulder. 'Fight where you will. I swear I intend no sacrifice. I would rather live.' He thought of the iron-coloured horse, and the dreams, which grew more frequent. They were true dreams. But he wouldn't tell Philokles the details.

'It is almost hubris, this assumption of doom.' Philokles put his cup down carefully. 'I tell you, if I can break this – this dream of ill omen, break it I will.' He grabbed the rib of the wagon tent and swung himself to the ground, brushing by Niceas, and walked off into the evening.

'You remember Hephaestes, here?' Niceas asked, jerking his thumb at the Sindi blacksmith.

Kineas swung down with the pitcher of wine. He glanced automatically at the king's laager and saw a man dismounting, his arms moving feverishly. Kineas made himself turn away and offered watered wine to Niceas, then to Eumenes, whose face had aged ten years in the last day, and finally to the smith.

The smith took the wine cup and set it carefully on the ground. 'I become man of you,' he said without preamble.

Kineas pursed his lips and shook his head. 'Say again,' he said in Sakje.

The smith nodded. 'My village is destroyed. I have no family. I will swear *gutyramas* to you.'

Kineas looked at Eumenes. 'I don't know that word.'

Eumenes shook his head. 'Some of our farmers hold land by gutyramas. It is more than tenancy – almost like joining a family. A loyalty bond, not just a deal for cash.' Eumenes shrugged. 'Farmers bound that way are better workers – and more demanding. Lawsuits, dowries – like I say, they feel they have become family, like being adopted as a cousin.'

Kineas spread his hands. 'I have no land to give you, smith. I hold no land.'

The smith rubbed the back of his neck. 'We broke men,' he said, and he pointed down the hill at the other Sindi refugees from the north. 'Some of us, the Cruel Hands accept – others, no man's man are. No family, no farm. Gone, in the smoke.' He looked up, met Kineas's eye. 'They take me for leading. Yes? I have nothing. I offer it, and them, of you. Me, I seek death, but for them, I seek life. Am I speaking so that you hear?'

Kineas nodded, wishing he had Ataelus, but Ataelus was

pursuing his dream of a horse herd with Srayanka and the Cruel Hands. To Niceas, he said, 'Can we feed them?'

'Fifty men? I expect we can. What would we do with them? Camp servants? We have enough.' Niceas raised an eyebrow.

Kineas nodded. He gestured to the smith. 'What's your name?' he asked.

'Temerix,' he said, then frowned.

'The Sindi form of Hephaestes,' Eumenes put in.

'Come with me, then,' he said. Finally, an excuse to go to the king.

He walked up the hill to the king's laager, followed by Temerix and Niceas. Nobody challenged them at the gate of the laager, and the king sat on the tongue of his wagon, straightening arrows with Marthax. Kam Baqca sat on the grass, her leather skirts gathered around her, sipping tea.

'Kineas!' the king said, getting to his feet. His pleasure was unfeigned.

Kineas stopped and gave a military salute, and then led the smith forward. He explained the situation in a few words, and the king watched him carefully, and then asked the smith sharp questions in unaccented Sindi.

The smith answered in single words.

The king turned to Kineas. 'If you do this thing, you may create tension with the Cruel Hands – these are their people. It seems to me that they've been allowed to fall through the cracks in the pot while we carried on the war. This man says you rescued his band, and he wants to swear his oath to you.' The king's displeasure was obvious. 'If I let him swear to you, I make you a lord,' he said. 'I am not sure that I am prepared to make you a lord – and I suspect I would insult my cousin. Srayanka will not forgive either of us. Knowing that, will you accept his oath, and be his lord?'

Kineas shook his head. 'I do not desire to be any man's lord.'

The king was visibly taken aback. Then he said, 'Just when I think I know you Greeks, you shock me again. That you must vote to make a war that is already upon you – that you will own a slave but will not take a man's oath of service.'

Kineas held the king's eye. 'I will not be his lord,' he said.

'I will take him and all his men in service, as psiloi, and I will pay them a wage and see that they are fed. And when Srayanka returns, I will see that those who wish her lordship receive it.'

The king nodded and rubbed his chin. He spoke again in Sindi, and after a while the smith nodded. He offered Kineas his hand, and they shook. And then Niceas took the smith away, to find him and his band a place to camp, instead of the wet river bank where they had been in hiding for days.

'What news?' Kineas asked, when they were gone.

The king glanced at Marthax, and then at Kam Baqca. The three held each other's eyes, excluding Kineas. Then they all turned to Kineas together. 'We wondered how long you could remain absent,' the king said.

Kineas took an arrow from the king's pile and held it up to the sun. The arrowhead had three blades, each wickedly barbed on the back, cast in bronze. 'I have to act the hipparch,' he said finally. 'What we did in the assembly – the effects will linger a long time. In effect, we deposed the archon.'

'Who may already be dead,' Kam Baqca said in her odd, Ionic Greek.

'You have seen it?'

'I see nothing but the monster on the sea of grass. But people tell me tales.'

The king nodded, and the distance Kineas had felt on the ride back from the Getae campaign was there, and deeper, too. There was pain in the king's eyes. 'I, too, have to act. I have dead this day, Kineas – too many dead. Because, as you said, Zopryon learned quickly. Thessalian cavalry smashed the Patient Wolves – a simple trap. A hundred empty saddles, and an angry clan.'

Kineas bent his head.

The king went on. 'Your tyrant killed those men. If you had been here to advise, they would not have ridden off so eagerly, so blindly, the second time.'

'Or they would have,' Marthax said with a harsh shrug. 'Don't make too much of it, Lord. We have dealt raking wounds and taken a bee sting in return.'

The king swung to Kineas. 'Just as you predicted, he learns quickly. Now the boat is fully in current, is it not? And I must ride it until it washes up at my destination or smashes on the rocks. This battle – it is close now, is it not?' He glared at both of them. 'I am now committed to the battle you wanted.'

Kineas stood still. He looked at Kam Baqca, and she swirled the tea in her cup and looked at the last leaves there. He could smell the resin and pine odour of her drug on the wind – there was a brazier lit at her feet. She raised her head and their eyes met. Her eyes were huge, deep, and brown, and in them ... *he could see the column moving across the sea of grass, as he swooped lower and lower, and he could see the bands of Sakje spread around the column for stades in all directions. The Macedonian column came on like a man's boot kicking an anthill, but the ants rode in closer, bolder than real ants, and every ant dealt a wound. But the seeing faded into another seeing, and the Macedonian column became a snake with a huge head, or a giant maggot, eating everything in its path and spewing wreckage out the tail – chewing on Sakje and Olbians, on triremes and city walls, exuding the excrement of burned homes and fields of stubble, fresh graves and unburied corpses.*

And she grimaced at him, a very male look on her made-up face. 'It is all I can see,' she said. There was pain in her voice. 'You too?'

'Yes,' said Kineas. 'It comes to me awake, now.'

She nodded. 'It will come more and more often. You are a strong dreamer.' She looked at her tea leaves. 'For the first time, I begin to hope for death, because I cannot bear to watch the monster cross the plains – the defiler, the tyrant. Everything it touches is polluted, stripped, killed. It will take me, soon enough.' She narrowed her eyes. 'My body will be dung for the monster,' she whispered.

Kineas glanced at the king, and Marthax. Marthax seemed to pretend he had heard nothing. The king turned away, embarrassed or saddened.

'It is all I can see,' she said again. 'I am no use to the king, and I fear to tell him anything lest I rush him to this battle. I have raised the spirits that will fight – I have done what I can. Now I just sit and drink tea and wait for doom.'

Kineas nodded. 'It is close,' he said. He found that, despite everything, he wanted to comfort her.

She looked at him across her teacup, and her eyes drew him again. He looked away rather than fall back into the dream. The smell of her drug was powerful. She said, 'Kineas – it is all balanced on a knife edge.'

The king ignored her and waved at the plains. 'We haven't slowed him as much as we hoped. His vanguard will be here tomorrow – or the next day at the latest.'

Kineas nodded.

The king gave a small shrug. 'Since we began to harass him, he has pressed harder. His army is wounded – as Marthax says, we have hit hard. The faster he moves, the more stragglers he has – and no straggler lives to see another dawn. But he is moving fast, now. Another day – perhaps two. He's leaving everything behind to make speed.'

Kineas nodded. 'Best recall the clans. We want the army on this side before Zopryon closes the ford.'

The king gave him an angry glance. 'I'm doing my best, Hipparch.'

Kineas leaned forward. 'Let me help.'

The battle was closer – closer by a week than he had expected. A week less of life. When he allowed himself to think about it, he was neither completely committed to the idea of death, nor had he thought through all of the ramifications of his dream. The battlefield, for instance. If his death dream was accurate, the battle would not be fought at the Great Bend. This thought had tripped across the stage of his mind before, but this time, fresh from the king and riding a surge of excitement and worry, Kineas elected to do something about it.

And the time was *now*. His battle was upon him – no more than two days away. He'd spent an hour thinking just *how* the battle would happen. Philokles had challenged his assumptions – Philokles was right.

He hailed Niceas, and ordered him to fetch Heron, the hipparch of Pantecapaeum. Heron had learned quite a few lessons at Cleitus's knee. If three weeks had not transformed him into the image of Hektor, if he had not yet learned to be courteous, professional, or polite, he had learned to be silent. He stood at every command meeting among the Greeks, a little distant from the others, a little hesitant to join in comment or laughter. He was a tall man, and he loomed over them, silent, and at times, sullen.

Kineas wanted to give the man a new start, and raise him in his own estimation.

'Heron,' he said, as the man came up.

'Hipparch,' Heron replied, with a civil salute. He was so tall that he appeared clumsy, and his legs were too long to look good on a horse. And he was dour – perhaps a reaction to being born ugly. He crossed his arms, not from nerves, but because they were so long that he had to do something with them. Kineas, who was too short to be accounted really handsome, felt some fellow feeling for the boy due to his ungainliness. Heron had something about him that suggested that when he was tested, he would not be found wanting – despite his attitude.

After offering him wine, Kineas went straight to business. 'I need the river scouted, north and south. The Sakje tell me there are no fords for a hundred stades – I'd like to know that myself. I'm going to give you the picked scouts of all the troops. Go south first – the greatest calamity, at this point, would be if Zopryon got between us and Olbia.' Kineas winced even as he made the comment. With the archon's treason, if Zopryon could slip past them to the south, he could rest his army at Olbia, receive supplies, and march up the river at his leisure. It had occurred to him that Zopryon might march straight to Olbia, trusting to the ferry at the river mouth to get his army across and into the city.

That was a possibility against which Kineas and the king had no plan. Kineas rubbed his right hand over his forehead and down his nose, sighed, and looked up at Heron, who stood silently.

'I need the river scouted, as far south as the bend of trees. Have your men test the water – really look at it. We can't afford a surprise. As soon as you have swept the south, come back here and go north.'

Heron straightened. 'Very well.' He saluted with ill grace. 'I perceive that you send me from the camp. Where do I find these picked scouts?'

Kineas gestured to Niceas. 'Crax, Sitalkes, Antigonus, and twenty more of your choice, Niceas. And Lykeles – with Laertes as acting hyperetes.'

Niceas's eyebrows twitched. 'Yes, Hipparch,' he said, with a shade of edge to his voice.

'Heron – this is a vital task. Do it well. Listen to Lykeles and Laertes. Ride like the wind. I need to know my flank is secure by nightfall tomorrow.'

Heron saluted. Nothing about the man suggested that he was pleased to be given an important mission – nor did he offer any hint of insubordination. He walked off, back stiff, and Niceas shook his head. 'Diodorus would have been more the mark, if you don't mind my saying.'

Kineas picked his chlamys off his equipment pile by the fire and threw it over his shoulders. 'I need Diodorus. We may be fighting by tomorrow night.' He shrugged. 'Call me a fool – something tells me that young Heron will do well – and he's the man I can spare.' He shivered. Darkness was falling, and the weight of all his responsibilities was pressing rational thought from his mind. Zopryon – where would he try to cross? Would he march to Olbia? The Olbians – would they fight? Would their newfound attempt at democracy last through a cold night before battle, or would they melt away? Food, firewood, fodder for horses, the number of lame mounts. Srayanka was still across the ford – so were half the Sakje horse and most of the clan leaders. Srayanka – he clamped down on those thoughts. 'Zeus guide me,' he muttered.

Niceas pressed a cup of warm tea into his hands, and he drank, and shivered when the warmth surged down his throat. 'Thanks,' he said. 'Now get me all the Greek officers – Memnon included. It's time to talk through how we will fight.'

Diodorus was the first in. Despite his worries, Kineas was pleased to see how naturally Diodorus had taken to command. Indeed, it was now hard to imagine that the man had been a gentleman trooper for four years of campaigning, grumbling about taking his shift on guard, complaining about the weight of his javelins. He appeared taller, and his splendid breastplate and crested helm, even his stance, with his legs a little spread and his hand on his hip, spoke of a commander – as did the slight hollows under his eyes.

'I've barely seen you,' Kineas said, taking his hand.

Diodorus had taken command of the pickets around the camp as soon as Kineas took command of the Olbians. He returned the pressure and took a cup of hot wine from one of the Sindi men around the fire. 'Cleomenes,' he said quietly. 'Bastard. Worse than home.'

Kineas raised an eyebrow, knowing that Diodorus meant the thirty tyrants in Athens. 'The vote wasn't even close. The men will be fine.'

Diodorus shook his head. 'I saw it coming. Philokles saw it coming – we all saw it, and we couldn't prevent it.' He took a drink of wine and glanced at Eumenes who stood with Ajax at the next fire. 'And that boy's father killed old Cleitus. It's *worse* than fucking Athens!' He glared. 'And now the bastard can swing south and have a base.'

Kineas nodded, watching Memnon's black cloak coming towards the fire. 'I'm taking precautions.'

'If he knows – he can cut straight south, march right past us, and cross at the ferry.' Diodorus drew a rough map in the scorched soil at the edge of the fire pit.

Kineas raised his hands to the gods. 'I don't think he will. I think his own image – his idea of who he is – will require him to come right up to our army and fight it.' He frowned. 'Cleomenes – I'm assuming he's in charge in the city – has raised the stakes. In exchange for personal power, he has traded our futures. Now, if we lose, Zopryon really will get the city. And if Zopryon knows that, all the more reason to fight a battle. He must think that one big fight and the whole sea of grass is his – the Euxine cities, the gold of the Scyths, everything.'

While they talked, the others had gathered, and the last light was gone from the sky, so that a ring of faces, pale and dark, listened intently as Diodorus and Kineas discussed the campaign. Memnon stood with his lieutenant, Licurgus, and the commander of the phalanx of Pantecapaeum, Kleisthenes. Nicomedes stood with Ajax, and Leucon with Eumenes and Niceas.

Kineas turned from Diodorus to face all of them. 'The waiting is over. Zopryon has made good time. He has, according to the king, abandoned his weak and his wounded to move faster in the last week, and he is almost upon us. Tomorrow the king will recall the clans who have harassed Zopryon's march. We will stand to from the rise of the sun. The phalanx of Olbia will draw up to the north of the ford, right here at the base of our hill. The phalanx of Pantecapaeum will draw up to the south of the ford. As soon as you are in place, you will drill in closing the ford.' Kineas drew in the black earth. 'The phalanx of Olbia will practise closing files and marching by ranks to the left – the phalanx of Pantecapaeum will practise marching by ranks to the right. You see how this will allow us to close the ford – quickly, without panic.'

All the officers nodded. Memnon snorted. 'We don't need to practise marching by ranks, Hipparch.' Kineas looked at Memnon. Memnon met his eye but shifted. 'Oh, all right. We'll march up and down a little.'

Kineas relented. 'Even if the men don't need the practice, it will help show the Sakje what we're about.'

'Fair enough,' Memnon said. 'What're you fancy horse boys doing while we pound the dirt?'

Kineas pointed off into the gloom to the west. 'Diodorus and Nicomedes will take their men across the ford at first light. They will establish a line of pickets five stades out from the ford. Diodorus will have the command. He will make sure that the ford is not surprised. He will pass every returning clan and provide them with a herald to pass the ford. Leucon will keep his men right here – as a reserve, and as messengers for me, and for the king, should he need them. Leucon will take the men of Pantecapaeum under his command until their hipparch returns. Everyone understand? We're going to provide security at the ford until the king's army has returned. The loss of the ford to a surprise would be a catastrophe.'

Ajax raised a hand. 'Are there other fords?'

Kineas rubbed his beard with his right hand. 'The Sakje say not. I have Heron of Pantecapaeum scouting the river for a hundred stades either way to make sure.' He made a sour face.

'I should have been scouting them three days ago. Now we're pressed for time. Any other questions?'

Memnon grunted. 'If they do come for the ford? What then?'

Kineas raised his voice. 'Tomorrow – and until I say different – if they make a dash for the ford, we close our ranks and stop them. It's not the battle I want – but we can't give up the ford until our army is back. So we have no plan for tomorrow beyond this – hold your ground.'

Memnon nodded. 'I like a simple plan. How big a fight will this be? As big as Issus?'

Kineas thought over what the king had said, and what he had seen in Kam Baqca's fire. 'Yes. As big as Issus.'

Memnon jerked his thumb at the huddle of Sindi men at the next fire. 'Where do you plan to put them?'

Kineas shook his head. 'I hadn't given it any thought,' he said, feeling foolish. Memnon had the ability to get straight under his professional skin.

Memnon grinned. 'Psiloi can't win a fight, but they can change one. I'll put them in the trees right by the ford, where they'll have a clear shot with their bows – right into the un shielded side of the taxeis. Leave it to me.'

Kineas agreed. 'So muster them with the hoplites,' he said. 'Anything else?'

Nicomedes leaned forward. 'What are the odds?' he asked.

Kineas gave the man a thin smile. 'Ask me tomorrow. Ask me after I lay eyes on his vanguard. Right now, we're all starting at shadows. My stomach is flipping like a flute girl in the last hour of a symposium, and every time I glance at the rising moon I think of ten more things I ought to have done.' He hoped it was the time for such frankness. 'If Zopryon will cooperate by coming here and camping across the river and offering the battle we've prepared for all summer – then, with the aid of the gods, I would say we were worth a sizeable bet.' He shrugged, thinking again that the Great Bend was *not* the site of his dream battle.

Eumenes' eyes brimmed with pain and hero worship. 'You will beat them,' he said.

'From your lips to the ears of the gods,' Kineas replied,

flinching from Eumenes' obvious passion. He poured wine from his cup as a libation, and his hand shook, and the wine flowed over his hand like dark blood.

20

With dawn came thunder that shook the earth, rivalling the hoof beats of the returning Sakje. Fog covered the sun and swathed the riverbanks for a stade, so that a man could only see the length of his spear, and every returning Sakje warrior was a cause for alarm. Ten horses sounded like a hundred – a hundred sounded like ten thousand. By the time the fog burned off, the nerves of the Greek contingent were stretched taut – but they had become accomplished at passing the returning clans across the ford.

The king came with the sun. He was on a plain riding horse, a short chestnut, and he wore no armour and rode alone. He pulled up next to Kineas and sat silently as Memnon and his officers marched the two phalanxes back and forth on the flat ground just short of the ford.

'I hope you approve,' Kineas said.

'Do you really think Zopryon will try to surprise the ford?' Satrax asked.

Kineas scratched his jaw with the butt of his whip. 'No,' he admitted. 'But we'd look like fools if he did and we weren't ready.'

Marthax rode up on the king's far side. He was on a warhorse, with his gorytos belted on and a short sword, although he wore no armour. He pointed across the river. 'Rain today. More rain tomorrow,' he said.

All three of them knew that rain could only benefit Zopryon.

Hour by hour, the clouds blew in from the east, and the sky darkened. Hour by hour, the Sakje came in from the west, some triumphant, some beaten. There were empty saddles, and bodies sprawled over the backs of horses; a bare-chested woman reared her horse at the edge of the ford to show the heads she had taken, and a troop of Sauromatae, eyes red-rimmed from fatigue, halted in front of the king to show him their trophies – hair, a helmet, several swords.

The king rode among them, congratulating the victorious, speaking softly to the wounded, teasing a reluctant clan leader and praising another for brave deeds.

Kineas dismounted to drink water and stretch his legs, and then remounted. In mid-afternoon, the thunder heads finally came to them, and the long line of darkness that seemed like the herald of the Macedonians moved into the river valley, and the rain began.

A few messengers had ridden up every hour since mid-morning, their hoof beats the only sign that time was moving, but as the rain came faster and harder, the number of messengers increased. The king had moved down the hill to the ford. As Kineas watched, the king's household knights joined him. He dismounted and two men began to help him into his armour.

Kineas rode down the hill with his own staff. He knew Ataelus as soon as the man rode out of the wall of rain to the west. Ataelus had been with Srayanka. Kineas found his heart beating faster.

Kineas pushed his horse through the king's household. They were grim-faced. Ataelus greeted him with a weary smile. 'Too tired for fighting,' he said. 'Too much damn fighting.'

The king had just settled his scale hauberk on his shoulders. 'Srayanka is covering the last group. She's pressed hard.'

Ataelus put a hand on Kineas's arm. 'Big fight – Cruel Hands and Standing Horses and some Patient Wolves. We trick them – they trick us – we trick them. Fight like ...' He swept his hand like a man stirring a pot, round and round. 'We shoot until for no arrows. Bronze Hats fight until horses fail. Then draw off, and the Lady Srayanka lets for go. Let Patient Wolves ride. Then let Hungry Wolves ride.' He pointed out into the rain. 'Just there. They come. And Cruel Hands come after.'

Kineas stared into the gloom. 'I have two troops across the stream – a hundred heavy horse. Let me fetch her in.'

Marthax nodded vehemently. 'Good. Take Greek horse and Sauromatae, here. Go!' With one hand he physically restrained the king. 'You sit here and wait,' he said. To Kineas, he called, 'Remember, brother! This is *not* the battle we want!'

The king had his armour on. He spoke in rapid Sakje, his

voice imperative. He was telling Marthax that he intended to ride to support Srayanka himself, with his household knights.

Kineas turned his horse back. 'Lord, you must not!' he said. Self-interest and the needs of the allies marched together, and he spoke with confidence. 'This is not a risk we can take!'

The king drew himself up, his mouth was hard under the sides of his helmet. 'Do I command here?' he asked.

Marthax grabbed his bridle. 'No!' he said. And to Kineas, he shouted. 'Ride!'

Kineas didn't hesitate. He turned his horse and rode for the ford. He had Niceas at his heels. 'Sound the rally,' he said. To Sitalkes, he called, 'My charger!'

The trumpet rang out, echoing strangely in the moist air. Kineas waved to Leucon, who could still see him. Sitalkes came with Thanatos. Kineas mounted his tall black and pushed him into the ford. The ford seemed vast in the rain. Kineas felt too slow – as if his men were riding in honey, not water.

'Are you calling us back?' called Nicomedes, from the far shore.

Kineas clenched his knees and rose on the horse's back. 'No! Form on your bank! Leave room for Leucon!'

Disembodied, Nicomedes called assent. He could be heard wheeling his men into line. Other voices could be heard to the south. The rain came down harder, trickling cold between the shoulder blades and back plate of bronze, running over the helmet to soak into a man's hair.

Thanatos's hooves were on gravel, and then on grass, and he was clear of the ford. Kineas put his horse to a canter and aimed at Nicomedes' voice. Niceas was right with him, still blowing the rally. It was hard to look straight into the rain, but Kineas finally saw Nicomedes – his cloak was unmistakable. His men were already formed in a solid block. Half a stade to the south, Diodorus was rallying his pickets and forming. Kineas reined in and pointed to Niceas. 'Leucon right there,' he said, pointing to the north of Nicomedes' troop. Leucon's men, and the troop from Pantecapaeum, were coming across the ford in good order. Beyond them, the heavily armoured Sauromatae were crossing. Just the way they moved showed that their mounts were tired.

Ataelus rode up. Kineas leaned over and put a hand on his back. 'I need to know exactly where Srayanka is,' he said. 'Can you link us up?'

Ataelus grinned. He blew his nose in his hand, jumped off his horse, and swung up on a remount he had on a lead. 'Sure,' he said. He waved and rode off into the rain.

Kineas rode to Leucon. 'I need Eumenes,' he said. Leucon nodded. Kineas continued. 'Hold the line. Don't lose your place. If we have to charge, halt the moment you hear the signal and retire in good order. If everything goes to shit, get back across the ford. We do *not* want a battle tonight. Understand?'

Leucon saluted. 'Line. Retire in order. Avoid a general engagement.'

Kineas returned the salute. 'You'll make a general yet.' He turned to Eumenes. 'Leave your troop and go to the Sauromatae. Stay with them and pass my commands. For the moment, they are my reserve. Try to explain reserve to them without twisting their reins.'

Eumenes nodded and rode away, shoulders slumped. Leucon had not yet said anything about his father's murder – but neither had he spoken a word to his hyperetes in three days, except to give an order.

Kineas rode back to Niceas. The line was formed – three dense blocks of men, with a looser line of Sauromatae in the rear.

'Sound: Advance,' Kineas said to Niceas.

The whole block began to walk forward. In twenty steps, the ford was gone behind them. In forty steps, they began to lose sight of the hills beyond the ford.

A band of Sakje appeared out of the rain, riding hard. Their first appearance gave alarm, but just as quickly they were identified – Patient Wolves. They showed their empty gorytos as they rode by, and indicated by gestures that the enemy was close.

Lightning flashed. In the time it took to illuminate the faces of his men, Kineas realized that this might be it. The fight. His death.

Silly thought – equally true for every man there.

Kineas rode along the front, too busy to dwell on mortality. He ordered all three troops to put their flank files out to prevent surprise. They passed another band of Patient Wolves, and then the first Cruel Hands – easily identified because every horse had the painted hand on its rump. Then, more and more – hundreds of them pouring by. Not routed – but drained. Done.

Ataelus rode up to him. 'She just ahead now,' he said. 'Bronze Hats not so close. Careful since heard for trumpets.' He pointed at Niceas for emphasis.

The rain was coming right into their faces. 'Halt!' Kineas called. Niceas played it.

They sat on their horses as the rain fell, drowning out the noise of the plain, and even whatever sound of fighting there might have been. Kineas couldn't hear anything but the beat of the rain on his helmet. He pulled the thing off, tucked it under his arm. He turned to Niceas, intending to speak, and Niceas pointed silently over Kineas's shoulder.

She was right in front of him, just a few horse lengths away. She was riding looking over her shoulder. Kineas tapped his stallion into motion and cantered up to her. The hoof beats warned her, and she turned in time to see him, and she gave him a tired smile. It was the first smile he'd had from her in a long time, even if it was only the smile of one commander to another.

'Almost, they are beating me,' she said. She was feeling in her gorytos for an arrow, and not finding any.

'Take your people straight through,' Kineas said – useless admonition. She had only a dozen of her household about her.

He put his hand to her face and withdrew it – it had gone there without his conscious volition. 'Straight through my line – I'll cover you,' he said, as much to re-establish their military roles as to inform her.

'Cruel Hands cover the rear. Always.' Her eyebrows were up, and her eyes still had a spark in them. Then she rolled her shoulders. 'Bowstrings wet. No more arrows. Long day.'

Kineas saw more and more Cruel Hands emerging from the murk. It wasn't just the rain – afternoon was turning to evening.

Srayanka raised a bone to her lips, and blew on it, and her trumpeter rode up. Hirene had a length of linen around her arm and blood on her saddle, but her face had fewer lines than

Srayanka's. She raised her trumpet and blew a two-tone note with a trill – a barbaric sound that rang harshly through the rain and was soaked up by the grass, and suddenly the rain was spitting Cruel Hands, pushing their jaded horses into a gallop, or changing horses, abandoning the most blown. Kineas had the impression of many wounds, and immense fatigue, and then the last of them were past him, streaming through the gaps between his troops.

'Get across the ford,' he said in his command voice. He pointed with his whip.

She raised an eyebrow and motioned with her whip, touched her heels to her mount, and galloped off, her back straight and her head high. As she rode off, he thought of all the things he might have said – instead of bellowing orders at her.

Instead, he turned to Ataelus. 'How far?' he asked, pointing into the rain. 'How far to the enemy?'

Ataelus pulled a strung bow from his gorytos, set an arrow to the string, and shot it in one fluid motion, the arrowhead pointed almost to the sky before he loosed, arcing away into the grey and dropping.

A horse screamed.

'Just there,' Ataelus said.

'Zeus, father of all. Poseidon, lord of horses.' Kineas swore, and then turned to Niceas. 'Sound: Advance!'

Niceas blew the signal as they walked forward. 'I thought we were avoiding a general engagement?'

'Sound: Trot!' Kineas called. He could feel his three blocks keeping their line, feel it in the sound of their hooves and the vibration of the ground. It could all be a vast trap.

He was half turned to order the charge, his throwing javelin just transferred to his right fist, when he saw the plumes, and then the whole man, emerge from the rain – two horse lengths away.

'Charge!' he bellowed. They were Thessalians – yellow and purple cloaks, good armour, big horses – and they were at a stand. Kineas's charger leaped from the trot to the gallop in two strides, and Kineas's javelin hit the Thessalian's horse.

Their ranks were well formed, firm and tight, but he took in their fatigue in his first glance. Kineas's horse shouldered past the wounded beast and pushed between the next two, lashing out with teeth and hooves to clear a way, and the whole troop flinched at his assault. Kineas used his second javelin like a sailor with a boarding pike, sweeping it to the right and left, tangling the troopers and knocking them off their mounts, and then the whole weight of his Olbians arrived, and the enemy formation shattered. Whatever their cautious officer had expected, a charge out of the rain by formed cavalry wasn't it.

They were gone in an instant – they ran like professionals, leaving only a handful of bodies on the ground. The rain swallowed them up.

Kineas rose on his horse's back and bellowed, 'Niceas!' in a voice that threatened to burst his lungs.

'Here!' replied his hyperetes. 'Here I am!'

'Sound: Recall!' Kineas pushed his horse out of the mob of his own troopers – too many of them were gone into the rain, showing their inexperience by pursuing the Thessalians. He rode back along the line of their advance, until he saw the damply gleaming shapes of the Sauromatae.

'Eumenes! We're retiring. We had a fight – no idea what we hit. We'll rally at the ford. Cover us.' He turned and rode back to his own men, who were falling in on the trumpets and turning about – a dangerous manoeuvre with the possibility of an unbeaten enemy somewhere in the rain. Kineas watched them – it seemed to take an aeon, and then another. He could see movement in the rain – bright colour to his right. Red cloaks. New enemy cavalry.

Nicomedes' troop was half a stade to the rear and well formed, Ajax's voice ordered men into the line, to close tight, close tight. Diodorus was well clear – gone into the rain. Leucon was having more trouble with the mix of men he had. Kineas rode over. 'Now, Leucon!' he called.

Leucon shook his head. The men of Pantecapaeum were having trouble finding their places in the rain and excitement. There were shouts to their front.

Niceas pointed. 'Too many unrallied men – and now they're getting snapped up. We need to get out of here.'

Kineas could feel the enemy cavalry gathering to his front. He heard a trumpet.

'Leucon!' he shouted. 'Away! Run for the ford!'

Leucon pushed his helmet back, swatted a man with the flat of his sword, and opened his mouth to shout an order. A javelin punched through his neck and he seemed to vomit blood, and then he was down, and a line of Thessalians came out of the rain and smashed into Leucon's troop.

Kineas's horse was away with his first touch – flying ignominiously for the ford. He was well out front – safe enough, and he looked back for Niceas, who was right at his heels.

The rain cleared a little, and he saw the Sauromatae charge straight through the broken line of Leucon's men. They struck the Thessalians with a sound like a hundred men beating a hundred copper kettles with spoons, and the Thessalians were stopped in their tracks.

Leucon's men were the youngest and best among the Olbian hippeis. The moment they saw the allied Sauromatae, they turned. The red cloaks were evenly matched. Javelins flew, and men fell. The whole line – both lines – threaded through the combat like shuttles on a loom, and then swirled into chaos in a matter of hoof beats.

Kineas tore his eyes away. Time would be counted in heartbeats, now. The engagement he didn't want was starting – half his command was committed, and if Zopryon had more cavalry to commit, he could win a sharp victory before nightfall. Kineas bore right, for Diodorus. Diodorus was there before him, his men already wheeled off to the left and reformed.

'Follow me!' Kineas yelled, and turned his horse. The stallion responded again – a magnificent animal, the best war mount he had ever possessed.

He led Diodorus's troop up the right flank of the enemy, guessing their location by sound and intuition. Their arrival panicked the red cloaks, and they broke, but this time they were tangled in the mêlée to their front and they took casualties breaking off. Their horses were done, and they died in dozens, cut down from behind or trapped in the mud on foundered horses – and the relative freshness of the Olbians began to tell. Then Kineas heard another voice, like a giant in the dark – Ajax, with Nicomedes' troop, closing in on the doomed red cloaks from the other flank. And even in the murk, he could see Eumenes, his sword wet with blood, exhorting the younger Olbians to rally, to press harder.

Scenting victory, Kineas harried them, unhorsed a trooper, cut another man's arm and then killed their trumpeter in three quick fights. In a flash of lightning he saw their commander in an ornate, gilded breastplate and he charged the man – a man he knew – but the officer declined the combat and galloped for the safety of the rear. His horse, at least, had the energy to run.

Phillip Kontos, Kineas thought. A man he respected – and now sought to kill.

Kineas pursued a half a stade, reined in, peered into the gloom – he was alone.

He realized that he was farther down the field than he had intended, and that he had lost his hyperetes. 'Rally!' he called, his voice hoarse, rising, cracking with the third repetition.

A Sauromatae rode up to him and pointed back to the ford, as if he was a young trooper who needed direction.

Ataelus came up out of the rain, grabbed at his reins, and shouted, 'Pikemen!' and pointed into the rain.

Kineas squinted and saw, far too close, a column of heavy infantry. He pulled his horse's head around. In the middle distance, he could hear Niceas's trumpet. He'd ridden too far – been a fool. Carried away in the charge.

He leaned forward on his horse's neck and put his head down, in case the Macedonians had archers. This was their army – he was right in among them, a stade or less from their pikemen. He pulled up at the first big knot of his own men – he was pleased to note that his horse still flowed over the ground – and shouted shrilly for them to fall back.

The pikemen – a full taxeis – were forming from column into their combat formation.

With gestures, with the flat of his sword, with Ataelus calling in Sakje, he moved his men back, back to the line of the first charge and then back to where Niceas was sounding the recall – Niceas was exactly where he ought to be. He had a cut on his bridle arm and his helmet was gone, and he was still blowing his trumpet, and his face as Kineas came out of the rain was like a father's with a strayed infant – love, relief, anger all born together.

Niceas put his trumpet on his hip and glared at Kineas. 'Where the fuck were you?' he yelled.

'Playing Achilles like a fool,' Kineas yelled back.

They were forming again. Kineas was proud of them – hard enough to form after a fight you win, harder to form after two, and Leucon's men had been shattered, lost their captain, and they were pushing into their ranks, ready for a third go. Their horses were done, and no one had a javelin, heavy or light.

Kineas expected it to be darker. It was as if no time had passed from the first encounter. Off in the rain, and the ground fog that was rising to meet it, a Macedonian trumpet sounded, and then another. A few stades to the south, there was shouting.

Niceas panted for a few breaths. 'Are we winning or losing?' he asked. Then he grinned. 'Aren't you the man who ordered us to avoid a general engagement?'

Kineas shrugged, his attention focused on the rallying troopers. 'I take your point, old man. Let's get across the river. Where are the Sauromatae?'

Niceas pointed to the centre of the line. 'Eumenes got them halted, all but a handful.'

Kineas rode to Eumenes. 'Take command of your troop,' he said. 'Leucon is dead.'

Eumenes' face fell – his mouth opened and shut like a gaffed fish, and nothing came out.

Kineas pointed again. 'Take command,' he said. His voice betrayed him, coming out as a squeak.

The reaction hit them all after they were successfully across the ford, riding in good order despite the rain and their own wounded. They were cold and wet and tired – too tired to cook or curry horses, and the officers had to bear down. Nicomedes and Ajax were as brutal as Kineas, using the whip of their tongues to berate any man whose horse was untended, or gear abandoned on the grass. Niceas pulled one of the younger men away from a fire and threw him to the ground.

Discipline was restored.

And then, after the first few minutes, the soul fatigue passed. Kineas thanked all the gods for the Sindi, who sprang into action, building fires, tending wounds, and cooking. Warriors came from the other camps – Olbian hoplites, and then a few Standing Horses, and some Patient Wolves. They came in the rain, with a jar of mead, or a skin of wine, or a haunch of cooked meat.

And the fires roared higher, pushing the rain back into the sky. Men ate their food, and drank some wine, or gifted mead, and the silence broke. Suddenly everyone had to talk, to tell his story.

Kineas still had his breastplate on, and his helmet under his arm, standing cloakless in the rain, watching for another outburst of insubordination, already beset with the next phalanx of worries.

Philokles had missed the whole engagement, but waiting had taken its own toil. Now he was half drunk, and he pawed at Kineas, trying to get his armour off.

'Don't be an idiot!' Kineas snapped. 'I don't want it off yet.'

'Who's an idiot?' Philokles answered. 'I didn't ride off into the Macedonian lines – Ajax says you were like a god. Are you looking for death? Or are you a fool?'

Kineas shook his head. 'I'm a poor general. Once I start fighting, I'm lost – blind. I focus on the man in front of me, and then the next.' He shrugged, his own reaction beginning to set in. 'I ran across an old – rival.'

'Put him down?' asked Philokles.

'He ran,' Kineas said.

Philokles pulled the helmet out from under Kineas's arm. 'Get this statuary off your hide, brother. Live a little. Step out of the tyrant's grasp for the evening. Go kiss Medea – if I can't bring you to sense, perhaps she can!'

Kineas relinquished his helmet. 'You're drunk, brother.'

'Bah! I am drunk. You should try it. Greek wine gives dreams from Greek gods – no dreams of death.'

'Who dreams of death?' asked Diodorus. He was rubbing his hair with his tunic, and was otherwise naked. 'That was the ugliest action I've ever been in.'

Ajax came up behind him. He was flushed. 'I wondered – it was like no fight you described.'

Kineas put an arm around Ajax. 'That was the animal,' he said to the young man, and gave him a squeeze. 'You did well.'

'Kineas dreams of death,' Philokles said into a moment of silence, and then shut his mouth with a snap.

Diodorus went on. 'Did we surprise them? Did they surprise us? I don't even know who won – what?' He looked at Philokles, and then at Kineas. 'You have dreamed your own death?'

Kineas fumbled with the sash he wore around his breastplate. 'Philokles is drunk.'

Diodorus took the Spartan cup from Philokles' hand and drained it. 'Good plan. Death dreams are all pigswill – I should know. I always dream my death before an action. I dreamed of death last night and doubtless I'll dream of it again tonight.'

Philokles gazed at his now-empty cup. 'Will it be tomorrow?' he asked quietly. He didn't seem so drunk, of a sudden.

Kineas got his sash untied and managed to open his breast and back plate. 'Maybe. I don't *know*.' He looked around the campfires. 'Where's Heron?'

Niceas appeared from the rain with Arni, Ajax's slave. Arni pulled the wet tunic over Kineas's head and pulled a drier one down over him.

Niceas shook his head. 'Heron isn't back. Neither are his men.'

'Crap,' Kineas said. 'Where's Ataelus?'

Niceas shrugged. 'He got a couple of horses at the end of the fight,' he said. 'I think he's wooing a girl of the Cruel Hands.'

Kineas pulled his wet cloak over his almost-dry tunic. 'I'll find him.' He hated to leave them – they were in the glow that comes after successful action, and he was headed for black depression. But something nagged him. Heron.

Kineas crossed the hill to the Cruel Hands, and his back was slapped many times. Sakje offered him wine, or mare's milk, or spiced tea in deep mugs, and he drank some of each as he passed from fire to fire, asking after Ataelus.

He found Srayanka's wagon first. He heard her laughter, and he rested his hand on the wheel, wondering – he had never

389

sought her out since the night by the river, and now he felt foolish, like a suitor waiting in the rain.

More laughter carried through the felt of the tent on the wagon bed. Kineas heard Parshtaevalt's deeper laugh, and he pulled himself up on the step and called 'hello!' in Greek.

Parshtaevalt's hand opened the flap. The tent was lit by a brazier and dense with smoke from the seeds and the stems – the pine-pitch scent flowed past him into the night.

'Hah!' called Parshtaevalt. He put a hand on Kineas's neck and hugged him, then pulled him through the door to the bench that ran the length of the wagon – seat by day, bed by night. The wagon was full of people, stifling with wet wool and smoke. Hands reached out and pushed him – prodded him – until he sank into a warm space between two bodies. One of them was Srayanka, and before he was on the bench, one of her hands had snaked into his tunic and her mouth closed over his. He kissed her so deeply that he breathed from her lungs, and she from his, and the fire in his skin burned his tunic dry as she curled around him on the bench. It was dark in the wagon – the red coals in the brazier threw no real light – and despite his knowledge that Hirene was under his left hand, he felt as if they were alone, and every breath of the air intensified his desire.

'You came,' she said around his kiss, as if she didn't believe it.

He had come looking for something. His hand was under her tunic, tracing the line where the soft ivory of her breast met the lusher skin of her nipple, and she sank her teeth into his arm, and he gasped, taking a deeper breath of the smoke off the brazier ...

The worm was close, the mandibles of its mouth chewing away at everything in its path, and his gorge rose as it ate Leucon's face off his skull ...

'Ataelus!' Kineas cried. He pushed her away. He wondered if he was going mad.

She grabbed his hand and he resisted, but she was strong, and she pulled him, pushed him, and suddenly he was falling – it was wet, and he was slumped at the wheel hub. She jumped down on the wet grass beside him.

'You are easy for the smoke,' she said. She admonished him with a finger. 'Breathe deep. Go under wagon and breathe.'

'Stay with me,' he said, but she shook her head.

'Too much, too fast. You breathe. I find Ataelax. He with Samahe. Do what we should do, but for Sastar Baqca and the king.' And she was gone.

His head was clear when she came back, with Ataelus behind her like a spare horse.

Kineas didn't feel like a commander and he knew he didn't look like one, but he pulled Ataelus close. 'I sent Heron – the hipparch from Pantecapaeum – downriver this morning to scout for fords.'

'No ford downriver,' Ataelus answered. There was another man with him – no, a woman. She had her arms crossed over her chest and anger dripped off her with the rainwater. 'This Samahe – wife for me.' He grinned. 'Twenty horse wife!'

Kineas shook his hand, which was inane. 'I need to know where Heron is and what he found.'

Ataelus frowned and looked at Kineas from under his brows. 'You ask me to ride off in the rain – now? For this Heron?'

Kineas said, 'Yes.'

Ataelus took a deep breath. 'For you?' he asked.

'For me,' Kineas said. He lacked the language to explain just why he was so worried, suddenly, about his missing hipparch – but he was.

When he was gone, Samahe protesting volubly after him, Kineas sat on the dry ground under her wagon. Srayanka sat against his back. They were silent for a long time. Finally, she said, 'If we win – when we win. You bring me twenty of horses?'

'Is that your price?' he asked.

She laughed – a low, rich laugh. 'I am beyond price,' she said in Sakje, leaning around to look at him. 'I want you like a mare in heat wants a stallion, and I would go with you for a handful of grass, like a priestess. That is one woman I am.' She threw back her head, and her profile was strong against the light of the nearest fire. 'But I am Ghân of the Cruel Hands, and there is no bride price to buy me.' She shrugged. 'The king would make me queen – and that would make Cruel Hands rich. I am woman, and I am *Ghân*.' She looked into his eyes. Hers were picked out with reflected campfires. 'But if we win this battle,' she said again. 'If we are free of the Sastar Baqca – will you ask me to wife?'

Kineas pushed his back into hers. 'If we live – I will ask you to wife.' He kissed her, felt the movement of her eyelashes against his cheeks. 'I know Baqca. What is *Sastar*?'

She wriggled slightly in his arms. 'What is the thing – the word you say when man rule over other men and will not hear them? Rule alone? No voice but that man?'

'Tyrant,' Kineas answered, after a moment.

'*Tyrant*' she echoed. 'Sastar is like tyrant. Sastar Baqca – the baqca that allows no other voice.' She turned and put her arms behind his head. 'No more Greek and Sakje.'

'No,' said Kineas. Death seemed far away, and everything seemed possible. 'I will marry you.' He kissed her again.

She grinned even through the kiss, pulled away and looked at him. 'Truly?' she asked. She smiled, kissed him and then pushed him away. 'Bring me Zopryon's head as my price, then.' She leaped to her feet.

Kineas got to his, still holding her hand. Their eyes were locked. She gave his hand a gentle pressure – and then she was stepping away.

The rain sobered him, and in moments it all came rushing back – the battle, plans, worries. *Where in Hades is Heron?* And the plain fact – *this is foolishness – I'll be dead.* But he forced a laugh and said, 'It's a high price.'

She slipped out from under the wagon and turned. 'It will make a good song,' she said with a smile. 'You know – they already sing of us?'

Kineas didn't know. 'Really?' he called after her.

She paused in the rain on the step up to the wagon. 'We may live for ever, in a song.'

He stopped at the king's laager to report, then walked, drenched, down the hill to issue his last orders at the campfires. The night was half spent when he pushed through the curtain into his wagon. He had the energy to strip his tunic, to hang his sodden cloak from the ridgepole, and then he lay down on the bed. He lay awake for a time, and again he wondered if the gods had sent madness to him. He didn't want to close his eyes. And then he did.

The worm was moving, a thousand legs pushing its obscene bulk across the wet grass to the river, a dozen obscene mouths chewing at anything that came under their jaws – dead horses, dead men, grass.

He circled above the worm, seeing it with two visions – as the worm was, the monster, and as the men and horses and wagons that composed the worm, like reading a scroll and understanding the whole of it at the same time, or like seeing every stone in a mosaic and seeing the whole design.

He pushed against the dream, and the owl turned away from the worm and flew south – the first time he had been in control in a dream. The owl beat its wings, and the stades flew by – grey and indistinct in the constant rain – but he saw horsemen moving on the west bank of the river, a dozen parties pushing south.

Then he let his dream self have its head and turn north, back to the worm on the sea of grass. It was horrible, but the horror had a familiarity to it – because he himself had been the legs of the worm, and the mouth. He knew the smell.

His dream self turned east, over the river, which had a dull glow in the dream rain, and then he was descending, and there was the tree – no longer a tower of green-black majesty. The tree was dying. The cedar bark was hard under his talons, the leaves and needles fallen away in swathes like a sick animal loses hair, exposing bare wood and rotten bark, and the top had already cracked and fallen away. He landed, grasping a solid branch, and it, too, cracked, and he was falling ... from his horse, an arrow in his throat, choking on the hard pain and the rush of blood – bitter copper and salt in his mouth, in his nose, and in his last moments of life he tried to see, tried to remember if the battle was won, but it all went away beyond his eyes leaving only her voice singing, and he couldn't remember her name – he listened to her ...

'Dawn, somewhere above the rain,' said a voice. A hand, pulling at his shoulder. 'Good news for you. Get up.'

'Huh?' he asked. He felt as if he'd been beaten like bread dough.

'Dawn. Eumenes is ready to ride. Your orders – are you awake?' asked Philokles. He was naked, and wet. 'Laertes is here, with a prisoner.'

Kineas sat up. The tunic he had stripped off before sleep was as wet now as it had been when he put his head down. So was his cloak. He threw the cloak over his shoulders and swung down from the wagon, stifled in the smell of wet wool. Philokles swung down behind him.

'It's not cold,' he said.

'We're not all Spartans,' Kineas said. In fact, he was, as always, hesitant to show his body naked. Even on the edge of battle. He smiled at his own vanity.

Ataelus was sitting at his fire with Laertes, Crax, Sitalkes and another warrior – a man lay at Laertes' feet, with curly blond hair and bare legs, covered by a dark red cloak – the prisoner, unless he was already a corpse. The rest of them were passing around a horn cup that steamed. Kineas intercepted it. 'Morning,' he said. The meaning of Ataelus' presence hit him through the last of his sleep. He put a hand on Crax's shoulder. 'Where is Heron?' he asked. And then he pointed at the stranger in the cloak. 'Who's he?'

Crax grinned. 'He's a fool. I caught him.' He prodded the recumbent form with his boot. 'Sitalkes hit him too hard.'

Kineas began to stretch his muscles. 'I think I need the whole story.'

Laertes grinned and snatched the cup back. 'Heron's thorough, Hipparch. Give him that. We went sixty – maybe even eighty stades, and we pushed our spears into every bank on the damn river.'

Sitalkes spoke quickly, tripping over the Greek in his excitement and showing a scalp on his spear, but Laertes spoke over him. He pulled an arm free of his cloak to point at Ataelus. 'Thank the gods you sent him,' he said. 'All the feeder streams are full – hard to cross themselves. We were lost in the dark when Ataelus found us.' He gestured at Sitalkes. 'We tangled with their patrols twice, but they couldn't make it across. This idiot,' Laertes ruffled Sitalkes's hair, 'killed a man with a javelin and then swam across to get his hair. Barbarian.'

Kineas felt the warmth of the tea spreading through his stomach. 'So there is a crossing south of here?'

Laertes shrugged, exchanged a glance with Ataelus. 'There's a dozen crossings – if you want to swim your horse, or if you can pick your way in single file. Nothing for an army – not really even a crossing for a patrol.'

Kineas rubbed his eyes. 'How'd you end up fighting these?' he asked, indicating the prisoner.

'They must have had boats,' Laertes said. 'Heron made us look for them, but we never found them. It took time, in the rain. And then we got lost.' He shrugged.

Ataelus grinned at the other warrior with him. Kineas realized she was his wife – Samahe. The Black One. She gave her husband a wry smile. 'I for find Greek horse,' she said. 'See in dark.'

Ataelus gave her the tea. 'Good wife,' he said. 'Find Greek horse – find Crax – find enemy all same-same.'

'Where is Heron?' Kineas asked. He looked at the prisoner again. The man looked familiar – or the cloak did.

Laertes held the horn cup out, and one of the camp slaves came and refilled it. 'Rolled in his cloak. He means to go north as soon as we have a rest.'

Kineas nodded. 'Give him my thanks. Get some rest yourselves.'

They all grinned, pleased with themselves and pleased with his praise, spare as it had been. They made him feel better.

Philokles took the cup and drained it. 'Eumenes is waiting,' he said acerbically. He wiped his mouth. 'I'm going out with him.' He put the cup on the ground. 'I'll see what I can get from our prisoner when I get back.'

Kineas walked down the hill, thinking about Macedonian patrols south of the ford. His intuition, which had burned all night, had been right. Then he understood what he had heard. Philokles was not often an active soldier. 'Why?' he asked. 'Why are you going out?'

The rain was soaking him again, and his beard was too full – it felt like an alien on his face. He wanted to shave. Too many days in the saddle.

Philokles shrugged. 'It is time to fight,' he said.

Eumenes was mounted at the head of Leucon's troop. The hippeis of Pantecapaeum were mounted as well, and beyond them in the rain were half of the phalanx of Pantecapaeum. Most of them were naked, holding their shields and a single, heavy spear. Beyond them, a pair of heavy Sakje wagons.

Kineas walked up to Eumenes. 'Straight across, retrieve the bodies, and get back.'

Eumenes had his eyes on the ford. 'We won't disappoint you. There will be no repeat of yesterday,' he said in a hard voice.

Kineas stepped in close, where he could feel the warmth of the horse. 'Yesterday could have happened to anyone. That's *war*, Eumenes. Claim the bodies and get back here and no heroics.'

Eumenes saluted.

A Sindi, one of Temerix's men, trotted up to Philokles and handed him a helmet, which he pushed on to the back of his head, then a heavy spear – hard, black, longer by a span than other men's, and as thick as Kineas's wrist. Philokles hung a shield on his shoulder – a plain bronze shield with no mark on it.

'You're going with him?' Kineas asked again. He was at a loss.

Philokles smiled grimly. 'Memnon made me the commander of this two hundred,' he said. He raised an eyebrow. 'The benefits of a Spartan education.' Philokles turned on his heel, his old red cloak billowing behind him. With a casual shake of his head, he dropped the helmet off his brow so that the cheek pieces covered his face. From the helmet came an inhuman voice – so different from Philokles' voice that Kineas would have said it was a different man's.

'We'll run all the way,' said the voice. 'Any man who falls behind is left for the birds. Ready?'

They growled. Spears beat on shields. Kineas watched them run off to the ford, keeping their space in close order, and wondered.

The expedition to cross the ford and retrieve the dead from yesterday's running fight was almost uncontested. Kineas kept the phalanx standing ready, held the balance of the Olbian horse under his hand, and then crossed himself for a quick reconnaissance in the second hour. Before the third hour the men of Pantecapaeum were back, still running, singing the paean of their city as they came. Behind them came the wagons, full to the beams with their grim cargo, and a handful of wounded who had survived a night in the rain. Last came Eumenes and his troop. They had seen a handful of Macedonians, as had Kineas. Eumenes had another prisoner.

Kineas called his officers, and they gathered around the fire by his wagon.

'I don't like it,' he said. 'I'm going to the king. Zopryon should have tried to close the ford.'

Eumenes didn't agree. 'I'm new to war, but I think they felt beaten last night, and retired from the ford to get clear – fearing the same battle we feared.'

Niceas gave the young man a proprietary grin. 'Sounds like sense to me,' he said.

Kineas nodded. 'It is possible. I have to guard against all the possibilities. Get the men under cover – rotate the pickets – and see to the horses. This weather will cost us more horses than a battle. Diodorus, you're in command of the pickets. Has anyone seen Heron?'

'Already gone,' Diodorus said. 'Tried to find you when you crossed the stream, and said your orders wouldn't wait and he was headed north with our scouts. He seemed to know what he was about. I sent Ataelus with him.'

Kineas couldn't stifle a grin. 'He ought to – he has all our best men. Send him to me the moment he returns, or any of his men. I'm for the king.'

Philokles, still an alien figure in a heavy helmet, spear in hand, spat expertly through his helmet. 'I'll see to the prisoners,' he said. 'Niceas has them separate. We'll see what they say.'

Kineas nodded. 'Eumenes – if you can stay awake, I need you.'

Eumenes nodded wearily, and Kineas dismissed the rest.

Up the hill, the view was better. As his legs brushed through the wet grass, Kineas could see the herds, well off to the north, and the camps of each of the clans. The rain would be debilitating for both armies, but the Sakje, with their huge herds of horses and their dry wagons for sleeping, would be more comfortable.

The sky was lightening, the clouds raising. Wisps of low cloud obscured his view, but on other lines he could see five stades or more, and although the rain was steady, it lacked last night's vehemence. In Athens he would have expected the rain to end towards evening.

To the west he could see a line of fires at the limit of his perception. The fires were small, and their smoke was black.

Almost out of firewood, Kineas thought. Out of wagons, out of food. He'd flirted with Zopryon twice in the rain, and despite the outcomes, he had a feeling for Zopryon's army.

They were desperate.

Kineas had a thought, so beautiful that it was dangerous. He didn't want to express it to himself, much less say it aloud to others, lest he somehow change the world by speaking of it. But it kept poking into his plans and his worries, and the thought was: Zopryon does not yet know that Cleomenes has betrayed the city.

21

The king was just summoning his clan leaders. He had a big felt tent, and his guardsmen had erected it in the clear space at the centre of his laager.

Kineas was still in armour from his reconnaissance. He kept his cloak around him, the more so as the clan leaders came in, Srayanka among them. She lay down on the rugs next to him. Marthax sat on his other side, and the king sat on a folding stool. He served them wine with his own hands, in heavy gold cups, glanced disapprovingly at Srayanka, and turned his head away.

The last of the chiefs came in, and a pair of Sauromatae, and then Kam Baqca. She bowed to the king, and slumped at his side, as if the energy of standing had exhausted her.

The king pointed his whip at Kineas. 'Our thanks to our allies. We would have had many empty saddles without your actions at the ford.'

Kineas rose and pointed a bare arm at the Sauromatae. 'They turned the tide,' he said bluntly. 'Without them, we might have been beaten. Even as it was, I lost young Leucon – one of my officers.'

The blonder of the two Sauromatae rose and returned his bow. He spoke rapidly to the king, and the king translated with pleasure.

'Prince Lot says that he questioned you as allies, and now he asks no more questions, and hopes that the quality of the offence was altered by the brotherhood on the field.'

Kineas smiled at the tall blond man.

The king nodded. 'It is good that we have the army together, and it is good that we struck Zopryon a blow at the edge of dark. Marthax?'

Marthax rose. He cracked his fingers and stretched his arms. In Greek he said, 'It is good.' Through Eumenes, he said, 'Zopryon flinched from the contest.' Eumenes translated, although, as was increasingly the case, Kineas understood almost every word. 'My sense is that he was afraid of what started in the dark and rain – and he retreated.'

The other chiefs roared approval.

Kineas could sense that their morale had shifted in the night. They were eager, and the king looked happier. Only Kam Baqca had hollows under her eyes and pale cheeks.

Kineas raised his hand and the king waved to him.

'I had scouts to the south,' he said. 'They saw patrols, and took a prisoner. Zopryon is looking for a ford. He has scouted us well – his men knew where to expect us last night, even in the rain.'

Srayanka spoke from the rug at his side. 'Those Thessalians are tough bastards,' she said.

Another chief across the tent swallowed his wine. 'And their companions are just as good,' he said.

Kineas nodded. 'As we said from the first – this is where he is desperate. He must either destroy this army or cross to the south and go to Olbia.' Kineas shrugged. Hesitantly, he enunciated his dearest thought. 'If he even knows of Cleomenes' treason – and nothing we have seen so far suggests he knows.' He grimaced at the irony of it – Zopryon's greatest advantage might be unknown to the man. The gods punished hubris in just such ways. He made a gesture learned from his nurse – pure superstition, to avert any part he might play in such hubris.

Kineas continued, 'He ought to push to the ford today. If he does not, we should consider pressing him again – sending raids across the river.'

Marthax rubbed his moustache and drank some wine. 'Already it is late in the day. And the rain soaks everything.'

The king nodded. 'There is standing water in the camp. It will be worse where the Macedonians are.'

Srayanka looked around the circle. 'I don't want to fight today,' she said, and other chiefs nodded with her, and Gaomavañt, lord of the Patient Wolves, rose to his feet. 'We need rest, Lord. The horses are weary, and the warriors – too many are hurt. The rain does not help.'

Lot of the Sauromatae shrugged, despite the weight of his

armour. He spoke through the king, who matched him gesture for gesture. 'We are not tired. Show us a line of bronze hats, and we will cut them down. The rain does not wet our lance heads. If you are tired, think how the bronze hats are today.'

Kineas shook his head. 'The taxeis are not tired. They can march through a hundred days of rain.' He looked at the king and shook his head again. 'We are drier – and more secure – than the Macedonians. We will rest better. You have more remounts to replace those who are lame. And – I hesitate to shout this to the gods, lest I offend by hubris – but nothing, *nothing* we have seen in two days suggests that Zopryon knows that Olbia is open to them. If my counsel carries weight here, then I suggest that the freshest clans cross the ford and block Zopryon's access to the south. Cut him off from any message. Strike his southern pickets and wear at them. A few hundred horse, at most – if they are cut off when Zopryon moves to the ford, they can harry his rear or simply ride off into the grass.'

The king rubbed his beard. He glanced at Marthax. 'Warlord?' he asked.

Marthax shrugged. 'What do we want, Lord?' he asked bluntly. 'The campaign has always come to this. Do we avoid battle? Or force battle and fight to destroy this enemy utterly – risking our own destruction? Did we not decide from the first to take that risk? We might have ridden into the grass in the spring – even now, we might be with the Messagetae. We are here. Enough counsel. Let us cut this Zopryon off from the south – that is sense – and goad him to the fight. Let him cross the ford in the morning.' Marthax's look at Kam Baqca was almost tender. 'We will be stung. But the hornet's nest will be destroyed utterly. So say I.'

The king glanced around the circle, but it was clear that the chiefs were with Marthax, and only the king hesitated. He said, 'I remind you that when we first planned this campaign, we discussed a parley at this precise moment. A token of submission.'

The chiefs growled. Next to Kineas, Srayanka stiffened and her face set.

The king looked around at them. He pointed to Kineas.

'Your friend the Spartan says that war is a tyrant, and nothing makes it more clear than this.' His bitterness was evident. 'The taste of blood has excited you. You want to risk all so that this menace may be destroyed, or so that we may all be remembered in song.' He glanced at Srayanka. 'Or so that past injustice may be wiped clean.'

The tent was silent while he toyed with his whip. None of them made a noise, and the sound of hoof beats carried clearly from outside.

The king looked at Kam Baqca, but she turned her face away and raised her hand, as if the king's eyes might scorch her. The hoof beats came closer, and stopped, and in the unnatural still-ness Kineas heard the sound as the rider's feet hit the ground.

The king flinched at Kam Baqca's reaction. Then he drew himself up, and Kineas, who knew the weight of command, could all but see the full load settle on the king's shoulders. He raised his whip and pointed at the lord of the Grass Cats.

'The king! I must see the king!' said a strong voice from the doorway of the tent.

The messenger was young, wearing nothing but a gorytos over breeches and boots and a short knife. He threw himself in front of the king.

'Lord – there is a herald at the ford demanding our submission. A herald from the bronze hats.'

As soon as Kineas saw Cleomenes sitting on a tall mare at Zopryon's side, he knew the worst.

The rain was clearing. A veil of cloud moved fitfully along the river valley, separating the two armies, but in the heavens, the sun was gradually conquering the element of water. Kineas looked up, and saw an eagle or a hawk far, far to the north – his right. A good omen. Below, on the earth, a hundred Macedonian cavalry sat a half-stade to the west, while a hundred of the king's household sat at the edge of the ford. And between them were two half-circles: the king of the Sakje, Marthax and Srayanka, Lot and Kineas. Across a horse length of grass: Zopryon, flanked by a Macedonian officer and Cleomenes, and a herald.

The good omen in the sky hardly balanced the disaster of Cleomenes' presence.

The Macedonian herald had just completed reading his master's requirements – the submission of the Sakje, a tribute of twenty thousand horses, and the immediate repudiation of the armies of Olbia and Pantecapaeum.

Kineas watched Cleomenes. Cleomenes met his eye and smiled.

When the herald was done, Zopryon nudged his horse into motion. He wore no helmet, but a diadem of white in his hair.

'I have Olbia in the palm of my hand,' he said. His words were arrogant. They belied the look on his face – fatigue, and worry. He went on. 'With Olbia as a base, I can ride against your towns. I will spend the autumn burning your crops. Save me the time. Submit.'

None of the Sakje flinched.

Cleomenes spoke to Kineas. 'You are wise to bring no man of Olbia to this parley, mercenary. But my men will find them, and tell them. And they will march away from you, and leave you to die with these. Traitor. False hireling. For you, my lord Zopryon will have no mercy.'

Kineas gave no more reaction than the Sakje. Instead, he turned to the king. And the king, who had sat slumped, relaxed, or perhaps tired while listening to the herald, now drew himself erect.

'When news of your herald came,' he said in his excellent Greek, 'I was in council with my chiefs. Ever they urge me to battle, and ever I hesitate, because to fight a battle is to submit the fate of my people to chance and death. O Zopryon, your words have cleared the air for me, as the sun burns away every fog, in the end. Do you know your Herodotus?'

Zopryon's face darkened. 'Do not toy with me. Submit, or take the consequence.'

Even now, Kineas could see that the man was in a hurry. Even with Olbia in hand, just three hundred stades away, the desperation was still there. A flicker of hope relit in Kineas's stomach.

The king reached out and took a basket from Srayanka, who rode at his side. 'Here are your tokens, O Zopryon.' He shrugged, and appeared as young as he really was. 'I hadn't time to catch a bird.'

He pushed his horse into motion. The horse took a few steps, and all of the Macedonians reacted. But the king handed the wicker basket to the herald. And then stopped his horse nose to nose with Zopryon's horse.

Zopryon motioned impatiently. The herald took a linen towel off the top of the basket, and a frog leaped clear. The herald dropped the basket in shock. He turned to his master. 'Vermin!' he said. 'Mice and frogs!'

The king reached into his gorytos and withdrew a handful of light arrows, which he threw on the ground at Zopryon's feet. 'I am the king of the Sakje. That is the answer of the Sakje. My allies may speak for themselves.' The king glanced at Kineas and sat straight. And then he turned his horse and rode away.

Cleomenes was as red as a Spartan's cloak. The herald's horse shied from the mice in the grass.

Kineas leaned forward. His hands were clenched with tension, but his voice carried well enough. 'His tokens mean just this, Zopryon. Unless you can swim like a frog, burrow like a mouse, or fly like a bird, we will destroy you with our arrows.'

Zopryon reacted angrily enough to confirm Kineas's suspicion that the man was at the edge. 'This embassage is ended, mercenary! Be gone before I order you dead.'

Kineas pushed his horse forward, floating on the promise of his dream. 'Try, Zopryon,' he said. 'Try to kill me.'

Zopryon turned his horse. 'You are mad. Drunk with power.'

Kineas laughed. It was a harsh laugh, a little forced, but it did the job. 'Does Alexander know you wear the diadem?' Kineas called. 'Do you have an ivory stool to match it?' He saw the shot go home. Zopryon whirled his horse. He put his hand on his sword hilt.

Kineas sat still, and his warhorse didn't stir.

Cleomenes leaned forward over his horse's neck. 'You are a dangerous man. And now you will die.'

Kineas stood his ground. His laugh was derisive, and he was proud that he could conjure it. And he needed to goad Zopryon.

He needed the man to commit to his desperation. 'Your horses are starving,' he yelled. 'Your men walk like corpses. You are burning your wagons for firewood.'

Zopryon was two horse lengths away. His hand was still on his sword, and his face was moving.

Kineas pointed at the king's arrows. 'Cleomenes,' he said mockingly. 'You have chosen unwisely.' He held the man's eyes. 'You are a fool. This army will never get to Olbia alive.'

Cleomenes didn't flinch. 'I demand that you give me my son, and all the men still loyal to the archon.'

Kineas shook his head. 'If I sent Eumenes to you,' he said, 'he would kill you himself.' To Zopryon, he said, 'Olbia is on our side of the river. Your scouts will have told you that there is no ford south of here. Whenever you think you can force the ford, come and face us. If your horses don't starve first.'

Zopryon's rage began to boil out of him, and Kineas rode away.

At the ford, he caught the king. 'He must not be allowed to march south.'

Marthax nodded. 'We know.'

'Let the Grass Cats cross the ford as soon as Varô their lord can be ready,' the king said. 'Let us show them their future.'

Kineas found that Kam Baqca was watching him. He met her eyes, and wondered if the same emptiness lay in his own.

The Grass Cats rode off across the ford as the rain tailed off to fitful spurts in early afternoon. And a damp sun made portions of the sky overhead lighter, if a man was an optimist.

Kineas ordered Diodorus to take a patrol across and scout the enemy camp – or their patrol line. He wanted to do it himself, but he needed sleep.

His nap was dreamless. But he had a sharp feeling of dream when it was the same damp arm that woke him, and Philokles' voice in his ear.

'Huh?' he asked, as before.

'Your prisoner?' Philokles said. 'The one Laertes brought? He's a Kelt. One of the archon's.'

'Athena, protectress. Shield of our fathers, lady of the olive.

All the gods.' Kineas swore, but he was out of his wagon into late afternoon light – a pale sky, sun too weak to cast a shadow but drier than rain. He followed Philokles to the fire pit, where the prisoner sat on a stone, watched by a trio of the blacksmith's friends. He had his head in his hands, and Kineas could see that the back of his head was swollen.

'Look at me,' Philokles ordered in his Ares voice.

The man raised his head, and Kineas knew him, despite the bruise over his eye.

'So,' Kineas said. 'It was not hubris. The gods smile on us – unless others slipped past.'

Philokles shook his head. 'A dozen Kelts and a pair of Macedonians and Cleomenes left the city together. Ataelus's wife discovered them in the dark, and led Heron's men to them. This one thinks they are all dead.'

Kineas rubbed his beard. *Balanced on a knife's edge.* If he and Srayanka – if she hadn't found Ataelus – if Ataelus didn't have a new wife to ride with him …

It wasn't over yet.

Kineas rubbed his face with cold water. 'Cleomenes made it to Zopryon,' he said. 'A day too late, I think. I hope.' He shrugged. 'I'm for hot water, a shave, and a strigil,' he said. 'Tomorrow, we fight.'

Philokles nodded. 'I'll comb my hair,' he said.

Marthax pushed more of his lightest, freshest cavalry across in late afternoon, with orders to cause as much chaos as possible among the Macedonians. The next hours saw a constant skirmish just out of sight of the ford. Sakje would ride back to change horses, get arrows, or tend a wound.

Kineas sent Diodorus to support them, and to gather what information he could.

There was yet an hour of light, or perhaps more, when Kineas saw the stir at the ford. He waved to Memnon, who approached at a run. Horsemen – Olbians – were coming across the ford at speed. He could see a Sakje messenger going up the hill to the king's laager. Another Sakje coming from the north, on their side of the river – galloping through the herds at a reckless pace.

And a Greek – Diodorus, as it proved – coming to Kineas at the gallop from the ford.

'They're moving,' Diodorus panted.

Kineas rubbed his trimmed beard. 'They're going to fight now?'

Diodorus struggled to catch his breath. Memnon arrived. 'They're going north. The parley must have been to cover them. The whole army is in motion. There's cavalry as a screen – we were lucky. And they're tired. We got a glimpse.'

Kineas stretched as tall on his mount as he could, as if he could see farther. The last of the rain was blowing away in the east, but the visibility was still soft, and the middle distance of a few stades was already losing colour. 'North?' he said.

The reckless Sakje rider was coming to him. A stade away, Kineas could see it was Ataelus. His heartbeat quickened. He had a sense – almost the sense of his baqca dreams – of knowledge. Ataelus was coming from Heron. Heron was searching north. Diodorus said the Macedonians were marching north.

Kineas could see it – Zopryon's desperate lunge. *The desperate boar gores kings.*

Ataelus didn't bother to dismount. He pulled up so close that horse sweat showered his audience. 'Heron finds ford. North. And Macedon find ford too.'

Kineas felt the weight of the inevitable future clamp down. Another ford – with a wide shingle and a big dead tree, no doubt.

The ford was just north of their northernmost herds – just by the shrine of the river god. Ataelus said that it was as wide as four wagons and no deeper than a man's knees, and that there were Macedonians on the far side – just a handful, but more arriving – and that Heron was determined to hold the ford as long as he could.

Kineas didn't wait to hear it all. He turned to Memnon. 'I'm off to see the king. Take the phalanx and march immediately. You have to beat the taxeis in the race. They have a head start, but you have the inside track.'

Memnon nodded. 'They won't cross tonight.'

Kineas shook his head. 'They'll try. Go!'

He turned to his own officers. 'Eumenes – your men are the most rested. Every man take two horses. Mount all the Sindi. Ride like every one of you bestrides a Pegasus. Nicomedes – go with him as soon as your men can mount. I'll push the slaves to get a wagon in motion and you'll have a late dinner. Thirty stades?' he asked Ataelus.

Ataelus shrugged. 'An hour's ride.'

'Diodorus – pull your men back from the ford. Rest now. You'll ride with me in an hour.' Kineas looked around. 'We must win the race to the ford.'

They all nodded.

Kineas said, 'This is his last throw. This will be the battle. He's stolen a march – and we know he can march fast. Now we show what we can do.'

Philokles put a hand on his shoulder. 'Enough orders,' he said. 'See you at the ford.'

Kineas's news only served to reinforce what the king had already heard.

Marthax was blunt. 'Maybe the ford. Maybe not the ford.' He made a motion with his hand. 'We cannot allow him to march away – go south, go to Olbia.'

The king looked five years older. 'We're taking the Sakje across the river,' he said. 'We will follow him, crush his rear guard, impede his march.'

Kineas took a deep breath. 'He will have a three-hour head start. He will march all night. You won't catch him until morning. If I'm right, he'll be crossing.' Kineas ran a hand through his hair. 'We have the smaller army and we intend to divide it?'

The king shook his head. 'We have the faster army. We watch all of his motions and we rejoin to fight.'

Kineas shook his head. 'He may force you to fight on the sea of grass – and I'll be hours away, unable to help.'

Marthax's face was set. He spoke rapidly, and the king translated. 'We have no choice. If he gets ahead of us to Olbia, we've lost.'

Kineas could see that their minds were made up. They were tired – everyone was tired, and there was no time to talk. He thought about a battlefield he had never seen, except in a dream. He thought about the king, his friend – and rival. Riding away to leave him.

He knew what mattered now. After a moment's hesitation, he said, 'Leave me a clan – I can't hold the ford with the Greeks alone.' He was more afraid of how the Olbians would feel, waking to find that they alone were to bear the weight of Macedon.

The king frowned, but Marthax nodded. 'Grass Cats. Standing Horses. You keep both. You know chiefs. Grass Cats fight all days – tired. Not ride all night. Standing Horses take hardest fight yesterday.' He sent Ataelus for the chiefs. Through the king, he said, 'I think Zopryon will go to the ford. We will catch him two hours after dawn – I think. You hold him. We will catch him.' The other chiefs were hurrying up the hills, those that weren't already across the river, fighting. Kineas saw Srayanka, already mounted, giving orders to her household knights. Philokles ran by her at the head of his light-armed two hundred, setting out at a run, and even as he watched, Philokles lifted his spear to her, and she shrieked a war cry in return that was taken up by her clan. Eumenes' troop was already vanishing into the gloom. Nicomedes' men were mostly armed, and the slaves had two wagons loaded – the whole column was moving, with Memnon's heavy phalanx marching at the rear.

Kineas was proud of them.

Kaliax of the Standing Horse came first. He was nursing a badly cut arm, and he was pale, but he agreed to serve at Kineas's command. Varô of the Grass Cats looked better – he spoke quickly, still full of the daimon of the fight, and he spoke eloquently in Sakje of the day-long skirmish beyond the ford, the puncturing of the enemy screen, the discovery that the enemy camp was being packed.

Kineas tried to be patient, but his heart was with the Olbians, moving swiftly up the river. They might be fighting in an hour. Right or wrong, Kineas wanted to be there. He had the eye for the ground, and his was the voice that all of the other Greeks would obey – even Memnon.

It occurred to him that he might die today – this very evening, if the fight started immediately. He felt his stomach clench, and his heart race. It was here. Now.

He wanted to see Srayanka again. The last time. She was at the foot of the hill, just the length of a racecourse away.

Instead, he turned to Varô and Kaliax. 'There will be fighting at the river god's shrine by nightfall,' he said. 'It is an hour's ride for you. How soon can you come?'

Kaliax flexed his injured hand. 'Sunset,' he said.

Varô nodded. 'Some of my Cats are still across the ford. We'll need remounts – food. Sunset at best.'

Kineas nodded grimly. He hadn't hoped for any better. 'Come on my right flank,' he said. He had to search for the words, and after a minute of confusion and worry, he slid off his mount, walked to a campfire, grabbed a burnt stick and a scrap of linen that covered a pot despite the protests of the Sindi woman at the fire. He put the linen over his knee and drew. 'River,' he said. Then two lines at right angles, like a road. 'The ford and the shrine,' he said, and the two chiefs nodded. He sketched a block, a simple rectangle. 'The Greeks,' he said. And another, crossing the river. 'Macedon.'

Both chiefs nodded. Kineas's stick was out of charcoal. He walked back to the fire and chose another. He drew a line, and then a broad, curving arrow. 'You come north,' he said. 'Swing east, away from the river, along the ridge.'

Both men nodded. 'Sunset,' said Varô.

'Go with the gods,' said Kineas.

He could feel the thing moving – the whole course of events, the preliminary to the battle, sweeping along like the river in the king's story. He wanted his warhorse and armour; wanted to make sure the slaves had sufficient food for a hot meal for every one of the Greek allies – wanted to see Srayanka.

He had no time to talk to Srayanka.

He would probably never see her again.

He mounted, took one look at the column of Olbians vanishing into the deep grass along the river, and rode down the south side of the hill to where she sat her horse, one hand on her hip and the other holding her whip. She smiled at him. 'Now,' she said. 'Now you will see how we fight.'

Something in Kineas was too weary to talk. He had only come to say goodbye, but she was so *alive*, so like a goddess – the Poet often said that men and women were like gods in their best moments, and there she was.

He didn't want to die. He wanted to be with her for ever.

His silence, and something in his eye moved her. She leaned forward, threw her arms around him, pressed her cheek against his, so that he felt the warmth of her and the bite of her gold gorget against his neck.

'Tomorrow,' she said. 'I will find you, or you will find me, and the Sastar Baqca will be lifted.'

He thought of many things to say. He realized, because he was a brave man, that what he wanted was her comfort – and that the best thing he could give her was his silence about the dream, so that she would ride to her battle with her hope un-diminished. He pressed her to him.

'You shaved,' she said, patting his cheek as their horses pulled them apart.

'Always look your best for battle,' he said. 'It's a Greek tradition.' He tried for humour, but she nodded seriously.

With that inane exchange, they parted. They were command-ers – they had roles to play.

Kineas looked at her one more time – and she was looking at him. Her eyes – across a widening length of grass – and then she turned to bark an order. He took a deep breath, and rode for the horse lines.

22

Arni had the command of all the slaves. The wagons were moving, and the remounts were coming along, but Arni had Kineas's warhorse ready, and stood at the animal's head, despite his other responsibilities.

'Master ordered me,' he said. He gave his lopsided smile. 'Blankets and gear with the baggage. Here's both your best javelins – and your armour. Clean chiton – Ajax said your best. So it's your best.'

Kineas grinned, his heart was lifted by seeing Srayanka, and because part of him didn't believe in fated death, and because, right or wrong, he'd planned the summer away for this battle, and it was his. He slid off his mount. It took too long to change his tunic, too long to get his feet comfortable in the long boots of the heavy cavalryman, too long to close his breastplate and tie his sash. Upriver, they might be dying now.

He took his fancy gilt helmet and put it on the back of his head, and threw his best cloak – blue as her eyes – over his shoulder.

'Start the fires as soon as you come up,' Kineas said to Arni. 'Choose the camp yourself. You've seen it done often enough. Get there in time to feed us, and I'll see you a free man. Tell your men – if we win, every one of you will be free.'

'My master said the same,' Arni said with satisfaction.

Diodorus came up with his helmet on. 'Ready,' he said. He gave Kineas half a smile. He was exhausted – and so would his men be.

Not as tired as the Macedonians, he reminded himself.

Kineas relinquished the reins of his best riding horse to Arni and mounted Thanatos. 'Pick a good camp,' he said, and set the stallion to run.

It was easy to follow the army. They had beaten a road in the tall grass as wide as Memnon's phalanx. It ran along the river for a few stades and then went straight as a bowstring at a tangent, cutting across the long sweep of the bend.

Kineas was impatient of the speed of Diodorus's troop. He forgave them their fatigue – they'd earned it – but he needed to *be there*. He found himself pulling ahead, and finally, he turned, rode back to Diodorus, and shook his head. 'Pardon me, old friend. I have to go.'

Diodorus waved. Kineas pointed with his whip at Niceas, and the two of them set off at a gallop.

He caught the phalanx at the top of the ridge that dominated the river valley. He waved to Memnon and kept going. Memnon would not expect a chat. He rode down the ridge, passing the first wagons that Arni had dispatched where they were delayed by soft ground. Men were cutting brush and tying it in bundles to hold the weight of the wagons. Kineas rode on. Beyond, the bulk of the phalanx of Pantecapaeum was clear of the marshy ground and there were officers shouting at them to close up, close up. Men were taking their shields off their backs and putting them on their arms.

Battle was close.

From here, on the last heights of the ridge, Kineas could see that there was fighting at the ford. Archers were firing on both sides, and there were bodies on the ground. He could see his own cavalry formed well clear of the ford itself, and he could see a body of infantry – it had to be Philokles – running up to form a line, stragglers trailing away behind them. Few men could run thirty stades over bad ground without pausing, even after a life of training. They might be so tired from the run that they'd be useless in a fight – but they were there.

Niceas pulled up behind him. 'Orders?' he asked. He looked calm, but one hand beat at his trumpet and the other was at his neck, rubbing at the smooth face of his owl. His horse dropped its head and its sides heaved. Kineas's stallion's head was up and alert – he appeared as though he'd gone for a walk.

Kineas patted his neck. 'You, my friend, are a champion.' He looked back at the chaos around the wagons and Memnon's phalanx behind. He shook his head. 'Tell Memnon to leave a few files to help the wagons and press on,' he said. 'I'm going down.'

From here, the whole field was clear. The river god's shrine was a cairn that stood on a short isthmus that stuck into the stream near the ford like the thumb on a wrestler's hand. The thumb and all the ground around it where it met the main bank were thick with big, old trees – oaks and big willows. Just north – upstream – of the thumb was the ford – in the light of the setting sun, the ford was obvious, perhaps because there were slingers standing in it to cast, but the water flowed, wide and shallow, and logs and a big rock betrayed the path of the ford. East of the ford, on the near bank, the river's floodplain stretched for stades – hard to judge in the red light of evening, but the grass was short, and the ground flat and damp.

The ford was half a stade wide, and the far side was as flat as the near side – flat and treeless. Perfect ground for the taxeis. There wasn't a sign of the Macedonian main body, and he could see for ten stades. He saw cavalry, and some peltasts, and men in cloaks – Thrake, he suspected.

He took one last look and pushed Thanatos down the last of the rise, through the reeds at the edge of the marsh that dominated the south end of the floodplain, and up a short rise on to the firmer grass along the river. He rode looking at the ground. His stallion's hooves squelched as he cantered, but it was firm enough under the surface water – and it would be drier tomorrow.

He cantered easily across the front of Philokles' two hundred – and they cheered. He raised his fist to them in salute as he rode past. He rode up to Nicomedes, who sat with Ajax in front of the line.

Nicomedes looked very fine – clean, neat, and calm – but the strength of his handclasp displayed his nerves. 'By all the gods, Kineas – I've never been so glad to see any man.' He grinned. 'Command of armies? You can have it. I've been in command an hour and I've aged a year.'

Ajax tipped his helmet back. 'He was cautious,' he said as a tease. Behind him, Heron trotted up to the command group and saluted. Kineas returned the salute and rode over to the gangly young man. 'Well done, sir. Well done.'

Heron stared at his hands. When he met Kineas's eye, his own were bright. 'Did my best,' he said. 'All I did was listen to your veterans.'

Niceas laughed. 'The world's full of men stupid enough to fuck that up,' he said gruffly. 'Take the hipparch's praise – you earned it.'

Kineas slapped his back, and his hand rang on the other man's armour. 'Well done,' he said again, and transferred his attention to Nicomedes.

Nicomedes pointed to the ford. 'I refused to be tempted into a fight in the water. If their slingers want to engage our Sindi, so be it. The Sindi seem happy enough with the fight, and none of us are being hurt.'

Kineas nodded curtly. 'You were correct. We only need to hold. I think they will try one rush before sunset.' He glanced at the line. Many of Philokles' men were down on their knees, or leaning to the ground, breathing hard – but more of them were already standing tall, shields resting on their insteps, spears in hand.

Kineas gestured to Eumenes, who rode up immediately. 'Who have you appointed as your hyperetes?' he asked.

'Cliomenedes,' Eumenes replied. Indeed, the boy was right behind him. The youngest of the boys who had made the winter ride – probably still among the youngest in the troop. Yet Kineas had seen his sword at work among the Getae – he wasn't really a boy.

'Very well. Take your troop to the south of Philokles, and cover his left flank. If we are pushed off the river bank, we retire south – so you will be the pivot. Nicomedes – where are the Sindi – at the shrine?'

'Yes. They went into the trees, and now all that comes out is arrows.' Nicomedes laughed with a nervous edge.

Kineas nodded. 'We'll leave them there.' He looked to the south and east to find Memnon's column. They were coming slowly across the marsh. Kineas gestured with his whip at Philokles, and then led the mounted officers towards the Spartan to reach him faster. He rubbed his beard, looked across the river again, felt his heartbeat increase, and reined in his horse with Philokles at his feet.

'They'll try for us in a few minutes, gentlemen. Philokles, those are Thrake; peltasts, really, but with big swords. They'll come for you at a rush, their flanks covered by the cavalry.'

Philokles had his big Corinthian helmet on the back of his head. He looked himself – a big, pleasant man. The philosopher. But when he spoke, he sounded like Ares.

'We'll stop them right here,' he said. 'I have never fought them myself – but I know them by repute. Only their first charge is worth a crap.' He smiled, and it was the sarcastic smile of Philokles. 'I think we can manage them.'

Kineas caught the eye of his cavalry officers and pointed at the very slight rise in the ground to the south. 'If we are broken, we rally to the south. Let the Thrake come – Philokles will hold them. When their cavalry comes across, they will be badly ordered – let them get across, and then charge them *before* they form. Look to me for the timing, but don't fear to make your own call. I'll ride with the infantry.'

In fact, it felt odd to be sitting on a horse, well clear of the front line, giving orders. But that was his work, now.

He rode back to the small phalanx – really, more like a hand-ful of *peltastoi*, with Philokles. The big Spartan gave him one grin, and then tipped his helmet back down on his head, and ran to the front of his men. He pointed across the river, and the two hundred gave a cheer like a thousand men, a cheer that sent a surge of energy through Kineas like a beneficial lightning bolt.

Across the river, the Macedonian slingers were retreating. On the far bank, clear in the fading light, Kineas could see the Thrake and the cavalry. And beyond them, *something*. It was hard to measure distance, and harder to detect troops moving on wet ground, without dust – but there was something there. A taxeis perhaps – still a few stades away.

The Thrake bellowed a cheer, and then another, and they raised their shields. There were quite a few of them. They beat their big swords against their shields, and they began a chant. Then they started across the ford. They kept no kind of order, and their ranks spread as they crossed.

Kineas had dismissed the handful of Sindi – the blacksmith's men – as unimportant, but from their position on the thumb, immune to the Thrake and unafraid, they shot arrows right into the side of the charge. The Thrake flinched away from the thumb, crowded to the north side of the ford and came up the bank too slowly, with much of the impetus of their charge lost to the water and the arrows. A chief rallied them at the river's edge, and led them forward – a hundred or more – and they crashed into the front of Philokles' men with a noise like a dozen blacksmiths working on as many forges. The chief leaped – a fantastic move – straight from the run of his charge up to the rim of the shield wall and then down, his long sword taking a Greek head even as he fell, but four spears pierced him before his body came to rest and the gap that he opened was filled in three thuds of Kineas's heart with dead men, Greek and Thrake, and then the *epilektoi* pushed from the second rank, and the wound in the phalanx was healed as they closed their shields.

More Thrake were coming up the river bank – every man seemed to make his own decision, and some ran off towards the base of the thumb, to end the galling fire of the archers, while others threw themselves into the fight in front of them.

Kineas tore his eyes away from the fight to watch the enemy cavalry. They were trapped in the ford – now they were the victims of the deadly archery, and they couldn't push forward because of the crowd of Thrake.

The width of an Athenian street away, Philokles' plume showed in the front rank, and his roar shook the air. Kineas saw the great black spear rise and fall – back and forth, held one-handed on the Spartan's shoulder, and he punched with it as if it had no weight – back and forth, like a machine for killing men. He was not alone – he was at the corner of his threatened line – yet he killed five men in as many breaths, the great black spear shooting forward with brutal economy, straight through a nose, into a mouth, into the soft flesh under a man's chin – and out, the broad blade never sinking past its greatest width. Philokles' arm was black at the hand, red as high as his shoulder, and he was red down his side where the blood of other men ran down his naked skin. Even as Kineas watched, the Greek line solidified, and Philokles' roar was answered by a push – a heave that threw the Thrake back on their heels, some men actually falling to the ground, and the line stepped over them, and spears in the rear rank rose and fell, the whole phalanx like a loom weaving death.

The Thrake broke. They were being massacred against the round shields, the strength of their charge was spent, and fear took them. They broke and fled into the ford, already choked with latecomers and their own cavalry supports.

Kineas rode up next to Philokles, who was leading his men forward. They were singing, and Kineas had to bellow to be heard. 'Halt!' he yelled. He poked Philokles' helmet with the butt of his javelin. 'Halt!'

The black spear whirled, and the butt-spite paused a fraction of a foot away from his face. Philokles glared at him with dull recognition. He shouted. His pipe player shrilled a call, and the victorious men of Pantecapaeum stopped. Kineas whirled his mount, put his heels to the stallion's flanks, and raced to Eumenes.

'Now!' he yelled. 'Into the ford!'

Eumenes wasn't ready. Clearly, he had been waiting for the fight to develop as Kineas had predicted.

It hadn't. Kineas had expected the rush of Thrake to push Philokles' little band back, to give the trap space to develop. Philokles' victory had happened too fast.

'Now!' Kineas bellowed.

Eumenes waved at Cliop. 'Sound: Advance!' he called.

Kineas rode away, wishing for Niceas. This was too slow – the trap would never be sprung, now. The men of Pantecapaeum had fought too well, and the Thrake had broken too soon. He waved to Nicomedes – harder to see now.

Nicomedes started for the ford, but halted before Kineas reached him.

There wasn't room for both troops abreast. Eumenes' men swept by, already at a gallop, and hit the river in a spray of water.

'Reform the line!' Kineas yelled. He waved with his sword, and Nicomedes led his cavalry back the little distance they had advanced. Philokles' men walked backwards, their shields to the enemy. Heron's troop had never advanced – they were too far to the flank to even see the fighting.

Niceas rode up. 'We'll have a camp in an hour,' he said. He pointed at the ford. 'What's that?'

Kineas shook his head. 'A trap gone wrong,' he said. 'Sound the recall.' Out in the ford, Eumenes' men were killing fugitive Thrake, but the enemy cavalry were already formed on the far bank.

Eumenes' men returned in good order, the sting of their rout expunged, and the ford was full of dead men, but the actual damage inflicted on the enemy was slight. He peered into the dusk, trying to read what lay on the other side of the ford. He felt that a taxeis had come up, but he saw no proof.

Behind him, on the ridge, a fire winked into life, and then another.

Memnon's column marched on to the edge of the dry ground and began to form.

Kineas watched the ford. He praised the men, riding along the line. He took the time to manoeuvre Memnon into the line, right in the centre, facing the ford, with the main phalanx of Pantecapaeum on his right and the epilektoi under Philokles on his left, and the cavalry covering their flanks. By the time they were all in line, Kineas couldn't see across the river. And there were fires all along the slope of the ridge behind him.

He gathered his officers again, and sent Niceas to get the Sindi blacksmith from his fortress of trees. When they were all present, he saluted them.

'We stopped them,' he said. 'We won the race. We almost hurt them badly. Now we have to hold them until the king comes.' He looked around in the last light at all the faces – new men and old friends. And Philokles – he couldn't adapt to Philokles as a killer.

'This is my plan. The whole army will retire to the ridge, to camp and eat. We'll hold the ford with a rotation of pickets – cavalry and infantry in every watch, four watches. But ...' He looked around, gathering eyes, making sure he had their attention. 'When they come, we give them the ford. I think they'll come at dawn – they'll push a whole taxeis across at a rush. Let them come.' He pointed to Temerix, who stood a little apart. 'You have enough arrows?' he asked in Sakje.

The blacksmith laughed. 'All we do for day and day is cut arrows,' he said.

'Can you hold the shrine? All night, and as long as you can in the day?' Kineas asked.

The blacksmith shrugged. 'I am your man,' he said. 'And I came here to die. River god's shrine is good place for man to die.'

Kineas shook his head, too tired to argue about ordering a man to his death. 'Don't die,' he said. 'Just hold it until they get across, and run to us.' He looked around the circle. 'The rest of you – form just as we are formed now, but here – at the edge of the marsh. We push up the little rise – that's our line.'

'With our flank on the river,' Philokles said. 'And the other flank in air.'

Kineas shook his head and pointed to the ridge. Even in the near darkness the silhouettes of riders were visible. 'Our friends from the Grass Cats and the Standing Horses will take care of the open flank,' he said. 'We let Zopryon – if he's here – come across. He'll be at right angles to our line – a terrible position to start a battle. He'll use more time to reform his line. And he'll have no way to expect it – which will cost him time. We advance at my word – and we'll pin them against the river.' He gave a small smile. 'Until they get their second taxies across – and then we give ground.' He motioned over his shoulder. 'We have a great deal of ground to give, gentlemen – about thirty stades. Stay together, keep the line, and don't get routed. As far as I am concerned, we can spend all day retreating. I want to hurt him early on, and then retreat until the king comes. That's all. And tonight – eat well, and sleep.'

They nodded – laughed a little. Their spirits were soaring.

Kineas mounted Thanatos again, and spared the ford one more look. It was lost in the darkness. The Macedonians had fires now, too.

Then he rode back to camp.

They cosseted him – the Sindi, the slaves, his comrades. His kit was already laid out, and he had a tent, ready pitched – the only tent among the hippeis, on a fine summer night with the stars like a canopy of glory across the sky. His cloak and armour vanished as soon as he had them off, and a bowl of cheese and meat and bread was put in his hands. Philokles came to the fire, the blood washed from his arms and side, wearing a tunic. He had a Spartan cup brimming with strong, unwatered wine, which he set on a rock by Kineas's hand. Just beyond the periphery of his vision, Arni and Sitalkes worked together on Thanatos, washing the mud from his legs, brushing the dirt and sweat from his coat, and he stood calmly enough and bore their attentions.

And beyond Thanatos, a hundred fires rose into the dark, towers of light and smoke from wood carefully gathered by slaves and free men, and at every fire, messes of horsemen and hoplites ate hot food and stared into the flames and thought about what morning would bring.

The old comrades – Lykeles and Laertes and Coenus and all the rest – came to his fire from their separate troops, and sat in a circle, but they left space for newer comrades; Eumenes was there, Ajax and Nicomedes, and Clio, hovering uncertainly around the edge of the firelight until Coenus, who had taught the boy all winter, waved him to the fire.

They were silent for a time. Kineas ate his food and drank the wine in silence, his eyes on the column of fire rising into the night. Sitalkes finished the big stallion to his own satisfaction and Arni took the horse away to the picket lines in the darkness, and the Getae boy – now a man, and a tall man at that – came and sat by Ajax.

Agis rose to his feet and cleared his throat, and hummed a little to himself – an agora ditty from Olbia. Then he bowed his head, raised it, and said:

'As through the deep glens of a parched mountain-side rageth wondrous-blazing fire, and the deep forest burneth, and the wind as it driveth it on whirleth the flame every whither, even so raged he every whither with his spear, like some god, ever pressing hard upon them that he slew; and the black earth ran with blood.

And as a man yoketh bulls broad of brow to tread

421

white barley in a well-ordered threshing-floor, and quickly is the grain trodden out beneath the feet of the loud-bellowing bulls; even so beneath great-souled Achilles his single-hooved horses trampled alike on the dead and on the shields; and with blood was all the axle sprinkled beneath, and the rims round about the car, for drops smote upon them from the horses' hooves and from the tyres. But the son of Peleas pressed on to win him glory, and with gore were his invincible hands bespattered ...'

And Agis continued the story until:

'Then the son of Peleas uttered a bitter cry, with a look at the broad heaven: "Father Zeus, how is it that not one of the gods taketh it upon him in my pitiless plight to save me from out the River? Thereafter let come upon me what may.

"None other of the heavenly gods do I blame so much, but only my dear mother, that beguiled me with false words, saying that beneath the wall of the mail-clad Trojans I should perish by the swift missiles of Apollo. Would that Hector had slain me, the best of the men bred here; then had a brave man been the slayer, and a brave man had he slain. But now by a miserable death was it appointed me to be cut off, pent in the great river, like a swine-herd boy whom a torrent sweepeth away as he maketh essay to cross it in winter."

So spake he, and forthwith Poseidon and Pallas Athene drew nigh and stood by his side, being likened in form to mortal men, and they clasped his hand in theirs and pledged him in words. And among them Poseidon, the Shaker of Earth, was first to speak: "Son of Peleas, tremble not thou overmuch, neither be anywise afraid, such helpers twain are we from the god – and Zeus approveth thereof – even I and Pallas Athene. Therefore is it not thy doom to be vanquished by a river; nay, he shall soon give respite, and thou of thyself shalt know it. But we will give thee wise counsel, if so be thou wilt hearken. Make not thine hands to cease from evil battle until within the framed walls of Ilios thou hast pent the Trojan host, whosoever escapeth. But for thyself, when thou hast bereft Hector of life, come thou back to the ships; lo, we grant thee to win glory.'"

He stopped there, well short of the death of Hector, declaiming that part of the tale brought men ill luck. When he bowed his head to show that he was done, the space beyond the fire was black with men standing in silence to hear him. And there was silence, thick and black as night, when he was done, as if by staying perfectly still, they could win more words from him, but he bowed his head again, and went back to his place, and sat. Then the men beyond the firelight sighed, and the sound was like the wind in tall trees.

Kineas stood, and offered libation to all the gods from Philokles' cup and their dwindling store of wine. He raised his voice and sang, 'I begin to sing about Poseidon …' And every man in earshot responded, and they all sang together.

'The great god, mover of the earth and fruitless sea,
God of the deep who is also lord of Helicon
And wide Aegae.
A two-fold office the gods allotted you,
O Shaker of the Earth,
To be a tamer of horses and a saviour of ships!
Hail, Poseidon, Holder of the Earth,
Dark-haired lord!
O blessed one, be kindly in heart and
Help those who ride on horses!'

Kineas had at his feet a wreath of oak leaves, made by Ajax and Eumenes working together by firelight. When the hymn was done, he lifted it from the ground, walked across the fire circle, and placed it without further words on the brow of Philokles.

When the wreath touched the Spartan, they roared, a single long note. And then the men were silent, feeling the nearness of the gods, and of death.

Niceas broke the silence, walking up to Agis. He put a hand on Agis's shoulder. 'Better than Guagemala,' he said.

Agis shrugged, clearly drained. 'When it comes to me,' he said, 'it is like a spirit speaks through me, or a god. I am no actor, and sometimes I can't believe that I can remember the passage.'

The other men who had known him for years all nodded. Even Kineas thought that the Megaran was god-touched.

But Ajax smiled. In the bright sun of battle, that boy was altogether gone, but he was beautiful in the firelight, and in his face lingered the boy who had followed them off to war from his father's house. 'I love to hear the Poet,' he said. 'It is almost – like the hymn, to listen on such a night, and the eve of battle?'

Nicomedes rolled his eyes, and Philokles gave a snort, almost the bray of a donkey, and Ajax's head went back in resentment.

'The Poet knew war,' Philokles said. 'And he did *not* love it. He told a great tale – the tale of one man's rage, and through that rage, the tale of what war is. Ajax, you are no longer a virgin.' A rude chuckle from the fire. 'War is madness, like the rage of Achilles.'

Ajax's chin was still up, and his voice was strong. 'Every man here made war today,' he said. 'You, Philokles, were a hero risen from the very lines of the Poet.'

Philokles stood up, and on his head sat the wreath, a crown of valour, and he seemed the tallest man at the fire, red and gold in the firelight. 'War makes men beasts,' he said. 'I fight like a wise and cunning beast – a predator. I killed nine men today – or perhaps ten.' He shrugged, and seemed to shrink. 'A wolf might say as much. And a wolf would stop killing when his hunger was sated. Only a *man* kills without need.'

Ajax, stung, said, 'If you hate it so, you need not fight!'

Philokles shook his head. The firelight played tricks with his face – his body was red and gold, but his face had black hollows for eyes, and his grin raised the hair on Kineas's neck. 'Hate it?' he said through his grin. 'Hate it? I love it like a drunkard loves wine – and like the drunkard, I prate about it when I'm sober.' He turned away, and plunged through the circle into the darkness beyond.

Kineas followed on his heels. He followed the Spartan along the ridge, past a campfire of Olbian hoplites, and then another, and down the hill a ways, stumbling on the uneven ground in the dark until he saw the pale shape of his friend's back settle. Philokles was sitting on a great rock that stuck up from the ground like an old man's last tooth. Kineas sat next to him.

'I am an ass,' Philokles said.

Kineas, who had seen a great deal of bad behaviour on the night before battle, punched the Spartan in the arm. 'Yes,' he said.

'He keeps his eyes so tightly closed to the horror. He wants war to be like the poem – he doesn't see how often they crash to the dusty earth clutching their guts.' Philokles' voice was soft. 'It is easy to kill a man, or a city, yes?'

'Too damned easy,' Kineas said.

Philokles nodded, talking to himself as much as to Kineas. 'If you train your whole life to be a warrior – offering nothing to the gods, learning no poet, perhaps even illiterate – you might make a superb killing man. Yes?'

Kineas nodded, unsure where the Spartan was going with his argument.

'You might be the finest fighter in the world. Deadly with a sword, deadly with a spear, mounted, on foot, with a rock, with a club, however you chose to fight. And you might spend all of your money on equipment for it – armour, shields, swords, the best of everything. Yes?'

'I'm sure you're going somewhere with this,' Kineas said, but his attempt to lighten the tone failed.

Philokles grabbed him by both shoulders. 'Just so that you could protect yourself, because it is so *easy* to be killed. You could imagine every threat that might come against you – every man who wanted your purse, every man who sought to steal your horse, or your armour. You might live your life in a wilderness, to be able to see the enemy coming – or perhaps you would fight for power, so that you could bid other men to protect you.'

'Like a tyrant,' Kineas said, because he thought he understood.

'Perhaps,' Philokles said dismissively. 'Because my point is that you can live like that – you can spend your entire life on security, either as a man or as a city. And a child with a sling stone can kill you dead in a moment. There you are – dead – and you have lived a life without a single virtue, except possibly courage – you are illiterate, brutish, and dead.'

Kineas began to see. 'Or?'

Philokles looked out over the water. 'Or you can live a life of virtue, so that men seek to protect you, or emulate you, or join you.'

Kineas thought about it for a moment, and then said, 'And yet we killed Socrates.'

Philokles turned back to him, his eyes sparkling. 'Socrates killed himself rather than relinquish virtue.' He made a rhetorical gesture, like a man about to speak before the assembly. 'The only armour is virtue. And the only excuse for violence is in the defence of virtue, and then, if we die, we die with virtue.'

Kineas allowed a slow smile to creep over his face. 'Now I think I know why I haven't heard of other *Spartan* philosophers.'

Philokles nodded. 'We're a violent lot. And it's always easier to die defending virtue than to live virtuously.'

Kineas had heard a great deal of philosophy in the hours before battle-dawns, but Philokles made more sense than the others. He gripped his hand. 'I think you and Ajax have more in common than you would have me believe.'

Philokles grunted.

'He's an ass, too. Listen to me, brother. I have a favour to ask.' Kineas's voice was light, but he put an arm around Philokles – a gesture he seldom made.

'Of course.'

'On the night before battle, I like to listen to Agis, and then I like to hear the voices of my friends. Because you are right – but tonight, we are not beasts. We are men. Come with me, back to the fire.'

426

Philokles had tears in his eyes that glittered like jewels in the moonlight. He wiped his eyes, and his fist brushed against the wreath in his hair. 'Why did you give me this thing?' he asked. 'I am no hero.'

Kineas pushed him off the rock, and the two climbed up the hill, their feet loud on the hard turf, so that Philokles might never have heard Kineas's reponse.

'Yes, you are,' Kineas said, but very softly.

23

And later that night before battle, they circled back round to the same again. Ajax couldn't leave war alone. Kineas, who had commanded men for too many years, knew that Ajax sought to justify on the eve of battle, the death he would face, and wreak, with the dawn.

'If we are beasts,' he said, after brooding for an hour, while the others spoke, and sang, and Lykeles danced a Spartan military dance to Philokles' astonishment. 'If we are beasts, how do we plan so carefully?'

Kineas leaned past Philokles, determined to avert disaster. 'Which plan of mine have you known to carry through the battle?' he asked.

Niceas laughed with the other veterans. Nicomedes glanced at Ajax as if embarrassed for his friend's bad manners – and kicked his outstretched ankle.

Ajax shook his head. 'We plan,' he began again, and something exploded in Kineas.

'It's a fucking shambles!' he said, too loud, silencing other conversations. 'Madness! Chaos!' He pointed at Ajax. 'You know better! You have seen the animal, night and day, for months. A man has to be in the grip of a delusion to believe that order can be imposed on war!'

Philokles put his hand on Kineas's shoulder. Ajax was recoiling, leaning away from Kineas as if his commander might strike him. Philokles spoke softly. 'We plan for war – to mitigate the chaos. We train so that our muscles will move in a certain sequence when our minds fall to panic and we become as beasts. In Sparta we perfect the making of men into automata.'

Nicomedes rose to his friend's defence. 'A dance troupe does the same, and so does a chorus – they train and train, so that they will automatically do what is right. But they are not beasts.'

Ajax was almost pleading. 'You,' he said, pointing across the fire at Niceas and Antigonus, at Lykeles and Coenus and

Andronicus, and all the old comrades. 'You are all men of war. Do you truly hate it?'

Philokles began to stand, but Antigonus rose to his feet – Antigonus, who never spoke in public, because he was ashamed of his bad Greek. He was a big man, covered in scars. He had fought his whole life, and he looked the part.

He liked Ajax – loved him, as they all did – and he gave the young man a smile that no one could resent. 'Somewhere,' he said in his bad Greek, 'there is a man so bestial that on the eve of a great battle, he proclaims his love for war.' Antigonus gave a rueful smile. 'I fear death too much to love war. But I love my comrades, so I will not flinch. That is all I can give, and all any comrade can ask.' He held aloft a skin, and shook it so that they could hear it slosh. 'No good will come if we talk of war tonight. I have wine. Let's drink.'

Memnon, who most often professed his love of war, smiled, took a drink, and stayed silent.

Later, Kineas, who wanted no anger on his conscience on his last night, went and flopped on the ground by Ajax. 'I snapped at you,' he said, 'because I, too, am afraid of death, and you seem immune.'

Ajax embraced him. 'How can they say such things?' he asked. 'When they are so like the heroes themselves?'

Kineas's eyes were suddenly hot with tears. 'They are better than the Poet's heroes,' he said. 'And they speak the truth.'

Wine and song, and the company of his friends, kept thoughts of death and the absence of Srayanka at bay until they went to their cloaks. Kineas walked among the fires, saying a few words to men who lingered awake, and then, spent, circled back to his own. As it chanced, Kineas chose not to lie in his tent alone, but threw his cloak next to Philokles, and found Ajax on his other side, as if a year had vanished from their lives and they were crossing the plains north of Tomis. He smiled at the warmth of his friends, and before death could haunt him, he was asleep.

But death caught him later, in his dreams.

He was wet with blood, and beneath him flowed a river of the stuff, and it smelled like every festered wound he had ever known, septic and evil, and he climbed to drag his body clear of the corruption. His hands were on the tree, his feet clear of the roots, and he climbed, wishing to take the form of an owl and fly free, but the blood on his hands prevented him somehow, and all he could do was climb. He thought that if he climbed high enough, he might see across the river, count the fires of the enemy, or see the worm, and know … He couldn't remember what he wanted to know. He climbed, bewildered, and the blood on his hands ran down his arms, and from his arms down his sides, and it burned where it touched fresh skin, burned like salt water on sunburn.

Sunburn on his face, clear of the water, salt in his eyes, and his hands tangled in the mane of the great horse, the water dragging at his legs and his heavy breastplate pressing him down at every attempt to mount.

A weapon rang off his helmet, turning it so that he was blind. A blade scored across his upper arm, scraped across the bronze of his cuirass and then bit into his bridle arm. The grey startled, bolted forward and dragged him out of the stream and up the bank he had so recently left, hanging from her mane, which panicked her so that she tossed her mighty head. Luck, and the strength of her neck, dragged him a hand's breadth higher than his best effort had reached before, so that he got a knee over her broad back.

He glanced around, and all the warriors behind him were strange – all Sakje, in magnificent armour, and he himself wore a vambrace of chased gold on the arm he could see through the slits of his helmet – he was dry, sitting tall on a horse the colour of dark metal, and the battle was won, the enemy broken, and across the river, the enemy tried to rally in the driftwood and by the single old dead tree that offered the only cover from their arrows, and he raised her whip, motioned three times, and they all began to cross the river.

He was ready for the arrow when it came, and he almost greeted it, he knew it so well, and then he was in the water – hands grabbing at him …

Again. He woke because Ajax was shaking him. 'That was an evil dream,' Ajax said.

Kineas had thrown his cloak free of his legs in his sleep. He was cold. Philokles had rolled away – probably looking for a quieter partner. A glance at the stars and the moon told him that he had slept well enough, and that dawn was less than an hour away. He rose. Ajax rose with him. Kineas pushed at him. 'You have an hour,' he said.

Ajax hung his head. 'I cannot sleep,' he said.

Kineas pushed him back down and threw his own old cloak over the younger man. 'It's a magic cloak,' he said. 'You'll sleep now.'

His fire was burning bright, and a dozen Grass Cats lay around it while two troop slaves heated water in a bronze kettle. One of the slaves handed him a bowl and he took it in silence, wolfed down the contents – odd, how the body continued the tyranny of its needs even when he had only hours left to live. He threw on a cloak and picked up a javelin – not even his own.

He felt very alive. He felt tall and strong, free. Even the fear of the last month – the fear of death, the fear of failure, the fears of love – were far away.

He walked to the horse lines and caught Thanatos. The horse was restless, and Kineas fed him carefully, whispering to him in the dark, and then mounted him bareback and rode down the ridge to the marsh, and across the marsh. A handful of Grass Cats greeted him – they were alert, and they all pointed across the river.

Something in the dark – lots of motion, and a steady hum of noise. The noise of an army. Kineas rode right down to the water's edge, the Grass Cats hard at his heels. No arrows whistled out of the dark. He could hear the hum even over the river noises.

Dawn was just two streaks of purple-pink against the dark sky, but already there was more light.

He had to know if Zopryon was there. And he suspected that they would be in a state of chaos as their column formed up. He pushed his horse into the stream.

One of the Grass Cats laughed, fear and delight mingled in a single giggle, and all of them slid into the water, their splashes covered by the steady cacophony on the far bank. Midstream, and they were still undetected.

Kineas felt a wild spirit rise in him – as if a god had dared him – and he pushed his horse forward, and the big stallion responded, rising from the water like Poseidon's own son and springing to a gallop in a few strides.

A man shouted, his guttural Macedonian clear in the dark, 'Who the fuck is that?'

'Scouts!' called Kineas. Thanatos's hooves were on solid ground now. He could see the head of column, men with their shields propped against their legs and their enormous pikes planted erect in the ground, and other men with torches. Relief washed over him. Win or lose – he had been right. The taxeis were here. Zopryon was here.

He galloped at the front of the phalanx. Men looked up – a little fearful in the dark, but hardly panicked. He put his javelin into a man who looked like an officer and turned Thanatos on his haunches. He saw all of the Grass Cats shooting, drawing and loosing and drawing and loosing with smooth and deadly efficiency, and then he put the stallion at the river. Behind him, he heard the Grass Cats laughing. The air was full of arrows in the dark, coming from both banks. Kineas kept his body low, and something passed a few inches from his face. The stallion hesitated a moment on the far bank and then they were up, safe. One of the Grass Cats had an arrow through his bicep, and another warrior, a woman, cut the head free and pulled the shaft out through the entry hole – all in a few strides of their mounts, without stopping.

Kineas had to prod Thanatos to turn – he was suddenly sluggish. He reined in at the base of the thumb, and Temerix emerged from the dark foliage at his call.

'Hold as long as you can. They'll come in half an hour. Then run back south before they cut you off. Understand?'

Temerix leaned on his axe, and the shadow hid his eyes. 'Yes, Lord.'

Kineas's horse was already in motion. 'I am not your lord,' he called over his shoulder. He thought guiltily that he had never arranged for the Sindi refugees to meet with Srayanka. Another task left uncompleted.

The stallion made such heavy work of climbing the ridge that Kineas dismounted and checked his hooves for stones, but they were clear. The animal's eyes were wild, and Kineas put a hand on his neck. 'Today,' he said. Then he remounted, and the horse finished the climb.

Kineas went straight to his own fire, where most of the officers were waiting. The light was already bright enough to show them the points of the Macedonian pikes across the river.

Memnon swatted him as soon as he dismounted. 'Are you a boy, or a strategist? Ares' prick, that was a stupid thing to do!' He grinned. 'Of course, since you lived, and since every spear in the army watched you do it, they'll all think you are a god.'

Kineas's face was red. He couldn't explain what had driven him across the river.

Niceas just shook his head. 'I thought I taught you better than that,' he said.

Ajax's eyes sparkled.

Philokles glared.

Ataelus came up mounted, and pointed to the south and east. 'Kam Baqca,' he said. 'And some friends.' He leaned down from the saddle. 'The Grass Cats say you airyanắm.'

Niceas touched his amulet and downed some tea. 'The Grass Cats are idiots, too.'

Kam Baqca came up the ridge in the full regalia of a priestess, with a high helmet of gold, topped by a fantastic winged animal. She had a gorget and scale armour all covered in gold, and she wore it over a hide coat of unblemished white. She rode a dapple grey mare, and behind her came another rider as magnificent, carrying the royal standard that should have been out on the plain with the king. The standard was a tall pole decorated with bronze birds and horsetails, and it was covered in bells that made an eerie noise like waves of the sea as she moved.

With her were half a hundred men and women as well armed and armoured as she. Every horse had a headdress that made the animal look like a fantastic beast – horn and leather worked to give each horse antlers and a crest of hair, and their horses, where their skin showed beneath all the armour, were painted red. Their manes were filled with mud and had dried erect. Most of the horses had scale armour of gold and bronze like the warriors, so that they might have been griffons or dragons born from myths.

They were the most barbaric sight Kineas had ever seen.

Behind them came Petrocolus, and the last troop of Olbian horse.

In the wedge of time before the fresh cavalry arrived, Kineas issued his orders, or rather, reviewed them. At his feet, they were already being carried out. Licurgus was forming the Olbian phalanx at the edge of the marsh, and the men of the main force of Pantecapaeum were filing down the hill and over the marsh, forming up as soon as they were clear of the wet ground.

Petrocolus came up on his right hand. He looked down the hill under his hand, and then saluted. 'We're in time,' he said wearily.

'A late guest is still a welcome guest,' Kineas said. He offered his hand and they clasped.

'We tried to catch Cleomenes,' Petrocolus said with a shrug.

'He made it to Zopryon,' Kineas said.

'I know,' Petrocolus said. 'So we pushed on here.'

Kineas leaned over and embraced the old man. 'Welcome.' Then his stomach rolled over, and he made his mouth move. 'Leucon is dead,' he said.

Petrocolus stiffened in his arms, and his face was grey as he pulled away. But he was a man of the old school, and he pulled himself erect. 'He died well?' Petrocolus asked.

'Saving his troop,' Kineas said.

Petrocolus grunted. 'Cleitus's whole line, dead. He has no other children alive. The archon will take his fortune.'

'No he won't,' said Kineas. 'When we are done here, you and Eumenes will go settle accounts in Olbia.'

'That viper's son still walks the earth?' Petrocolus spat.

'Do not hold Eumenes responsible for his father's treason,' Kineas said.

Petrocolus avoided his eye and spat again.

Kam Baqca came up on his left side. Her face was a white mask of paint, and the paint and the gold rendered her inhuman.

'I thought you would go with the king,' Kineas said.

'This is where the monster must be stopped,' she said. 'So this is where I will die. I am ready.' The inhuman face turned towards him. 'Are you ready?' she asked.

Their eyes met, and hers were calm and deep. The hint of a smile cracked the paint at the corner of her mouth. 'I see it to the end,' she said. 'And it is still balanced on the edge of a sword – indeed, on the point of an arrow.'

'I'm ready,' he said. He had his armour on, and all his finery – a little worn from two days in the saddle, but still fine. 'And the king?' he asked.

'Gone to the sea of grass,' she answered.

'Will he come in time?' Kineas asked.

'Not for me.' she answered.

Kineas nodded. He motioned to Sitalkes, waiting patiently, like all the men of his troop, for his turn to descend the ridge. 'Stay at my shoulder and carry my spears,' he said.

The young Getae saluted like a Greek and took his javelins. Kineas pushed past the horses of the other officers to where a troop slave stood with Thanatos. The big animal was trembling. Kineas vaulted on to his back, and the stallion grunted, slumped – and fell.

Kineas just managed to get clear without tangling in his cloak.

'What the fuck?' he said. He pointed to the slave. 'Get me another mount.'

There was an arrow. Ironically, it was a Sindi arrow – it stuck out of the big stallion's chest with just the fletching showing. The poor beast. And he'd never seen.

'Here they come,' Cleitus said.

Kineas ran to the edge of the ridge. The taxeis was coming out of the ford. Their ranks were disordered and they were bunching to the north side of the ford. Kineas knew immediately it was the rawer of the two taxeis he'd seen.

He turned back to his officers. 'Here we go,' he said, his heart pounding in his chest and all the calm of the early morning drained away. His hands shook like leaves in the wind. 'You know the plan,' he said, his voice high with tension and fear.

Philokles had his helmet on the back of his head. Once again, he was naked except for the baldric of his sword over his shoulder. The black spear was in his hand. He handed it to Kam Baqca and stepped forward to Kineas and embraced him. 'Go with the gods, brother,' he said. Then he took his spear from the icon on horseback, and clasped her hands. 'Go with the gods,' he said to her.

Philokles' men were already standing in their ranks to the left of the Olbian phalanx. Now Philokles tossed his helmet down over his oiled, beautifully combed hair, tossed his spear, and ran straight down the face of the ridge, disdaining the trail, so that he ran across the face of his men before Arni could bring Kineas a fresh horse. His men roared.

Niceas handed Kineas an apple. It was sound, despite its age. 'Kam Baqca brought a bag,' he said.

Kineas took a bite, and the smell caught him, so that he thought of Ecbatana and Persopolis, of Alexander and Artemis, and victory.

At his feet, the raw Macedonian taxeis was trying to restore its order. The blacksmith's men on the thumb were merciless. They poured arrows into the shieldless flank of the taxeis . Men were dying – not many, but enough to make the whole block flinch away from the thumb, just as they had when they crossed the ford. Until their own psiloi came up and cleared the thumb, they had to take the harassment. And having crossed, they had to wheel to the right to face Memnon's angled line – a difficult manoeuvre at the best of times, rendered more difficult by the arrows of the Sindi.

The raw taxeis was followed by the veterans. They crossed in perfect order and started to form to the left of the younger block. The First Taxeis was supposed to be anchored on the river, while the veterans had the more difficult task of covering the endless open ground on their left, where Sakje scouts already rode in close to put arrows into the phalangites.

From his vantage, Kineas could see the cavalry preparing to cross next. Zopryon was committed now.

'He's made a mistake,' Kineas said quietly. He took another bite of apple.

Niceas was mocking. 'Enough of a mistake to save us at odds of three to one?' He waved, and the arc of his arm encompassed the whole field at their feet. 'How long do you think our city hoplites will hold that? And where the *fuck* is the king?'

Kineas took another bite of his apple and chewed carefully, because it covered his nerves and put something in his stomach besides cramps. 'Those are the questions,' he said.

Niceas nodded. 'Your stupid heroics cost him time, I'll give you that.' He turned to look at Kineas. 'Will he let you die here to win the lady, Hipparch?'

Red-cloaked companions were coming up on the right, flanking the veteran phalanx, and behind them, more cavalry – companions and Thessalians. Kontos would be there, now, trying to get his men formed to face the Sakje. Men on exhausted horses.

Kineas made his decision. He tossed the apple core as far as he could – another boyish gesture – and mounted his spare warhorse, a big Sakje gelding. Big, but nothing on Thanatos. 'Petrocolus – stay right here. Form to the right of the Sakje.' He pulled the horse's head round. 'Follow me,' he said to Niceas, and drove the horse down the trail.

Straight across the marsh – the trail was all mud, but the ground was already drier – and then across the front of Eumenes' troop of horse. 'Hold here for my order,' he said to Eumenes.

Eumenes saluted.

Kineas rode to Memnon. The Macedonians were half a stade away, and Memnon never took his eyes from them.

Kineas reined in. 'We're going to attack – right now. I need you to push the raw taxeis to the right,' he said. 'Every pace matters. Let them come as far down the field as you dare, and then try to push them to the right.'

Memnon still had his shield on his foot and his helmet on the back of his head. He took his eyes off the Macedonian line long enough to flash Kineas a victor's smile. 'Didn't I tell you it would come to this? The spear push. Against Macedon.' He turned away from Kineas, saying, 'Best ride clear, Hipparch. This is where things get dirty.' And as soon as Kineas had his horse in motion, Memnon bellowed, 'Spears and shields!' like an old bull accepting a challenge. As Kineas rode down the front ranks, every Olbian pulled his helmet down over his head, set his shield on his arm, and lifted his shield. Kineas drew his sword and lifted it in salute, and they started to cheer.

'Silence!' roared Memnon. 'Cheering is for amateurs.'

And they were silent.

To his right, the phalanx of Pantecapaeum copied their motions. Indeed, not a single pace separated the two formations.

Kineas came to the front of Philokles' men. Philokles himself was at the front right corner. Kineas leaned down. The eyes in the helmet were alien, ferocious, bestial. 'When you hit, push *right*,' Kineas yelled. 'Every pace will count!' Kineas pointed down the field, where the Macedonians were coming on, just a hundred paces or so away. The veteran phalanx marched as if on parade. The other phalanx was still being galled by the arrows of the Sindi, and its files closest to the river were disordered. Men on that flank had their eyes on the oak trees next to them, and arrows came out of the trees at point-blank range to punch men screaming from their feet. Not many men, but enough. The front rank had an enormous bend in it, and the middle ranks were not closing up – and the whole taxeis was angling away from their tormentors on the riverbank.

A space fifty paces wide had opened between the rightmost file of the phalanx and the riverbank as they tried to avoid the arrows.

'I see it,' said the voice of Ares from Philokles' helmet.

Kineas rose erect on his mount. 'Go with the gods,' he said, and rode down the line to where Eumenes waited. As he came up, Eumenes was pointing at the gap. 'Don't point!' Kineas said. At this range, a single gesture could alert one of the enemy officers to their peril.

Memnon had his men in motion. Their spears were down, their shields up, and the whole line went forward as one. And the Macedonian pikes were coming down, and beyond them, the heavy cavalry was moving toward Kineas's right flank.

Time for the Grass Cats and the Standing Horses. Time for Nicomedes and Heron.

But they were on their own. Kineas was here.

There was a roar from the Olbians or the Pantacapaeans – or both. And an answering roar from the Macedonians. Just to Kineas's right, Philokles' men moved faster, breaking into a trot.

The Macedonian pikes were longer than the old-style hoplite spears. A man had to be very brave to face the prospect of pushing his body, his shield and his head through the wall of pike points.

Philokles' men were brave, and they had proven their mettle the day before. They went into the iron forest without hesitation, at the trot, and Kineas heard Philokles' war voice roar, 'Now!' and then the lines met, shield to shield. From Kineas's place on horseback, he could see the Spartan's transverse plume of scarlet, and he saw the eddy of carnage the Spartan left behind him, and the whole of the epilektoi made a noise like cattle, or thunder, and the Macedonians, whose front hadn't been perfectly formed to start, moved. It was all a matter of two paces – the epilektoi struck, and then, two paces later, the Olbian spears were in, Memnon's challenge carrying even over the sound of war. The raw phalanx of Macedonians contracted and men fell as they lost their balance and suddenly Philokles' plume moved forward three paces – five. The Macedonians were struggling to restore their order. A lot of men were dying.

Kineas rode to the head of Eumenes' troop. He faced the men. 'We will go right along the edge of the phalanx,' he said. 'At my order, we will turn and charge. There will be no room. There will be no time. The river waits for a man who pushes too fast on the left, and the spears will eat a man who pushes too far to the right.'

Philokles' charge had gained them another five paces. They had a gap of perhaps sixty paces between the Macedonian flank and the river.

Kineas tried to catch every eye. 'We will turn the block, just as on the drill field. It must be done well. Everyone see it? This is where you show that you learned your lessons.'

Time was flowing away.

He took his spears from Sitalkes. Even Sitalkes looked grim.

Kineas had no time for men, even those he loved. He turned for Niceas. Niceas nodded, his bridle hand at his throat. He was murmuring his prayer to Athena.

'Walk!' Kineas ordered. As soon as the block of fifty was moving, he ordered: 'Trot!' To the right, the epilektoi were faltering.

Even disadvantaged, the Macedonians were deeper, their files stronger. They were pushing hard.

The transverse plume was still leaving an eddy of death.

Memnon's men were locked. There were horses dying farther to the right, and Kineas could hear their screams like a demand for his attention, but he had chosen his foe.

And almost at his feet, the terrified eyes of the rightmost file leader in the young taxeis locked with his. Kineas rode past him, along the highway of the empty ground where the new men had flinched from the Sindi.

The deeper he got, the more ruin he'd cause.

The rightmost file was raising their pikes. Kineas didn't think that one file could stop him, but neither did he care to lose men. 'Right! Turn!' Kineas yelled.

Ten paces separated him from the flank of the pikes. An absurd distance. The men behind the right files were already defeated. His heart swelled with a dark joy.

'Charge!' he said.

They were only fifty men, but the taxeis couldn't endure the invasion of their files, and men in a phalanx panic when they sense an enemy behind them – for good reason. Kineas threw one of his javelins into the unshielded side of a pikeman, and then he was among them, wielding his heavy javelin two-handed, reaching out over his horse's neck to plunge it down into his foes while his horse bowled men over or kicked them. He struck and struck again, more concerned to sow havoc than to finish off wounded men. His good javelin was suddenly gone, jammed into a man's skull where the helmet failed to cover his cheeks, and then the Egyptian sword was rising and falling – the Macedonians had heavy glued linen cuirasses, and idle blows did no damage to them, but their backs were turning under his weapon.

They broke slowly, a file at a time, and the irony of the Olbian charge was that the collapse of the riverward taxeis occurred after the Olbian attack had lost all of its impetus in the press of bodies. But the pressure on their front was relentless, and the threat of the cavalry was enough. The rear ranks flowed away, and then the whole mass, almost three thousand men, was pouring away.

The Olbian horse had to let them go. They were already spent, and they were only half a hundred. Niceas was blowing his trumpet, and they were slow to rally – the flank of the veteran taxeis was open, but the Olbians were too slow, too tired, and the veterans had seen the threat; their flank files turned smartly and their pikes came down, while their main force pressed to the front, forcing the lightly armed men of Pantecapaeum and the Olbian phalanx back, foot by foot.

Kineas didn't like the sound of the battle on the right. He glanced at the sun – still early morning, for all that he felt that he had fought all day. Kineas reined in by Eumenes, who had lost his helmet. 'You have the command here.' Kineas pointed at the gap, the road that still ran all the way to the ford. 'Do all the damage you can,' he said.

Eumenes looked at his tired men and the gap. 'Are we winning?' he asked.

Kineas shrugged. 'You just broke a Macedonian taxeis,' he said. 'What more do you want?'

'Where's the king?' asked Eumenes.

Good question, thought Kineas, as he rode for the right flank.

He rode up the ridge with Niceas and Sitalkes at his heels. He had to see.

The rout of the riverside phalanx had evened the score, but no more, and the veterans were holding Memnon's men or even pushing them back. Zopryon's main effort was falling to the right of the Olbian infantry.

There was a cavalry mêlée to the right of the spearmen – companions and Thessalians, Olbians and Sakje. It stretched from the right flank of Memnon's men all the way to the north end of the ridge.

In Persia, there had always been dust. Dust was kind – it hid the bestial panorama beneath a shroud of earth. The Poet called it the *battle haze*. The damp ground of the sea of grass was not so kind, and Kineas was looking down at a cauldron of death with no disguise, no shroud of dust. The armoured mass of Macedon had fallen like the smith's hammer on Nicomedes' troop and the Grass Cats. Kaliax of the Standing Horse had hidden in the tall grass to the north and west of the ridge, had swept into the flank of the Macedonians, and stopped their advance – but that was all. The whole fight was balanced, a great circular mêlée of cavalry that stretched from Kineas's feet to the north of the ridge, three stades of dying men and horses.

The balance was about to be broken. There were fresh Macedonians coming across the ford. They had to push through the broken taxeis, but someone would rally the raw men soon.

Balanced on the point of an arrow, Kineas thought. But only until the fresh Macedonian horse pressed into the Sakje on the far right. Then the cavalry fight would unravel like a skein of yarn, and the Thessalians would fall on the flank of Memnon's infantry, and the rout would start.

'Where is the king?' Kineas asked the sky, and the gods.

Under his eye, Sakje shot Macedonians at arm's length, and Macedonian lances emptied saddles, and men fought with spears and swords, or bare hands and daggers. Kineas fought the urge to do something. It was hard to sit and watch.

His reserve was pitifully small. His attempt to deliver a great blow against Zopryon's line and withdraw had gone awry. There was no longer any hope of withdrawal. Like two wrestlers, the two armies could only fight until one was beaten – they were locked close.

Kineas thought he saw Zopryon. A big Macedonian in a purple cloak was pushing up the bank of the ford, and even as he watched, the man pointed at the cavalry mêlée and shouted. An arrow plucked the man at Zopryon's side from his horse.

The Sindi on the thumb were still fighting, still slowing Zopryon's manoeuvres across the ford.

Kam Baqca was at his side. She gestured with her whip – more like a staff of white wood. 'I curse them, and they die,' she said. 'The grass curls around the legs of their horses. The worms open holes for their hooves.'

Kineas drank from a gourd of water handed to him by one of the slaves. 'Zopryon's horses are exhausted. Even with his advantage in numbers, he's having trouble.' He grimaced. 'I was a fool to make a stand. I cannot break off. And the king is *late*.' He met her eyes. 'I need you to charge.'

'Yes. I will charge. I will hold him,' she answered. But she returned his smile – a singularly sweet smile, like that of a young girl receiving praise. 'I am ready to die now,' she said. 'And now is the time. For me.'

Kineas shook his head. 'And for me?'

'Not yet, I think,' she said. 'Goodbye, Baqca. Perhaps this will teach you the humility I never learned.'

She motioned with her staff, and her escort formed around her at the top of the ridge. They formed an arrowhead, with Kam Baqca and the standard at the tip.

Kineas wanted to remonstrate that they couldn't ride straight down the ridge, but they were Sakje, and he knew them.

She flashed him one last smile. 'Charge!' she shouted in a man's voice.

They fell down the hill like an avalanche of horseflesh, and they punched through the nearest ranks of Macedonians like a cleaver through meat. Dozens fell. Nicomedes' beleaguered troop was saved, and the survivors rode clear, dismounted, drank water.

Kam Baqca's risk allowed her to cut straight into the heart of the cauldron, and her fifty riders were like an arrow of gold flying through swirl of fog and mud.

Kineas sat with Sitalkes at his shoulder and watched the charge. So great was their impetus, and so hot burned their fire, that the cauldron of the mêlée moved away from the marsh's edge. In the centre, the Macedonian cavalry flinched away from Memnon's men.

Kineas pulled his gaze away from the Sakje priestess. At his feet the veteran taxeis was no longer pushing Memnon back. Philokles' young epilektoi were into their flank files. From the height Kineas could see Philokles' plume, could hear his battle rage. Even as he watched, Philokles tipped his great shield, slammed it into a new opponent and rolled his enemy's shield down with the force of his arm and then killed him with a brutal spear lunge into the man's unprotected throat. The men behind Philokles' victim shifted uneasily.

Farther to the west, between the thumb of oaks and the flank of the veterans, the empty grass was filling with peltasts and

Thrakes, and there were Thrake cloaks amidst the trees, hand to hand with the Sindi, who had stayed at their post to the end, and whose arrows had been the margin on the left.

Eumenes would charge the Thrake, and win, or lose. Either way, the left would hold.

Philokles and Memnon were spear to spear with the best Macedon had to offer, and nothing Kineas could do would change their fight.

At the north end of the ridge, Grass Cats and Olbians milled at the edge of the maelstrom, leaderless.

The golden arrowhead had gone deep, and the beast was wounded, but golden men and women were falling now. Kineas could no longer see Zopryon, but he could read the man's thoughts. Zopryon must think that the golden arrow was the last throw – and that the golden helm was the king of the Sakje.

And off to the west, another flash of gold came across the river and out on the sea of grass. His heart rose. *The king.*

It was just mid-morning, and he needed an hour. One more distraction would buy time, and keep men alive. If the right held, then the centre would hold, and the king would come to find the men of Olbia alive. If the right collapsed, then the king would come only to build pyres for the dead. And if the king's delay was deliberate ...

Kineas turned to Petrocolus, who looked older than his fifty years. 'Follow me,' he said.

Without a word, he rode down the north flank of the ridge. Even from the last of the ridge he could still see the horsetail standard, well out on the plain. He wondered what would happen if he refused his fate and rode away.

He laughed. He motioned to Nicomedes' men where they were drinking water, and they remounted to follow him, swelling his numbers.

Farther east, there were Grass Cats getting remounts, and a dozen of Diodorus's troopers – and Diodorus.

'These gentlemen gave us fresh horses,' Diodorus said. His helmet was gone, and his red hair was almost blond in the sun. He had a nasty wound across his shoulder and one of the straps

444

on his breastplate was severed. 'It's been warm work here. I thought we were going to withdraw?'

Kineas shrugged. 'Too late.'

Diodorus started to struggle with his breastplate, and Sitalkes handed him a length of leather. The two of them worked to tie the breastplate tighter. Niceas was organizing the survivors into a single troop.

'Where's the king?' Diodorus asked.

Kineas pointed out to the west with his whip. 'The king is coming,' he said. Men stopped what they were doing to listen, and he shouted it, pointing across the mêlée and the rising dust. 'The king is coming!' and the word spread like a grassfire on the plains.

Diodorus gave his cynical half-smile. 'Of course he is,' he said, and slapped Kineas on the back plate. 'Let's ride to meet him.'

Kineas made a motion with his whip, and the Olbians fell in on him, and Grass Cats rode in a loose knot at their right.

As they rode north, more men joined them – wounded men, and men who had, perhaps, had enough of the fight, and now felt differently. Kineas didn't harangue them. He just gathered them, his eyes on the horsetail standard.

Every Sakje eye was on the horsetail standard, and every Macedonian eye. Sacred to the one – royal to the other. Kineas gathered his men while the maelstrom swirled to a new centre. He kept them moving north, pecking at the mêlée to disengage those who could be pulled free.

The ground was losing its moisture, and the dust of the deadly battle haze was finally starting to rise.

Kineas watched the battle as he pushed north. The Macedonian horses were done – ruined by the campaign, not the battle – and they could never pursue when the Sakje gave ground, so that he was able to take men out of the battle lines and the Macedonians could do nothing in response but watch.

It took time, and he saw too much. He saw Nicomedes' body pinned under Ajax's horse – just a spear's length from the mangled remains of Cleomenes the traitor. He saw Lykeles with a broken lance straight through his body, and gentle, priestly Agis would sing no more of the Poet's words with a sword cut across his face and neck. The Olbian cavalry had held the worst of the first Macedonian charge, and paid.

And Varô of the Grass Cats was surrounded by his household with a ring of dead enemies like a hill fort. The survivors were grim-faced, but they rallied under the leadership of Varo's daughter, Urvara. He gathered them and moved north, while the attention of his enemy was locked on the horsetail standard.

And then the standard fell.

Every Sakje gave voice together, and despite the distortion of a thousand voices, Kineas knew the word. '*Baqca!*' They cried.

By then, Kineas had almost two hundred men – Olbians and men of Pantecapaeum, Diodorus and Andronicus, Coenus, Ataelus, Heron and Laertes with a length of linen tied around his bridle hand; two dozen Grass Cats and a handful of bloody Standing Horses as well as Niceas, Petrocolus and his troop. He was as far around the flank as he could spare the time to go, and he prayed to Athena that his two hundred men would, like Kam Baqca's charge, distract Zopryon and his army for a few more minutes. The sun was high in the sky above the dust.

He pointed to where the standard had fallen. 'That's where Zopryon is!' he called, his voice still strong. Sitalkes put a javelin in his hand.

He looked at his friends. There was no tree across the stream; he was on the wrong horse, no ford, the whole thing was insane. But the feeling of victory that suffused him was the same, and so he knew that this would be the time. And he meant to see it finished.

'Zopryon's head is Srayanka's bride price!' he yelled, and his voice held. They laughed, because of who they were, Hellenes and Sakje laughing together, and their laughter was terrible.

'Charge!' he said, for the last time.

The Macedonian horses could barely stumble along, and many of the Macedonian cavalrymen were fighting dismounted. His two hundred appeared out of the dust and bit into the red-cloaked companions to his front as a complete surprise, and they were knocked flat. Many died, and many more fought back like desperate men.

Kineas found Phillip Kontos in the battle haze. The man's horse reared, throwing back his magnificent cloak, and Kineas knew him, and gave a yell. Kontos knew him, too – and they came together with a crash of armour and horses, chest to chest. Kontos was his match, blow for blow, and their horses bit at each other, the enemy officer's stallion a better mount than his, but luck was against him, and Kineas's weakest blow went past his guard and fingers sprayed away from his adversary's sword hand like twigs from an axe – and the man fell against the mane of his horse and from there to the ground. Kineas circled him, wanting his horse and his javelins. Kontos clutched the ruins of his sword hand and looked up at him, battle rage spent, and before Kineas could consider mercy, Ataelus shot him dead.

Kineas whirled his brute of a horse and looked around. The battle had moved past him. Ahead, Coenus was dismounted, collecting javelins, and Sitalkes was finishing an opponent. Ataelus pushed past him to shoot, and every time he had an arrow knocked, he reared his horse for an extra span of height, and every arrow emptied another saddle. While Kineas pushed his horse into motion. Diodorus engaged an officer, cut hard with his heavy javelin, and a Thessalian lance caught him in the back plate and unhorsed him.

Kineas dug in, knees and heels, and his horse responded, flowing over the ground. Kineas's sword flicked out – right through the eyes and nose of the Thessalian – a blow rang against his helmet and he cut backwards underarmed, and saw Ataelus behind him, rising to shoot even as Kineas's new enemy whirled his javelin to strike again. Kineas's sword cut the man's thigh and Ataelus's arrow emerged from the bronze of his helmet, and then Kineas had Diodorus's wrist in his hand and he got him up behind without stabbing him with the sword while Ataelus continued to fire point-blank into the mêlée.

I'm not a general anymore, Kineas thought. He saw Kontos's riderless horse, rode at it and it shied, but Ataelus was there with a lasso. Diodorus slipped off his gelding and got a leg over the strange horse. 'Apollo, he's a giant!' he called.

They were almost alone – a minute away from the combat and it had moved south. The ground had dried, and the dust was rising faster – the familiar dust that gathered over every mêlée. Nothing was visible a javelin's throw away – closer than that, men were just shapes moving in the dust, like ghosts.

Kineas took a breath, looked around, put his heels to his gelding, and the brute responded. Kineas had time to be pleased, and then he was back in the madness.

Something had changed. The noise was different and the whole shifting mass of the fight was moving west like an ocean current. Kineas pressed after it. A flurry of blows – his sword bit deep and locked in the bone of a man's arm, and it was gone behind him in the brawl. He had no time to regret its loss – he had a dagger, and his whip – and he used both, pressing his next opponent close, slashing the Sakje weapon across the man's face and then finishing him with the dagger, clutching his mount with his knees to keep from slipping.

Something caught him in the hip – a flare of pain and then nothing more, and there was a javelin trapped between his leg and his horse. He grabbed at it, pulled it clear of his girth strap and fell straight to the ground as the strap gave under him.

He never felt the blow that put him down.

Horses hooves all around him, grunts, the scream of a horse, and he couldn't get his feet under him – right leg wouldn't answer. Dust in his mouth, filling his throat – a horse stepped on him and stepped away without testing his breastplate with its whole weight, and he still had no breath – dust everywhere, and hooves, and a javelin.

'Kineas!' screamed Coenus. He whirled a javelin, swinging it two-handed like a Thrake sword, clearing a space around his commander, and Sitalkes was there – he still had a javelin to throw, and he threw hard, killing the man at Kineas's right, and then he unhorsed another and pushed his horse past Kineas, and Coenus had one of his wrists and Niceas had the other – he was up.

Ataelus had another horse. He grinned, his face a mask of grime with two burning blue eyes. Somewhere beside him, voices cheered 'Apollo!' and Ataelus reached for his gorytos and came away without an arrow.

Kineas's right hip was aflame and the leg was unresponsive.

He could just stay astride the new horse – it hurt his balls to canter because he couldn't get his knees to lock. He looked right and left – he could see nothing but battle haze and shadowy figures, but the sound to his left was the Paean of Apollo and he could *hear* as the Olbian hoplites pressed forward. He didn't need to be able to *see* what was happening – invisible in the murk, the veteran Macedonians were giving way.

Somewhere in the dust, the king was finally on the field. Nothing else would have the same effect.

They had won. Kineas knew the feeling, having felt it in the dream – the certainty of victory.

He glanced around at his friends, and then, without a word, he pushed into the cloud again, feeling the strength of a god despite his wound, the daimon that lifts a man above himself in the eye of the battle storm, knowing that these were his last moments and determined to ride fate's horse to the very end. He followed Sitalkes, who left a swathe of dead the width of his reach, because the enemy was in the cloud, and because that's where the rest of his friends were, now.

And Srayanka.

There were grunts and calls and animal screams, but the song had changed – the battlefield was a hymn to victory for the Greeks, rout for the Macedonians – and there was cheering from the ford. 'Apollo!' again from the left. 'Athena!' from Coenus at his right hand.

The Macedonian army was dying.

Kineas had a javelin – too long and too heavy and the gods knew where he'd gotten it – he thrust it at a Macedonian face and the man went down, taking the javelin with him, and Kineas's horse was astride the broken body of Kam Baqca, gold and dirt mingled beneath his horse's hooves – another red cloak, and Sitalkes swept him from the saddle – the dust was rising faster, or the sun was stronger – the falling red cloak had the horsetail standard in his fist. Kineas hit him – hit him again, lashing him with the whip, screaming his war cry in the man's panicked face. Sitalkes got a hand on the standard, and together they killed the man, and Sitalkes held the standard high. Sakje voices cheered – fresh voices, and closer, now.

More Macedonians – where were they coming from? Kineas's head snapped back as something hit him a hard blow – he couldn't see, but he hung on, his whip rising and falling, and then he was free, like a ship at sea that cuts loose an anchor, and he had his reins and the gelding was still under his command. He whirled his whip, his arm feeling like a chunk of wood; the tendrils of the weapon caught at an enemy helmet. As soon as it tore free, he saw Sitalkes cut a man from his horse and a dismounted Macedonian cut at his side, clanging against his breastplate, and Sitalkes fell amid the hooves, gone in the dust – the standard going down again. Coenus killed the Macedonian, and Ataelus caught the standard.

Kineas was eye to eye with Zopryon. There was no shock – the man was where he ought to have been, at the centre of the battle cloud. Kineas had long enough to see defeat in his eyes – and rage.

Kineas lashed him with the whip, two quick blows, and one of them went home, a tendril of the lash wrapping under the brim of the man's gilt helmet and taking an eye, but Zopryon's back slash with his sword cut through the Sakje whip, leaving Kineas with a handle of gold and no weapon. Kineas leaned forward, and the gelding responded, rushing the bigger horse and catching him broadside on. The gelding's teeth bit hard, and the stallion struck back – but Kineas caught Zopryon's rising sword arm with his left hand and trapped it with his right, used the other man's strength and his strong left leg against his horse's spine to clasp him tight and pull him down – and they were in the dust, the horses a storm of teeth and hooves above them. Kineas fell on top, and their bronze breastplates bounced and winded them both. Kineas got an arm around the man's neck – nose to nose, Zopryon's breath was foul like a bad wound, and his eyes were those of an injured boar.

Zopryon, by luck or skill, forced Kineas back against his injured leg and Kineas screamed. Twice, Zopryon got the pommel of his sword against Kineas's helmet, and his head rang with the blows, and darkness threatened.

Kineas had only one good leg, but rage and thirty years of wrestling broke the Macedonian's bridle arm in a scream of sweat and blood. The crack of the arm seemed like the loudest sound on the battlefield – but pain, rage, desperation, strength born of despair allowed Zopryon to roll back, rise to his knees in the dust, and, ignoring his shattered left arm, cock his sword for a killing blow.

Kineas went for his second dagger, trapped by his injured leg – too slow.

The first arrow went into the Macedonian just above the circle where his neck emerged from his breastplate. And then he seemed to grow arrows like some trick of a stage machine – one, then four.

Kineas was on one knee, and he couldn't think very well, but he raised his head, and her blue eyes were there above a tall horse, and above them the dust rose like a funeral pyre. And even as he looked at her, the dust opened and he was looking at the sky. The sky above the dust was blue and in the distance, far out over the plain, clouds rose in pristine white. Up there, in the ether, all was peace. An eagle, best of omens, turned a lazy circle to his right. Closer, less auspicious birds circled.

A hand grasped his, hard as iron on the calloused side, and soft as doeskin on the back under his thumb.

And darkness took him.

He was sitting on a horse in the middle of a river – a shallow river, with rocks under his horse's feet and pink water flowing over and around the rocks. The ford – it was a ford – was full of bodies. Men and horses, all dead, and the white water burbling over the rocks was stained with blood.

The river was enormous. He lifted his head and saw the far side, where piles of driftwood made the riverbank look like the shore of the sea, and a single dead tree rose above the red rocks of the shore. There were other men behind him, all around him, and they were singing. He was astride a strange horse tall and dark, and he felt the weight of strange armour.

'Is this any river you have ever seen?' Kam Baqca asked mockingly.

'No,' he admitted, feeling like a boy with his tutor.

'The hubris of men, and their vanity, is beyond measurement.'

She laughed, and he looked at her, and the white of her face paint could not obscure the rot that had taken most of the flesh of her cheeks.

'You're dead!' he said.

'My body is dead,' she said.

'And mine?' he asked. Even as he spoke he looked down, and the skin of his arm was firm and marked with all the scars that life had given him.

She laughed again. 'Go back,' she said. 'It is not yet your time.'

There were three of them, sitting on the branches of the tree, and each was more hideous than the last. The one on the lowest branch reached above her and took something from the crone on the next branch, and when she looked at him, she had just one eye, but that was as bright as a young girl's. She held up her hand, and from it dangled a thread, or perhaps a single hair of a child, and it was bright gold and shone with its own light, although it was shorter than the width of a man's finger.

'Not much left,' she said, and she cackled. 'But better than nothing, eh?'

'Enough to father a child or two,' giggled one of her hideous sisters.

'Enough to defeat a god,' roared the one on the highest branch. 'But only if you hurry!'

AUTHOR'S NOTE

Very little survives of the Scythian language, and I am an author, not a linguist. I chose to represent some Scythic words with Avestan, and some with modern Siberian words, and some with Ossetic words, all with the intention of showing how difficult a language barrier is, even when many words share common roots. I have very little skill with Classical Greek, and none with any of the other languages mentioned, and any errors in translation are entirely my own.

ACKNOWLEDGEMENTS

A book – really, a series – like this does not spring full blown from an author like Athena from the brow of Zeus. Kineas and his world began with my desire to write a book that would allow me to discuss the serious issues of war and politics that are around all of us today. I was returning to school and returning to my first love – Classical history. And I wanted to write a book that my friend, Christine Szego, would carry in her store – Bakka-Phoenix bookstore in Toronto. The combination – Classical history, the philosophy of war, and a certain shamanistic element – gave rise to the volume you hold in your hand. Along the way, I met Professor Wallace and Professor Young, both very learned men with long association to the University of Toronto. Professor Wallace answered any question that I asked him, providing me with sources and sources and sources, introducing me to the labyrinthine wonders of Diodorus Siculus, and finally, to T. Cuyler Young. Cuyler was kind enough to start my education on the Persian Empire of Alexander's day, and to discuss the possibility that Alexander was not infallible, or even close to it. I wish to give my profoundest thanks and gratitude to these two men for their help in re-creating the world of fourth-century BC Greece, and the theory of Alexander's campaigns that underpins this series of novels. Any brilliant scholarship is theirs, and any errors of scholarship are certainly mine. I will never forget the pleasure of sitting in Professor Wallace's office, nor in Cuyler's living room, eating chocolate cake and debating the myth of Alexander's invincibility.

I'd also like to thank the staff of the University of Toronto's Classics department for their ongoing support, and for reviving my dormant interest in Classical Greek, as well as the staff of the University of Toronto and the

Toronto Metro Reference Library for their dedication and constant support.

I'd like to thank my old friends Matt Heppe and Robert Sulentic for their support in reading the novel, commenting on it, and helping me avoid anachronisms. Both men have encyclopedic knowledge of Classical and Hellenistic military history, and again, any errors are mine.

I couldn't have approached so many Greek texts without the Perseus Project. This online resource, sponsored by Tufts University, gives online access to almost all classical texts in Greek and in English. Without it I would still be working on the second line of *Medea*, never mind the *Iliad* or the *Hymn to Demeter*.

I owe a debt of thanks to my excellent editor, Bill Massey, at Orion, for giving this book a try, for his good humor in the face of authorial dicta, and for his support at every stage. I'd also like to thank Shelley Power, my agent, for her unflagging efforts on my behalf.

Finally, I would like to thank the muses of the Luna Café, who serve both coffee and good humor, and without whom there would certainly not have been a book. And all my thanks – a lifetime of them – for my wife Sarah.

If you have enjoyed *Tyrant*

Look out for the thrilling sequel

TYRANT: STORM OF ARROWS

Available in Orion paperback

The conqueror of Asia stalked into his tent and tossed his golden helmet at the armour stand by the camp bed. It hit the wooden post with a bronze clang. The servants froze.

'Where the *fuck* are my recruits?' he yelled. 'Antipater promised me eight *thousand* new infantry. He sent three thousand Thracians and some mutinous Greeks! I want my Macedonians!'

Members of his staff followed him into the tent, led by Hephaestion. Hephaestion was not afraid of his royal master, certainly not his master's temper tantrums, and his bronze-haired head was high. He was smiling.

Behind him, Eumenes and Callisthenes were more hesitant.

Alexander scratched his head with both hands, trying to get the sweat and the dirt out of his hair. 'Don't stand in the doorway like sheep. Come in or get the fuck out.'

Hephaestion handed him a cup of wine, poured another for himself. 'Drink, friend,' he said.

Alexander drank. 'It's not fair. If people would just do as they were told ...'

Hephaestion raised an eyebrow, and they both laughed. Just like that.

Alexander swirled the wine in his cup and looked at Eumenes. 'Did he say why?'

Eumenes – shorter, not godlike in any way – accepted a goblet from Hephaestion, who rarely served anyone but the Great King himself, and met his lord's eyes. They were mismatched, blue and brown, the blue eye ringed in black and opened just a little too wide. Eumenes sometimes thought that his master was a god, and other times that he was mad. Either way, Eumenes, a brave man and veteran of a dozen hard fights, disliked meeting Alexander's eyes.

Eumenes of Cardia was a Greek and not a Macedonian, which made the bearing of bad tidings all the harder. Men competed to bring Alexander good news. When the news was bad, men conspired to avoid being the goat. Eumenes, the foreigner, the smaller man, was the goat.

'Lord,' he said carefully, 'would you like to read the letter, or shall I tell you what I think?' In the right mood, Alexander craved straight talk. Eumenes lacked Hephaestion's touch with his lord, but they had an emergency and he needed Alexander to act like a king.

'Just tell me,' Alexander shot back.

Eumenes looked at Hephaestion and received no sign at all. 'Reading between the lines, I would say that Antipater sent an army to conquer the Euxine cities – and perhaps the Sakje tribes.'

'Sakje?' Alexander asked.

'The Western Scyths,' Callisthenes answered.

'Amazons?' Alexander asked.

Callisthenes snorted contemptuously. Alexander whirled on him. 'Why are you here, sir?' he asked.

Callisthenes raised an eyebrow. 'Because you can't tell the difference between a Scythian and an Amazon.'

Alexander seemed pleased with this remark. He flung himself on a couch. Hephaestion came and lay with him. Servants brought food and more wine.

'So Antipater made a campaign against the Scythians,' he said.

'Not in person. He sent Zopryon.'

'Shit for brains,' Alexander said. 'I assume he cocked it up?'

Eumenes nodded. 'I think that's where we lost our missing recruits.'

Alexander snorted. 'They're off chasing Amazons, eh?'

Eumenes shook his head. 'No, lord. If I'm right, and my sources are firm on this point, all our recruits are dead.'

Alexander rolled off the couch and stood. 'Zeus Ammon my father. Zopryon lost a whole *taxeis*?'

'Zopryon lost a whole army, lord.' Eumenes waited for the explosion. 'And died himself.'

Alexander stood rigid by the couch. Hephaestion reached out and put a hand on his hip, but Alexander struck the hand away. Hephaestion frowned.

460

'They almost defeated my father. Philip, my father. He was wounded – wounded badly.' Alexander was speaking very softly.

Eumenes could remember it. He nodded. 'Yes, lord.'

'And Darius – these Sakje defeated Darius.' Alexander's face was immobile. He stood like a schoolboy reciting for his tutor.

Callisthenes shrugged. 'Not so much defeated as avoided, if Herodotus is to be believed. They made Darius look like an ass, though.'

Alexander glared at him.

Callisthenes raised a shaggy eyebrow. 'Of course, it took Athens to *defeat* Darius.'

Alexander's face burned as the blood rushed to his cheeks. 'Athens *checked* Darius. Sparta *checked* Xerxes. *I* conquered Asia. Macedon. Not Athens and not Sparta.'

The philosopher glared at Alexander, who met his look and held it. Long seconds passed. Then the philosopher shrugged again. 'As you say,' Callisthenes said, with a nod.

A tense silence filled the tent. Outside, the new recruits could be heard being shepherded to their quarters in the sprawling camp – a camp so big and so well built that men already called it a city.

Alexander sat on the couch again. 'And Cyrus,' he said, as if continuing an earlier conversation.

They all looked at him, until understanding dawned on Callisthenes. 'Yes,' he said. 'Yes, as you say, Alexander. Cyrus lost his life fighting the Massagetae. Well to the east of here.'

'Massagetae?' Alexander brightened. 'Amazons?'

'The Massagetae are the Eastern Scythians,' Callisthenes said. 'Their women do fight, and they sometimes have warrior queens. They pay tribute to the King of Kings. There are Massagetae serving with Bessus and with Spitamenes. The queen of the Massagetae is Zarina.'

Alexander raised his goblet in salute to Callisthenes. 'You do know some useful things.' He drank, staring out of the door of his tent.

Eumenes fidgeted after the silence stretched on too long. Callisthenes didn't fidget. He watched Alexander.

461

Alexander ran his fingers through Hephaestion's hair. Then he watched a Persian boy retrieve his helmet and polish it with a cloth before hanging it on the armour stand. Alexander gave the boy a smile.

Callisthenes continued to watch him.

'Antipater has cost us more than a few thousand recruits,' Alexander said some minutes later. He leaned back so that his golden curls mixed with Hephaestion's longer hair. 'Our own legend of invincibility is worth a pair of *taxeis* and five hundred Companions.'

'You are invincible,' Hephaestion said. From another man, it would have been fawning. From Hephaestion, it was a simple statement of fact.

Alexander allowed himself a small smile. 'I cannot be everywhere,' he said. He rolled off the couch again and motioned to the silent slave who waited at the foot of the bed. 'Take my armour,' he said.

The silent man opened his breastplate and put it on the armour stand. Alexander shrugged out of his tunic and stood naked, the marks of the armour clear on his all-too-human flesh.

Naked, neither tall nor especially beautiful, Alexander picked up his wine, found it empty and held it out for a refill. Slaves tripped over themselves to correct the error.

Callisthenes laughed at their eagerness and their fear. Alexander smirked. 'Persians make such *good* slaves,' he said. He drank off the whole cup and held it out again, and the pantomime was repeated. Even the Cardian had to laugh. The slaves knew they were being made a game of, and that made them more afraid. Wine was spilled, and more slaves appeared to clean it up.

'I can't be everywhere,' Alexander repeated. 'And Macedon cannot afford to appear weak. These Scythians must be punished. Their victory over Zopryon must be made to look the stroke of ill-fortune that it was. When Bessus is brought to heel, we should spend a season crushing the Massagetae.'

Callisthenes sensed the dismay of the other men. 'Alexander,' he began carefully, 'the Massagetae live far to the north and east, beyond the Kush. And they live on the sea of grass, which

Herodotus says runs for fifty thousand stades. We will not crush them in one season.'

Alexander looked up and smiled. It was a happy smile, and it removed years of tension, war and drink from his face. 'I can only spare them a season,' Alexander said. 'They're just barbarians. Besides, I want an Amazon.'

Hephaestion struck the king playfully, and they ended up wrestling on the floor.

PART I

FUNERAL GAMES

1

The sun shone on the Borysthenes river, the rain swell moving like a horse herd and glittering like the rain-wet grass in the sun. The Sakje camp was crisp and clean after days of rain, much of the horse dung vanished into the the general mud that filled every street, the felt yurts and the wagons bright as if new-made. Kineas had taken the sun as a sign and risen from his bed, despite the fresh pain of his wounds and the recent fear of death.

'You should find the stone,' the girl said. She was eleven or twelve years old, dressed in caribou hide, with a red cloak blowing in the wind. Kineas had seen her before around the camp, a slight figure with red-brown hair and a silver-grey horse from the royal herd.

Kineas crouched down, wincing at the intense pain that shot from his hip, down his leg and through his groin. Everything hurt and most actions made him dizzy. 'What stone?' he asked. She had big eyes, deep blue eyes with a black rim that made her appear possessed, or mad.

'It is a *baqça* thing, is it not? To find the stone?' She shrugged, put her hands behind her and rocked her hips back and forth, back and forth, so that her hair swayed around her face. She was dirty and smelled of horse.

His Sakje didn't run to endearments for children. 'I'm sorry,' he said. 'I don't understand.'

She favoured him with the look that children save for adults too slow to understand them. 'The *stone*,' she said. 'For the king's barrow.' Seeing his incomprehension, she pointed at an old barrow, the kurgan of some ancient horse-lord that rose by the great bend. 'At the peak of every barrow, the *baqça* places a stone. You should go and find it. My father says so.'

Kineas grinned, as much from pain as from understanding. 'And who is your father, child?' he asked, although even as he said the words, he knew where he had seen that long-nosed profile and the fine bones of her hands.

'Kam Baqça was my father,' she said, and ran away, laughing.

He knew as soon as she spoke that he had seen the stone in dreams – seen it and dismissed it. He feared his dreams now, and denied them if he could.

But he gathered a dozen of his Sindi retainers and a few Greeks: Diodorus and Niceas because they were friends, and Anarxes, a gentleman of Olbia, because Eumenes was wounded and Anarxes had the duty. Together, they rode down the river a dozen stades.

'What are we looking for?' Diodorus asked. He, too, was recovering from a wound, and his red hair gleamed where it emerged from a bandage that swathed his whole head, under a Sakje cap of fox fur and red wool. Temerix, the Sindi smith, rode over.

'We're looking for a stone,' Kineas said.

'For kurgan,' Temerix said, as if this was the most natural thing in the world. 'Lord Kineas sees it in dreams. We come find it.'

Young Anarxes' eyes were as wide as funeral coins at this open talk of his hipparch's godlike powers.

Diodorus raised an eyebrow and nodded slowly. He reached into his cloak and produced a clay flask, from which he took a long pull. He offered it around. 'Did it ever occur to you that life was simpler when we were just mercenaries?' he asked.

Kineas and Niceas exchanged a look.

Diodorus pointed with the fist that held the flask. 'Look. Kineas is wearing a Thracian cloak. Anarxes here, as fine a wrestler as we've ever seen – an Olympian, by Apollo – is wearing Sakje *trousers* as if that were the most natural thing in the world. All our men wear their caps.' Diodorus touched his bandages and the Sakje cap perched atop them. 'Are we even Greeks any more?' he asked. He took another drink of wine from his flask and handed it to Kineas.

Kineas shrugged. 'We're still Greeks. Did travel to Persia make you Persian?'

Diodorus was serious. 'It made me a lot more Persian than I was before I went there. Remember Ecbatana? I'll never think of Greece the same way again.'

'What are you saying?' Kineas asked.

'There's a rumour that you and Srayanka aim to take us all the way east to fight Alexander,' Diodorus said. 'I've heard you talk around it. You mean it, don't you?'

Kineas shook his head. 'Lot is insistent and Srayanka wants to support him. The queen of the Massagetae has sent messengers to the Assagatje. They had another yesterday.' He drank.

Diodorus grunted. 'Hey! Hey, that's my wine!' He seized the flask. 'We have unfinished business before we go riding off to fight the boy king. The tyrant, for instance.' He looked out at the horizon. On their right, the Borysthenes flowed down to the Euxine Sea. On the left, the sea of grass rippled in the wind as far as the eye could see, and then another forty thousand stades, or so Herodotus claimed. 'I don't want to fight Alexander. I don't want to see more fascinating barbarians. I'd like to retire to Olbia and be rich.'

Kineas rode along, hips moving with his mount. He hurt, and despite weeks in a cot in Srayanka's wagon, or because of them, he felt sore in every muscle. 'Things change,' Kineas said.

Diodorus nodded. 'Too true. The peace faction took over in Athens while we were winning this campaign.'

Kineas laughed, which also hurt. 'Athens seems very far away.'

Diodorus nodded. He handed his flask to the silent Temerix. 'That's what I mean. When I left Athens with you, I thought my heart would break. When we were cracking Darius's empire, I used to dream of the Parthenon. Then we fought this campaign. Now Athens is too far away to remember and I'm a gentlemen of Olbia. Now I dream of finding a wife and buying a farm on the Euxine.' He paused. 'I'm afraid that I'll end up in a yurt on the sea of grass.'

Kineas had stopped his horse unconsciously. He was looking straight at the stone he'd seen in his dream, and the day seemed colder. 'Hera,' Kineas said. He spoke aloud a prayer for divine protection.

Diodorus was looking at him.

'It's just as I dreamed it.' Kineas's voice was hushed. 'The stone is broader at the top. When we dig it up, the bottom will be shaped like a horse's head. We'll flip it over and the horse head will mark Satrax's grave.'

Diodorus shook his head, but as the Sindi dug away at the deep soil around the stone, he became thoughtful, and when the shape of the stone's hidden base was revealed, he rubbed his beard in annoyance.

'Remember when we were just mercenaries?' Diodorus said, again.